THE WOOING OF KATIE MAY

THE WOOING OF KATIE MAY

Harriet Hudson

HEADLINE

First published in 1992
by HEADLINE BOOK PUBLISHING PLC

10 9 8 7 6 5 4 3 2 1

British Library Cataloguing in Publication Data

Hudson, Harriet
Wooing of Katie May
I. Title
823.914 [F]

ISBN 0–7472–0524–8

Typeset in 11/13pt Plantin by
Falcon Typographic Art Ltd, Fife, Scotland

Printed and bound in Great Britain by
Richard Clay Ltd, Bungay, Suffolk

HEADLINE BOOK PUBLISHING PLC
Headline House
79 Great Titchfield Street
London W1P 7FN

For my father-in-law
David Myers
whose infectious enthusiasm
sent me to visit the Tabor Opera House

Acknowledgements

The house and village of Bocton Bugley are fictitious, as are the characters of this novel. Leadville, however, still thrives in Colorado, though its great silver mining days are long over. On Harrison Avenue, now the main thoroughfare of the town, the Tabor Opera House, still an active theatre, bears proud witness to Leadville's dramatic past. Much of the opera House's decor and layout is unchanged, and the atmosphere of earlier times is strong. I am grateful to Mrs Evelyn Furman for information about the Opera House in early times, much contained in her fascinating book *The Tabor Opera House*. In Leadville the names of Tabor and Baby Doe are still as prominent as though the scandal had taken place yesterday. Baby Doe, despite the former Mrs Tabor's predictions, remained faithful to him to the end, even after he lost his fortune when the silver market collapsed. She died a recluse in a shack by Tabor's Matchless mine, which she refused to sell because he had told her that one day silver would regain its value. The day did not come in her lifetime, nor since.

I am grateful also to the geologist A. C. Benfield for his interest in the mining chapters, much of the information for which was drawn from Fossett's *Colorado: Its Gold and Silver Mines*, New York, 1880. My thanks also to Peter Lambert, Lionel Leventhal, Meg and Peter Ryan, Carolyn and Christopher Maude, Adrian Turner and Carol Tyler. To my agent Dorothy Lumley of the Dorian Literary Agency, and my editor Jane Morpeth, my deep appreciation of their help and encouragement.

Among the modern books I have consulted are *Kent Lore* by Alan Bignell (Hale, 1983); *Maidstone and Ashford Railway* by Elwyn L. Evans (Hollingbourne Society, 1984); and *Leadville: Colorado's Magic City* by Edward Blair (Pruett Publishing Co, Colorado, 1980). It was in *Kent Lore* that I first found reference to the legend that Richard III's illegitimate son, Richard Plantagenet, fled from Bosworth Field to Kent where he became a brick-layer on the Eastwell estate. This part of the story is contained in two issues of the *Gentlemen's Magazine*. The legend has a gap, however; there is no word of what Richard was doing between the ages of sixteen at Bosworth, and seventy-odd, when Sir Thomas Moyle discovered him reading a Latin textbook on his estate. In the following pages, I have augmented the legend accordingly.

Prologue

Nicholas Stowerton had been dead for over two hundred years on the day of the last treasure trove in 1841, yet his legacy cast its dark shadow over that bright summer's day. His ghost looked on, awakened from its slumbers, at his beloved Kentish manor of Bocton, as the Stowerton children gathered, unconscious of the brewing storm. Six sons – and Sophy.

Bocton Manor had been empty for twenty years, its ownership still in dispute. Soon it would be settled, but today the seeds of strife were to be sown in a new generation and he could do nothing to prevent it. Once again the fates had picked the Stowertons for their sport. Just as on that day in 1573, he foresaw what would happen but for all his misgivings was powerless to stop the wheel from turning. And, after all, had not Will Shakespeare said it truly? 'The fault . . . lies not in our stars but in ourselves.'

The ghost of Nicholas Stowerton shrugged and laughed. *So, let the play begin, my Queen!*

At ten the wagonettes set out from nearby Stowerton House, one with seven neatly clad children crammed in it, and the other with servants and food for the picnic. The carriages carrying Nathaniel and Bridget Stowerton led the procession to Bocton for the yearly children's game held on the anniversary of the battle of Bosworth in deference to the old legend that Richard III's jewels were hidden somewhere within the walls of Bocton Manor. Nonsense, of course, for Nicholas himself had built this red-brick manor house on the site of his ancestors' dwelling, in the reign of Good Queen Bess, almost a hundred years after Bosworth Field. Since then Bocton had been fought over by generations of Stowertons, each claiming it for their own.

'I'll win the cup,' declared Robert confidently, nonchalantly. 'I usually do.' The eldest at sixteen he was naturally superior, too old for childish games, too acquisitive to cede his claim.

'You won't,' muttered Jeremiah, two years his junior, fixing dark vengeful eyes upon him.

George's owlish amiable grin: 'It's Joseph's turn. Fair's fair,' he put in quietly, the words almost lost in Alfred's happy shout: 'Who cares? Who cares who wins?'

Joseph had heard. 'Yes, it's my turn,' he took up childishly, full of fierce determination, emboldened out of his usual reserve. 'Mine, mine, *mine*!'

'But *I* want it,' thought three-year-old Albert, silent, watchful, holding his sister's hand.

1

Six-year-old Sophy, anxious, loving: 'Please let this be a happy day,' she beseeched God, closing her eyes and apologising for the informality of her prayer. *'Please.'*

Suddenly, inexplicably, she was afraid.

And the wagonette turned in at the gates of Bocton Manor.

Chapter One

·

'Never forget you are a Stowerton, my dear,' said Alfred, somewhat reprovingly.

'Father,' Katharine began helplessly, 'don't you understand? Obadiah's heard a rumour that Bocton is to be *sold*.'

A bewildered look appeared on Alfred's pink-cheeked face, then quickly passed away again. 'Excellent though Mr Trant's building accomplishments are, my dear,' he told her happily, 'he does not appreciate the Stowerton tradition. Indeed, how could he?' he continued reasonably. 'He is a Trant.' His tones suggested Obadiah was indeed to be pitied, as was anyone who did not carry the Stowerton name. 'The Stowertons have *always* lived at Bocton.'

'Then why has it been empty for nearly sixty years?' she enquired gently.

Her father looked hurt. 'A little misunderstanding,' he said firmly, 'such as happens in all families.'

Katharine laughed outright, despite her anxiety. A little misunderstanding indeed! Enough to drive four of the six sons of Nathaniel Stowerton to the far ends of the earth. Enough for the sons of Matthew Stowerton to battle for over twenty years before that. Yet seeing her father sitting there in his old Norfolk jacket, threadbare in places, with, incongruously, a huge cravat that was said to have belonged to Beau Brummell, a wave of affection swept over her. But how could she, at twenty-three, hope now to pour out all her worries as she had when a child? Then his beneficent charm had been a comforting and sheltering blanket, until gradually she had come to realise that comfort provided no answers and that love alone filled no stomachs.

'Do you not think,' she replied lightly, 'that the Stowertons are a little more *extreme* than most families in their misunderstandings?'

They were sitting in the Stowerton Room. How grand that sounded for a cramped Dower House, and who but Father could have so named it? The room was small, and every inch of wall space and furniture top was filled with portraits of Stowertons or prints of Bocton – or so Katharine had thought until one day she had made the shattering discovery that not all the portraits were of Stowertons. Alfred had merely acquired any he could obtain cheaply enough that looked sufficiently patrician. 'They could have been Stowertons, my dear,' was his plaintive defence when taxed with this 'white' fraud. She forgave him his veniality for here, surrounded by his ancestors and would-be ancestors, was the one place he could still be the illustrious descendant of an honourable house.

3

Besides, there was something else far more serious amiss with the Stowertom Room, something that made her realise that there were deep mysteries attached to the Stowerton family, mysteries she could not hope to comprehend. There were no photographs. Alfred was one of the seven children of Nathaniel Stowerton, yet apart from one old daguerreotype of his parents standing stiffly to attention, no record of his immediate family stood in the room. And try as she might, Katharine could get no indication as to why. They were simply names in the huge family Bible now. Nothing more. She had pored over the heavy volume as a child, reciting the names almost as a litany: Robert, Jeremiah, George, Alfred, Joseph, Sophy – and another through whose name a pen had deeply scored an obliterating line. And try as she would, she could never make out the name beneath.

'Where did they go, Father?' she asked time and time again. 'Why did they go?'

Her father merely looked hunted and picked up the *Sporting Times*, a sure sign that all conversation was at an end, and eventually she gave up asking. Dimly she remembered huge shapes that loomed over her in childhood, just shapes, never faces. But they had vanished and only Uncle Robert was left, the eldest, watchful and quiet – and Aunt Sophy.

After Mother had gone, she had asked Aunt Sophy about those giant figures of the past. 'Suppose they come back?' she asked wistfully.

'It won't happen, my love,' replied Sophy sadly.

'But why not? Anything is *possible!*' cried Katharine with the confidence of an eight year old.

Once, greatly daring, she had even asked Sophy about that fascinating blacked-out name. Her aunt had laid down her work and spoken so firmly for her that Katharine had not asked again, much as she had puzzled over it.

'You must not ask, Katharine. There are some matters that must be buried. Families are difficult,' Sophy broke off, bending over her sewing again so that Katharine would not see the tears in her eyes.

Bocton had been Katharine's playground from her earliest days. She remembered toddling round with kind Archie Thomas, the gamekeeper. It was always a place of magic with its red brick and smell of old wood, its passageways and staircases, its deserted courtyards and sweet-smelling gardens. A place of light and laughter. There had been a playmate too, hadn't there? A fair-haired boy who teased and laughed at her, but gently enough so that she devotedly toddled after him. Was he a relative? Thomas's son? No, not the latter, for he too had disappeared. A cousin perhaps, but not Philip for sure. Philip was Robert's son and ever-present. It wasn't David either, his younger brother, and her own age of twenty-three in this year of 1879. Had the fair-haired boy existed at all, or was he a product of her lonely imagination, a spirit of Bocton itself, as he climbed trees so high he was lost in their branches? She would look pleadingly upwards, longing for him to reappear, to come again. Perhaps one magic day he'd take her

4

up, so that she too could share that leafy world high above. But he had vanished, and she was the only person left to love Bocton.

The house had suffered from greed, possessiveness, neglect, sun and storm, but somehow its soul had survived them all. Yet now, if by any terrible chance the rumour was true, it was to be sold.

'Where did Trant hear this extraordinary rumour?' asked Alfred querulously from behind his newspaper, unable to concentrate on important matters while such irritating details were disturbing Katharine.

'I don't know,' she replied soberly. 'But I'm going to find out.'

Katharine pushed open the heavy silvered oak door of Bocton Manor's porch. It creaked protestingly on its hinges, as the familiar smell of disuse and decay filled her nostrils. Futile anger seized her once more, used as she was to it, that the old house, so proud, so mellow, could have been allowed to fall into such disrepair, a haven for bats, mice and wood fungus, and anything else that cared to invade what the Stowertons had abandoned.

Obadiah Trant was already at work in the study at the foot of the East Wing, trying to repair the old panelling which had been put up earlier in the century and had rotted badly. He stood up as she came in, his rounded figure swathed in a huge canvas and leather apron, and his mouth full of nails which he carefully removed one by one before he spoke.

'Dere be summat odd 'ere, Miss Katharine,' he pronounced, frowning at the rotten wood.

'Never mind that for the moment, Obadiah. Have you found out anything more about that rumour?' she burst out anxiously, her face troubled.

'Yus,' he told her simply. ''Tis the new railway.'

'The *railway*?' For a moment she was gripped by fear, then she laughed in relief. 'Oh no, you've got it all wrong, Obadiah. The plans allow for the new railway line to run through a tip of the estate, that's all. The railway company won't be buying the manor itself. Why should they?'

'Dat's what I do 'ear,' Obadiah muttered obstinately. 'Dat's what folk do say. And dey'll probably be knocking dis old 'ouse doon. Won't do for no station now, will it? So Sir Robert, 'e –'

Uncle Robert? A slow clutch of fear fastened over Katharine's heart. If the rumours Obadiah had heard brought in Uncle Robert, then anything was possible.

Even selling Bocton? No, surely that was fantasy, a rumour spreading, distorting . . . Even Uncle Robert wouldn't do that. But the fear grew and grew. Uncle Robert and Cousin Philip might be capable of anything.

For years there had been talk of a railway link between Maidstone and Ashford, but this time it seemed serious. Plans had been published earlier this year, and a bill was now before Parliament, in which both the London, Chatham and Dover Railway and the South Eastern Railway

5

were mentioned as likely builders. It meant this area of Kent would be prosperous once again, no longer a backwater. For Katharine, it had immediately meant that her plan to hold a school at the old manor was now an exciting possibility. Bocton Bugley, nestling between Lenham and Charing, was remote, not even near a main thoroughfare, and in current circumstances no one would travel to a school there. Then had come the news of the proposed railway. There would at least be a station at Lenham, perhaps even – her imagination had run away with her – in years to come when her school was established, a Bocton Bugley Halt.

The school, she planned, would not only save Bocton, but would mean she would earn money of her own. There were so few things that women could do – only nursing or teaching. She was no use at nursing. A governess? Even if she wanted to, Father would never allow it. No, it had to be a school for the children of gentlefolk; since the Education Acts nine years ago, schooling had been open to all, but there was still a demand for private schools. And whether she liked it or not, her sister Meg, four years younger than Katharine, was going to have to help her run it.

She had gone to Uncle Robert, determined to counter any argument he might put in her way. He had said little, which had puzzled her at the time. Surely it made more sense to have Bocton repaired and a commercial enterprise than to have it fall down through neglect? Reluctantly he had given her permission to inspect Bocton with Obadiah in order to work out her costs. Then, he said hastily, and only then would he consider the matter again.

Now, with sinking heart, she wondered if the reason for his lack of enthusiasm did indeed involve the new railway. Uncle Robert was a director of the powerful South Eastern Railway, one of the two companies put forward as builders of the proposed railway line. The London, Chatham and Dover Railway was the more popular contender, and were behind the plans just published. But the earlier proposals of 1874 and 1865 that had come to nothing had each been the brainchild of the South Eastern Railway, and they would fight tooth and nail to get what they wanted this time – or at least to prevent LCDR getting it.

Her first impulse was to rush to Stowerton House immediately, to demand of Uncle Robert whether there was truth in this rumour. Obadiah watched her pityingly.

'Now don't you be afretting, Miss Katharine. A rumour it is, an' tomorrow there'll likely be a dozen more to take its place. You be paying me to work, not tell you stories about things dat'll never 'appen.'

But suppose they did? Resolutely Katharine tried to suppress her concern, and to concentrate on Bocton. She left Obadiah in the study, and went to strip the fast-growing ivy from the front wall, where it was growing over the window of the Queen's Reception Room on the first floor. She had been working for about thirty minutes when there was a shout.

'Come along 'ere, Miss Katharine, an' yew do look at dis!'

6

Startled by the unexpected noise and note of intense disapproval in the voice, Katharine swayed on the ladder precariously balanced against the old red-brick wall. Ten feet away, Obadiah's plump face, on which his usual expression of doubtful melancholy had been replaced by indignation, popped out of a hole in what had once been a fine mullioned window, his cap and hair now covered in dirty white plaster.

'What is it, Obadiah?'

Katharine scrambled down the ladder, impatiently cursing her long dress. How ridiculous to have to clamber up ladders in tight, trained skirts, she thought, overlooking the fact that even in this advanced year of 1879 ladies were not expected to climb ladders. Hurrying inside, she began to laugh as her eyes fell on Obadiah. As well as the plaster, cobwebs adorned his apron, waistcoat, high collar and shirt, and even clung to his eyebrows.

''Ere, miss,' he remarked lugubriously. In his hand he held towards her two plaster-festooned staves, looking for all the world like a latter-day Friar Tuck with a broken bow. 'Yew do look at dis!' he repeated.

Seeing his expression, she stopped laughing instantly and rearranged her features into an expression of worried sympathy. 'Is anything wrong?' she asked fatuously. Of course there was.

'Yus, dere is,' he said truculently. 'Someone's been a-doing of no good 'ere, Miss Katharine. Look what dey done. Lazy devils, begging your pardon, dat's what dey was. Can't be bothered to pull de place down an' build decent in its place. Oh no, dey 'as to build *round* it, an' now see what a trarble I've got.' He walked back through the large doorway into the study, every inch of his broad back displaying his indignation at the trials that beset master builders. Majestically, and still quivering with outrage, he pointed.

Katharine, meekly behind him, obediently looked. On the front-facing wall, where Obadiah had been stripping off the panelling, bringing the centuries-old crumbling plaster away with it, the smell of damp was overpowering, but she could see nothing to excite his indignation.

'What is it, Obadiah?' she asked, puzzled.

'What yew gart 'ere, miss,' Obadiah confirmed in tones of gloom, 'is an 'allouse.'

'A *what*?'

'Vun of dem mediaeval places. Dis aren't a nice Tooder place after all. Oh no. It's an 'allouse.' He sighed deeply at having to impart this bad news. In the hole Obadiah had made Katharine could see two silvery oak posts exposed, and between them vertical oak staves, and hazel strips wound round them, where the pug that once covered it had fallen away through damp.

'Mediaeval?' she said blankly. 'How can it be? Sir Nicholas built this manor in Queen Elizabeth's reign in the sixteenth century, after pulling down the old house.'

His chest puffed up. 'Ho, no. I thinks all 'e did, miss, was build two

7

new wings nice and solid in brick, either side of the old 'ouse, and to join them 'e just put a brick wall rahnd the outside of de old 'ouse so it all looked the same. Den 'e plastered over the inside, so's yew couldn't see dem ugly beams. 'E just left de old 'ouse 'idden away.' His voice rose in indignation at the enormity of this architectural crime.

'So this study, although it's got the East Wing joined on to it behind, is actually part of the old house? A whole mediaeval building is hidden here?'

Katharine gazed round at the old panelling and fireplaces, the dirt-encrusted ceilings and Georgian wall-coverings. Her face lit up with interest, making Obadiah think suddenly that if Miss Katharine didn't wear that pretty chestnut-coloured hair of hers scraped back that way, she might be quite a good-looking maid, for all her seriousness. Not as pretty as Miss Meg, 'course, but passable. But there was no denying she was a little peculiar was Miss Katharine, her head stuck in her books and always running up ladders an' all. Strange how interested she was in this old place. He looked disparagingly round the desolate manor. The old place'd fall down soon. Best thing for it if it were to be sold and pulled down, he reckoned. Give him his nice cottage built last year with its inside valve closet. The trouble with Miss Katharine was, she felt things too much. Not like Miss Meg.

Excitement was almost bubbling out of Katharine now, driving all thought of the terrible rumours from her head. Perhaps here was the very house that Thomas had built, or perhaps his son William Stoorton. The implications began to tumble over each other in her mind. Just suppose the old legends were true . . .

There had been Stowertons at Bocton Bugley since the time of Queen Elizabeth, and, some argued, for five centuries before that. Her father, in his youth, with more enthusiasm and energy than he now bestowed upon such matters, had painted a detailed family tree, decorated with the Stowerton armorial bearings and miniature paintings of Stowerton forebears, tracing the family back, albeit with a hiccup, to one John de Stour who had been granted the right of free warren at Bocton by William I. This had intrigued her as a child. What was this right of free warren?

'The right to hunt coneys,' her father said absently. 'Rabbits, we call them.'

Rabbits? But who would want to hunt rabbits, except Thomas the gamekeeper? Did that mean he too came of a special family? She was temporarily ashamed of being a Stowerton, afraid for days that she would be sent out to hunt rabbits. Then Archie Thomas had explained to her that he was the only poacher he was going to allow on to Bocton land, and, relieved, she stopped crying at night.

Bocton meant a manor granted by charter, she had been told, and the Bugley came from a Saxon lady called Bucge who owned much land in the area. A younger Katharine had confused Bucge with Boudicca and kept a wary eye out for a fierce lady driving chariots over Bocton Bugley land. But she never came. The hamlet was called Bocton Bugley to distinguish it from other Boctons in the area, most of which now spelled it Boughton. The house, however, remained just Bocton Manor. Unlived in since Matthew Stowerton, her great-grandfather, had died in 1820, it had been damaged by storms, wind, frost and fungus. Tiles had fallen from the roofs exposing the inside timbers to the elements, where, bereft of attention, they slowly rotted. Ivy infiltrated itself via unrepaired windows and roofs. A great storm in 1875 had brought a huge oak crashing through the roof of the West Wing, and bats and birds found a new refuge.

And all the while Katharine agonised for the house. Much as she loved it, there was little she could do to protect it, save to patch up the worst of the damage as best she could with what materials Obadiah could find lying around. There were no pennies to spare to spend on Bocton. What Obadiah did was out of loyalty to the Stowertons, not for reward.

She, Father and Meg lived cramped into the damp Dower House, built by a somewhat guilty Stowerton in the last century for his widowed mother. All the while Uncle Robert – Sir Robert Stowerton – lived in the splendid Palladian Stowerton House near Chilham; it was smaller than Bocton, grander than Bocton, and infinitely more comfortable. Not a penny did he spend on repairs to the old house. It was not practical from the business point of view, he explained coldly whenever she tackled him on the subject. There was no one to live there. How infuriating that Bocton should be in the hands of such a man – and the thought that Philip, his elder son, would one day inherit it was even worse. There had to be something she could do. Bocton had to be financially rewarding for Uncle Robert. Very well, she would present him with such a plan, she had thought, a plan that would bring Bocton back to life – and so had been born the idea of the school. It should really be a family home, but there was no family now.

As she entered the wood on her way home, Katharine paused to glance back at the house, shrouded now in a mist of summer green of the trees. It was drizzling with rain, and the house seemed almost unreal, receding from her grasp. A few cows clustered under the trees by the edge of the wood, looked up at her, as she hurried on towards home, mooing indignantly, as though she were responsible for their damp condition.

The harsh call of a jay first alerted her, then the sound of a horse and carriage trotting towards her along the pathway. It couldn't be Archie Thomas, or Obadiah Trant, for he had already driven away in his builder's cart with old Pug, as he called his horse: 'Parentage uncertain but gets de job done.' Her heart sank.

She glanced quickly down at her damp dress, aware of lank and bedraggled hair under her boater and boots caked in mud. Of all the times to have to face Cousin Philip – just when she wanted to get her chaotic thoughts in order about how best to tackle Uncle Robert about the rumour. His round smug face stared at her complacently as he brought the horse to a halt and jumped awkwardly down from the phaeton. He was almost insolent in his correctness in his formal morning coat, sweeping off his top hat with too perfect politeness. His eyes flickered up and down her almost possessively, as if lord of the manor already. Debating the merits of exercising his droits de seigneur, she thought, trying to hold her ground and not step backwards in instinctive revulsion.

Gouch, or Grouch as Father persisted in calling him, remained seated, with merely a perfunctory touch of his bowler hat, his glittering and watchful eyes on her. Gouch was Uncle Robert's steward and looked after all his estates, though Bocton received only a cursory eye from time to time.

'The man's a Pecksniff,' declared her father roundly. 'A hypocrite. A Uriah Heep,' he embellished, mixing his Dickens novels unconcernedly. 'I don't trust him. I wouldn't put my money on him.'

'You haven't any money, Father,' Meg had pointed out brightly. 'Not after last week.'

Unusually she earned a stern glare from her father, followed by a hasty: 'You are so right, my dear, but if I had, I wouldn't.'

And neither would she, thought Katharine, looking Grouch straight in the face. He should not realise how much he intimidated her. Then she braced herself to try to talk calmly to Philip. His eyes missed nothing, neither the specks in her hair nor the dirty hands.

'You have been to Bocton, Cousin.'

'I have your father's permission,' she retorted quickly, then regretted it. Philip, so unctuously polite, was like a sweet confection smeared with poison, very different from his aloof, disdainful father. When she was a child, it had been the same; six years older than she, he had appointed himself her 'protector', against her will and unnecessarily, and she had learned that one did not hand hostages to fortune with Philip or his father.

Now all caution went to the winds, however, as words burst from her. 'Bocton,' she said flatly. 'Is the rumour true? That it's going to be sold?' It was out, and bitterly though she regretted speaking she could not take the words back. Did she imagine the quick flash in Gouch's eye, the sudden stillness of Philip's plump body?

'My dear Katharine,' he said quickly, 'you are distressed. The rain – may I drive you home?'

'Forget the rain,' she said impatiently, aware suddenly of the sight she presented. *'Is it true?'*

'Your usual common sense seems to have deserted you, Cousin,' he said, as if amused. 'Are you not due to put your proposals for a school there to my father tomorrow? How could Bocton be sold?' he said smoothly.

She stared at him. It seemed ridiculous. He was right, of course – they could not sell Bocton – and yet . . .

'My father is delighted that you are taking such an interest in the old place,' Philip continued smoothly.

'If he had taken more interest himself, it would hardly be necessary,' she was unable to prevent herself from saying.

10

His eyes flashed suddenly and it was all she could do not to step backwards, as if a snake's venom-laden tongue had shot forth.

Katharine had done her best over the years to make good the worst of the damage at Bocton, but with no money to spare and only her own hands to work with, she had had to turn herself into a handyman, poring over building manuals, learning to wield tools properly. Obadiah had become her trusty friend, advising her, even helping her in his free time to patch up the worst of the damage from time to time, but the big storm of '75 had beaten them both, and the longer the damage went unrepaired the more Bocton suffered.

Full of enthusiasm two years ago, she had asked the newly founded Society for the Preservation of Ancient Buildings for advice. A young man had duly toured Bocton, and become almost as interested as Miss Stowerton herself. But when the matter of repairs was put to Sir Robert, he had refused point-blank. If Bocton was to be repaired, it would be done 'properly'. Sash windows should replace those old Tudor ones, the ornamented chimneys rebuilt, turrets and battlements added. It should be a house to be proud of.

'Sir Robert is a most generous man,' Gouch put in sanctimoniously, 'both to his staff – and to his relatives.'

Katharine flushed angrily. He was pointing out what they all knew: that Alfred Stowerton and his daughters lived in the Dower House rent-free.

'He is my uncle,' she said coldly. 'I believe *I* should know just how generous Sir Robert is.'

'My father is eagerly waiting to hear your plans and estimates,' Philip put in in a studiedly bored tone. 'And I shall myself have the pleasure of being present, of course.'

Shaken by the encounter, and trying to ignore an insidious feeling that they were mocking her, which added to her fears, Katharine hurried past Home Farm, and the mill, back to the Dower House on the far side of the park from the manor. Clearly there had been little love lost between the original dowager and her son. Home Farm was still part of the estate, but the farmer in the old days had been obliged to sell all his produce to the house – at low prices. Now he was an independent tenant, as was the miller. Bocton retained its feudal estate but not its customs. Sir Robert was a good landlord by some standards. On a strictly business footing, Katharine thought wryly. Provided the rent was paid, he did his part, but he showed little mercy for those who fell by the wayside for whatever reason. It was left to Katharine and Aunt Sophy to sort out problems such as that of John Beane when he broke his leg and couldn't pay his rent because of the poor harvest.

Katharine ran up the path to the Dower House, and almost flew through the door, banging it behind her. 'Where's Father, Maggie?' she burst out as belatedly she wiped her boots. Looking ruefully at the wet gingham, she decided that there was no time to change, despite the fact that Father would disapprove. He liked them to keep up standards. Maggie was their one maid, one of Farmer Beane's

11

daughters, and so grateful for Miss Katharine's help to her family that she did not object to her tiny pittance of a wage, which was all that could be afforded.

'In the Stowerton Room, miss.'

'Is he – ' Katharine hesitated.

'No, miss. We're run out.' No need to ask of what. Brandy, of course. Maggie understood the situation perfectly.

It was hardly any wonder that funds ran short, Katharine acknowledged. She gave her father an allowance with the hopeful idea that his winnings on horses must cover all his drink – except for her home-made wine. They were desperate times indeed when he turned to that. He wheedled more money somehow, sometimes even from Maggie, until Katharine found out and put a stop to it. But no one, least of all she, could be angry with Alfred Stowerton for long.

All her adult life she had scrimped and saved, merely to keep them alive and to keep Papa happy with his horses – not riding them, but gambling on them. Sometimes, it was true, he even won, but more often he lost. On such days he would be downcast, telling her she was a good girl and he did not deserve such a daughter. Yet the fact remained that if it had not been for Godfather they would have starved. Godfather was always slightly mysterious to Katharine. Always so correct, so formal – and a little sad – on his six-monthly visits to their home to bring money for the next half-year. He was tall, distinguished-looking in his frock coat; she always wanted to tell him not to look so unhappy, but never had the courage. 'Yes, thank you, Mr Dean,' she would say in reply to his polite questions as to her lessons. Everyone relaxed when he left, even Aunt Sophy.

Godfather was a distant cousin of Mother's, Father explained vaguely, who had a great deal of money and a conviction that it was his duty to help those less fortunate than himself. He had not come into their lives – she never even knew she had one – until after Mother had left and Aunt Sophy had moved in, meek, biddable and timid. 'Mouse', Papa called her. Aunt Sophy had done only one surprising thing in her life. When Katharine was sixteen she had moved out again, saying firmly that devoted though she was to them, she wished to live alone. When scandalised voices were raised, she bowed to convention and took a companion to live with her in the Lodge.

It was after she had taken over the endless household budgeting that the remnants of Katharine's childish adoration of her feckless father had finally crumbled into loving exasperation. Between the mysterious disappearance of her mother and her sixteenth birthday she had subconsciously realised that all could not be well with a way of life such as her father's, prancing through each day without heed for the next. After her sixteenth birthday Katharine knew for certain that the family reins must rest in her hands if they were to survive for there was no hope of her father changing, or of her sister's doing anything other than following in his footsteps.

Katharine drew a deep breath before entering the room, trying not

12

to forget that she was a Stowerton. A smile forced itself from her. This was her father's gravest reproach to either of his daughters when they earned his displeasure. That his own gambling and drinking might earn him the same treatment never seemed to occur to him, and had it done so he would have dismissed it out of hand, for these were occupations worthy of a gentleman.

She had intended to tell her father calmly what had happened, and of the plans she was already beginning to formulate, but once again impetuosity took over.

'Obadiah's heard more, Father – that it might be connected with the new railway. I met Grouch and Philip. They deny it, of course, but *could* it be true, do you think?'

'The railway? Dear me, how distressing!' Alfred's mild blue eyes were troubled, then they cleared. 'I expect we'll be all right here though,' he declared happily, picking up his glass of Madeira, to which he had been forced in the absence of brandy. 'Robert would never let them turn us out.'

'Bocton, Father, *Bocton*,' she cried unbelievingly. 'You can't mean you don't care?'

'Of course I care, my dear,' he said hastily, aware of a false move. 'It would mean the end of your splendid plan to run a school there. Perhaps Robert will find you somewhere else,' he said placatingly.

Katharine gazed at him, agonised, but took a grip on herself before speaking again.

'Father, the idea of the school was primarily to save Bocton – *that*'s the important thing. With the money we make, we could pay for the repairs, and with you and Meg teaching as well as myself, we could charge perhaps fifty pounds a year.'

Alfred Stowerton held up his hand. 'A moment, my dear,' he said thoughtfully. 'Did you mention teaching – *my* teaching?'

'Why, yes, I would teach the younger children, Meg dancing, art, music and so forth, and you the classics pupils.' This, she had planned, would be sure to appeal to him.

'My dear, I could not possibly do so. *Teach*? That is no occupation for a gentleman.' He was clearly painfully shocked.

'But, Father,' her heart sank although she had half expected this, 'would you not like to live in Bocton again, to be Alfred Stowerton of Bocton Manor?'

'My dear, that is hardly the point.' He sighed deeply. 'Do you not think it a trifle demeaning to run a commercial establishment? The classics should be free for everyone. Would you not think it beneath your social standing as a Stowerton, to charge for such instruction?'

'Social standing, Father? What standing can we have?' she asked wearily. 'We live in a crumbling dower house, far too small for the three of us and Maggie, and we are totally dependent on the money Godfather gives us.'

How she hated to be dependent on anybody, even someone as nice as Godfather. Who *was* he? Some kind of remote cousin, her father always said vaguely, and Godfather politely scotched any tentative questions

13

from her. Kind though he was, she was determined to end the situation if she could.

'Never forget you are a Stowerton, my dear,' he interrupted, happy that he had found the only possible answer to such outrageous statements.

'Of course, Father. I'm sorry,' she said penitently. Indeed, she was. She should have known better than to try to persuade her father that he should take an active part in the school. If school there was to be. If this rumour were unfounded. She dismissed the terrible thoughts and decided to leave the question of Father's teaching until he became piqued at being left out of the project. Then she would tell him that she intended to teach classics herself. That would horrify him. A woman teach classics! She could almost hear his reaction now.

She smiled ruefully. She was an excellent classicist. How frustrating it was to love so many things that women were not supposed to be good at. Classics for one. Building for another. If she had not become the handyman of the family, who would? She had learned early to wield hammer and saw, but was always careful that she should not be seen repairing anything by her father; he never thought to question who carried out the repairs or how they could be afforded. Yet skirts were so hampering. How could you climb up to roofs in full skirts without danger, let alone with modesty? She had remembered talk of lady mountaineers like Meta Brevoort who wore breeches under their skirts, the latter being discarded and hidden behind rocks when out of sight of civilised eyes. She had begun to contemplate how sensible this might be for her while working on the house, but a mere mention to Aunt Sophy, the dressmaker of the family, and the house had almost fallen about her ears. She had had to make her own bloomers, bad seamstress though she was, and their existence remained a closely guarded secret from everyone but Obadiah.

'But,' she said cunningly, changing tactics, 'Father, there may not be a school if Uncle Robert sells our heritage.'

Alfred set down the glass of Madeira carefully, arrested by the magic word 'heritage'.

'By George,' he roared suddenly, making her jump, 'sell Bocton? The idea's ridiculous. The ancestors will be shivering in their frames.' He cast his predecessors a comradely glance. 'My dear, to our chargers. Fully armed, let us ride on Stowerton House. There is work to be done.'

Meg Stowerton examined her doeskin gloves critically. Katharine had tried to clean them for her with stale bread, but there was no denying she needed new ones. Katharine had simply told her they could not be afforded. It was too bad – who appointed Katharine keeper of the Stowerton purse anyway? Now they were going to Uncle Robert's and Katharine knew she, Meg, never felt up to such visits unless she was on top form. Oh well, Katharine was a dear really, and at least she had given way over this new spot muslin dress with the yellow ribbons. She glanced at Katharine sitting across from her in Uncle Robert's carriage.

14

Father always insisted on Uncle Robert sending the brougham and not driving in their own old dogcart to Stowerton House. Meg thought he was quite right to insist. After all, they were Stowertons too.

Meg was dubious about her proposed role as school teacher. All that it had in favour of it was that it was a change, and, after all, it need not entail too much work. Cousin David had told her he might help, and she might meet some influential families. She never met anyone normally. She pouted; she was already nineteen. It wasn't fair, she didn't stand a chance of meeting anyone in her own station of life. Uncle Robert and Aunt Millicent rarely had balls, not since David's twenty-first birthday three years ago, and she hadn't been out of the schoolroom then. Her spirits rose slightly at the thought of meeting Cousin David; he wasn't such a dried-up old stick as Philip and he did adore her so. It was nice to be adored. Not that she could ever marry him; being the younger son, he had no money. Such a pity that Philip was so old – almost *thirty* – and had inherited his mother's large frame. He was decidedly plump, if not fat, whereas David was slim, almost good-looking in a way. She wondered if she could stand being married to Cousin Philip and decided not – provided Katharine married him, to keep the money in the family. She pouted again, thinking of the good fortune that always rained down on the heroines in the romances of Lady Wittisham, her favourite novelist. It wasn't fair. Why didn't someone attractive come along?

Katharine sensed the tension as soon as they entered the elegant morning room of Stowerton House. Surely they would not be so much on edge if it were merely the school and her estimates they had to discuss? She must be careful, and wait her moment. Uncle Robert, Cousin Philip, Gouch – only Cousin David greeted her with anything like warmth, though he had a decidedly warmer welcome for Meg. She was sorry that Aunt Millicent was not there. She at least was warm and welcoming, if always overshadowed by her husband's presence.

If the large table, fifteen feet in length, was meant to intimidate her, it succeeded. She felt small for all her inches and her best formal dark blue taffeta dress.

Sir Robert was a slight man only a little taller than she herself; today he was as usual impeccably dressed in frock coat and striped trousers, and as urbane in manner as Philip. His eyes watchful behind the oval gold-rimmed spectacles, Robert greeted his more corpulent and expansive younger brother with barely concealed distaste, as the Ancient Mariner might his albatross. He reached for his albert watch chain and studied his watch rather pointedly.

'My dear Robert, you look as though you preside over the Bank of England at the very least,' Alfred greeted him cordially.

'And you, Alfred.' He cast a glance at his brother's for once carefully valeted morning coat, grey trousers and high starched collar. 'I am honoured indeed.'

'I never forget I am a Stowerton, Robert,' retorted Alfred, surprised, sitting unasked at the foot of the table, facing his brother fifteen feet away.

15

Robert glanced at him uneasily. One never knew with Alfred. A strange fellow – that business with his wife for instance . . .

Katharine tried to steady herself, looking quickly round the table: Philip staring at her with pale eyes that betrayed nothing; Meg fluttering modestly, aware of and apparently avoiding David's devoted look. And Grouch, always Grouch.

'I have the figures, Uncle Robert,' she began carefully, restraining herself from bursting out with the question most on her mind. They would be waiting for her to raise the subject, after her meeting with Philip yesterday.

'I am glad to hear it, Katharine. If you would pass them to Mr Gouch?'

'I would prefer to explain them myself, Uncle Robert,' she replied firmly.

'In business, Katharine, you will learn that figures speak for themselves,' Robert commented drily. Nevertheless he motioned her impatiently to continue.

They listened in complete silence, yet she had the impression they were not really listening. Swept away for the moment by her own enthusiasm for the project, however, she continued to the end. She looked round the table, but only David's friendly eyes looked in her direction. 'Well done, Katharine,' he said enthusiastically.

'The figures you quote,' broke in Sir Robert quickly, 'do not seem to take account of rent, merely repayment of the loan.'

'Rent?' she repeated, dumbfounded.

'Quite. To Sir Robert,' interjected Gouch smoothly.

'But the improvements I shall make to the manor –'

'At your own desire, for your own purposes, with a loan from us,' said Philip offhandedly.

'Nonsense,' she declared roundly. 'To save Bocton for the family. Or isn't that what you have in mind at all?' She had flung down her gauntlet, and looked steadily round the table. 'Is it true that you plan to sell it for the new railway?'

The look that immediately passed between Gouch, Uncle Robert and Philip did not escape her.

'It is under consideration,' said Robert in his thin voice. 'As is your own plan.'

She dismissed this impatiently as the placebo it was.

'But I've seen the proposal for the railway line to link Maidstone and Ashford,' Katharine retorted. 'The railway would affect only a small corner of the estate.'

'No,' broke in Philip smugly, and unwisely. 'By law the railway could be obliged to buy the whole estate.'

'*Could* be?' queried Alfred sharply and surprisingly. 'It would be your choice then?'

'Precisely,' snapped Robert.

'Father,' said David, puzzled, hardly believing that he had known nothing of this, 'you can't mean you'd sell the old manor and estate? Away from the family?'

16

'Railways represent prosperity, David,' Robert said sharply. 'We must support them with business enterprise.'

'You mean there's more money to be made from selling the whole estate than from my school,' Katharine said flatly.

'You hardly despise money yourself, my dear. You seem remarkably eager to make some.'

'To keep Bocton, Uncle, not to sell it,' she pointed out quietly, almost unable to take in that that what she had feared was being confirmed. 'Bocton has been in our family for many centuries. And what would the railway company do with it? Why not sell part of the estate to the railway and keep the rest? It would help the school –'

'Impossible,' said Gouch dismissively.

She caught another look between him and Uncle Robert, which at first puzzled her. Then she understood. It wasn't the money at all – not primarily at any rate. Bocton was a pawn in the game of chess between the two railway companies. 'It's all settled, isn't it?' she blurted out. 'You're going to use Bocton as a bargaining point. You'll refuse to sell to the London, Chatham and Dover Railway except on such exorbitant terms that they could never afford it.'

'I am a director of the South Eastern Railway,' said Robert coldly. 'It seems natural for me to give preference to them.'

'By George, Robert,' shouted Alfred, who had been thinking things over, and now suddenly thumped the table, 'there's more for you than the price of the land, isn't there?'

Robert shrugged almost indifferently. 'In fact, yes. The South Eastern Railway has exciting plans for the estate. It will need a brick works, perhaps a tiling factory close at hand. Industry can be developed at Bocton. I have plans possibly for a brewery, to take advantage both of the waters of the Stour and of the new railway for carriage.'

The ponds, the river – all to be diverted to a factory . . . This was worse than Katharine had ever imagined, even in the long nights when she had lain awake worrying over Bocton's fate.

'Since you are *suddenly*,' Robert continued, emphasising the word, 'so interested, Alfred, I could explain that the South Eastern Railway envisages a line running south of Maidstone to Bocton Bugley and then up to Chilham, where it will of course join with our Ashford to Canterbury line.'

And Bocton stood in the way, no more than a pile of bricks by their reckoning, to be bargained for and signed away at the stroke of a pen, Katharine realised bitterly.

'Highly convenient for your estate here. What plans do you have for Stowerton Park, eh?' Alfred said, flushed.

'As you say,' Robert agreed drily, 'I do see advantages for my interests here. I must say, Alfred, I feared your private pursuits had ill fitted you for the practicalities of business, but you show a –'

'Practicalities of business my foot, Robert! Father would turn in his grave,' Alfred roared.

They would knock down Bocton, reduce it to rubble, re-use the bricks for factories, create worksheds, turn gardens to lime yards, stables to storage for beer barrels. How easily Katharine could foresee the destruction of the past, which should live to guide the future, a heritage not theirs but held in trust. Never! Not while she could do something about it! She stilled the nausea rising from her stomach. She must remain dispassionate.

What came to her, however, was no reasoned argument. It rose like a monstrous chimera in her mind, then obsessed it. No logic to it, no rational justification, but the one weapon left to her. The weapon that no Stowerton had ever thought to use again. The weapon that had so often been used to hurt Bocton in the past, had proved the cause of its present neglect, but now might be its salvation.

Katharine spoke clearly, in a calm voice that did not seem to be her own: 'You will never sell Bocton either to the London, Chatham and Dover Railway or to the South Eastern Railway.'

'Indeed, my dear?' Robert was patronising now, assured of his victory. 'And just what can you do to prevent my doing so? Must I remind you that Bocton and its estates are my property?'

'That is open to question,' she replied quietly, but unable to keep a tremor of excitement from her voice now.

Robert's head jerked up, eyes fixed on her.

She looked back at him coolly, and took a deep breath. 'You ask what I can do? Not can, *shall*. I shall reopen THE CASE.'

18

Chapter Two

'My dear, what a jewel I have in you.' Alfred beamed happily, sitting himself down with a sigh in his favourite armchair, relaxed now that they were away from the ears of Robert's coachman. 'What a jest! What bravado! Did you see Robert's face? And Mr Pecksniff Grouch's? My love, I had not thought you such a wit.'

'I am serious, Father,' said Katharine, astonished that he could think otherwise. Meg began to titter.

'Come, come, my dear, no need to continue the joke,' replied her father, a trifle uneasily.

Meg burst into outright giggles. 'Did you see Philip's face? I thought I should burst.'

'I am *serious*,' said Katharine angrily.

This time the look on her face silenced them. Carefully Alfred cleared his throat. This needed thought. He cleared his throat again.

'My dear, even supposing you are – um – in earnest, you have no legal standing in the matter.' The note of hope in his voice suggested that this unfortunate furore might evaporate, and he could pick up his *Illustrated London News* and ensconce himself with the sporting column once again.

'I realise that,' she retorted passionately, 'but you know the situation is unjust. *You* will reopen The Case, Father. You have taught us enough about it over the years,' she added cunningly.

Alfred's eyes bulged. 'Me?' he spluttered feebly. He looked wildly round for escape, but there was none. Katharine had firmly planted herself against the door, and since it was now raining heavily outside he saw no escape through the garden windows either. 'My dear –'

'Do you not wish to see Bocton thriving once more, Father? Do you want to see it reduced to a pile of bricks when Uncle Robert sells it to become a brewery or brick factory? Besides . . .' She paused. Should she speak, or keep the secret still? No, she must tell them now. 'Father, Mr Trant thinks the old mediaeval house is still *there* inside the brick walls that Nicholas Stowerton built. The *old* house, Father. Just think – the jewels might really be there if the house dates back to before Bosworth.' She didn't believe it for a moment, but Richard III's jewels were the best of all possible carrots to dangle before her father.

'When we find the jewels, my loves,' he would declare happily in their youth, 'the jewels, you will see. All will be well.' And Mother had been satisfied – for a time. Until at last even she believed him no longer. 'The jewels, Alfred,' she had told him forthrightly, 'have as much chance of turning up as Richard III himself.'

A momentary wistful gleam appeared in Alfred's eye as he contemplated the likelihood of legends proving true against the upset that Katharine's pronouncement would cause if put into action. The latter won hands down. The gleam disappeared. 'Progress, my dear,' he murmured feebly. 'We must look to the future.'

'Nonsense,' she declared roundly. 'The whole estate does not have to be sold for the railway. The only progress in knocking down Bocton will be found in Uncle Robert's banking account.'

'Katharine, my dear, we must be practical,' pleaded Alfred. Even she laughed at that, despite her concern. Alfred looked hurt. 'I cannot reopen The Case on my own,' he pointed out with relief. 'I have – had – four other brothers,' he said craftily. 'Besides, my dear,' clutching at a sudden straw that helpfully presented itself, 'if you reopen The Case, what about Father's brothers, my Uncle Frederick and Uncle Jacob? Could one not argue they too still had a claim? You remember that after my grandfather died, although they fought The Case for over twenty years, it was only abandoned, and not decided. Suppose they were to reappear?'

'Great-uncle Frederick was killed at Canton in 1841, as you well know,' Katharine said patiently, and demolished the straw. 'Great-uncle Jacob disappeared without trace after he abandoned The Case in 1845, and is now legally presumed dead. Uncle Robert is the owner now,' she said bitterly, 'or rather, he is in possession, and you, Father, are the only one who can dispute it.'

Alfred sought wildly for inspiration. Katharine could be so difficult when she fixed on these mad ideas. 'Money,' he declared, thankfully. 'We have no money to pay a lawyer.'

'I've thought of that,' said Katharine calmly. Her head had been buzzing with plans ever since they left the meeting at Stowerton Place. The room had resounded with mocking laughter at her declaration, until her face burned with anger and embarrassment. Even Meg and Father had joined in at first, until they saw her face and fell silent, reserving their mirth for a more private occasion. Only Cousin David looked at her with anything like sympathy – as a younger son he would, of course, she thought wryly. Philip's snake-like eyes glinted fury at her, through the apparent mirth, for even mentioning the forbidden subject, which by tacit agreement, in view of their dependent position, was never referred to.

Only a trace of unease in Uncle Robert's watchful eyes had given her the strength to continue. He was worried. Why? The answer was obvious, she thought later, sitting in her small room at the Dower House, looking out at the apples beginning to ripen on the tree outside. Uncle Robert couldn't seriously be worried that he would lose The Case, even if he believed she was in earnest. The odds against their victory would be enormous. Then why? The answer came to her like a calming shower.

If ownership of the land were under dispute in the High Court at Westminster, it could not be sold.

How could she get the money to buy even this limited time? They had none. Sophy had only her allowance from Robert. Godfather did quite enough for them already. Yet there had to be a way . . . Katharine sat at the window, looking out into the night sky. All over the world there were Stowertons. Stowertons who had left Bocton for one reason or another, but perhaps not because they did not love it. Other skies shone over them now, yet perhaps they remembered it still? Surely they must. Other Stowertons who thought as she did, perhaps, to whose lives Bocton was in some way as integral as it was to hers. The family. Not just Robert and Philip and Aunt Sophy, but a family that stretched back over the centuries, and now like an oak, having grown full strong had spread its branches, reaching out all over the world. The root that gave them this strength remained constant, and the root was Bocton.

It was Aunt Sophy who made it possible. She heard Katharine out in silence, then hastily looked down at the lap of her deep purple taffeta dress. If it had been anyone other than Aunt Sophy, Katharine would have sworn she was trying to suppress laughter.

'Your Uncle Robert will not be pleased,' she pointed out mildly.

'I've no choice,' said Katharine hotly. '*We've* no choice. You see, don't you, Aunt Sophy, that Bocton can't be allowed to be knocked down and replaced by a factory?'

Sophy too loved Bocton. She had played in its gardens, run round its mazes, climbed its trees and explored the rambling rooms of the empty house. She was over twenty years older than Katharine, however, and knew that the course of the law once started could be a heavy stone, impossible to stop in its relentless journey. But there were other factors much more important than the house – which caught at Sophy's heart, made her wonder if this wild impossibility might indeed be practical, or whether the hope she had harboured all these years was merely romantic folly.

'You can do nothing without your father,' she said at last. 'You realise there are problems.'

'You mean Father's brothers,' said Katharine forthrightly.

'Yes. No case could be started without their being included; all the surviving sons have equal claim, and as there *are* surviving sons, as a woman, I have no claim.'

'Then we'll have to contact them,' said Katharine excitedly, as a whole field of possibilities opened up. 'Is there any reason why not? I know Father never talks of them but –'

'Oh, my dear,' said Sophy helplessly. 'My dear child.'

'Why did they go? Aunt Sophy, please tell me.'

Sophy got up abruptly as though she could not face her niece. 'They all had their reasons, my dear: disappointed hopes, expectations of a brighter future overseas, longing for foreign lands. But primarily –' her voice faltered '– they left because they were Stowertons.'

'Because they were –' Katharine repeated blankly.

Sophy swung round, her skirts rustling, her usually mild face pink. 'It's a kind of curse, Katharine. As though the Good Lord blessed the

21

Stowertons with charm, with wit, with loving kindness – and then to balance matters up He refused to give them the gift of tolerance. I heard all the stories your father used to tell you, but what he never explained to you was the misery, the heartaches, it caused as brother fought brother. For years there would be peace, and then it would break out again. Endlessly, endlessly.'

'It could change,' said Katharine hopefully. 'Couldn't it?'

Could it? A flame of hope flared in Sophy's heart. Her brothers, home and at peace after all this time. Even . . . No, perhaps that was too much to ask. 'You must persuade your father first,' she said slowly.

'And how do I persuade him, Aunt Sophy?'

'There is only one way to persuade Alfred of anything, Katharine. Convince him it's a good bet.' The words sounded odd, coming from her prim lips. 'I think,' said Sophy, 'you'd better let me talk to him. And if I succeed, then I will pay for you to have a preliminary discussion on the matter with my solicitors.'

Katharine stared at her curiously. 'But you can't afford it, Aunt Sophy.'

'I can,' said Sophy, going pink, 'and I would like to. You realise, of course, that Robert will not take kindly even to these initial steps. Suppose he withdraws the Dower House from you?'

Katharine gasped. 'Surely he could not do that?'

'I see no reason why he should not,' said Sophy. 'Or this Lodge from me.'

'Aunt, I hadn't thought!' The consequences of her actions were beginning to dawn on her belatedly.

Sophy reached out and held her hands. 'You're a brave girl, Katharine. If you believe in this enough, you'll do it, and you'll win.'

Stowerton and Stowerton was popularly thought to have been one of the models for *Jarndyce and Jarndyce*, the legal case that dragged on and on in the Court of Chancery in Mr Dickens' *Bleak House*. Father had told Katharine many times of how her grandfather, Nathaniel, had met a young office boy called Charles Dickens during a visit to his solicitors, Messrs Ellis and Blackmore. For one of her father's fanciful imagination, this practically constituted a personal introduction to the great man. But even *Jarndyce and Jarndyce* had been dwarfed in most respects by *Stowerton and Stowerton*. *Stowerton and Stowerton*, however, differed in one major particular. It concerned inheritance, true, but centred on the custom of gavelkind.

Kent is a strange county. It has always had its own ways of doing things and these are hard to change. For centuries it had had its own common law, enshrined in a Customal of Kent that overrode every other law except one made by the king himself, and arguably even that.

Legend has it that when William the Conqueror fought his way through to London, he was so impressed with the fighting qualities of the men of Kent (and the Kentish Men as those living on the other side of the Medway are called) that he granted them the right to continue the old Saxon custom of gavelkind, which principally gave them the right to divide their land on death between all the sons of the family, and not bequeath it, according to the new custom brought in by the Normans, to the eldest son alone.

Entranced by her proud heritage, Katharine had believed the legend, but reading the old law books in her father's library, struggling with ancient spelling and quaint language, she had come to realise that legend was largely that; only the fact that Kent was prosperous and its customs so strongly embedded in the land had led to the survival of its ancient ways.

Kentish families, however, proved as quarrelsome and litigious as those of the rest of England – indeed, perhaps more so. Not all lands in Kent remained subject to the custom of gavelkind. Many manors, granted by the king himself, or by an overlord, were held in knight's service, with homage or military service due as rent. Such manors passed, as came to be the common law of England, to the eldest son only. Only those that could be proven for 'time out of mind' to have been subject to the custom of gavelkind could be claimed by all the surviving sons, and not merely the eldest.

Anxious to keep estates intact and not to be forced to divide them amongst several heirs, which they saw as a threat to a family's power and standing, landowners tried many means to avoid the custom of gavelkind. They tried by creating an estate in fee tail; they tried by bequeathing money and possessions to younger sons, on condition that the will was not contested; they ignored the custom in the hope that younger sons would not wish to get embroiled with pleading and proving gavelkind; finally, as time went on, many applied to Parliament for a disgavelling statute to allow their property to pass undisputed to their eldest son.

But none of these measures, for one reason or another, had the slightest effect on *Stowerton and Stowerton*, which raged on, with intermittent pauses, down the centuries.

Yet Bocton itself remained curiously untouched by the battles around it, amid its green woods and fertile fields. Over the years Bucge's homestead had acquired further lands, other smaller manors with their own farms, mills and cottages, and by the time of the Domesday Book was a sizeable estate.

When Henry de Stour acquired the lands late in the reign of Edward I, he built himself a fine manor house. His heirs quarrelled so long and so expensively over the inheritance that the house was quite neglected and the family impoverished, until one Thomas Stoorton, as the family was by now known, grew rich from his support of the Yorkist side in the Wars of the Roses. While the white rose flourished, so did the Stoortons, and their wealth carried them comfortably into the Tudor era, in a fine new manor house with fashionably jettied upper storeys at either end of the great hall.

All would have been well had not Thomas's son, William Stoorton, impetuous and romantically minded, remembered a misguided loyalty

23

to the House of York when he talked by chance, in 1524, while visiting one of his other manors that had accrued to Bocton over the ages, to a brick-layer who claimed to be the illegitimate son of Richard III. He brought him to Bocton, so the story went, that his ancestry might be traced with the help of its fine library and the jewels he claimed as Richard's authenticated. But William was called away in the midst of these interesting discussions by a summons to court. In the hopeful belief that the King would be as charmed as he was by the discovery, he gave Henry full details. The King was indeed interested – but not charmed. William was imprisoned for treason and lost in swift succession his lands, his liberty, and his head. The brick-layer, warned of the approach of the King's Men, disappeared and lived into an impoverished old age on the nearby estate of Eastwell, dying twenty-six years later. No more was heard of the jewels, but persistent rumour had it that the Stoortons knew well where they were.

Bocton languished neglected, a forgotten manor in the hands of the Crown, until Queen Elizabeth granted it and all its subsidiaries to Sir Nicholas Stowerton, a good-looking and astute young man, grandson of the unfortunate William, brought up by distant relations. Nicholas wisely continued to charm Her Majesty, lest any lingering suspicions of Stowerton loyalty remained.

Visiting the nearby manor of Boughton Malherbe in 1573, Her Majesty took a detour at Nicholas' innocent suggestion, though not to stay. She was disapproving. Was this the manor of Bocton? This cramped old-fashioned timber-framed building was not fitting for one of his station. She bade Nicholas pull it down and build another. Money? Her Majesty glared. But his smile was even more irresistible than her love of a tight purse. With a smile she bade him pay her homage of a red rose. And, she added, attend Court on Midsummer's Day each year.

Sir Nicholas issued instructions to his master builder, and rode away to serve his Queen abroad. When he returned the grand new manor of Bocton Bugley awaited him. Gone were the oak-timbered frame and the wattle and daub; in their place a mansion three times the size, built in fashionable Kentish red brick with peg-tiled roof; two long wings flanked a long hall, enfolding an open paved courtyard at the rear between them, leading to the lake and formal gardens. In front of the house, rambling flower gardens had been transformed into quaint knot gardens and yew walks.

Sir Nicholas smiled in pleasure, leaped down from his horse and strode into his new domain, resolved to avoid strife for the rest of his life. This he succeeded in doing, but even he could not control what happened after that.

There was no getting round the fact that William Stoorton had been found guilty of high treason. And high treason was the one incontrovertible cause for lands to revert to the Crown, whether subject to gavelkind or no. If the Crown retained them, they would in due course descend, with the Crown itself, to the eldest male heir. What happened if the Crown granted them out again was a moot point. However, a learned judge, Sir Anthonie Browne, gave it as his authoritative opinion that so strong was the custom of gavelkind that the land must once again revert to a legal situation where all sons inherited.

The younger sons of Sir Nicholas Stowerton therefore lost no time in claiming to a jury that the lands of Bocton had 'time out of mind' been subject to gavelkind, and should continue to be so. The eldest son immediately informed the jury, firstly that it was the Crown's prerogative to change the nature of gavelkind lands, and that Queen Elizabeth in demanding Knight's Service of a rose from Sir Nicholas had thereby most certainly done so; secondly the Queen could not revert the lands to Sir Nicholas on the same terms as his forebears without seeming to condone the treason of his grandfather, and thirdly (by subtle innuendo) that Sir Anthonie Browne, when delivering his judgment on gavelkind, had clearly been well past his years of usefulness to society.

Disputes continued sporadically over the years, but at Bocton itself nothing much changed, save that it adapted itself to the new challenges of growing hops, cherries and watercress. One Stowerton grew extremely rich on its fertile lands, and built his younger brother Stowerton House to replace the old manor of Northwell, then watched in envy as he lived in more comfort and in better repair than did the owner of Bocton itself.

Bocton slumbered on for a hundred and fifty years, until vicious dispute once more broke out when Sir Matthew Stowerton unwisely died intestate in 1820. Waiting to hear the result of a minor bout of legal wrangling, he had deferred making his will till he knew the full extent of his property. Such was his joy when the jury found in his favour that he promptly expired. Then had begun the latest and most famous of the *Stowerton and Stowerton* cases in the Court of Chancery which had already been raging for some years when the young Charles Dickens first heard of it, and was to proceed for another eighteen before it petered out.

As a child Katharine was torn by what she read of her family history. One part of her despaired that the Stowertons were quite, quite mad, and the other part was spellbound by the tales her father told her.

'Never forget you are a Stowerton,' he would declare grandly at the end of each re-enactment of family history, often with Sophy dragged in to support him. Katharine loved best his account of the gavelkind action in the reign of Richard II, which had been decided by trial of battle – a verdict overruled twenty years later, since according to the Custom of Kent a gavelkind trial could only be held by judge and jury.

'Have at you, base varlet,' Father would snarl, paper helmet on head and poker for weapon. Sometimes, she recalled now, looking back to those far-off days, she was Father's opponent, sometimes that fair-haired boy, wearing a wastepaper basket and armed with Father's best stick. Who had he been, that boy? She asked Father once, who muttered something and retired behind his newspaper –

as always when she dared ask something about the past that she did not understand. In those days to fight at law had seemed a great and glorious thing to him. Now, she thought wryly, Father had changed, and she was going to take his place, seized by the age-old Stowerton madness.

When Sir Matthew died, his eldest son, Nathaniel, Alfred's father, prepared to step quietly into his inheritance, but Frederick and Jacob were both made of true Stowerton mettle. Hitherto neither had taken much account of Bocton, Frederick having his head full of foreign lands, and Jacob because he was too young. But Jacob was not too young to appreciate what might be passing out of his reach for ever, and persuaded his elder brother to reopen The Case. Frederick had obligingly done so.

Property lawyers' eyes gleamed at the prospect of such succulent fare as a case of gavelkind. Their enthusiasm lasted longer than Frederick's, who joined the East India Company and went east to seek the fortune he undoubtedly needed to continue The Case. He died in the campaign at Canton, leaving Jacob to continue alone. He battled on until 1845 when his money ran out, at which point the court, though not the lawyers, heaved a sigh of relief as he withdrew his suit. Nathaniel was thus left in control of Bocton, Stowerton and Charham manors, offering Jacob as a peace offering rents from the mill and the farm, amounting to £12 per year. Jacob refused this generous offer and disappeared.

Fourteen years later, with his death imminent, Nathaniel decided to update his 1835 will, and took steps to have Jacob legally presumed dead in order to leave Robert a clear path to his inheritance. With the same bad timing as his father, Nathaniel died before either end had been achieved, leaving his 1835 will valid. Under it, Robert inherited everything, although Nathaniel had had five other sons and a daughter. He provided a sum of money for each and dismissed them from his conscience in the happy belief that Robert would 'look after them'.

His other children had by now no such rosy-tinted view of their brother; three of them had already departed for different points of the globe by the time Nathaniel died early in 1860, a fourth soon followed. Robert took steps to speed the legal presumption of Jacob's death, and the Family Bible was closed. What was past, was past, and gavelkind and the misfortunes it had wreaked on the Stowerton family were most certainly part of it.

'Gavelkind?' Mr Pinpole's voice rose in a positive shriek. It occurred to Alfred for the first time that he might possibly enjoy this meeting as he saw Pineapple, as he had mentally dubbed him on account of his shape, struggling for words in the neat offices of Foggett, Dodson and Pinpole in Canterbury. 'Did you say gavelkind?' Unfortunately, his voice was raised so loud that suddenly two doors flew open simultaneously and his two partners, both like Pinpole in old-fashioned double-breasted frock coats, stood quivering with excitement on the thresholds.

'Mr Pinpole, pray,' breathed Mr Foggett, another Pineapple in shape, but both shorter and proportionally slimmer, 'this is most unethical, but if gavelkind is mentioned, may we attend?'

Mr Dodson, tall and thin, overtopped them both, a tree trunk between the fruit. 'I would be most obliged, Mr Pinpole. A real gavelkind would be most instructive.' His deep gravelly voice was almost wistful.

Mr Pinpole considered. Normally he would indignantly reject such intrusions into his professional jurisdiction, but mention of gavelkind made him cautious. Other heads and a joint sharing of responsibilities might be politic.

Katharine took a deep breath. 'We would like to know what the legal position is regarding Bocton. Does Sir Robert have a right to sell it, or does it not belong to all of Sir Nathaniel's sons under gavelkind?'

At the mention of the word noses twitched appreciatively again; at the mention of Robert Stowerton wary glances were exchanged. Imperceptibly they seemed to flow together, until they stood in line, three pairs of hands clasped firmly behind backs.

'The last case at Chancery, I recall, ended in your father, Sir Nathaniel, Mr Stowerton, entering upon sole inheritance of all the estates,' Pinpole vouchsafed cautiously.

'Only because The Case petered out for lack of money,' said Katharine firmly.

'Money. Ah,' said Mr Foggett. More glances.

'And it passed to Sir Robert by entail?'

'By will,' said Katharine.

'Then I regret,' said Pinpole in some surprise that they should even have been consulted, and more than a little disappointment, 'there is nothing to be done. Even if we could establish the lands are subject to gavelkind, and it is a big proviso –'

'A big proviso,' chorused his partners, equally disappointed.

'– to fight a specific will is hard indeed. We live in modern times, Mr Stowerton.'

'Then the old times were better,' declared Alfred, who had taken a distinct dislike to Mr Pinpole's wagging finger. 'Why, Sophy here wasn't even born when that will was made.' He rose majestically to his feet. 'Come, Katharine.'

'One moment, Mr Stowerton. I hesitate to ask such a question,' Mr Foggett was inexplicably almost dancing up and down in excitement, 'yet how old are you, Miss Stowerton?'

'Mr Foggett!' Mr Pinpole glanced at the senior partner with some disapproval. 'A lady!'

'I am forty-four, Mr Foggett,' replied Sophy, quite composed. 'Though I can't see what my age has to do with gavelkind.'

'Mr Foggett!' cried Dodson suddenly, echoed by a: 'Can you be thinking . . . ?' shrieked by Mr Pinpole. They beamed at each other, and all shook hands.

'And when,' asked Mr Foggett in a tense whisper, turning to their prospective clients, 'did Sir Nathaniel enter into his inheritance of Bocton?'

27

'Year the case died out,' said Alfred uneasily, not liking the sudden hopeful tone in their voices, since he had by now lost much of his former enthusiasm. 'Forty-five.'

'The *Wills Act*,' shrieked Pinpole, Foggett and Dodson in unison. 'There's a chance, a positive chance!'

'Oh, Mr Foggett,' breathed Mr Dodson in excitement to his senior partner, 'we haven't had a good will since the war.'

'It's tempting.' Pineapple was positively beaming.

'Not without money,' said Alfred desperately. 'We haven't any.'

'Details, details,' Pinpole said loftily.

Mr Foggett stood weightily considering the matter, then glanced up at his two partners. 'I believe –'

'Yes, Mr Foggett?' The suspense was terrible.

'We must consult the potential co-parceners.'

'You mean Father's brothers? They are abroad as you know,' cried Katharine eagerly, not daring to look at her father's face. 'We must advertise,' determined not to let them change their minds.

'Advertise?' Pinpole looked blank.

'Aunt Sophy tells me she has not heard from them for some years,' Katharine admitted reluctantly. 'But they are sure to respond when they know about Bocton, and one of the four must have money.'

'Three,' glared Alfred.

'Our youngest brother is no longer considered a member of the family,' Sophy explained quietly.

Alfred crossed his arms mulishly.

'Nevertheless, I fear the judicial system would still regard him as one,' said Pineapple firmly.

'Why?' Alfred asked belligerently.

'All brothers have a right to be consulted first to see whether they wish to be co-parceners, that is, parties to the suit, and in the event of victory all must enter into the estate.'

Alfred's eyes bulged. 'You mean he – *he* would get part of the estate. No, definitely no.' He rose to his feet again and was pulled down by Sophy and Katharine.

'Alfred,' said Sophy firmly, 'would you ever refuse to back a possible winner because a wrong 'un was racing?'

He considered this year's 100th Derby and his fortunate win on Lord Norrey's Sir Bevys. 'Oh, very well,' he muttered. Nothing would have stopped him backing that colt, he thought complacently, and he'd come in at twenty to one. And, true, he had hardly given a thought to the rest of the field.

'I believe I know where Joseph is,' said Sophy softly, 'but we can advertise in the newspapers, can we not, as well as writing to their last addresses?'

After some consideration, it was decided to summon them to a family meeting for the following April. 'But it's so long off,' objected Katharine appalled.

'Rome wasn't built in a day, Miss Stowerton,' said Mr Pinpole reprovingly.

'But Bocton can fall down in one,' she pointed out, alarmed. 'Suppose Uncle Robert sells and Bocton is knocked down next week?'

'I suppose we could enter a writ of ejectment immediately,' said Mr Pinpole doubtfully. 'It's irregular, but —'

'So was Hannibal!' injected Alfred, his imagination suddenly fired. 'Elephants and vinegar, Mr Pinpole, elephants and vinegar.'

'I doubt if the High Court will see it quite in that light, Mr Stowerton,' replied Pinpole drily. 'Nevertheless, I take it I have your agreement for this preliminary step? I should point out that at the moment all formal steps can be in your name alone, Mr Stowerton. Miss Sophy, as a woman, has no claim.'

Katharine held her breath. Fortunately Alfred had been transported to the Alps, to the route he was convinced the great Hannibal must have taken. He saw himself heading a long procession of Stowerton elephants safely through the Alps to victory. Marching ahead of the clan. 'By George, we'll make a fight of it, eh, Katharine?'

She flung her arms round him, swept away by affection. 'Yes, Father. Oh, *yes*.'

Alfred turned grandly to Messrs Pinpole, Foggett and Dodson. 'You may,' he announced, 'approach my brother Joseph Stowerton, my brother Jeremiah Stowerton, my brother George Stowerton. And —' his face grew pink '— that blasted fellow Albert!'

Meg, for once in her life, was thinking seriously. She couldn't believe at first that Katharine had been in earnest. Now that she had been told what had happened at the solicitor's, alarm bells were ringing furiously in Meg's head. Suppose Katharine succeeded in her ridiculous claim? And whether she did or not, the family would once more be split asunder. Philip would no longer be certain to inherit. She would be cut off from Stowerton House, the one avenue open to her at the moment that promised the life Meg was convinced should be hers. The possibility of her receiving money of her own through The Case was remote indeed compared with the near certainty of obtaining it through marriage to Philip. The latter, she had suddenly realised, since Katharine had sprung her news upon her, was the only sure way to money. True, he was a bore, but there was no denying that he was the heir and David was the younger son. Why was the world so contrary?

'Does that mean Philip wouldn't succeed?' Meg asked carefully, not betraying her own interest.

'Yes. Not to the whole estate anyway. Bocton and Charham, possibly even Stowerton, would be split between Father and all five of our uncles. It wouldn't be practical just like that, so some kind of financial settlement would have to be made. The mill and the farm, of course . . .' Her voice trailed off, as she foresaw one problem after another should they win. But the important thing was that Bocton should be saved. Who precisely would own it then must come second.

'I think you're being horrid to Uncle Robert,' said Meg, pouting. 'Who cares about that stupid pile of bricks?'

'I do, and you should, Meg,' said Katharine, appalled at her sister's flippancy. 'That stupid pile of bricks has all our family history in it. It's our past *and* our future. You can't just knock it down.'

'It's the present that is important,' said Meg mutinously, though not loudly enough for Katharine to hear.

'I am so sorry, Philip.' Meg's eyes filled with tears.

Philip looked at her. Cousin Meg, empty-headed but biddable. And pretty too. Not like Katharine. He was filled with rage against Cousin Katharine and this nonsense about gavelkind. The Stowertons had been a laughing stock over the centuries, but for the last quarter of a century it had died down and they had won the respect that was their due from their neighbours. Now Katharine was threatening to start it all again. She couldn't, of course. She had no money. They lived on Father's charity so far as the house was concerned. What Meg had just told him was distinctly worrying, however.

'I trust the solicitors laughed at their preposterous idea?' enquired Philip casually.

Meg hesitated, but Philip was waiting for an answer. 'Katharine said they have agreed to advertise to ask our uncles to attend a family meeting. It's all nonsense. As if they'd come. After all –'

'When?' Philip's voice was sharp.

'In April, I believe,' she said. After all, what harm could she do telling Philip what would soon be public knowledge from the newspapers?

'Indeed,' he said offhandedly, whilst thinking that in seven months much could happen. And then he heard her continuing: 'But they're going to issue a writ of something or other now.'

His eyes fixed themselves absently on the Reynolds portrait of younger Master Matthew Stowerton. All this under threat? 'Ejectment,' he said slowly. 'A writ of ejectment now? Are they indeed?'

Joseph Stowerton walked absentmindedly along the Corso. For once he was oblivious of the beautiful blue Pacific Ocean in front of him and of the new small shops and restaurants that were beginning to spring up on both sides of this wide avenue. Today he was cautiously optimistic about the future. He'd got the land to build the new hotel. There was no doubt about it, Manly was going to be prosperous. Already the numbers of day visitors from Sydney and further afield were growing. Now more land was being released for sale, and he was going to be one of the first to take advantage. For once the fates were looking kindly on Joseph Stowerton. Australia – an open land, a golden land, the land of the future.

When he had first come here, he'd settled in Sydney, living at Petty's Hotel until his small store of money had run out. It was there he'd met Emily, nineteen in 1857 to his twenty-five. She was a waitress, and on her day off they'd taken the ferry to Manly, the small community established in the cove in Sydney Harbour, named after Governor Phillip's description of the Aboriginal inhabitants who greeted him in

1788: 'their confidence and manly behaviour made me give the name of Manly to this place'. When Joseph and Emily had first come here, the whole place didn't have more than 200 residents, but he'd seen immediately that his future lay in Manly. Already far-sighted people were trying to buy up land, and with the ferry service established between Sydney and Manly's golden beaches in 1854, people were beginning to visit it. Perhaps Manly could be a holiday spot like Margate? Certainly the weather was better. He mopped his brow. Only December, and already 90°.

He'd married Emily – the one thing in his life that he *had* done right – and she'd taught him that out in this land, only work got you places. Not your name. So he forgot all about being a Stowerton and worked. By golly, he'd worked. But it hadn't fully paid off. Not yet. They'd opened a bar; it burned down. They tried again, and by scrimping and saving managed to build an inn up on Fairy Bower overlooking Cabbage Tree Bay. Now it was doing well, but not well enough. Bars for casual parties were not good enough for him. Hotels would be where the money lay. Hotels overlooking this golden beach. He exulted, but cautiously.

'My wife shall be a lady,' he told himself in some recollection of an old-timer striking gold somewhere. Then he grunted in displeasure at this betrayal of his origins. Was England in him still? The future was here, not in old weary countries, stifled by their past and by their albatross of colonies. Australia would be a nation on its own soon. It was marching forward.

The sweat was running off him as he climbed the steep hillside, to the mocking call of a kookaburra. He cursed the high collar and formal suiting that Emily had persuaded him to wear to the meeting this morning. He was glad to reach the shade of the old ti-trees, and enter the long low cool building. Emily was washing glasses in the kitchen and looked up, a smile on her round pleasant face. He was so engrossed in what he had to tell her that he didn't notice the smile was strained.

'That's good, Joseph,' she said warmly. 'I knew you'd do it.'

'What's that, Emily?' His sharp eyes saw her fidgeting with something in the bar – could it be, hiding it from him?

'Just a letter, Joseph.'

Quickly he picked it up, reading the warning in her eyes.

'It's from England,' he said, his voice gone suddenly flat, turning the envelope over and over in his hands. God-almighty, he might have known it couldn't be as easy as that. There had to be some cursed thing to mar his just reward. Swearing, he thumped his hand down upon the letter. 'Open it,' he said thickly. 'Open it.'

'You'll go.' Emily's voice held no note of query.

'No!' His own was almost violent. '*Now?*'

The reserved and almost gruff young man she'd met over twenty years ago had changed, matured now into a gentler, happier man, one as determined as ever to succeed but loving with it, not afraid to speak

31

his mind – or his love. But still there was something she could not reach – for she knew its origins went way back before the time she knew him, before Australia.

A bitterness, a hatred that could not be eradicated by her. And side by side with the hatred was something else. A deep love perhaps? She did not know. All she knew was that it was tied up with his family – and a place called Bocton.

'I can run the inn. And as for the new hotel, I reckon the land won't spoil for six months. And young Henry can keep an eye.'

Henry, their son, was nineteen, working on the *Illustrated Sydney News*. Jemima, their only other child, was now seventeen. After Jemima, there'd been three that didn't live.

'No!' he shouted. 'England is past. So is Bocton.'

'And your family?'

'Family!' He laughed bitterly. 'What's my *family* ever done for me?'

'That's why you must go, Joe,' she said quietly. 'A man with venom in his soul can't think straight. And you need to, what with the hotel and all. Jus' get rid of that, then come back to me, Joseph.'

Inside, she was frightened. Very frightened. What if he didn't come back? What if the love of this Bocton, of England, proved too much?

Heads were bent. 'Amen,' declared Jeremiah Stowerton finally before attacking in silence the old-fashioned chicken corn pie deemed fit for their household, in which Puritan values sat oddly with the splendour of their surroundings. His three children and martinet wife Augusta, having echoed a dutiful amen, followed his example.

Today Luke felt it would choke him. For his sisters' sake he stayed in this house of hypocrisy, which built its stark life on an insatiable greed for money. Partly too through an obscure and unsought-for pity for his silent, grim mother, caught in this dark world that she herself had caused to be created. Without his presence his sisters' life in this bleak household would be hopeless indeed. He had escaped it, mentally at least. His years at Yale University had shown him other kinds of life, not ruled solely by money and by a doom and destruction religion; a life in which love and not fear could be master, in which learning and zest could open the way to fulfilment. In the four years after Yale he had stayed away at first, writing for newspapers, travelling in his own country, longing to see other lands, to find out how others lived. But a plea from his sisters when they moved to a place called Leadville in Colorado had brought him reluctantly back, back to fight the battle he had been fighting all his life. Now it was different, though. His armour was complete, fortified by his years away and by his writing; it warded off attacks with light and glancing rapidity.

Jeremiah scowled at his son, his black hair and dark eyes making him look like a hell-fire preacher of the religion he followed.

'Nothing. I shall do nothing.'

What he deemed his son's 'flippant attitude to life' nonplussed Jeremiah, who bemoaned to his God that his son trod this world too lightly. His mother retreated from him further still, locked by her own choice into a way of life that had been hers from birth, and which had first attracted her husband to her, perhaps seeing in it an escape from the Stowerton heritage, or perhaps something else. However, if it was the answer to his problem, yet it spelled the doom of his children. He thought he had escaped from the Stowertons, but now Luke was a constant reminder to him of the worst of all the Stowerton faults. Fair-haired, tall, laughing his way through the world, he was as feckless as Alfred, as Nick Stowerton himself . . . and Luke let his father continue to think that way. It was his way to survival. Some day he told himself, he would find a new sort of life. Perhaps even create one for his sisters.

Today, unbelievably, the chance was here. But he must be careful. Not by a muscle did he show that anything other than a desire to irritate his father lay beneath his thrown-down gauntlet.

'Why?' he demanded lightly.

His sisters stared aghast. How could even Luke dare to break silence at luncheon! They sat breathless, waiting for retribution to fall.

'Luke!' rapped Augusta sharply.

He smiled at her reassuringly but unflinchingly.

Jeremiah ignored his question, though he breathed the more heavily.

'Why?' demanded Luke again, this time more urgently, although still in control. He must remain controlled. A muscle twitched at the corner of his mouth. It might have been amusement; it might have been tension.

Jeremiah laid down his knife and fork, wiped his lips with his napkin, and stared at his son. 'This is not the time –' he began.

'Then tell me the time, Father,' retorted Luke pleasantly, his hands clenched tightly round his water glass.

'Very well!' Jeremiah roared, standing up. 'It shall be now.'

Martha shrank back, remembering how she always confused Father with Moses when she was small, and wondering now whether she had been much mistaken.

'I shall not disgrace a table blessed by the Lord with argument. Follow me.' Without a backward look, Jeremiah walked majestically from the room.

Mary burst into tears, but her mother bade her be quiet and continue her luncheon.

Luke followed his father down the long hallway to his study, relieved that the die had now been cast.

Not many brick houses like the Stowertons' existed yet in Leadville. Indeed, 'Cloud City' as it was so nearly named, because of its altitude two miles above sea-level, had only been in existence for a little over a year. Before that there had been mountains, trees, gulches – and abandoned placer gold workings. Jeremiah Stowerton had first brought his family to America in 1859, when his finely attuned nose for money had twitched at the news of gold found at Pike's Peak, in what was then barren and unclaimed territory.

33

'Pike's Peak or Bust' had been the rallying cry for thousands. Most came east in groups from California, disappointed in dreams of easy gold there, many falling prey to Indians or illness en route. Jeremiah Stowerton came west, however. Across the Atlantic he sailed, shaking the dust of Bocton from his life for ever in search of brighter goals. But he didn't travel to Pike's Peak or even Denver; he settled in New York, foreseeing that gold needed to be organised, marketed, sold – and profit made. And gold was found, not only in Pike's Peak but all over what was first the Territory, and now State, of Colorado. Jeremiah Stowerton learned, and prospered in mining stock, but the great prize eluded him. Money. Money he pursued as an ideal; it was to be made, and made in quantity. Only in that way could he revenge himself on the fates that had cast him as younger brother to Robert.

And one day, while he was on a routine visit to his Denver branch, a rough hobo came staggering into his office, a miner, bleary-eyed and drunk. His secretary, apologising profusely, rushed in to throw the man out. But Jeremiah stopped him. For the miner told a fantastic tale. A tale not of gold but of lead, and moreover silver-bearing carbonate of lead. Jeremiah's nose had more than twitched. Like a water-diviner with a hazel twig, it had positively quivered and bounced.

From the civilised streets of New York the Stowerton family had promptly moved to Leadville, a rumbustious lawless mining camp full of the scum of the earth and a few more determined men. One of them was Horace Tabor, a man who like Jeremiah had backed a hunch and now, only eighteen months later, owned mines and money beyond anyone's wildest imagination. Even Jeremiah's. Clinging to old puritanical habits, as a safeguard for his soul, Jeremiah pursued the dream and then the reality of money as it danced round each enticing corner.

Luke watched his progress and sickened. He remembered the world of his childhood. Was it real or merely dreamed from his imagination, a vision of paradise to set against this treadmill to Hades? Were there really green fields and meadows dappled in sunlight, full of the scents of flowers? Were there really woods, full not of tall spruce and aspens but carpeted with anemones and bluebells? Was there ever a world where nature had its way, undespoiled by the greed of men?

He had wanted to travel to pursue that dream. Just to see what other worlds were like. But he couldn't. He had been ready to go without a penny, to set out on his metaphorical wagon with 'Pike's Peak or Bust' written on it, though *his* gold was a different sort to his father's. Then his sister Mary had pleaded for his return. How could he leave them unprotected from Father's maniacal search for riches, in what he'd heard was the lawless life of Leadville?

So he had returned. But now his chance had come.

Luke followed Jeremiah into the study. *The Times* was lying still on the large desk. His eyes went to it. Just a plain advertisement announcing: 'Bocton. All parties of the Stowerton family interested in the future of the Bocton estate to attend on 15 April 1880 with a view to discussing its future.'

Bocton. When Luke had seen the announcement, quite by chance this morning, he had remembered. It was Bocton, that place of green woods and meadows. And more than that – he racked his brains – a house, and childhood games, and companions. He could remember little more about it, yet the thought of it set his pulses racing.

'You presume to dispute my decision?' Jeremiah began without preamble. He never knew quite where he was with Luke; the boy's levity, ill becoming a man of twenty-seven, was something that puzzled him. He told himself that discipline and hard work would knock it out of him. But it hadn't. He frowned. Luke, with his fair hair and dark blue eyes, was in such contrast to himself and Augusta. Luke was a throwback to his Stowerton forebears, part of that past Jeremiah did not care to recall – and now was forced to.

'Why are you scared of returning, Father?' Luke asked, lounging against the bookcase. 'Did you lock up a skeleton in the closet before you left?'

Jeremiah spluttered. 'Scared!' he retaliated scornfully. 'It's time you realised life is a serious business, boy. Once you gallivant along side turnings, you're lost.'

'You mean the pursuit of money is a serious business, Father,' Luke said provokingly. It was an effort, but only by so doing could he take the sting from his father's power.

'And what's wrong with that?'

'Nothing. Provided you don't turn into a pillar of silver.'

'Twaddle! I've no time to go. Who's to look after my interests here, eh?' It was a rhetorical question; it wouldn't be his idle son. Luke lacked application.

'Then I shall go.'

Jeremiah stared at him, the anger which had temporarily subsided sweeping back over him. 'No,' he said peremptorily.

'Father, you've more money than any of us can possibly spend. Don't you wonder how your brothers are and what's happened to them? You haven't written since you left – we only saw this *Times* by chance – it's two months old.'

Jeremiah rose abruptly. 'Get out!' he screamed suddenly.

Even Luke flinched at the unexpected venom in his voice, but he stayed. 'No,' he said steadily. 'I have a right to know about our family. About my uncles. About Bocton. You never talk of any of them, and we *should* know.'

Jeremiah stared from the window, shaking with emotion. Tell him? Tell him of George, whose aimlessness had sent him wandering footloose all over the country, turning up from time to time seeking more funds, to be overwhelmed with the affection they all poured on him? Tell him of Alfred, who'd never keep a penny in his pocket if he could throw it away? Tell him of Sophy, who never did anything in her life? Tell him of Albert? Tell him of Joseph, unable to speak up for himself, who couldn't hope to win against – *Robert*. Above all, impossible to tell him of Robert. All his early life, Robert had been there, two years his senior, blocking his every move, aloof, superior, snakelike, hateful. Always *there*. Finally, stopping Father from giving him the money he needed to start a business. He could hear it now, Robert's high pedantic voice: 'A *business*, Father? That doesn't seem right. Not for a Stowerton.'

But he'd had his revenge. Oh, yes. He'd had Millicent, the girl Robert had long courted, whom he, Jeremiah, had taken first in the long grass, who'd shown a passion in her rounded limbs that had enslaved him. He hadn't intended that, because in the end, as usual, Robert had won. She'd married him because he was the eldest son, and would inherit the whole estate. Money . . . No, he'd never return. He hated her, as he hated Robert. They were cut from his life. Now, when his body stirred and could not be subdued, he blamed *her*. Always *her*.

'It's past. Over,' he said flatly to Luke, the passion dying from his voice.

'But what do you think they want to discuss, Father? Are you not curious?'

Jeremiah swung round. Luke stared in amazement for something that might almost have been a smile came to his lips for a second.

'Gavelkind, Luke,' he said slowly. 'I suspect they wish to reopen The Case.' And he began to explain. Then he stopped short. Why had he not realised? Revenge could be his. It was so simple. If gavelkind could be shown to apply, Robert would lose his inheritance. And Millicent would suffer.

'Go,' he almost choked out.

'No, I want –' Luke misunderstood.

'I mean, go to England,' said Jeremiah impatiently. '*Go!*'

Mabel Stowerton sat in the garden of her hotel in Baghdad, considering the paragraph she had somewhat belatedly seen in *The Times*. She glared at the Arab who had advanced optimistically towards her, entranced at seeing an English lady alone, and not in the least put off by the serviceable tweed skirt and battered old hat. He changed his mind rapidly, and retired.

Bocton? Interested in its future? Mabel thought long and carefully, and then laughed. She'd intended to go to Albania in April. Still, there might never be another chance like this. She owed it to George to go.

'*Chéri!*' The voice of Louise, formerly Comtesse de Fréjus, now Madame Stowerton, rang out plaintively. Albert wandered in from the garden of their villa on the hillside of La Californie in Cannes, his entrance timed to a nicety. The sweetness in her voice did not disguise the underlying note of steel, but they understood each other now and, while he would obey, it would be in his own time.

'There is a letter for you. From England. It has been somewhat delayed. It was addressed to Rome.' There was only the slightest emphasis on 'Rome'. To all outward appearances, Louise was more interested in the rearrangement of the elegant folds of her rose chiffon teagown than in correspondence from overseas.

Albert Stowerton regarded the envelope somewhat nervously when he saw from the embossed stamp that it was clearly a business letter. Not more trouble, surely?

He ripped it open, aware of her curious eyes upon him. He looked at it and began to laugh.

'What is this?' his countess demanded suspiciously.

In between bursts of laughter that shook a figure that was still elegant, despite last year's fortieth birthday, he managed to explain:

'They want me to attend a family meeting, *ma rose*, to discuss the future of Bocton. *Chéri*, perhaps they are thinking of reopening The Case!'

Even the countess smiled. 'And what,' she said carefully, examining her still exquisite face in the mirror, 'shall you say? You cannot, of course, go.' She turned round and met his gaze.

Albert looked innocently back at her and reflected. A smile curled round his lips – a malicious one. 'Do you know, my dear, I think I *shall* go. It might be most amusing.'

'But what if – ?' the countess began sharply.

'This is a Stowerton affair,' he interrupted quickly. 'No danger of that.'

She relaxed. 'Do you wish to take Louis with you?' she asked casually. 'It might be instructive for him to meet his English relatives.'

And a safeguard for you, he thought to himself. How well he understood her, and she him. 'If he wishes it, naturally,' was all he said. After all, it would hardly spoil, and might well enhance, the drama of the occasion. It was not every day that a prodigal son was not only admitted back into the fold, but positively invited. Especially one who had every intention of remaining prodigal.

Chapter Three

'Stud an' mud,' said Obadiah disapprovingly. 'Or wattle an' daub, as 'is lordship called it.' Animal dung had no place on the walls of a decent house, in Obadiah's opinion. 'Primitive, that's what dem mediaeval builders were. An' lazy. 'Course,' he paused, trying to be fair, 'dere's no denying some folks find it interesting. The lad [this was Obadiah's thirty-year-old son Jethro], 'e went to work over 'eadcorn way for a lordship. Almost a lordship, anyways,' he amended. 'When he got dere, 'is lordship was all set to pull 'is 'ouse down, just to see if 'e got dis mediaeval house inside. Member of this 'ere Kent Archaeological Society, 'e is. Mostly dey likes a nice church, but 'im, 'e says 'e likes old houses, because 'e reckoned dere was lots of houses in Kent where de old places had been covered up an' 'idden by new walls. Quite right too. 'Ow dese mediaevals expected an 'ouse to last built of wood and dung beats me. I went over to give the lad a bit of advice, that 'ow I recognised yours, yer see.' He cast a disparaging look towards the hole in the study wall before resuming his inspection of the entrance hall.

He pointed towards the ceiling over the great hall and stairway with his yardstick. 'If yew was to ask me, Miss Katharine, dey built dis ceiling to cover up the roof in Tooder times. In de ole days, dey couldn't be bothered with no ceilings.' De 'old days' to Obadiah meant anything before Good Queen Bess invented England, right back to Julius Caesar, Katharine had discovered through her long association with him.

'Is that going to cause trouble, Obadiah?' she ventured to ask him, torn between concern and a desire to laugh at his outraged expression.

'Nah,' he admitted somewhat reluctantly. ''Ere be trouble,' pointing at the front wall. 'When de lazy devils put de false front on, dere was an 'ole left between de old and new walls on de lower storey, 'acos of de jetty at either end – dat's where de upper storey overhung de lower. So de new wall, it come straight down, like a decent brick wall should.'

Bit by bit Katharine disentangled Obadiah's theory that in the great hall where Nicholas Stowerton added the stairway and upper corridor surrounding the hall at first floor level, the builders had to extend the floor out to match up with the jettied rooms at either end, knocking away in all probability a great many of the old framing beams underneath.

'Bocton has stood up for three hundred years, Obadiah,' she pointed out firmly, in the well-established pattern of doubt and persuasion that had taken place between them in the last few years.

He sniffed. 'Ve'll see,' he said darkly. 'Ve don't know 'ow much 'as been eaten yet.'

'Eaten?' she repeated, startled.

'De liddle beetles,' he said happily. 'Munching away now for a tharsand years or more.' His understanding of the centuries was somewhat lacking. 'You want to be careful what you do touch, Miss Katharine. Whole house could fall dahn at a kick of a calf's hoof. Don't you start meddling wid dem beams.'

She laid her hand on his arm. 'Don't worry, Obadiah,' she said, determined not to be daunted. 'We'll get Bocton restored somehow. Perhaps we'll find Richard III's jewels . . .' She laughed.

''Et won't be coming to no 'arm during de winter, Miss Katharine,' he assured her. 'We'll tuck 'ers up all nice.' But he so nearly was wrong.

Katharine had waited uneasily after her dramatic declaration in September, wondering what Robert's next step would be. Alfred did not seem concerned, even when the half-expected letter arrived threatening to turn them out of the Dower House.

'Do nothing, my dear. That's my motto,' he announced grandly and predictably. 'Ignore it. It will go away.' For once he seemed to be right, for no formal solicitor's letter followed. In fact Robert was too astute to turn them out. He was well aware that, for all his own money, Alfred Stowerton was held in higher esteem locally than he was himself, and for the moment with the railway negotiations so precariously poised, he could not afford to alienate public sympathy.

His next move, however, was completely unexpected and unrecognised then for what it was.

Early in October Katharine was harvesting the last of the James Grieve apples, and was perched on the ladder in the small orchard she had created at the back of their vegetable garden. Properly stored in their attic, these apples would last them throughout the winter, and the less than perfect ones went into making apple wine and cider. It was a difficult job since she had no help. Meg turned her pretty nose up at such down to earth employment, manufacturing an excuse of 'mending'. Mending in fact was a diplomatic word for sewing artificial flowers on to the train of her new winter dress. Maggie was too busy with household chores – and no one would think of asking Father.

Suddenly she became aware, even through her absorption, that she was not alone. The drone of bees and birdsong had been replaced by a heavy silence. She glanced down expecting perhaps to see her father. It was not. It was Philip, intense eyes set in his heavy rounded face fixed on her ankles and, since she had lifted her skirts for climbing, partly exposed legs; and since she was almost directly above him, he could probably see further still. A shiver of disgust ran through her.

'What are you doing here?' she cried sharply, climbing as quickly as she could down the ladder.

'Paying a social call, Cousin Katharine – and enjoying *our* property,' he replied coolly, emphasising the 'our' to ensure she realised that the orchard did not belong with Dower House land. He did not look as if he had come to enjoy country pursuits, dressed in his impeccable morning coat and striped trousers.

'I'm glad you say *our*,' she retorted sweetly, rearranging her skirts, and furious at being caught so off guard. Skirts were ridiculous for this sort of work. A labourer's tasks demanded a labourer's clothes, and she would see in future she wore them, and be blowed to what people thought.

He attempted a smile, but failed for it resembled a sneer. 'Father's and mine, of course.'

'That is open to argument,' she said levelly.

'Cousin Katharine, I have not come to quarrel with you,' he replied mildly. 'On the contrary, I have come to help.'

She regarded him suspiciously. Philip, help? 'Good,' she said lightly. 'There's another basket there. Start on the next tree.'

He regarded the basket with distaste. 'I mean with advice.'

'I did not know you were an expert on apple growing,' she said innocently.

'Cousin Katharine,' he retorted, somewhat rattled, 'cannot we talk reasonably? You know I have always admired you –'

'No,' she said, before she thought, 'I did not know that.'

'It is the truth,' he said. 'Let us go somewhere where we can converse. Somewhere less wet.' His eyes flashed briefly down to the long grass which had dampened his polished black boots, and the hem of her skirts. He took her arm firmly to escort her back into the Dower House garden and it was all she could do not to recoil from his touch.

Once there, and seated in the small arbour, she felt more able to cope with Philip, less overpowered by his presence. How ridiculous to think that way about him, though. It was only Cousin Philip, whom she had grown up with, although he was six years older than she. He had always been there, hovering, never participating – if he had been more likeable he would have been an almost pitiable figure compared with David, a favourite with all the family.

'You must not think I am not proud to be a Stowerton,' he remarked. 'I believe in our heritage too. However, your reopening The Case can only harm the family.' She stiffened mutinously as he continued: 'Even if all the brothers were to come and to agree to proceed – and as women you and Aunt Sophy, of course, have no legal standing in the matter – the result can only be that the family will be torn apart once more by feud. Surely you do not wish that?' he asked politely. Her eyes flashed but he ignored the danger signals. 'Whatever money you have – and I am not quite sure, Cousin Katharine, how you intend to finance this venture – will go to the lawyers, just as it has over the centuries. You know what damage it has done to the family fortunes in the past. How can you consider reopening such wounds again? You who pretend to have the interests of family and Bocton at heart.'

'*Pretend?*' she said sharply, disconcerted by this new angle on her actions.

'I apologise,' he said instantly. 'Of course, you do not pretend. I know you are a person of great integrity.' He appeared sincere. 'I have come here with a suggestion. Forget this ill-advised gauntlet. The time to repair our fortunes is now, with the railway companies so interested. Father and I now propose that we sell the estate, but retain the house and the land immediately around it. We will put part of it at least in order so that you may live there and run your school. Furthermore,' he added carefully, 'so that you may share in the proceeds of the sale after it has gone through, we will transfer ownership of Bocton to you.'

Own Bocton? The world seemed to swim round her. 'Philip!' All other thoughts fled save that she could be the owner of Bocton. No one could sell it then. 'I've misjudged you, I'm sorry,' she continued warmly. 'It's a very generous offer. I will discuss it with Father.'

A fleeting expression of annoyance crossed his face, but he wisely said nothing. 'Of course,' he murmured.

'But why are you doing this, Philip?' she asked, puzzled. Something told her to be careful. Did leopards change spots? And was not Philip too catlike in his underhandedness? In the silence of perhaps seconds, her eyes fell on the old sundial with its worn inscription: 'Only count the happy hours. *Carpe diem.*'

Seize the day. She should do it. Bocton would be hers. And yet, and yet . . .

'Katharine.' He leaned forward, suddenly seizing her hand. Then, with a muttered 'Forgive me', quickly moved to sit beside her on the bench, drew her to him and kissed her full on the lips, pressing her body close to his.

She tore herself away, repulsed by the contact with his body, at the feel of his warm hands through her dress, as much as by the kiss itself. 'Philip! What on earth do you think you're doing?' Bewilderment followed shock.

'Forgive me,' he said, but he looked smug not contrite. 'Seeing you here, so beautiful, surrounded by these bright flowers – I can't think what came over me. Yet I don't regret it. Not for one moment.' He held on to her hand. 'Do you?'

'Cousin Philip,' she interrupted, withdrawing her hand and repressing her instant desire to tell him just how much she regretted it. 'I am not a beauty,' she informed him tartly.

'Ah, to me, Katharine. Always to me.'

'Cousin Philip, I am grateful to you for your offer of Bocton,' she said, her voice trembling a little. 'I will think about it.'

Think about it? he sneered disdainfully to himself, watching her hurry back into the orchard. How dare she? Think about it indeed! She'd accept – both Bocton and him. He shrugged. It might not be so bad after all. A man of intelligence could win any woman he wanted – and adapt her to his needs.

'It means losing the land, Father, but we'd save Bocton.'

Why was she not happier? Why was she not overjoyed with victory? She had told her father everything – except about the kiss. She didn't like even remembering the touch of Philip's thick lips on hers. There

41

had only been one love in her life, a local schoolteacher who had come to instruct her in Greek. One day he had kissed the earnest pale-faced sixteen-year-old, overcome by a mutual passion for the less erotic of Ovid's poems, but he had departed from Bocton Bugley taking with him not a classicist but the buxom miller's daughter. She had never cared for Ovid since. Now marriage was something she had relegated for consideration after the main purpose of her life was achieved. She didn't want to be like Meg, thinking of nothing but marriage and clothes. Yet she didn't want to be an Aunt Sophy either, though with some uneasiness she realised how likely that might be, especially if she were to be a schoolmistress at Bocton. But if the alternative were someone like Philip, it would be a blessed life indeed!

'You don't like their offer, do you, Father?' she said, correctly interpreting his silence when she'd finished.

He jumped, startled. 'I am sorry, my dear. I was miles away. I was thinking of my last winner.'

'Oh, *Father*!' Horses, always horses.

'Don't be exasperated, Katharine. It is relevant. You see, I was intending to put my money on Loyal Duty. Good form, good jockey – everything looked good. Just at the last possible moment, however, I thought – no, I won't. I'll put it on My Pride.'

'What does this have to do with Bocton?' she asked patiently.

'It's the same situation. Instinct, my dear. Have Robert and Philip ever done us a good turn before?'

'No,' she said, racking her brains.

'Then why should they now?'

'To stop The Case perhaps. But we know what the odds are against our even beginning it. We haven't the money.'

'Don't you think they realise that?' Alfred said.

'Yes, but – Father, are you telling me they really think it might happen, and that we *might* win?'

'I haven't the slightest idea. But do you not think it strange they should be talking of putting Bocton in *your* name and not in mine?'

'Father!' She was horrified that in her enthusiasm at the idea of owning Bocton, she hadn't even thought about this aspect. Of course it was odd.

Alfred smiled benignly. 'If I were charitable, I would assume that since you are their main obstacle, they wish to placate you, banking on my not objecting. But I am not always charitable.'

'But this way we would own Bocton outright; even if we won The Case, we would have to split the properties somehow.'

'Just a sniff, Katharine. Just the smell of bad horseflesh in my nostrils.'

'So what do I do, Father?'

Alfred took a pinch of snuff. 'Gamble, my dear. Gamble.' And picked up the *Sporting Times* again. In another week or two he would be driven to Maidstone to take the railway train to London, and then to Newmarket. Bliss swept through him. What more could life offer?

*   *   *

42

Katharine turned down Robert's offer, politely but firmly, but lay awake night after night fretting lest she had put Bocton out of her reach for ever. However, soon proof arrived that these leopards had indeed not changed their spots. Early in November she arranged to meet Obadiah at Bocton in order to discuss what they should do about protecting the house for the winter; when she arrived, however, she found not Obadiah but Gouch and two or three men in overalls. She stopped, hidden for the moment by the trees of the Yew Walk, puzzled. Was Gouch, too, worried about what the winter might do to the building? Surely not.

Had Uncle Robert relented? Was he obtaining estimates of how much it would cost to repair the house? Convinced this must be so, she hurried towards them, eager to be part of it. Then something happened that made her realise she was wrong. The men walked up to the front door, one of them kicking it disparagingly with a foot – and another swinging a hammer contemptuously through one of the delicate amber-leaded panes in the small window on the side of the porch. At once she realised why they were here.

Scarcely knowing what she was doing, she sped towards them, shouting at them: 'You're going to knock it down, aren't you? *Aren't you?*' Of course, of course. How could she have been such an idiot as to think Uncle Robert had good intentions?

Gouch stopped the men with a word, and turned to greet her coolly.

'You can't do it,' she choked as she reached them.

He caught her by the arm, holding her back from trying to reach the door and bar them from entering.

'Now what makes you think that, Miss Stowerton?' he enquired blandly, as she struggled in his grasp and then tore free.

'That!' She pointed to the small heap of shattered glass. 'That glass is three hundred years old and you've smashed it in seconds.'

'H'accident, Mr Gouch,' sniggered a labourer, nudging his companion. 'We're 'ere to turn this dump into a palace fit for Her Gracious Majesty 'erself, ain't that so?'

Gouch said nothing but prepared to push past Katharine into the building. She flung herself before the inner door, and he hauled her out of his way with an impatient grunt.

''E 'urting yew, Miss Katharine?' Obadiah suddenly appeared in the porch, bristling with truculence, a plump knight on a white charger. Dear old Pug was in fact peacefully grazing on the lawn, finding himself suddenly free, trundling the cart behind him.

Gouch let her go, glaring at Obadiah. 'You're trespassing, Trant. Both of you can go and leave us to our work.'

'Best come away, Miss Katharine,' Obadiah whispered, and, sick at heart, she turned her back on Bocton. Obadiah drove her home, and she rushed to find her father. He was not there, but waiting in the morning room, on an unexpected visit, was Godfather, impeccably handsome as ever in his formal London attire. And it was to him she blurted out the story.

43

'Mr Dean!' She clutched at his arm as he rose to meet her, anxiety making her incoherent.

Alexander Dean listened gravely. 'If you are right, an injunction is in order.' Within thirty minutes, having added Aunt Sophy to the party, they were on their way to Canterbury, in Dean's hired brougham.

'The County Court is not empowered to deal with estates of the magnitude of Bocton,' declared Mr Pinpole agitatedly. He did not like being taken by surprise with demands to act quickly. It was not the way Foggett, Dodson and Pinpole liked to do things.

'Then we will go to Westminster,' said Godfather firmly.

'To Westminster,' echoed Mr Pinpole, this clearly being a concept that took even more time to grapple with. 'Next week –'

'Today!' said Alexander Dean inexorably.

It had taken twenty-four hours to get the injunction, and Katharine was terrified as to what she might find when she next went to Bocton. As though coming back after a long absence, she saw the red-brick front, welcoming even in November. It was undamaged. Gouch's party had clearly been on inspection only. From then on she watched and worried over Bocton like a mother hen, as though it might disappear before her eyes. Obadiah, muttering about winter being no time for joinery, fixed protective sheeting over the worst of the holes, and vanished, popping up again in March like a cuckoo.

Robert had been silent over the winter on the question of Bocton; the dutiful Christmas gathering was strained, the air crackling with tension. Katharine assumed this was because of her, but realised later it was not. Her uncle was occupied with the problems of the railway. Unable to outbid the London, Chatham and Dover Railway in their bartering for land north of Bocton, the South Eastern Railway were frustrated in their plans to put forward a practical plan to Parliament to support their claim to build the new line. All their energy went into opposing the LCDR scheme, by trying to get the bill, which had not yet been debated, rejected by Parliament.

These facts had come to light during an acrimonious public meeting at the Star Hotel, Maidstone, in February, which Katharine had attended. The mention made of 'an influential landowner in the neighbourhood, who is a director of the South Eastern Railway' had made her smile. But she had rapidly ceased to smile when it had been revealed that landowners and directors of the South Eastern were making last ditch attempts at preventing the more popular LCDR (because they improved service and lowered fares) from gaining speedy parliamentary approval for the link.

With rival plans before Parliament, bitter arguments were still raging all around this part of Kent, and in this spring of 1880, Bocton waited to know its fate. True, the injunction helped, but until the matter was finally settled, Katharine fretted and worried.

At Godfather's suggestion, she had asked the Society for the Preservation of Ancient Buildings to send someone to view the property again, in order that the beauties – and plight – of Bocton should be made more widely known. Uncle Robert would not dare to ignore the injunction and might even feel under some pressure to repair the old house, though this was doubtful. At the very least it would be guidance for her as to what should be done and how. The Society had promised to send someone down, and with this in mind, as well as the forthcoming family meeting, after which surely all the members would wish to inspect Bocton, Katharine decided to do the best she could to present it in its most favourable light.

There was only one problem. In retaliation for the injunction, Robert had forbidden her to visit Bocton, and the locks had been changed. The first she ignored. The second presented only slightly more difficulty. Despite the chilly weather she threw herself with gusto into stripping ivy from walls, tidying broken masonry opening windows to air rooms where lack of glass was not already performing this function. Everything now depended on 15 April.

On Wednesday 14 April Joseph Stowerton climbed aboard the London, Chatham and Dover Railway train bound for Canterbury. He had deliberately bought a third-class ticket. No Stowerton ever travelled third-class, or even second. Faces turned to look at him as the train steamed slowly back towards the scenes of his youth, observing his bronzed face, grim expression, and quaintly cut clothes. A foreigner, they realised, and turned away, dismissive of this alien presence. They didn't know he was English, Joseph thought sardonically, interpreting their attitude. He was as English as they were, and perhaps more, his family stretching back way beyond the days of Good Queen Bess. A sudden surge of family pride – and even excitement – at what might lie ahead took hold of him.

Luke Stowerton was wandering along the woodland path, taking time to savour this new land where fresh green leaves replaced the dust of mines. There were no bears in these woods, like those back home. No brightly coloured blue jays, no chicadees. Just a thrush singing. Didn't Browning write about April in England, and thrushes?

Hold hard, Luke, don't get carried away, he warned himself. Take things real easy. Remember what Father told you, when at last you persuaded him to tell you something of what you are about to face.

'Look out for the Stowertons, Luke. They've squabbled for six centuries and they aren't going to stop now. Some of them are good, some bad, some stupid, and some downright mean. And they aren't always as they seem.'

It was a surprising thing for Father to say – especially when it was about all he did say. He just clammed up after that, explaining nothing about the family squabbles. He had never said anything about England in the past, merely that they were all Americans now, no longer English. Of course, Luke remembered some things hazily from his own youth. He even remembered some of the Stowertons, enormous figures magnified by childhood. Were they real or had he confused them with giants and ogres from fairy tales? He recalled some kind of mock battle, one of his uncles in a helmet and wielding a poker, himself the opposition. 'Go on, Uncle Alfred, go on. Try to hit my sword,' he heard his youthful voice saying. Wasn't there a little girl there? And a beautiful woman, like a princess? Or was that a fairy tale too? No, for Alfred was no fairy tale. And wasn't that battle over gavelkind?

He had been incredulous when, in reply to his questioning, his father had explained tersely what gavelkind was and the problems it had brought.

Surely that could have nothing to do with the magical place he remembered from his childhood? Or if it had, then Bocton itself must surely show the signs.

Yet he'd come to England all the same. Ten to one, this was a trick of some kind to get money out of his family. In trying to escape the endless domination of the pursuit of money at home, he might find the same lust here. For all his eagerness to see the family roots, he must not overlook the fact that these roots might now be rotten, fine timber turned to powder. But he'd be ready for them, ever vigilant.

He emerged from the woodland into overgrown gardens. His attention was caught first by an old iron statue rusted amid the weeds, then by the entrance to an enclosed garden. He wandered over to it and into the garden, and found it cared for, full of daffodils, its brick paths curving and twisting into an intricate pattern, culminating in an old sundial at the centre. Then he looked up – and saw Bocton.

So this was it. He drew a deep breath. No dream; it was there just as he had imagined it. How could he have forgotten that this place really existed, the house he'd loved and left behind when he was seven? His family had lived at Charham then, an uncomfortable house and soulless. Bocton had not been like that at all.

He had come here frequently with old Grimmer, Grandfather's steward with whom he was great friends, and while Grimmer went about his business on the estate, Luke would play in the house; it had taken a deep hold on his imagination, instilling a love deep within him that had unconsciously endured through all the years in America, the something inside him that reminded him he was English. Just as Father and Mother never forgot it either with their strict adherence to formality. Was that where the sombre heavy Puritanism that dominated all their lives came from too? The Puritanism that contrasted so oddly with Father's headlong pursuit of money.

As he approached, Luke saw the house was sad, crying out with emptiness and neglect. Indignant on its behalf, he walked up to the huge door with the ridiculous notion that he might pass through it and find himself a child once again. It was locked. Stupid of him to think the house was waiting just for him with open arms. Even if it were, it could wait. He was in no hurry, he would take his time. Yet as he put his hand on the huge old iron handle, it felt as if he were claiming his own. He noticed the broken leaded window panes at the side of the porch and wondered who these Stowertons might be that they could let this happen.

Where there was one broken window, however, there might be others. He found another with glass missing at the front of the house – not large enough for him to crawl through. He wandered on round the building, admiring the huge ornamented chimneys and mullioned windows, the gently curved gables at either end with their fine ornamental stonework, a pattern repeated over the porch entrance. At the back overlooking the paved courtyard between the two wings, he found what he was looking for: a gaping hole for a window. He jumped in, finding himself on the far side of the huge main hall of the house. The smell of damp was overpowering. Ah, yes, he remembered now. Oh, how he remembered. The dark panelled hall, the games of hide and seek with – with whom? Cousin Philip, he supposed, two years his senior. Not that he was fun to play with. There was Cousin David – and wasn't that little girl there? He frowned, wishing he'd demanded his father tell him more, instead of: 'You'll meet them all soon enough.'

Why had he had the impression that there was a strong reason Father did not wish to go too fully into the past – or to go to England himself, despite the excellent excuses he gave for having to remain in charge at Leadville?

Luke crossed into what had obviously been some kind of study, judging by the old decaying desk and the bookshelves. In one place the panelling had been pulled away, and, curious, he went to investigate. How thick these old walls were. Brick, then a wide gap of perhaps a foot, then wooden posts, laths, plaster. Sure was a strange way of building. His attention caught by a movement, he glanced through the dusty window and saw a woman walking up to the front of the building. No, a girl, though with her hair all scraped back and that old hat crammed on her head, no wonder he was confused. A cleaner? No, too much determination in that walk.

Not knowing quite why, he ran quickly up the main staircase, peering over the balustrade to see her come in. But the front door did not open, so obviously she had no key either. This was intriguing. There were scrabblings beneath him, and moving along the corridor, he saw a long white-stockinged leg waving into the room, followed by a skirted rear. The girl caught a heel in her skirts as she reached down for the floor, tumbling over with some kind of unappreciative utterance to fit the situation. He could have sworn it was in Latin. Amused, he decided to stay where he was rather than rush to pick her up.

She had scrambled to her feet now, but her next move was unexpected. She was taking off her skirts and petticoats. Gentlemanly scruples suggested he shouldn't watch, but curiosity ignored them. Clad in long white frilly drawers and shift, she disappeared into the study with her skirts bundled up, and reappeared in the funniest garment since Calamity Jane. Breeches, he supposed, would be the nearest description, though those baggy long pants looked more like something out of the *Arabian Nights*.

Greatly diverted, he settled down to await what would happen next.

Katharine Stowerton, having assured herself that Gouch was not around, was embarking on a final inspection before tomorrow's meeting, to ensure that all was ready should Father's brothers wish to inspect Bocton. Early tomorrow she would put daffodils in the hallway, to give an air of brightness to the dark house with its wallpaper and plaster peeling through damp.

'Dat roof,' Obadiah had told her gloomily last autumn, 'dere's trouble in dere.' He had given it as his opinion that water had seeped in where the Elizabethan chimney had been inserted into the old mediaeval hall through unmaintained flashings; the water penetrating out from the flue was causing visible problems above the great inglenook fireplace. And what was going on in the roof itself was anyone's guess at the moment.

Where Obadiah had made an access to the roof void, she had clambered up, fearful at first of the height, then forgetting it as the flickering candle, helped by holes to the daylight beyond where tiles had fallen, revealed the beauty of the massive construction. The original timber framing of the great hall was intact: the graceful crown posts with their braces to the collar beam in the apex of the roof, the huge oak tie beams – this was the massive structure that Thomas Stoorton himself had erected in the mid- to late-fifteenth century. She felt almost an interloper, staring back into 400 years of history – and perhaps, who knew, further back than that.

Today, however, she was concerned with the East Wing, the one that was more nearly habitable than the West. Here too water penetration had occurred through fallen tiles and chimney seepage. Apart from rot, the soft woods had attracted –

'De liddle beetle,' Obadiah had remarked with gloomy relish, as he had descended from his first inspection last autumn. "E do want some medicine poured over 'im, 'e do.'

Today her role was quickly to try to patch up the holes in the ceiling where damp had caused rotten joists and falling plaster, so that they would not look too obvious. Only she and Obadiah would know they were there. The roof space above this second storey had once been used as attic bedrooms, with a rickety staircase still leading to them at the far end of the wing.

She had brought a bucket of plaster up with her, and was preparing to cover the thin laths of wood that Obadiah had laid temporarily across the hole. Only this room remained, the Queen's Chamber: one smaller hole which she coped reasonably easily with, and a second, larger, one over the old four-poster bed in the middle of the floor. She was faced with having to balance precariously on some books piled on the bed.

What was that? Surely the noise came from above? A rat? She looked up nervously, but there were no further sounds. She was imagining things, she told herself firmly.

A few feet above her head, Luke Stowerton craned forward to peer through his view hole, eager not to miss a moment of this entertainment. A woman covered in plaster? England sure had changed from what he'd heard about it. He tried to imagine remote and starchy Mother in unmentionables, and failed. He leaned forward over his inspection hole.

There was that noise again. Katharine looked up sharply. That was a floorboard creaking with more than a rat on it, surely?

A yowl. A miaow.

A *cat*? How could it be? Had one got trapped up there?

Katharine jumped up on to the bed and tried to peer into the tiny attic room above.

'Puss?' she called tentatively. 'Here now, this way,' reaching up her arms.

There was an ominous creak as Luke shifted his weight, and Obadiah's temporary repair gave way. Luke's long body came hurtling through rotten joists and plaster to land five feet beneath on the old four-poster, knocking Katharine backwards with him, but managing to avoid too much damage by dexterously rolling much of his weight to one side of her.

There was a moment's appalled silence as they sorted themselves out, and recovered their wind. Katharine tried to wriggle free of this tall stranger who gazed so impudently at her with blue eyes, but was trapped by her baggy pantaloons. He did not seem inclined to move.

'Miaow,' he said meekly, grinning at her.

'Could you,' she managed to gasp incoherently, 'kindly roll away from me!?'

'Gee, I'm sorry, ma'am,' he said contritely, obeying slowly.

'Are you planning to knock the rest of Bocton down too?' she panted, finally extricating herself. 'If so, I should inform you that there is an injunction –'

'No, ma'am, I'd rather help you put it back up,' he said, biting back the laughter. 'Are you hurt?' He glanced at the pieces of timber that had fallen down after him.

'No, I don't think so.' She tried to brush some of the plaster off her. Then she looked at him, belatedly taking in what he'd said about putting Bocton in order and that he was not from these parts. 'Protection of Ancient Buildings, that's it, isn't it?' she cried, aghast. '*That's* why you're here?' He had been inspecting the roof, and had fallen through it. She was full of alarm now lest this man whose arrival she had so impatiently awaited, deem Bocton too bad to save. Of all the things to happen.

'I guess it is, ma'am,' he answered politely, lolling back on the bed despite its rotted cover, adorned with the dust of ages to which had now been added rotten timber and plaster.

'Oh, Mr – Mr –'

'Arch, ma'am. Gabriel Arch,' he supplied promptly.

'Mr Arch, I am so sorry. I had no idea you were coming today. You must think this a strange welcome.' She looked despairing down at her pantaloons, and up at the hole. 'Not all Bocton is like this,' she tried to say brightly. 'Most of the masonry is sound. It looks much worse than it is, I assure you. If you will give me a moment, I can show you.'

'That's real nice of you,' he told her. 'I'll be back, but right now I've a bruise coming up on my behind as big as that hole up there. I guess I'll get back and get me a mustard bath.'

She flushed, interpreting this unconventional reply as rejection. 'Certainly. I'm sorry. If there's anything I can answer now . . .'

'Why, yes, ma'am. You could tell me how you got to be a builder's lad.'

'I am not a builder's apprentice, Mr Arch,' she replied heatedly, struggling to retain her dignity as she realised the sight she must present.

'I'm sorry to hear that, ma'am.' He struggled off the bed with a groan.

'Why?' she asked, amazed.

'I never kissed a builder's lad before.'

'I, Mr Arch, am Katharine May Stowerton,' she retorted, outraged, and wondered why his blue eyes danced so.

'Well then, Katie May,' he said softly, 'I guess I'll just have to kiss you instead.'

Katharine seethed as she marched away from this unfortunate encounter, forgetting that she was still in her pantaloons. As she exited through the window she was drawn back by a mocking: 'Aren't you forgetting somethin', ma'am?' and a strong brown hand assisted her back over the sill. She was forced to the conclusion that he must have watched her undress, until she comforted herself that perhaps he had seen her walking up to the house and deduced what she had done.

With that strange accent and dialect he must come from a long way away: Yorkshire perhaps, even Scotland or Wales. And she had always imagined the Society to consist of Londoners, completely unlike this broad-shouldered, sun-burned young man. Perhaps he'd just visited Italy. Perhaps that was where he'd learned to kiss. She gulped. How dared he take advantage of the fact that they were alone? But he was from the Society. She would have to meet him again, for she'd offered to show him around Bocton. Suppose he kissed her again? She pushed this disturbing thought from her mind. True, she had sometimes imagined that if she married at all, it would be to someone who shared her interests, someone from the Society even. But not like him! Definitely not like him. However sweetly he kissed.

Albert Stowerton stretched out on his comfortable bed in Brown's Hotel – and contemplated his immediate future with some pleasure. Now that he was back in England, he was positively relishing the thought of a visit to Kent. After all, whatever their reservations, they'd *asked* him to come. He'd take Louis out tonight, to a music hall perhaps. He remembered Evans' Supper Rooms from his youth. Or perhaps a theatre. The Haymarket, Drury Lane. He'd been only twenty-one when he'd left England to marry Louise, and hadn't been back since, save for that one visit. A smile played round his lips. Oh yes, how he'd enjoy seeing them all again. Just the thought of their faces made him laugh.

It had all turned out for the best. True, Louise was eight years older than he, but she was still an attractive woman; and she understood that men needed freedom. And money. He sighed, thinking of her with affection. How they'd laugh together when he returned. Or perhaps he wouldn't tell her about it after all. Some small remnant of what could have been family loyalty tugged at his woefully underused conscience.

Katharine dressed with great care for the meeting. How did one impress long-lost relations from far-off lands (if any in fact arrived) with your competence as a business woman, and at the same time offer them a warm welcome back to the family? In the end, she gave up the task without regret and donned her old taffeta dress, gloves and cape. She put on a severe-looking hat, then frowned at her reflection in the mirror. No, it wasn't right. She took it off and, greatly daring, donned the other one, with the roses and feathers, adding, since it was spring, a fresh daffodil amidst the artificial flowers. A new life for Bocton, that's what she would win. Was the hat too frivolous? Yes, but let it stay.

But however daringly dressed she felt she was, her opinion changed when she saw Meg, adorned more like a May Queen than for a business meeting in April. Every item from her Gainsborough hat to her kid leather shoes seemed chosen to emphasise fragility and feminine helplessness. Fragility, however, was not a quality Katharine associated with her determined young sister.

No carriage from Uncle Robert today, Katharine thought wryly, as Father handed her up into Aunt Sophy's trap, driven by Ned Higgins, an odd-job man from the village.

Sophy, despite her earlier anxiety, was looking forward to her day with surprising excitement. Overriding all her fears was the thought that she might see her brothers again. Her early years had been spent surrounded by adoring elder brothers, the petted single daughter of the family. Gradually it had changed. One by one they had left. Reasons were given, but even as a girl she knew they were not the true ones. She retained a dim memory of rows that harshly split the gentle haze of childhood. She had never been aware of them until that fateful day, the day whose memory she had consciously buried. Was it just from then that the rows had started or had they always been there, bursting their way into the open on a summer's day, given focus and nourishment? A day that had been inevitable and irrevocable.

Mr Pinpole positively flew out of his office to greet them, agog with unsolicitor-like excitement, Mr Foggett and Dodson palpitating behind him. Even the clerks looked animated.

'Such a day of it,' Pinpole beamed. 'Earlier this morning, why, there was a queue outside the office!' There was great pride in his voice. 'I need hardly tell you, Mr Stowerton, that we expected only one or two answers to our letters and advertisements. Mr Stowerton,' he said somewhat reprovingly, 'the Stowertons appear to be a *very* large family – I had not realised. No less than forty-five persons arrived, claiming to be Stowertons. It was quite a task, quite a task.' He mopped his pineapple brow with a large purple handkerchief. 'Twenty were, however, charlatans. We disposed most quickly of those. The other twenty-five –' he paused '– really, I don't know quite what we could have done had Mr Foggett not had the most ingenious idea.'

Mr Foggett looked modest.

'What?' asked Katharine, intrigued.

'He suggested each pay as a guarantee of good faith their 6s 8d consultation fee, and eighteen people positively vanished.'

Alfred snorted. 'They were genuine Stowertons all right. Trust a Stowerton to disappear when he's asked to put his hand in his pocket.'

'Father!' wailed Meg, all for keeping up appearances on this important day.

'This leaves seven,' said Pinpole, tactfully ignoring this, 'of whom –'

'Did they pay up?' asked Alfred with interest.

'Not yet, Mr Stowerton,' said Foggett with asperity.

'Then they're Stowertons too,' said Alfred complacently. Talking, talking, that was how you could forget who might be waiting in there for you. He couldn't blame Katharine – she'd done this in all innocence – and perhaps it was inevitable anyway, this armageddon, this reckoning.

As she walked in, Katharine's confidence evaporated. What had she expected? A roomful of Fathers and Aunt Sophys? No, these were strangers at the table, not family, a lions' den. This was the reality of her defiant clarion call. 'Childe Roland to the Dark Tower came,' she thought to herself wildly. 'Dauntless the slughorn to his lips he put.' Well, she had done that too – and this was the result. Seven strangers – no, *six* strangers.

Katharine stared, horrified, at Mr Arch who was gazing at her quizzically, correct and formal in morning coat and striped trousers, albeit with a most eye-catching burgundy-coloured cravat just inside the collar. He had lied – he wasn't an Arch at all, and not from the Society for the Protection of Ancient Buildings. He was a Stowerton, spying out the land. How dared he! She cast him one furious look, then tried to ignore him. But such a bad start made her tongue-tied, her carefully rehearsed welcomes flying from her head, and she stood mute as Aunt Sophy and her father were surrounded by their family, excited murmurs of reunion filling the room.

Only one man stood apart, an ironic smile on his face. Puzzled, Luke went to talk to him until Mr Pinpole quickly called the gathering to order, proposing that he introduce each person in turn. He prepared to be in his element as the gathering reluctantly reseated themselves round the table.

'Mr Joseph Stowerton.' Awkwardly Joseph stood up again, hating this formal meeting. Uncle Joseph – younger than her father, thought Katharine. Wasn't he the one who went to Australia? He didn't look like Father at all. His hair was darker, he was bearded and burnt by the sun, but most of all there were lines of worry etched into his face. For all that, he looked a kind man, one she would look forward to meeting presently. How could Father have lost touch with him? What made him leave?

'Mr Albert Stowerton.' So this was the black sheep; the one not even Sophy would talk about. But he looked so interesting, so innocent. What crime could this handsome, still young-looking man have committed, so serious that his name had been crossed from the Family Bible? Involuntarily, her eyes went to her father, studiedly talking to Sophy, head turned away from his brother – for brother he was. Not all the pen-strokes in the world could eradicate that, Katharine thought. Perhaps this case would iron out small misunderstandings and bring peace, not another battlefield.

'Mr Louis Stowerton, Mr Albert's son.' Katharine heard a slight intake of breath from Meg – and no wonder. Louis, though slightly insolent-looking, was the handsomest young man Katharine had ever seen. Dark hair, liquid brown eyes, fine classical features . . . She made a mental note to keep an eye on Meg – if she could. To her, this young man looked as though he would put himself before any woman he chose.

'*Enchanté.*' Louis bowed to the company, catching Katharine's eye. One eyebrow rose quizzically as if he knew exactly what she was thinking. Then his gaze swept briefly round this panoply of new relations – and settled on Meg, where it remained.

'Mrs George Stowerton.'

'Mabel! By God, I didn't recognise you,' said Alfred, bounding round to the other side of the table to embrace her. 'Where's George?' he enquired anxiously, suddenly realising whom he had missed in the excitement.

'Dead,' Mabel retorted bluntly, a stocky figure in thick tweed skirt and jacket, pork-pie hat crammed down on to her head. 'It was his own fault. Dear old George. He had this gift of getting on with people, speaking languages well, that sort of thing. Especially in Africa. Had this idea he could mediate between Wolseley and the Ashantis. He'd done it before for the army out East. I told him the Ashantis were a different kettle of fish, but he wouldn't listen, and got a bullet through him as a result.'

'Oh,' said Sophy faintly.

Mabel turned to her, all compassion. 'There, Sophy, sorry to have broken it so abruptly. Happened six years ago – '74. Forgot you didn't know. I'm a tactless old thing.'

George dead? Sophy, Albert, Joseph and Alfred's thoughts flew to their brother. They had not seen him for twenty years or more, but could not believe that George of all people would no longer smile at them in his affable, lazy way.

'I thought he would be the last of us to go,' said Alfred at last, speaking for them all.

'George!' cried Joseph, stunned. 'He –' He looked at Alfred, at

53

Sophy, at Albert. 'You wouldn't understand,' he said abruptly. 'He looked after me.'

'Good old George,' said Alfred sadly. 'He looked after all of us.'

'I don't recall his looking after me,' said Albert coolly.

'You looked after yourself, you, you –' Alfred suddenly forgot his intention of not speaking to the fellow.

'Alfred,' warned Sophy, laying her hand on his arm, and her brother subsided.

'You're right, Sophy. He's not worth it,' he muttered.

'Mr Luke Stowerton,' interposed Mr Pinpole hastily. Katharine watched without surprise as Gabriel Arch got to his feet, surveying the company with interested eye, towering above them. 'The only son of Mr Jeremiah Stowerton.'

'Jeremiah's boy, eh? I remember you, don't I?' said Alfred, happy again now that attention was diverted from Albert.

Jeremiah? But Jeremiah went to America, didn't he? In one of the gold rushes? thought Katharine, interested despite her fury. So that odd accent was American, not Scots or Welsh. She felt foolish and looked quickly away from his amused blue eyes. She noticed uneasily that he had no such scruples but was staring in frank admiration at her – or was it Meg? – wafting his air of the new world into the old.

That left two more, the oddest of them all. Two short women, quaintly and identically dressed, of about fifty, with straight short hair and slanted dark eyes in their pink and white faces.

'Shall we, Primrose?' said one excitedly to the other.

'Indubitably,' said the other with a gasp.

They stood up. 'The Misses Stowerton,' they chorused in unison, and promptly sat down again. Katharine almost laughed. In their bundle of clothes, which appeared to be layers of tunics one over the other, they looked like Tweedledum and Tweedledee from Mr Carroll's story.

Mr Pinpole cleared his throat. 'The Misses Stowerton, Miss Violet and Miss Primrose, say they are the daughters of Mr Frederick Stowerton.' Slight emphasis on 'say'.

Frederick? But the only Frederick was grandfather's brother, killed in 1841 in China. That would explain the odd clothes, certainly!

'I remember Uncle Fred!' shouted Alfred, clearly delighted, as visions of munificent gifts of toy soldiers and of a larger than life figure in scarlet uniform returned to him.

'Yes,' said Violet. 'We've come to claim Bocton.' She looked round for approval and found only puzzlement. 'Father always told us we owned it. And we're glad, because we like it here, don't we, Primrose?'

'Indubitably,' said Primrose with another gasp.

Mr Pinpole cleared his throat, but this time in extreme agitation.

'How are you, Alfred?' Albert's voice drawled from the far end of the table. 'I notice you failed to give me the welcome you accorded Joseph here.'

Alfred glared straight in front of him. For a moment Katharine feared he would say nothing, and she gave him an appealing look.

'I am, as you see, Albert, most well. I thank you for your concern.' He crossed his arms, duty done. Katharine, relieved, saw Joseph shoot a puzzled look at her father, as if unaware of trouble. Perhaps it had happened after he left? But had there not been letters at least at first – no, it would be just like Father, and Aunt Sophy too, to ignore whatever had happened, Father in order to blot it from his mind, Sophy in order to preserve a façade – a hope – of family unity. Katharine could remember no more letters coming from abroad after she was about six.

Luke Stowerton looked round the table curiously. So this was it. This was the Stowerton family. He could already sense that buried deep here were tensions that had not died, as sharp as any that existed in Jeremiah's household. Something odd here. Why, for instance, had they all left home with so little contact since? And how come this strange mixture? Why had Alfred been the only son, apart from Robert, to stay? He was obviously Katharine's father, the man he remembered fighting battles with. She the little girl. She looked mighty fine today, for all she wasn't looking at him. Not like Miss Margaret Stowerton. He winked at her, and was rewarded by a flutter of long eyelashes. He'd met plenty like Cousin Meg. But Katharine was more interesting. Quite unlike Leadville ladies. Or Yale ones come to that.

Mr Pinpole cleared his throat. 'Miss Katharine Stowerton.'

Nervously, she rose to her feet. This was the all-important moment, as she explained in detail why they had summoned the Stowertons together. They listened intently, apart from Miss Violet and Miss Primrose who looked vaguely round from time to time, with the occasional smile of satisfaction at each other. 'There's no question but that Bocton must not be sold,' Katharine finished at last.

'Why not?' enquired Luke with interest. 'Is there nothing to be gained from its sale, since so few of the family now reside in England?'

Katharine was immediately aware that she was being tested. She had to make the right answer to this annoying man, an answer that would appeal to someone from America – and she had no idea what America was like except from the accounts Mr Dickens and Mrs Trollope had written, and they had little opinion of it. And she had to convince the others too. How could she appeal to them all? She could only speak the truth honestly as she saw it, she decided, for surely Bocton was magnificent enough to speak for itself.

'It is our home,' she explained simply. 'Stowertons have lived there over the centuries, and we were all born Stowertons. No matter what has happened to you since, or where you live, no one can change that. Our family heritage is part of us all. You've all built on what it gave you or your parents in the past. We can't lose it now just for the sake of money. We have a duty to save it. Over past centuries we took enough from the people around here; they all served Bocton. In former days that's the way the world worked. Bocton was no better or worse than any other manor. But it came to mean something to the village, and still does. A symbol of the country they were born into. None of you can escape that, however much you try.'

'And what of the new world, niece?' said Joseph almost aggressively. 'Don't you reckon we have a duty to our new homes too?'

'Yes,' said Katharine, having expected this argument, 'but the new world grew because of the old – and now the old needs your help.'

There was a sudden stillness. 'Help?' enquired Albert eventually.

'Yes,' said Katharine steadily. 'We want to bring an action against Uncle Robert, on a claim of gavelkind.'

A short silence, broken by a shout. 'I knew it!' Joseph cried.

Albert chuckled. Mabel cackled. Luke said nothing. The twins clapped, still smiling politely.

'By God, you Stowertons haven't changed. Robert wants to sell the estate, and you need our money to help you stop him,' Joseph said, outraged.

Katharine flushed red. 'Yes,' she said defiantly. 'Legal action needs money. But it's to be a family thing. To save Bocton for the family.'

'And what good would it be to me out in Australia? And with Jeremiah in America, and Mabel heaven knows where?'

'Good?' Katharine flushed. 'Bocton will be saved. Don't you remember Bocton? Don't you care about it? Come to see it, *then* you'll know why.'

Oh, yes, they remembered Bocton – and much more too. It should have been the last place on earth they would want to come to, but here they all were – drawn back by some invisible magnet.

'What chance do we have of winning?' Luke asked matter-of-factly.

Albert laughed sardonically. 'The family's been asking that for six hundred years, Luke. You expect a lawyer to answer in less?'

Messrs Pinpole, Foggett and Dodson drew themselves up to full height, trying to ignore this slur on their profession. 'It is not possible to predict with accuracy, Mr Stowerton,' Mr Foggett replied stiffly.

Albert laughed. 'I'm sure it's not,' he sneered.

'Nevertheless, we do believe you have a case,' Mr Pinpole took over, ignoring Albert's contribution. 'A difficult one, but legally logical and valid. Sir Robert claims his entitlement to the estates of Stowerton, Charham and Bocton under Sir Nathaniel's will. However, Sir Nathaniel's last will was never signed, and his earlier will of 1835 therefore remains valid, bequeathing all his lands to Sir Robert. In 1837 a most important Wills Act was passed. Thereafter all lands in the testator's ownership at the time of death passed according to will. Before that date, however, and the Act did not apply retrospectively, only lands in the testator's possession at the time of *making the will* passed according to its directions. Any lands acquired later would have to be the subject of a new devise. At the time of making the will, in this instance, only Stowerton, which had been given to Sir Nathaniel on his marriage, was actually in his legal possession. The other lands did not finally become his until Jacob Stowerton withdrew his claim to a share of the estate according to the Custom of Kent in 1845.'

'So where does that leave us?' demanded Joseph, puzzled.

'It means that all surviving sons or representatives of deceased sons can make a claim for the estate if –'

'If?' taunted Albert, detecting a slight hesitation before the last word.

'If the lands can be proved to be subject to gavelkind "time out of mind". Otherwise everything remains in Sir Robert's ownership. I take it you all know what gavelkind is?'

It was a rhetorical question. No Stowerton could fail to know. Even Violet and Primrose looked knowledgeable.

'And what,' said Luke, 'are the chances of proving that?'

'It would, of course, be open to much argument,' said Mr Pinpole.

'You mean it would be a gamble, Mr Pinpole,' put in Alfred brightly.

'Precisely, Mr Stowerton.'

'A gamble by Uncle Alfred here, Uncle Joseph, Uncle Albert, Aunt Sophy –' Luke pointed out drily.

'Not me, Luke,' she said. 'Women don't count, unless there are no surviving sons or their issue.'

'But I do, paying on my father's behalf,' completed Luke.

'And me,' put in Mabel firmly.

'Not you, Mrs Stowerton,' said Mr Pinpole. 'You cannot claim on behalf of a dead spouse, I'm afraid. Not unless you have issue.'

'Issue?' Mabel looked vague. 'I've got some somewhere.'

Meg giggled, diverted from her game of modestly avoiding Louis's eyes.

'Good God, Mabel, you can't have forgotten,' said Alfred, outraged.

She stared at him indignantly. 'Of course not. I just forget which school he's at. There have been so many.'

Mr Pinpole took up his pen.

'And your son would be – ?'

'Fourteen – no, fifteen.'

He sighed. 'His name?'

'Agamemnon. And there's Helen too. She's at school somewhere else.'

Katharine bit back a smile.

'George wanted to call him Achilles, but I persuaded him out of it. I brought Gam's birth certificate.' She fished around in a battered suitcase.

'Very well, Mrs Stowerton. And that concludes the theoretical claimants,' said Mr Pinpole thankfully.

'What about us, Mr Pinpole?' Tweedledum and Tweedledee rose to their feet indignantly.

'Dear ladies, I fear on grounds of sex you are ruled out.'

'Oh no,' said Violet brightly. 'We are the sole surviving issue, you see. So our – um – gender is no barrier.'

'But your departed father, Frederick Stowerton, would have no standing in this case,' Mr Pinpole told them somewhat crossly.

'Not this case, no,' whispered Primrose bravely. 'We thought we'd reopen the last one.'

'What?' screeched Pinpole, his eyeglass falling from his eye on to the birth certificate of Agamemnon Stowerton.

'Oh my, oh my, what a case,' breathed Foggett happily.

'It was never settled, you know,' Violet said brightly. 'Father died, and we heard that Uncle Jacob could not afford to continue. But the grounds remain valid.'

'But this is ridiculous,' said Pinpole in most unlawyerlike terms. 'If you reopened that case, then Sir Nathaniel's whole tenure would once again come under doubt, and invalidate not only Sir Robert's tenure, but all of these good people's claim.' He waved a feeble hand at the assembled company.

'You couldn't really want all the trouble of reopening that case, would you?' cried Katharine, horrified at this new chimera.

'Oh, yes,' said Violet brightly.

'Indubitably,' agreed Primrose.

There was something that might have been a groan from Mr Pinpole, an exclamation of excitement from Mr Foggett. But they were lost in the general hubbub as Alfred, Sophy, Joseph, Katharine – and even Albert – leapt to the defence of their own prior claims for action. But the excitement was cut short as the door opened, and the last of the Stowerton clan walked in, an anxious clerk hovering behind him, burbling, 'He said he had as much right . . .'

'I am a Stowerton, Pinpole,' said Robert coldly, as he handed hat and gloves to the clerk. 'Your advertisement bade all Stowertons with an interest in Bocton to attend, did it not?'

Horrorstruck, Mr Pinpole could only nod dumbly. Slowly Joseph got to his feet, his eyes fixed on his eldest brother. He murmured something that Katharine did not hear. For she was aware, looking round the room, that for her, and perhaps for some at least of those present, the meeting had stepped from unreal fantasy into something different. With Robert's arrival, the group unified, not into something pleasant, but something held together by the long forgotten tentacles of the past. Katharine felt it, Luke felt it. For Alfred it crystallised into the unbelievable fact that he was actually sitting in the same room as that blasted fellow.

'*Merde*,' observed Albert pleasantly, 'it *is* a pleasant family reunion.'

So she had to wait yet longer. Katharine's spirits sank lower and lower on their homeward journey. Robert's unexpected arrival had achieved two objects: firstly that their decision on whether to proceed with the case would be deferred until 1 June; and secondly, that Uncle Robert was deftly taking control of the situation. For all of the visitors had been offered, and accepted, the hospitality of Stowerton House for the length of their stay.

Katharine raged. Uncle Robert thought he had won, that with

everyone under his roof, on the pretext of a family reunion, his case could insidiously be put – and hers demolished. Even her fighting spirit quailed at the thought of the effort ahead. Father chatted happily of Joseph, and times past, then sadly of his memories of George. Meg chattered about the attractions of Louis Stowerton *and* of Luke Stowerton. Katharine gritted her teeth. But worse was to come.

As soon as they entered the front door she knew something was wrong. Maggie was hovering in the hallway. 'You've got a visitor, Miss – that is, you all have,' she said.

'All?' asked Alfred perplexed. 'I've seen enough strangers for one day. I have to read the *Pink 'Un* before luncheon.'

'Still on the horses, Alfred?' a voice rang out from the parlour.

Alfred turned white. Hazily remembering, Katharine wondered why she trembled so unaccountably.

Alfred spun round, trying to escape through the front door, but Katharine and Meg were in his way, and he found himself trapped as an exotic perfume filled the hallway; a dark-haired beauty, wearing a toque hat with long feathers at every conceivable angle, flowing layers of chiffon and lace swirling around her, burst out through the parlour door and embraced him.

'Darling,' she said in a throaty voice.

Katharine did not need to see her face. Meg would have been too young, but she herself could never forget it. She cried one word as the chiffon and lace transferred themselves to her, enfolding her in their embrace, but the sound was strangled.

'*Mother!*'

Chapter Four

'How are you, Elizabeth?' enquired Alfred hollowly, seeing no escape. 'Still gallivanting around the desert?'

'*Chéri!*' Elizabeth Stowerton was deeply hurt. 'Do I look as if I have come from the desert?' Certainly her bright green, boldly striped pleated dress, with its plain silk overskirt, and the wide-brimmed straw hat with its outrageous luscious artificial fruits clustered on top amid plentiful bows did not suggest she had recently seen anywhere east of Vienna. 'Ah, but those delightful days!' She smiled reminiscently. 'Those sweet desert nights. Dearest Medjuel.' Then she whirled on Katharine, throwing herself into her arms. 'Never forget,' she almost sobbed, 'beloved daughter, that love is *all*.'

Katharine dutifully allowed herself to be embraced and kissed once more, and was at once bathed in exotic perfumes that did indeed suggest a sheikh of Araby rather than the Garden of England. Elizabeth then turned her attention to Meg, who with an overdone shriek of delight threw herself into her mother's arms.

'You're not planning to come back here for good, are you?' cried Alfred, suddenly alarmed by this display of motherly affection.

A delicious deep laugh, and a white doeskin-gloved hand smoothed his cheek. 'Good gracious, no,' she replied. 'Here? Back with Mighty Millicent and Silent Sophy? I can't imagine the horror of it.'

'That's all right then.' Relieved, Alfred relaxed, leading the way into the tiny morning room in the hope that its chilliness might rid the house of this unfortunate visitation more quickly than the parlour.

Unfortunately the implications of his statements had belatedly struck Elizabeth. 'Don't you want me here?' she cried indignantly. 'Don't you love me any more?'

Seeing the large tears beginning to well in the dark eyes, a situation so well remembered from the past, Alfred soothed her hastily. 'Devoted, always yours, Elizabeth. Heart and soul,' he assured her. She looked suspicious but somewhat mollified as she sat down in the shabby armchair and regarded her family.

'Isn't this fun?' she beamed.

Katharine had seen her mother only once in the sixteen years since she had so mysteriously vanished from her young life, when Meg was only four and she eight. However, on her sixteenth birthday, Alfred and Sophy decided that Katharine had entered adult years, and in order to get the matter disposed of quickly bestowed the same privilege on Meg.

They were taken to London for the day by a gloomy Alfred and

60

decidedly nervous Aunt Sophy, where in a hotel room a strange sight had greeted them – a woman with jet-black hair hidden beneath a strange headdress and wearing flowing white robes, sitting cross-legged on the floor and looking like a picture from Mr Lane's *Arabian Nights*, had stood up in one graceful movement, thrown her arms around them, and embraced them passionately, until their cheeks were wet with her tears. Alfred had then belatedly and abruptly informed Meg that this was her mother; Katharine had with a deep sense of shock already recognised her. She had adored her beautiful mother though without affectionate love, for Elizabeth was unpredictable, swamping her children with love one day, remote and self-absorbed the next. Not like Father whose constant, comforting presence meant home, even if he too was unpredictable in his way. Those early years had been a rocky sea on which her craft of childhood bobbed uneasily, and when her mother left the gap was quickly filled with the pleasures of a more peaceful existence, even if one of routine.

A stilted half-hour had followed in the hotel, with both Katharine and Meg tongue-tied. Was she returning home? When it was clear that she was not, Katharine's first reaction had been relief and if a pang for some other adventurous life shot through her, it was quickly forgotten. Elizabeth had made a solemn farewell speech to her daughters, embracing them formally once more. 'Never forget, my doves, that love is all. Follow the stars of the desert night, and not the pebbles of a humdrum path.'

That encounter had left a deep impression on both Elizabeth's daughters, but for different reasons. Katharine had reflected that desert nights might often be cold and uncomfortable. Meg had thought only of those stars – while travelling in comfort, of course. Father had explained hurriedly to them, ignoring all questions, that Elizabeth had left home to explore the world, and had yet somehow managed to convey the fact, without dwelling on detail, that these explorations had not been unaccompanied, and indeed had been forced upon her not so much by a compulsion to see far-off lands as by the disapproval of the society she had left behind.

Since then Katharine had discovered by careful questioning of Sophy that Elizabeth had left England with a gentleman friend, and when he later abandoned her, promptly solaced her broken heart with a Prussian prince. Three years later, finding Prussian lovemaking no more to her liking than English, she had travelled further east and in Damascus fallen in love with a desert sheikh and shared his roving desert life interspersed at intervals with six months spent in relative civilisation in Damascus. For some years now Western society had heard nothing of Elizabeth Stowerton, though it did not forget her. It was a new and unwelcome development for her husband that desert life no longer held the attraction it had.

'What do you want, Elizabeth?' he asked warily.

'*Chéri, pas devant les enfants.*' She put her white-gloved finger mysteriously to her lips.

'I am twenty-three, Mother,' said Katharine nettled. 'Not twelve.'

61

'My little baby! Are you really twenty-three? Darling!' She gazed absentmindedly at Katharine. 'Do you know, darling, I cannot help but feel that you would look so lovely if you didn't wear your hair in that unbecoming chignon. Why not just the merest curl at the front? It would look more . . . alluring.'

Katharine stiffened as Meg chimed in: 'Oh, you can't tell Katharine anything, Mother. She's determined to be as ugly as Aunt Sophy.' Anyone who did not share Meg's love of curls and ringlets was ugly to her, particularly those who did not care. Like Katharine.

'I saw the advertisement, Alfred, for all the Stowertons to gather here, and I thought what better time to ask you for a divorce? So I just quickly came out on the steamer from Paris –'

'I've told you before, Elizabeth, no divorce,' interrupted Alfred angrily.

'But, darling, I want to marry Klaus and bear his children. How can I do that if I'm married to you? *You* would not wish to support another baby and it would legally be yours.'

'You're too old to have another baby,' he was goaded into saying.

'How ungallant you are, Alfred. But then you always were, you dear dunderhead. Anyway, I am *not* too old,' somewhat indignant. 'I am only forty-four and I want to be the Baroness von Freiturm.'

'Haven't I enough worries looking after these two?' Alfred asked theatrically. 'Without this?'

Katharine bit back a comment, deeming it wiser not to intervene.

'Robert's giving a family dinner tonight,' Alfred went on heatedly. 'We've got the whole future of Bocton to discuss. I have meetings with lawyers, with brothers, with –'

'Gentlemen of the turf,' put in Meg irrepressibly, and he gave her an indulgent frown.

'Brothers? A family dinner? Oh, splendid. I shall enjoy that.'

'No,' shouted Alfred, having fallen headlong into the trap and seeing disaster looming. 'You are no longer a member of this family.'

'But I am, dearest Alfred.' She looked hurt again. 'You will not give me a divorce. Remember?'

Meg giggled. 'Oh, do let Mother come to the dinner.'

Alfred whirled on her angrily. 'You know nothing about it, miss. It's out of the question. *No!*'

'Very well, Alfred,' Elizabeth sighed meekly. 'I shall have to return to Lenham Place. I'm staying with the Pearseys. So sweet of them. But dull. How dull they are! Still, just for one night I must endure it. Now, dearest, I won't go without seeing you again. And that's a promise. We have to make arrangements for the divorce.'

'No,' yelped Alfred in a strangled voice, but Elizabeth seemed not to hear.

'Enjoy your dinner, darlings.' And she wafted out, the sound of her little buttoned shoes clip-clopping on the patched lineoleum resounding in the silence she left behind her.

The day could hardly get worse, Katharine thought despondently as she dressed for dinner. First the meeting this morning. It hadn't been disastrous exactly, just had not produced the result she had expected. What precisely had she thought would happen? That, like Joan of Arc, she would hold up her banner of Bocton, that the Stowertons would fall in behind her and march to her tune? Yes, she thought ruefully, perhaps that's just what she had thought. And look what had happened. A roomful of people each with their own thoughts, their own views. And she had just over six weeks in which to persuade these disparate people into her way of thinking – but meanwhile they were living under Uncle Robert's roof.

And now to crown everything Mother had appeared.

However had Father come to marry her, he so placid and she so wayward? And yet, Katharine supposed, they had something in common. Perhaps too much. Each was completely swept away by what they desired at the moment, Mother by love and her father by a love of a different sort. Neither of them thought of consequences. Both of them assumed that they could butterfly their way through life without thought for winter. But someone in the house had to plan and think ahead – if the family was to survive from day to day. It wasn't going to be Meg, but why did it have to be her, Katharine? she thought mutinously. Suppose she too put love over all? Father and Meg took her for granted, and she had not minded before, so why suddenly rebel? She must not so do now at all costs for she had to persuade the family to save Bocton and, an even harder task, they had to act together in order to do so.

So why the hesitation? Perhaps because one of them was Luke Stowerton, and somewhere on the path to Bocton a Jack o' Lantern swung his ensnaring light.

'Katie May.'

Why, oh why, did Luke have to be the first person she saw after greeting Uncle Robert and Aunt Millicent? Robert, sober as usual in grey satin waistcoat and black tie, had greeted her benignly as if to show that on this important family reunion she was forgiven her girlish folly in trying to stir up discord. Philip was the other side of the room but already moving towards her when Luke Stowerton, wavy fair hair vigorously pummelled into submission, and a red silk cummerbund the sole relief to the stark formality of his black attire, seized a glass of champagne from a footman and pushed it into her hand.

'That dress becomes you more than yesterday's costume.' His eyes scanned the dark blue moiré dress and matching satin shoes, dwelling for a moment on the low neckline.

Her chin went up. 'I'm surprised you have the audacity to refer to yesterday, Mr Stowerton. And who gave you permission to call me Katie May?' she demanded, on a less lofty level.

'Our fathers,' he replied meekly. 'We are related. I could refer to you as Cousin Katharine, but that would involve your calling me Cousin Luke, which makes me sound as stuffy as a tax collector.'

'And Mr Gabriel Arch does not?' she enquired.

'I thought that rather clever – the Archangel Gabriel swooping from the heavens. And now I am found out.' He looked rueful. 'From archangel to apostle in one day. It is a humiliating descent.' He cocked his head on one side and considered her thoughtfully when this brought no reaction. 'Do you never laugh, Cousin Katie?'

'Why, yes, I –' she began, caught off balance by this unexpected attack.

'I guess not too often. I watched you while you spoke this morning. So serious, so impassioned. You really love this place, don't you? But what makes you *laugh*, Katie May?' he asked softly.

'I –' She was disconcerted, cheeks flaming. 'I suppose –' She stopped. It occurred to her with some surprise that it was a long time since she had really laughed. But there was little to laugh about. To tread life with too happy a foot, like Mother, was dangerous. 'I don't know,' she finished weakly, hardly knowing why she answered this nonsense at all.

'Then I will find out, Cousin Katharine, and that is a promise.'

'What is?' Meg came rustling up in her pink-patterned organza dress and silk petticoats. 'Cousin Luke, I am Meg, your cousin. We did not really meet this morning.' Her eyelashes fluttered slightly as she gazed at him, fully aware that Louis had come up behind her.

Luke took both her hands and kissed them lightly. 'Cousin Meg, I remember well the roses of England, but I thought they only grew in gardens.'

As he straightened up, he saw Louis looking coolly at him, appraisingly. Louis, however, like his father was a gambler and knew well when to play and when to stay his hand.

Meg smiled at Luke, deliciously torn between the more certain prospect of Philip and the entrancing excitement of the new. 'Cousin Luke, would you escort me in to dinner? Boring Cousin David is advancing this way, and I simply could not bear to sit next to him.' It would do no harm to let Louis wait.

'Ah, *ma cousine*,' Louis murmured, '*je suis desolé*. But perhaps Cousin Luke has already requested the pleasure of escorting Mademoiselle Katharine?'

'Oh, no, of course not,' Meg said, opening her eyes wide. 'Katharine can go in with David. Or even you,' she added munificently. 'I may come with you, may I not, Cousin Luke?'

'I should be delighted,' Luke said lightly, giving her his arm and casting a quizzical look at Katharine, which she pretended not to see. Scornfully, she watched them go as Philip, the small black moustache that he had grown over the winter quivering importantly, came possessively to take her arm. Speedily she turned to Louis.

At first everything went well at dinner. The talk flitted from China (Violet and Primrose, clad in identical but peculiar button-through garments of dark brown moiré silk, sat resolutely together, despite Millicent's table arrangement, which had decreed otherwise) to Australia, America, Cannes, and the fashionable cities of Europe. Animated laughter and discussion took place as wine smoothed over any awkwardness. Even Katharine relaxed, fascinated by this talk of

foreign lands, by the unusual twins and their chatter of life in China, by
Luke's descriptions of the wide open prairies of America, of cowboys,
of the savage Indian wars that were still continuing, and by Joseph, not
to be outdone, with his tales of the Aboriginal natives of Australia, of
how convicts of yesterday had become the prosperous farmers of today,
and of how the new nation was growing. Albert and Louis amused them
with tales of the English in Cannes and the excesses of visiting royalty,
now the railway ran from St Petersburg all the way to Cannes. They had
an eager audience at least in Meg, who had positioned herself between
Luke and Louis, again in defiance of Millicent's decree.

So when did the mood change? Katharine afterwards reflected.
Perhaps imperceptibly it was after the conversation returned to family
matters. Innocent enough to begin with . . .

'And what are you doing with yourself, Sophy?' roared Mabel into a
sudden hush after she had been telling them about her forthcoming visit
to Albania and of travels in the past. It was a way of life she had adopted
with George, taken a fancy to, and continued after his death.

Sophy, insignificant in grey silk, looked up as if in surprise at being
addressed. 'Oh, I live quietly,' she replied softly. 'A dull life compared
to yours, Mabel.'

'You always did. Too devoted to looking after other people. Don't
believe in it myself. Does you credit though, but see where it's
got you.'

'You could have married,' said Joseph suddenly. 'What happened
to that curate you liked?'

'He married someone else,' replied Sophy quietly, a faint flush in
her cheeks. She did not add that it was at her suggestion.

'Why didn't Uncle Jeremiah come himself, Cousin Luke?' asked
Katharine quickly, to save her aunt further embarrassment.

A snorting laugh from Joseph, and Robert, ignoring this, looked
enquiringly at Luke. He too wanted to know why Jeremiah hadn't
come, though he could guess. He didn't have the nerve to face him,
that's why. He'd shown him who was master in their youth, and
Jeremiah wouldn't forget it.

'He is needed at the mines,' explained Luke with composure.
'Leadville is a mighty exciting place at the moment, but you can't
afford to walk away from your claims and workings for six months.'

'*You* can though, eh?' pointed out Mabel blithely.

He glanced at her. 'I'm a free spirit, like yourself, Aunt Mabel,' he
replied lightly.

'You're a well set-up lad. Not married yet? Like your father though,
I'll be bound.

He looked puzzled, but she deliberately turned her attention
elsewhere.

'Pray give my regards to your father, Luke,' said Robert formally.

'Regards!' said Joseph forthrightly. 'Would have been a sly kick in
the old days. You were always scrapping.'

Robert's pale eyes gleamed. Scrapping was somewhat of an
understatement. He clearly recalled all the fights and the rivalries

that had upset Sophy and driven their mother to despair. Robert, however, looked round the family table with some satisfaction at his own strategy. It was by far the best plan to bring everyone together, gauge what opposition he might have. He had six weeks to persuade all these people to drop The Case, or two cases as it had apparently become. True, the LCDR were certain now of obtaining the right to build the new railway, but with Bocton confirmed his and the injunction lifted, there might still be room for exploitation of the old place.

His eyes rested thoughtfully on Luke, Jeremiah's son, trying to size him up. Jeremiah couldn't be that interested in Bocton or he would have come himself, despite everything. Or perhaps, he thought uneasily as a sudden idea came to him, this was Jeremiah's way of getting back at him. Though if there was any revenge to be carried out . . .

Strange to be back in this room, Joseph reflected. He remembered it so clearly as it had been in Father's day. All seated round this table, boys of varying ages and little Sophy. There had been some good times before they all started leaving one by one. He frowned. *Had* they been that good? Was there not uneasiness in Robert's face? Wasn't he glad that Jeremiah was not here? Robert and Jeremiah – always fighting, hating each other, and yet Jeremiah had stayed, not leaving until after Joseph himself had gone. George had gone last apparently. George the Peacemaker. Robert had been the snake in their childhood Arcadia, always watching, never participating. Father's sneak. Because he was the eldest, he said. The Heir. Albert was a mere toddler, Sophy the precious darling of the family, and in the middle Alfred. No one could dislike Alfred. Joseph looked at him now: oldfashioned short dress coat, greying hair beginning to recede, black lace-up shoes, and ancient embroidered waist-coat – and this was the brother he remembered so well. Absent-minded Alfred, who drove them all to distraction, even amiable clumsy George who was always putting his foot in it. Why had it all changed? And how had it happened?

Albert chatted pleasantly to Sophy and the aunts on his other side. There he could do no harm, Millicent had calculated. He had been too young to know the halcyon days that lingered in Joseph's mind. Albert only remembered with glee all the fights that so upset Sophy and which Mother and Father were helpless to control. He had decided his own role was that of 'good little boy', so he caused no trouble – then – but merely watched. They starting leaving one by one, and when he was twenty-one, good biddable charming Albert left too. Within a year he was married to Louise, and a year after that he was a father. He was turning out well, just as they all predicted. Then Albert had come back one day, drawn by curiosity to see the family in which he had no role. But when he came back, he wasn't good any longer.

'Where's the cup, Robert?' asked Joseph suddenly, looking round the room and realising what it was that he had subconsciously missed.

Sophy looked up quickly. So it would happen now. Perhaps it was better this way. It must surely be on everyone's minds, as it was on hers – or was it? Could she have been mistaken? Did that momentous day not haunt them as it did her?

'You're right, Joseph,' said Albert in surprise. 'It has gone. I'd almost forgotten about it.'

'It's put away,' answered Robert shortly.

'Why?' persisted Joseph. 'It was always kept on that mantelpiece.'

'I put it away,' said Robert coolly, 'because there didn't seem –' he looked round the table defiantly '– any point in keeping it there. You had all left.'

'I remember it,' said Albert suddenly. 'But not what it was for – why was it so important?'

Sophy looked quickly round at her brothers, but saw no sign on their faces that they remembered it as she did. Perhaps it was she who was wrong – perhaps it had merely been another storm to them, one to blow over and leave the skies of childhood clear again? No, she could not be wrong. Not about this.

'It was just something we competed for as children,' said Robert offhandedly, his thin voice rising slightly.

'Until your foolish feud with Jeremiah got out of hand,' said Alfred forthrightly, remembering vaguely that one day it had all been different.

Should she speak? Somehow pull them back from this hidden quicksand?

Robert shot a look at Alfred. 'You are quite wrong. As usual. Besides, in any family there are differences. There was nothing unusual about my relationship with Jeremiah.'

'Something was unusual somewhere,' said Joseph, considering. 'Everything was splendid, and then for no reason it all got out of hand. But when?'

'I don't know,' said Robert flatly. There was a sudden tension in the room.

Sophy's hands were clenched in her lap, her knuckles showing white where her gloves were drawn back. To speak? Or to stifle it once more. No, if there were to be hope, there had to be understanding.

'George always said the Stowertons were cursed,' said Mabel happily, munching a piece of Stilton. 'Nothing anyone can do about it. Been so over the centuries, and it'll go on like that. That's why he left. For some peace and quiet.' She gave a bark of laughter.

George, his kind, understanding elder brother. Joseph suddenly wanted to cry, grown man that he was.

'It was a mistake,' he cried thickly, 'coming back here. George was right. We're better off apart. The only hope for the Stowertons.'

'No,' cried Sophy.

Her brothers stared at her in surprise, she so rarely spoke.

'Now look, Joseph,' said Alfred angrily, 'you've upset Sophy. You know how tender-hearted she is.'

'Alfred, no,' she said, more composed now. 'But you have it wrong – don't you see, any of you?' she said bitterly to her six brothers. 'Don't you remember the day of the last treasure trove . . . ?'

The day *had* to be fine. It *had* to be sunny. The day of the treasure trove
had come at last. Eleven-year-old Alfred Stowerton opened his eyes,
having thus commanded the heavens to obey him. And gave a sigh of
relief. Heaven had obediently consented, and the sun was streaming in
through the tall windows of Stowerton House. He jumped out of bed,
had a cursory wash in the bowl, then wakened nine-year-old Joseph.
The day was too exciting to waste time washing. At ten o'clock they
would all depart for Bocton, the children in large wagonettes with the
servants and the picnic, followed by Mother and Father in the carriage.
Not just an ordinary picnic. The annual treasure trove picnic.

Every August, on the anniversary of the Battle of Bosworth and in
honour of the legend of the missing jewels of Richard III, Nat and
Bridget Stowerton held a treasure trove race in the gardens of the old
manor of Bocton. Here the Wars of the Roses were re-enacted, the
children divided into two teams of Yorkists and Lancastrians; but the
outcome of the war was decided not by longbows and pikes but by the
race to find the cup. Everyone got something, Sophy a necklace, the
boys toy soldiers or swords. But the honour went with the silver cup on
which not only the team of the year would be engraved but the name of
the actual finder. It was the highest honour in the family to be recorded
on Richard III's cup. One year the family spaniel, appropriately named
Bosworth, nosed it out and Nat had solemnly engraved his name too
on the cup.

The only person whose name was not yet engraved, apart from
three-year-old Albert, who was too young to play, was Joseph. They
all knew quite how much it meant to him to win. Perhaps this year
he would; indeed, he should if *he* had anything to do with it, vowed
Alfred.

The sun was misty that day, like childhood itself seen through the
haze of later life. Father and Mother sat on chairs by the lake, the
footman and butler superintending the preparation of the picnic. Cries
of laughter came from all directions as one by one clues were pored over
and puzzled out.

'I'll beat you this year, Robert, see if I don't,' yelled Lancastrian
Jeremiah, in charge of one team.

In charge of the other, Yorkist Robert was sixteen, though
his brother, two years his junior, outstripped him in looks and
physique. Robert had learned to take care of himself, however,
and was an effective fighter – when he thought Father was not
watching. For his fighting was not always by orthodox means.
George, two years younger than Jeremiah, would usually intervene,
trying to stop them, barging in clumsily and ending up making
things worse.

In and out of the manor, up and down the stairs, into attics and
closets, butteries and laundry, on to the courtyard and into the gardens
amongst empty conservatories, up untended fruit trees, pushing aside
sweet-smelling rosemary, lavender and sage in the straggly, overgrown
herb garden, swarming through the wild self-sown flowers – love in

a mist, larkspur, snapdragons – in their warriors' quest: the treasure trove cup.

Joseph pushed his way through the overgrown bushes to the disused beehive. Here it would be, he knew it. This year the cup would be his. He felt exalted, twice his size, glory within his reach. As Eve in paradise, he opened the hive and stretched his hand towards its gleaming silver temptation. But even as he did so, there was a voice behind him, persuasive, reasonable, convincing. 'Leave it, Joseph. Let's find your prize sword first. The cup will keep. I knew you'd find it first. I'll tell them you've found it.' And because he trusted his brother, he did so. He could never remember clearly quite what happened then. All he knew was that when he next reached the hive the cup was in Robert's hand.

His brothers came running as they heard Joseph's cries, listened to his tale, and used it. Jeremiah's eyes glowed in triumph. 'You pig, Robert,' he hissed, 'stealing from a youngster. I'm going to kill you.'

He pitched in. All the scores of childhood formerly forgotten rose to the surface as he saw his chance to remove Robert's superiority for good in the eyes of his brothers. Fighting with arms, legs, fists; pummelling, punching his way to a revenge he had not till then realised was called for. George dancing round, half umpiring, half egging them on, first Robert, then Jeremiah, and urging his younger brothers to keep out of it.

'Stay away!' in high-pitched tones. 'It's not Robert's fault.'

Joseph let out an inarticulate cry. Not Robert's fault? When he – for it must have been he – told him to leave the cup there? The snake, the snake! Usurping, grabbing for his own. Always his own. The elder brother. With a sob he hurled himself into the fray, clawing at Robert's face till the blood ran and Alfred dragged him off; Jeremiah clung tenaciously, yelling insults at Robert. But he was winning. His wiry disciplined strength was overcoming Jeremiah's loose, wild, ill-directed blows of rage. The underdog, Alfred, pushed a stumbling Joseph towards Sophy, and joined in to help Jeremiah, as his sister sobbed impotently and Albert watched – and learned.

With a strength Alfred did not know was in him, as Jeremiah weakened, he aimed a punch at Robert which caught him full in the face – just as Jehovah thundered above them.

'Enough!' decreed Nathaniel Stowerton. Instantly subdued, they rolled apart. But even Father could not quell the animosity that crackled between the four.

'It was mine,' cried Joseph, desperate. Didn't anyone believe him?

'I found it,' glared Robert stiltedly, his eye and cheek already swollen and turning black, bloody scratches dripping on to his muddied white shirt.

'It was Joseph's turn,' murmured George quietly.

'Robert's a pig,' cried inarticulate Alfred, unable to make sense of the jumble in his mind.

Robert glared at him. Alfred would pay for this. But not with blows, oh no. There were better ways of humiliating him. And Jeremiah . . .

He smiled condescendingly at him. How he would pay! Yet he, Robert, had won and that was more important than a bruised body.

Dishevelled black hair tumbling over his face, dark eyes glaring malevolently, Jeremiah limped away like a wounded dog. There had to be a way . . .

Sophy stopped him leaving with her tears, tears for she knew not what. But they halted Jeremiah, and slowly he returned to the group, avoiding Robert's eye.

'No more snivelling,' cried Jehovah. 'You'll have Albert at it.'

But Albert wasn't crying. He was enjoying it.

'Bring me the cup, my son,' Nathaniel ordered Robert in heavy tones.

'But –' he began, astounded.

'Bring it.'

Silenced, Robert bent to pick up the silver trophy, lying disregarded on its side in the bushes where it had been kicked in the struggle.

'The name to be engraved on the cup for *this* year –' Joseph looked up, hopeful, expectant, of justice at last '– will be Robert's. Not yours, Joseph.' He stared open-mouthed, then fought back the rush of tears. Was this not a just world? Was not Father just? What kind of future lay ahead if such basic premises were false?

'But there will be no more treasure troves,' said Nathaniel, a Jehovah in judgment.

Jehovah did not relent, and Bocton fell silent . . . Until Katharine had come.

The day of the treasure trove . . . Each brother remembered it now with sickening clarity. How could they have forgotten? The day had brought into the open something that had lain festering, waiting for its chance, but was now irreparable. It went on to harden into first, resentment, then bitter rivalry and hatred, suppressed only by the dictates of family life and a common love of Sophy. But little by little venom accumulated, and resulted in their leaving one by one. All save Sophy – and Alfred. For Alfred, there was a special humiliation: the humiliation of dependency.

So there was some kind of unfinished business, was there? Luke thought grimly. No wonder Father had sent him, and not come himself.

'*That's* why I came back,' murmured Joseph wonderingly.

'My dear Joseph, we are grown men. Do you still wish to win the cup?' Robert asked lightly, hearing his words.

Joseph flushed angrily. 'I reckon so,' he said slowly, looking his brother straight in the eye. 'You took it from me once.'

Robert's face did not betray the annoyance he felt at having made a false step.

'Looks like the Stowertons are off again,' roared Mabel happily. 'Gavelkind, eh? Give me Albania any day.'

Alfred hopefully tried to pour oil on troubled waters. 'What's past

70

is past. Let's just enjoy ourselves.' He looked around, hoping for more of Robert's excellent claret.

'Hear, hear,' said Sophy valiantly, but without his optimism.

But their hopes were doomed. The doors were flung open and sweeping in in advance of an agonised butler, Elizabeth Stowerton, clad in the lowest-necked evening dress Katharine had ever seen, with bright orange satin stripes and a long train, her black hair tied back with a large matching bow under a diamond tiara and two long necklaces of solid gold round her neck complemented by several bracelets, stood poised on the threshold. Like the statue of Mozart's Commendatore, she was late for dinner, but made no less effective an entrance.

'Mother,' cried Katharine outraged, as Alfred groaned aloud, and Millicent, with the calm of a hostess with nothing more to lose, rose to her feet like an automaton, saying feebly, 'How nice to see you again, Elizabeth.' Those who did not know her, those who had merely heard of her, and those who knew her only too well, gazed at her as if hypnotised.

Elizabeth surveyed them, a mocking smile on her lips. Then she noticed the one she was seeking. He was cowering distinctly.

'Albert,' she cried cheerfully, 'how wonderful to see you. How is your rupture nowadays? Still wearing that funny little truss, are you?'

He did not appear to share her enthusiasm for their reunion. Casting an agonised look at his son, he rose to his feet, struggling to regain his usual calm detachment. 'Elizabeth, I had no idea you would be present.' An inimical look at Alfred.

'Nor did Alfred,' she rejoined cheerfully. 'Darling,' she addressed her husband, 'can I sit by you?'

'Why don't you sit by me, Elizabeth?' said Millicent faintly, trying to save the situation with as little chance of success as Lord Cardigan reversing his decision to send in the Light Brigade. Elizabeth would be as far as possible from Albert here, was her one thought.

'No thank you, Millicent. I get on better with men.' The statement's simple truth robbed the words of insult. 'Ah,' Elizabeth continued happily, 'Meg darling, I'll sit there between these handsome young men. You go to sit by Millicent, darling.'

Meg's pretty mouth fell unbecomingly open as Elizabeth bore down upon her, and Louis showed every sign of enthusiasm for his new neighbour – to Albert's considerable disquiet.

Luke turned to Elizabeth as he resumed his seat. 'Were you not clad in that most modern and becoming dress, I would undoubtedly cast you as the skeleton at the feast.'

'I am so glad,' she announced happily, 'that at least one of the family can appreciate the important matters of life.'

Albert, a drowning black sheep, relived the iniquities of his past life as they flashed before his eyes. His revenge for his enforced goodness had been all too easy. Handsome, married to a rich French countess, they'd welcomed him back on his visit to Kent with open arms. Especially Elizabeth. 'Yes, do stay with us, Albert dear,' she'd said, smiling at him with dark soulful eyes. Odd the way he'd never noticed them before. After all, he'd known Alfred's wife for long enough. 'The children are away staying with my parents. We don't have much room here,' a moué of disgust, 'but it's more fun than life with Mountainous Millicent and Robert the Rat.'

So Albert had stayed. It suited his plans excellently, and when he left two weeks later he took Elizabeth with him and forgot to return to his countess. Quite whose idea the latter part was, he was never quite sure. They had lived in Rome where news from London society travelled slowly and that from France scarcely quicker. Even when in this case it did arrive, few cared.

Albert, however, had discovered his own self-centred ruthlessness was outclassed by Elizabeth's. For three years the countess waited. She had made enquiries and discovered that Elizabeth had no money. She knew her Albert, and though it took longer than she expected, back he came – and this time stayed. Those excursions he thereafter took, though frequent, were always from the home base.

For Elizabeth there was no going back, and even had there been such a route, she would not have taken it. Love beckoned once more, a tantalising will o' the wisp, that led her from country to country.

For Alfred it had been a period of such pain that he had thought at first he could never recover. But one day, five years after her defection, he had woken up and thought quite rationally about the matter. Women, after all, were much like horses. They often let you down. Of the two he thought he'd stick to horses in future, for the penalties were purely financial.

'Are all our family dinners going to be as exciting as that?' Luke asked, as Katharine hurried up to him, somewhat annoyed that he had arrived at Bocton first, as though by so doing he was intruding on something that was hers alone. Then she realised how foolish she was being. After all, he had already seen the house at its worst. Now he was lounging almost proprietorially against the porch wall, basking in the sun that fell full on his face.

'No,' she told him, embarrassed. 'You said you wanted me to show you Bocton, Cousin Luke –' she broke off. She couldn't talk about Mother at the moment. Not to Luke Stowerton.

'Luke,' he reminded her. 'Just Luke. Are you going to tell me about your mother?' he asked.

'We're here to see Bocton,' she replied firmly.

'But you're not wearing your breeches today,' he pointed out.

'They're not breeches, Cousin Luke, they are pantaloons or bloomers. Don't ladies wear them in America? You seem fascinated by them.'

He gave her an amused look and took her arm. 'Back home most women don't even speak of them, let alone wear 'em. They are "unmentionables" in polite New York society.'

'Here too,' she told him primly. 'But I think it's foolish. Hypocritical. Legs should be called legs.'

'And with legs like yours, they should be seen too,' he cut in.

She flushed red and he took her hand. 'I'm sorry, Katie May. You're so mighty easy to tease, so solemn and all.' She looked down in surprise at her hand in his, and promptly removed it. She could not forget her scorn when he had taken Meg in to dinner. If he thought she was another Meg, to be flattered so easily, he was wrong, and she would show him so.

'I have to be solemn,' she said defiantly. Surely he could see why, now he'd met Father and Mother?

'No one *has* to be solemn,' he said gently. 'It's what they choose for themselves.' He should know, with a father like Jeremiah and Augusta for a mother. Everyone had his own means of escape. 'Now, it's over twenty years since I saw this place, Katie, and I'm kind of impatient to know about it. I've walked round the outside again while I was waiting – it sure needs work doing on it. What makes you think it's worth saving?' He regarded her bright-eyed as she rose to the challenge, like he'd known she would, and they began to walk round the outside again.

'Worth saving? Of course it's worth saving. Those things you saw – they're minor.'

'That hole through the West Wing?' he enquired drily.

'That can be repaired – in time,' she modified honestly.

He laughed. 'Tell me all, Katie May, tell me everything.'

Diffidently she explained about the Stowerton family arms over the porch door in the ornamental stonework, then with gathering excitement told him of the conceits and emblems with which Nicholas Stowerton, like all Tudors, had loved to embellish his house.

'Like this?' he enquired, peering at a carved stone inscription on the base of the old chimney stack:

> Grow rich in that which never taketh rust
> Whatever fades but fading pleasure brings

He read it out with some difficulty because of crumbling lichen-encrusted stonework. 'Why did they do it?'

Katharine considered. 'I think because they were in love with life. It seemed to have such enormous possibilities that exuberance just burst out of them. That's from a sonnet by Sir Philip Sidney – on the virtues of higher things than earthly love.'

'"Thy necessity is yet greater than mine" . . . that Sidney?'

She nodded, surprised that he should know.

He grinned at her surprise. 'We do have books in America. So Sidney built the house?'

'Oh, *no*. This house,' she chose her words carefully, 'was built by Sir Nicholas Stowerton. Queen Elizabeth granted him the manor in 1572 after it had reverted to the Crown through the treason of another branch of the family. The story goes that she was so disgusted when she visited him in 1573 and found only an old-fashioned lime-washed timber-framed house that she actually gave him the money to build the new house, and returned to stay at Boughton Malherbe instead –

that's a few miles away. In fact,' Katharine added suddenly, for the resemblance had been troubling her and now she had placed it, 'you look a little like Nicholas – there's a miniature of him by Hilliard in Father's study.'

Luke cocked an eye at her. 'Handsome fellow, was he?' smiling, ridiculously disconcerting her.

'My handsome Nick, my old Saint Nicholas,' quoth the Queen. 'The devil may dance in your pocket, Nick, but what care I?'

She looked at his new manor of Bocton, every brick paid for by herself; no other man, not even Robin, had charmed her to such extravagance. She sighed. The light of the devil was in his eyes, not his pocket.

'What would I do without my merry Nick?' she murmured, while the practical side of her was speedily estimating the cost of this magnificence, automatically checking that he had been honest with her. Nick and she understood each other – he understood how much she wanted to be off and away, and how she could not because she was a queen; he understood the distance between them, knew when to cross it, and when to hold back. Nick Stowerton, who would follow the drum beat and return to tell her of foreign lands and ways, and of whom she could trust and whom she should watch. Of Nick himself, she had no doubt now; she had watched carefully, and for all his devilment he was as pure gold as the locks that fell about his shoulders.

Or if he wasn't, he should be shorter by the head . . . She smiled grimly. She had not forgotten these Men of Kent were notoriously prone to treason.

'"Grow rich in that which never taketh rust . . ."' She cackled as she read the pious conceit on the chimney stack, for this day at Bocton she was in forgiving mood. 'Take care, Nick, you devil's spawn, lest grown rich, you forget from whom your riches came.'

'My queen,' swore handsome Nick Stowerton, the laughter shining from his blue eyes, and the sun gleaming on yellow-gold hair, 'that will I never do.'

Luke Stowerton stared up at the ornamented brickwork of the gable above the mullioned window, as they returned to the porch. The gentle curves were echoed by those of its larger siblings to left and right, at the ends of the two wings flanking the central building, and the same curves subtly reflected in the dressed stone above the mullioned windows, satisfying and soothing the eye, carrying it upwards towards the ridges of the red-tiled roofs, and the tall graceful ornamented chimneys beyond.

And Robert wanted to pull this building down? It seemed to him that the world was turning ugly. Out there in Leadville men had been fighting and killing for the precious silver ever since it was first discovered there three years ago, even though there was plenty for all. They tumbled over each other like ants in an anthill. No, not like ants, for insects worked together industriously for the good of the whole. Only men tore their fellows to pieces for sheer greed. Money was the honeypot to which they swarmed. In Leadville he watched it daily; now it appeared it lurked even in the green woods of Kent.

'Why,' he asked Katharine abruptly, 'is the door here and not centrally between the two wings? Everything else is so symmetrical and balanced, but this is out of place.'

Katharine thought she knew why, but was not going to tell Luke Stowerton. The old house within was her secret, and would only be shown when she chose. 'I think it looks right here,' was all she said. 'After all, the Elizabethans were God-fearing folk and perfection belongs to God.'

He looked at her for a moment, but only said, 'Let's go inside.'

'Let's see the East Wing first,' she suggested as casually as she could.

'No,' he said mildly. 'I believe in facing the worst. That's if your dress –' He hesitated politely.

She lifted her chin. 'I am perfectly all right, thank you, Cousin Luke.' In fact she was regretting her sudden impulse to put on the delicate muslin dress.

The rooms seemed oppressive away from the sunlight, with their dark panelling and damp smells. Far from needing to be shown over the house, Luke seemed perfectly capable of seeing himself round, tapping panelling, examining 'live' plaster, testing floorboards. Halfway down the West Wing, she stopped reluctantly. 'You can't get any further,' she explained. 'It's not safe. There's a garden door if you want to see the far end.' Cautiously Luke edged himself into the devastation, which from inside the building showed its true extent. The walls were bulging out ominously, both ceilings were completely down, and the oak tree lay wedged still across the main ceiling beams and joists.

'The main roof timbers were broken,' explained Katharine, 'and the walls are crumbling a little, but –'

'A little!' exclaimed Luke. 'You aren't planning on mending this yourself, are you?' he drawled.

'No,' she replied. 'Obadiah's going to help me.'

He looked at her suspiciously, but she seemed perfectly serious. 'Is he now?' he commented resignedly.

'They say oak trees cry out when they fall,' she said ruefully, 'but I think when this one fell that Bocton cried with it.'

They went back into the East Wing in silence, where he continued his explorations, as she watched, running up the curving staircase at the far end to the attics. 'I used to do that when I was a kid,' he told her, returning at last and continuing the tour.

'Behind here,' she told him, pointing to the fireplace where a Georgian grate had been installed late last century, 'Obadiah thinks there must be the old Elizabethan inglenook fireplace as on the other side in the entrance hall – I'd like to tear it out and see,' she added wistfully.

'Katharine, the whole house is falling about your ears and you want to tear down the one thing that still seems to be standing up?' he asked ironically, as they went up to the next floor.

'It's all quite easy to repair really,' she said, anxious that Bocton was not making a good impression. 'It's worse than it looks,' she reassured, shouting after him as he disappeared into the attic rooms. 'Apart from the West Wing, there's only the roof to repair, and some repointing, and the windows.' Her voice faltered as he pulled at a beam above his head which disintegrated into powdered wood that showered down through the hole by which Mr Gabriel Arch had so ignominiously descended.

'Do be careful,' she shouted, anguished, brushing the dust off herself. Then a reluctant smile came to her lips as she realised the incongruity of what she was now saying. Luke swung himself cautiously down through the hole on to the bed. She hastily moved away.

'How bad does your builder think the roof is?' he asked briefly.

'There are some rotted tenons,' she said bravely, 'in the joints, but Obadiah's bracing those, and some rotted joist ends where the water got in, but really it's in good condition . . .' Her voice faltered before his steady eye.

'I'd rather try and hold back the Red Sea,' he said succinctly.

'But –' she gazed at him, appalled '– does that mean you won't help? That you don't think it's worth saving? Oh, surely you can see beyond the dry rot and the beams – just look at the whole house. Can you really look out at all that and not want to save it?' She gestured through the leaded windows out into the gardens. From this side view you could not see quite how overgrown they were and some idea of the original shape and excitement of the layout was clear, especially bathed in the greenness of May. 'Nicholas Stowerton once slept in this room,' she continued desperately when he did not answer. 'Perhaps even Good Queen Bess.'

'Together?' he enquired.

'Oh, can't you ever be serious?' she cried, anguished. 'What are you staring at?' she demanded as his eyes fixed on her.

'Forgive me, Cousin Katharine, you have woodworm in your bosom.' To her indignation, his hands lightly brushed the powder from her low-necked dress, touching her skin, ceasing before she had fully taken in what he was doing.

'Thank you,' she said stiffly. 'As I was saying –'

'About the love life of Good Queen Bess?'

'No!' she snapped, then thought better of her tone, and changed to one of conciliation. 'The gentleman from the Society for the Protection of Ancient Buildings will shortly come to give advice. Please don't decide before then. You can come too – he'll tell you how worthwhile it is.'

'Very well.' Luke had had no intention of making a snap decision anyway. 'Does he know about rot?'

'He knows about everything.'

'Then I must meet him. He might be able to tell me about that hole in the old study wall,' he said vaguely.

She jumped, then tried to conceal her reaction and replied

nonchalantly: 'That's just where Obadiah tore away the panelling to inspect the –'

'Rot,' he concluded succinctly.

'How dare you!' she retorted angrily.

He raised an eyebrow. 'Rot. The beam down there at the bottom was quite clearly affected by wet rot. I did not mean to imply you were not telling me the truth, Cousin Kate. A person of your integrity would never do such a thing.'

'I apologise, Cousin Luke,' she told him, feeling somehow she had been out-manoeuvred.

'I accept your apology, dear Kate. Now pray accompany me to the gardens and tell me what lies behind that study wall.' It was a command.

Seeing she had no choice, she led the way out into the gardens, determined that at least he should see them at their best, and glad, irrationally glad, that she had kept the old knot garden in some kind of order, freeing it from weeds, planting it with daffodils, gilliflowers, Sweet Williams, nasturtiums – flowers to bloom from April round to October, multiplying themselves into a riot of colour, just as the Elizabethans themselves had loved. Intricate little brick paths, half hidden by tumbling plants and shrubs, curled round on themselves, yet inexorably led the wanderer to the centre, the old sundial.

Then, as once again she appeared to have no choice, she began to explain about the old mediaeval house still lying tucked inside Bocton, aware all the time of his eye on her, of his closeness to her on the old love-seat tucked in the corner of the garden.

'And what did this old house look like?' he asked.

'Obadiah's not certain, but from old houses where the timber-framing is still visible on the outside, and which might have been built on the same pattern, it looks as if the house was constructed as one central hall open to the roof with no chimney –'

'No chimney? In this climate?' Luke shivered.

'Oh, they had a fire, but it was in the middle of the hall and so blackened the beams as there was no chimney. When we get into the main roof to look at the beams there, we'll know whether we were right.'

'And so now will you tell me why that porch isn't central?' he asked mildly.

She flushed. 'Because it's built on to the old doorway. The two ends of the hall were respectively the private quarters of the owner and his wife, and the buttery and storerooms and so on. Dividing the buttery from the hall was a passage through the house to the other side.'

He watched her curiously, wondering if she knew how lovely she was with the sun glinting on that chestnut hair, and her brown eyes so animated and far away as she talked of Bocton, lighting up her oval face with its fine features.

'And just what's so exciting about this old house to you, Katie May?' he asked.

She paused, considering. 'Because it's been hidden away, because

77

it's at least hundred years older than the Tudor house, perhaps even older than that, and it's the very house where Richard Plantagenet might have stayed and hidden his jewels.'

'Anything to do with that treasure trove?'

'Yes,' she said, wondering at his sharpness, and explaining about the old legend.

When she had finished, he sighed. 'Legends – the past, Katharine. We're in a second age of expansion now. New continents opening up, new lands. Don't you think Robert's right? That we should be looking to the future, not the past?'

'No,' she said simply. 'I mean, yes, but they're part of each other. We can't be sensible about the future, if we forget about the past.'

'Maybe,' he said dismissively, wandering up to the old sundial, with its injunction to seize the day engraved upon it. 'What's this?' He knelt down, seeing another inscription carved in stone around its base.

'"*Tyme wanes awaye*
As flowers decaye",' she quoted from memory.

He grimaced. 'Cheerful, weren't they?' he commented. 'Bocton's a decaying flower, I guess.'

'Not if we win The Case,' she said stoutly. 'I will open Bocton as a school, and raise enough to pay all the other owners rent.'

'A school?' he asked incredulously. 'With you as schoolmistress?'

'Why not?' she asked indignantly. 'You think I am not capable?'

'Capable, yes.'

'Then why –'

'You'll be buried here, deeper than these flowers,' he said decisively. 'That's why. Overgrown and unregarded. Now wouldn't that be a waste?'

'A waste? I can teach Latin!' she exclaimed.

'Look at these flowers, Katie May. You know, I remember these pretty ones from when I was only knee high to a frog. Sweet William, isn't it?' He bent and picked one. 'Now I recall reading the Elizabethans reckoned these flowers were only to be used to adorn the bosoms of the beautiful.' He leaned forward and poked the flower in the lace on the neckline of her dress.

'I'm not beautiful,' she said belligerently, insulted, entranced.

He did not answer, but simply pulled the ribbon that held back her hair and before she could stop him was removing pins so that the chestnut curls fell about her shoulders. 'If there were a pond here, you'd see,' he told her, admiring the softness that the curls added to her face.

Suddenly she found her voice and the hazel eyes blazed. 'I, Cousin Luke, am not a mere doll, to be dressed and undressed at your whim!' Sweeping on all the more enraged by the twitch at his lips, and oblivious of what made him smile; 'I'll have you know that women are *people*, not dolls; we have brains like you, feelings like you, dreams like you. And one day you men will find that we can rule the world like you.'

To her fury he merely laughed, replying softly: 'Shall I come to teach at your school, Cousin Katharine?'

'I wouldn't have you as a teacher,' she said deliberately, 'if Plato himself pleaded with me.' And with a whisk of her sprigged muslin skirts strode off in as deliberately an unfeminine a manner as she could.

Luke continued to wander through the grounds when she had gone, gazing at the back of Bocton with the old courtyard and fountain nestling between the two wings, birds nesting in the eaves and wistaria growing up the walls. Partly he was thinking about Bocton, but mostly about Katharine. He was certainly going to take his time over a decision on Bocton. Could he, much as he wanted, invest his father's money in this ruin, however lovely? He had been going to take his time over Katharine too. He remembered what his father had said. There were good Stowertons, bad ones, mean ones, and some you had to be careful of. But he didn't need to think any longer. She was a girl who believed in something, whatever its value, and was going to do something about it; a girl who looked funnier than he had ever believed possible, all covered with plaster and wielding a hammer with the ease that most women waved fans. A girl with chestnut hair and hazel eyes the colours of the woods, a girl he couldn't tumble in the hills like those back in Yale, and quite unlike the few prim starchy girls in Leadville, all so concerned with position and money – but a girl he hadn't made laugh yet. He smiled. He guessed he'd go a-wooing Cousin Kate.

But it was not Kate but Meg who was standing over him as he sat abstractedly in the late afternoon sun. He leapt to his feet apologetically.

'Oh dear, I thought Katharine was still here,' she said innocently.

'You thought nothing of the sort,' he said gently, mockingly.

She blushed prettily. 'Perhaps I did just think you might still be here too,' she conceded, peeping up at him from under her eyelashes. 'Shall we walk back through the gardens, Cousin Luke?'

'How delightful that would be,' he said gravely, and offered her his arm.

Katharine removed the pins from her hair that night one by one and brushed it vigorously. How could she have been so foolish? It only went to show how easily you could be taken in by the butterflies of this world. And she had almost taken him seriously. How stupid of her. Beautiful! What nonsense. It was her own fault. She'd told him he looked like Nicholas Stowerton and that had encouraged him. He would behave the same to any girl. Had he not walked off instantly with Meg when she approached him before the dinner? And now apparently had had an assignation with her at Bocton? She did not blame him, nor her sister, who had babbled incessantly at supper of the charms of Cousin Luke who had persuaded her into rambling the gardens with him. Meg was pretty, bubbling, full of life; no wonder she was attracted to Luke and he to her. He was an outrageous flirt, though. He had kissed her, he had even touched her breast – well, not again. She would be distant, cool, and perfectly polite.

She needed his support. His *cousinly* support, to help save Bocton. He would not be able to fault her behaviour – nor penetrate her defences.

Yet all the same, as she fell asleep at last that night, she was fingering a lock of her long chestnut hair.

Chapter Five

He must have arrived already for a brougham was drawn up in front of Bocton Manor. Katharine broke into a run, gathering her skirts impatiently. That was no hired conveyance. A coat of arms displayed on the door told her the Honourable Roderick Mayfield, son of Lady Mayfield, was already inspecting Bocton. She had been so determined to be there first, in order she supposed to defend the old house against criticism. She wanted to explain, to defend its apparent defects. Now Mr Mayfield might already have made his own judgements.

A week ago the representative of the Society for the Protection of Ancient Buildings had paid his visit, but it had not turned out to be the meeting she had envisaged. Uncle Robert had flatly refused to allow him entrance, unless not only he but all claimants to Bocton were present.

Katharine had recognised this gambit for what it was. It was not out of fairness he had decreed this, but so that he could point out one by one, so cleverly, all Bocton's faults, magnifying each problem, debating each one endlessly with the Society's representative. As a result, all the while Joseph, Albert, Louis, Mabel – and Luke – were listening, quietly, uneasily, while Robert carried on a duologue with the society's representative. She could almost pinpoint the decisive moment that Bocton's fate seemed sealed as the man had explained that restoration work should be clearly distinguishable from the old; the old historic building should be seen for what it was, not renovated to hide the wear and tear of years; all clumsy additions and 'improvement' since should be stripped away to expose the old house.

'You mean,' said Robert, falsely appalled, 'that it will look a hotch-potch?'

The representative was disconcerted. No, that was not what he had meant.

'Oh, I understand. That we should not add modern improvements, windows and chimneys? As Mr Morris says, we are trustees for those who come after us.'

'Exactly,' agreed the young man, thankful Robert was so easy to convince.

'It can still be a home,' Katharine said quickly, glancing at doubtful faces after he left.

'With decaying woodwork still visible?' enquired Robert.

'Nasty things, beetles,' declared Mabel after a moment. 'I wouldn't want to eat my luncheon under these beams. I don't see this could be made into a home. Or a school, come to that.' She gave a barking laugh. 'Have the youngsters falling through the old ceilings. Beams giving way.'

'We can repair them,' said Katharine eagerly. 'Mr Trant was telling me how you can repair the joists, splice in new pieces of timber –'

'A lot of work to repair all that,' said Joseph doubtfully. 'Quicker to build something from scratch.' He thought of Australia, its virgin land, its optimistic promise. Build, yes, not repair.

'In France, at Carcassonne for example, Monsieur Viollet-le-Duc has restored mediaeval buildings very successfully,' said Albert, staring up at the house. 'I think the same could be done here. I think these societies are too particular.'

'Never been particular yourself, have you, Albert,' growled Alfred.

Albert raised his eyebrows. 'On the contrary, Alfred. I am most particular. I choose most carefully – in clothes, in snuff, and in my – ah –'

His voice dropped delicately, and Alfred's hands clenched tightly.

Obadiah had came to her rescue when she poured out the story afterwards. 'Now don't yew be afretting, Miss Katharine. Dis uncle of yours, 'e didn't say nothin' about yew not taking no other visitors round now, did 'e? Why don't I ask Mr Roderick to look at it, then? 'E do be de genlem'n wid de 'ouse wid de 'allouse inside. 'E be respected, for all he do live in 'eadcorn,' he added disparagingly, as befitted a man of the downs.

So Katharine had fixed all her hopes on Mayfield's visit – for surely if a man of his stature were to pronounce Bocton easily repairable and worth saving because of its mediaeval origins, the family would be impressed.

She could see a tall figure staring up at the Stowerton armorial bearings in the stonework over the porch, and nervousness overtook her as she walked quickly up to him. She was suddenly aware that what she had previously thought of as a serviceable everyday businesslike dress of brown linen was merely countrified before this elegantly attired gentleman who looked more suited for an At Home than for exploring a tumbledown country house, full of dust and insects.

Perhaps it was the seriousness of the expression in the deep grey eyes set in the lean face, for all he could only be in his late thirties, that made her ill at ease.

'Mr Mayfield, I do hope you'll feel it's worth your coming.'

'A pleasure, Miss Stowerton.' He bowed. '*Audacibus annue coeptis*: look kindly on our –'

'Why, that's Virgil,' she said ingenuously. 'My favourite poet.'

'Indeed,' he said, clearly surprised that a woman should have such inclinations. 'Then, Miss Stowerton, *fervet opus*. Let us begin. I must confess, I am entranced by what I have already seen. The dressed stone on the gables, the devices, the emblems, the chimneys. In sad repair, I regret to say, yet I am eager to see inside.'

'Are you?' she said hesitantly, 'There is a certain amount of dust inside. And the roof –'

Roderick Mayfield gestured upwards. 'Your builder's lad will do all the inspection for me, Miss Stowerton.'

'Builder's lad? But Obadiah isn't coming. Nor his son.' Even as she spoke a sinking feeling overtook her. She looked up at the cluster of four ornamental chimneys, two of which were crumbling badly. There was a ladder over the roof, and there was a figure crawling along it. The face was not in sight, but those long legs were unmistakable.

'That's not a builder,' she said slowly. 'That's my Cousin Luke.'

'Oh.' Roderick Mayfield's face grew pink. 'I apologise. I had no idea,' he said stiffly. 'The clothes . . .'

Luke came swiftly down the ladder, his face almost invisible under a battered bowler hat which Katharine instantly recognised as Obadiah's working hat which he left inside Bocton. His clothes and Obadiah's enveloping canvas apron were covered in brick dust and dirt. Oblivious of his unconventional attire, he strode across and kissed her on the cheek, to her annoyance.

'*Cousin* Luke,' she reiterated meaningfully, 'may I introduce the Honourable Roderick Mayfield, who is here to advise *me* on Bocton.' Another emphasis on 'me'.

'I'll sure be glad to hear what you have to say,' said Luke wholeheartedly. 'It's not often I gets to hear a real English gentleman talking and all.'

She looked at him suspiciously, but Mayfield seemed mollified. 'You are not from these parts, I take it, Mr Stowerton.'

'Me? Nossir. I guess I've bin away for a while,' agreed Luke. 'Jus' come back to see the ole homestead. Pity it's so old and all. I guess I'll just follow you round. Don't you go taking any notice of me, though. I'll be as quiet as a chickadee on toast.'

Katharine closed her eyes, agonised. How could she keep him quiet before he spoiled everything?

'Quite,' said Roderick stiffly. 'Do you have any objection, Miss Stowerton?'

'Mr Stowerton is one of the prospective owners of the house,' she said. 'He has a right.'

'Gee, I sure love these quaint old places,' Luke told him blandly. 'Back where I come from the oldest homestead is two years old.'

'I think we can do better for you than that,' said Roderick smugly.

Katharine led them into the house, longing to warn Mr Mayfield that Luke was leading him on. Why couldn't he see it? That gleam in Luke's eye. Surely not only she could be conscious of it? She led them on a quick tour of the whole house so that he could get an idea of the layout of the house. Luke followed on behind, occasionally making some bright remark, which they both ignored.

The four-poster bed in the state bedroom immediately seized Mr Mayfield's attention. Katharine could sense Luke's fidgeting behind her. 'This has been treated abominably,' Mayfield announced severely. 'Not only left in the damp to deteriorate, but the original trappings torn down. And look at this rotten timber left here.'

Katharine had to suppress an insane desire to giggle, as she thought

83

of Luke hurtling down through the roof, and had to repress an instinct to turn round to see his reaction. 'This,' she said quickly, 'is said to be the bed that Queen Elizabeth slept in when she came to inspect the new manor of Bocton after Sir Nicholas had rebuilt it – at her expense.'

'And a mighty uncomfortable one it is too. Is it not, Cousin Katharine?' said Luke innocently.

'Of course,' she swept on hastily, ignoring him, but feeling her cheeks growing red, 'there's no proof that this was the state bedroom, only tradition, and this was obviously the best bed.'

'You will recall, Miss Stowerton, that the Bard of Avon left his second-best bed to his wife?' said Roderick Mayfield.

'Of course,' she said, and smiled at him, drawn to his obvious appreciation of their literary heritage.

'This would not have been part of the mediaeval house, though that adjoining room which overlooks the front of Bocton would have been.'

'The Queen's reception room,' said Katharine eagerly, trying to ignore Luke who was ferreting about round the fireplace.

'Precisely, Miss Stowerton. So, now, having seen the plan of the Tudor house, I will investigate as to whether the whole mediaeval house exists here or merely fragments of it.'

'Why, back in Leadville we don't make so much fuss about lill' ole wooden houses,' put in Luke helpfully, as he obediently trotted downstairs after them into the study. 'We build 'em, knock 'em down, or pick 'em up and pop them round the corner. If you don't like where you live, you picks up your house – wid a bit of help of course – and puts it somewhere else. Nothing to it. Ain't never heard of –'

Neither Katharine nor Mayfield was listening to Luke's monologue, both peering into Obadiah's hole in the panelling, made somewhat larger for his visit. 'Panels – wall post – a brace . . . Yes, I do believe, – Miss Stowerton, it's still here. At this point at any rate. You see the staves that held the wattle and daub?'

'That the stuff made of animal dung?' enquired Luke brightly.

Roderick Mayfield shuddered. 'If you care to put it that way.'

'Ain't that something. To think for four hundred years a load of cowshit –'

'Mr Stowerton! There are ladies present.'

'Gee, I'm sorry, Katharine. I guess I'd best keep my mouth shut.' He watched meekly while Mayfield continued to expound on the structure of the old house.

'Look,' said Katharine, 'I think if we just pull some more away –' She picked up the hammer and chisel she always left there and began to wrench away more of the old panelling.

'Miss Stowerton!' Roderick was astounded. 'Your hands.'

'Allow me, Cousin Kate,' Luke came forward. 'I guess I'd better save your lily-white hands. You're not used to this. Man's work.'

Katharine glared at him, both mortified and annoyed that Roderick Mayfield should be so shocked at her wielding hammer and chisel. Any annoyance at him, however, was vastly outweighed by her fury at Luke's performance, as he solemnly took the tools from her.

'You notice the gap between this inner mediaeval wall on the ground floor level and the outside Tudor wall – about a foot . . . up as far as where the upper storey was jettied out. The upper storey, the room you call the Queen's Reception Room, was where the former private apartments were for the owner and his family. Sleeping and working rooms, with the kitchens and the buttery down at the other end. The fire of course would be –'

'Where was the closet?' Luke broke in.

'I beg your pardon,' Sir Roderick stared at him aghast for mentioning this delicate subject.

'The water closet,' repeated Luke. 'Don't you have 'em here? Outside was it? Mighty long way for the ladies to come down in their long dresses and all.'

'My cousin has a great interest in domestic history,' murmured Katharine through clenched teeth.

'This is hardly a fit subject –'

'Before a lady,' finished Luke. 'Ah, but Cousin Kate is different. Cousin Kate's like you. A historian, Mr Mayfield.'

'It is possible some arrangement was made whereby a closet jutted out from the upper storey at the side or rear. A – er – garderobe,' said Mayfield stiffly.

'I'd sure like to see that.'

'The roof,' said Katharine hastily, seeing Mr Mayfield's embarrassment, 'let us go to see the roof. Wait till you see the beams. They're magnificent.'

'You've seen them?' Mayfield asked in surprise.

'Well, yes.' Belatedly she once again recalled that climbing ladders was not a ladylike pursuit and it was after all necessary to keep Mr Mayfield on her side. 'I just climbed up a little way and peered in,' she said, flustered. In fact, she'd crawled along quite a distance inside, captivated by the enormous tie beams, and huge crown posts, majestically soaring upwards.

Behind her Luke snorted with laughter. 'You'd like me to climb up and report down to you, Mr Mayfield?' he asked, eyes rather too obviously on the visitor's tight-fitting coat and trousers.

Mayfield hesitated. 'I shall climb myself,' he said curtly, clearly not wishing to lose face before this foreign yokel.

Luke and Katharine stared at his elegantly clad legs, as he stood on the ladder, his head in the hole created where the ceiling had fallen, light shed by the holes in the tiling. Presently he descended.

'It is poetry, Miss Stowerton. Sheer poetry. The crown posts, the braces, the purlins, smoke-blackened beams. There,' he announced reverently, 'is history.'

'Rot,' said Luke. 'Wet rot,' he added hastily, 'where the chimney has been inserted.'

Mayfield continued to address Katharine. 'I wonder if you would

85

care to visit Hurstdene? My mother would be delighted to entertain you to tea, and we could discuss Bocton at greater length.'

'I sure would enjoy that,' said Luke warmly.

Roderick opened and shut his mouth several times, and wisely decided to ignore it. 'Shall we say next Tuesday, *Miss Stowerton?*' he emphasised.

'I should be very pleased,' said Katharine, thankful that here was a chance to redeem Bocton's chances.

Roderick bent low over Katharine's hand, gave a cool nod to Luke, and began to climb into his waiting carriage.

'*Macte nova virtute, puer, sic itur ad astra,*' called Luke cheerfully.

A foot wavered in mid-step as Mayfield rapidly took in the implications of Luke's farewell.

'My favourite, Virgil,' added Luke calmly, as the brougham drove off with Mayfield staring rigidly forwards.

'How dare you?' Katharine burst out angrily.

'How dare I what? Quote Virgil? Dearest Kate, you cannot monopolise the classics for yourself.'

'Humiliate him.'

'Not a chance. You have to be human to be humiliated, Katharine.'

'But he may be Bocton's last chance,' she said desperately. 'I want him to convince the family of Bocton's worth.'

'*I'm* probably Bocton's last chance – or part of it, and it doesn't need a dried-up stick like him to tell me something I ought to be able to see with my own eyes, feel with my own heart. I thought you'd like to see me taking an interest in the house.'

'Yes, but –' There was a flaw in his argument, but she could not define it. 'I just wish . . .'

'You wish too much,' he said lightly. 'You should laugh your way to what you want. See how easy it is,' he said softly, his fingers at the corners of her mouth, forcing it into a smile.

'But it isn't,' she said indignantly, shaking free of him. He didn't understand. How could he? Money was no object to him. He could never understand how much she hated living on other people's charity, how she was determined not to do so for the rest of her life, and just how determined she was to save Bocton.

'Oh, Katie May,' Luke replied softly, 'it is.'

Joseph walked slowly down the staircase at Stowerton House. In his large high-ceilinged bedroom he could breathe, staring out over the downland beyond the park. But downstairs, he felt trapped, back in the miasma of his youth, the toils of family inexorably reaching for him again. And he seemed powerless to resist them. When Robert had suggested – commanded? – Mabel, Albert, young Luke and himself to stay with them at Stowerton House, only Albert had had the sense to say no, that he'd remain in his Maidstone inn. Joseph had welcomed it at first. Robert had seemed sincere in his desire to be reacquainted with his family, despite the circumstances, assuring them that whatever decision was reached it would not affect his regard for them. Nor indeed had he put pressure on them regarding Bocton.

No, the unease he felt here went back over twenty years, earlier than that if Sophy were right. To the day of the treasure trove? Or earlier still? He remembered George clumsily shambling down the staircase, an owl-faced amiable fourteen-year-old. He'd never changed. What he was at eight, he was at twenty-eight. Dear George. Of all of them, why did it have to be him who died early? Even now, he felt a welling up of emotion at something lost for ever. Had it not been for Emily, he would indeed be a ship without a rudder. Without her here, however, without George, he felt as defenceless against Robert's domination as he had as a child. George had always protected him, been between them, and now that he was dead it was too late for Joseph to develop his own defences.

He walked into the dining room. Trust Millicent to insist on formal breakfast. Shades of Father; small set faces surrounding the huge table, all with their own enmities and feuds, all suppressing them in order not to upset their parents. If he'd stayed here, he'd never have met Emily. He'd have been stuck forever in the morass that engulfed him here, forever under Robert's cool authority, always with the feeling that he was trapped in a maze, the middle of which could never be reached. Everything stemmed back to Robert. If this case succeeded, then Robert would suffer; it would be a means of revenge – yet then Joseph would be part owner of Bocton; would that not mean he would be trapped in the maze forever? If only George were here to tell him what to do. Amiable, happy-go-lucky George, the one who held the family together, in the face of Robert's domination.

'Millicent tells me you've been to Bocton again, Joseph,' said Robert, politely helping him to devilled kidneys.

'It's a fine old building, Robert,' he grunted, trying not to give an inch. 'We don't have places like that in Australia. Katharine has a point. It ought not to be pulled down.' Even saying it gave him satisfaction, a small revenge for the day of the treasure trove. Yet the maze still trapped him, a mist over that summer's day so long ago.

'It is a quite ridiculous notion of Katharine's, dragging you halfway across the world for a whim of her own. For her good, not yours.'

'We're grown men,' retorted Joseph stubbornly. 'We all came. I suppose we all had unfinished business here.' He glared down at the kidneys, unable to look Robert in the face even now. 'Albert with Alfred, Mabel for George. And Jeremiah . . .'

'What about Jeremiah?' asked Robert quickly, his pale face flushed.

'You know, Robert. It's buried now, and I doubt if that son of his knows. You *do* remember Jeremiah, don't you, Robert?'

Silence.

'I didn't know why I came till Sophy told us,' Joseph said slowly.

'I won my place on that cup,' said Robert venomously, losing his composure. 'I have nothing to reproach myself with.'

'Then why did you put it away?' Bitterness crept into Joseph's

voice even now. 'It should have been mine.' He stopped, amazed
that so much feeling still existed within him. He wasn't a child any
longer, yet suddenly everything centred on that cup. The old feelings
of helplessness against Robert came back. Robert who controlled all
of them with quiet cunning. Robert who had everything. Well, he was
not going to have Bocton. Not if Joseph could do anything to prevent
it. And he could.

Meg hummed to herself as she closed the pink parasol to enter the
village stores at Bocton Bugley. It was a small village, small enough that
there was no chance of missing Luke Stowerton, who had announced
his intention of going there to see old Mr Coppen, the retired saddler
whom he recalled from his childhood.

Meg rarely visited the village shop; this was Katharine or Maggie's
task, and she was greeted in restrained cool terms as she waited to be
served, seating herself without question on the one chair provided for
customers. It provided an excellent view of the street, and she was
able to time her exit to coincide with Luke's leaving the small tile-hung
cottage opposite.

'Cousin Meg,' he said in amusement. 'What a delightful surprise.'

'Oh, Luke.' She gave him her hand as if bestowing a gift. 'I am so
pleased to see you. I walked here, you see, and I fear it might rain.'

'Cousin Meg, you are an English rose,' he teased, twirling and
opening her parasol. He glanced into the clear blue sky. 'And roses
bloom best in the rain, I am told.'

'But I am tired, Luke,' she pouted, looking meaningfully at his
sturdy horse.

'Then you must ride, and I shall walk,' he said promptly, knowing
this was not what she intended at all.

He assisted her to mount and took the reins to lead the horse
himself.

The back of his head did not please Meg at all; as they came into
the lane that skirted the Bocton estate, a remedy came to mind.

'Cousin Luke, there are some delightful cowslips in that meadow.
Do you think we might stop?'

Obediently he helped her down, and she remained close to him
rather longer than was strictly necessary.

'Oh, I do hope you will stay in England,' she said ingenuously and
truthfully.

'Now what makes you think I could do that, Meg, when I live way
over there in Colorado?' he said lightly.

'I thought perhaps –' a little gasp '– Bocton. Of course,' she went
on rapidly, 'I have equal right to it with Katharine. Our share, that
is. That makes us partners, doesn't it?' She dimpled.

'I guess it does, Meg. And a prettier partner I sure never did have,'
he said lightly.

'Oh, *Luke*, I do like you,' she blushed. 'And – this horse is very
strong. Do you not think we could ride back together? I should
feel safer.'

'Sure,' he agreed, helping her up and swinging up himself, holding her lightly to him.

'I feel better now,' she declared happily, wriggling so that his hand was close under her breast.

'Haven't you forgotten something?' he whispered in her ear.

'What?'

'Your flowers.'

'Oh!' She turned and laughed at him, eyes sparkling.

'Where have you been, Meg?' said Katharine despairingly. 'I've been waiting for those nails before I could leave for Bocton.'

'I'm sorry, Katharine,' said Meg meekly, burying her head in the bouquet of wild flowers. 'Aren't these lovely? Cousin Luke picked them for me.'

Katharine seized her nails and stumped off to the manor house in a thoroughly bad temper. She told herself it was because of the nails, but the hammer she was clasping so fiercely was for some reason aimed in her mind less for the tie beam lap dovetail joint than for Luke Stowerton.

Alfred paced round the Stowerton Room in great agitation, glowering. Not only had he not been able to read the *Sporting Times*, but of all people he could see Albert marching up the garden path, large as life. What the devil did he want? Perhaps he still expected to see Elizabeth here? Thank heavens she had gone back to Paris, without what she'd come for. Divorce of all things! If he'd wanted a divorce, the time to do it would have been when she first ran off with his brother, not now when he'd simply appear ridiculous, not aggrieved. That terrible time came back to him.

True, on due reflection, he was now slightly more able to think of Albert as much sinned against as sinning, but that was no excuse.

'What do *you* want?' he roared belligerently, guarding the French windows like Cerberus as Albert arrived, nonchalantly swinging a walking cane. There must be a carriage somewhere; no hard work like riding for Albert.

'I had called on Robert and he was so kind as to leave me here while he visits the old manor.' Albert smiled, almost seeming to read his thoughts.

'And don't you want to see the old manor?' Alfred growled.

'I thought I'd renew acquaintance with my older brother first,' said Albert disarmingly. 'I must say, Alfred, you've made yourself very comfortable here,' looking at the shabby armchairs and piles of books and newspapers. He was almost jealous until he reflected that amours would be difficult to conduct in such an environment and he would miss the Provençal sun. Not to mention Louise. All the same, a fleeting pang for home and what had been seized him, as it had not at Stowerton. There he was always the youngest, the disregarded, the onlooker – and the one who waited. Anyway, it wasn't the same without George. George was the only one he'd had any time for. No, he'd burned his boats and left. There was nothing in England for Albert Stowerton. He'd look at Bocton before he finally made his decision, but already he'd fulfilled his purpose: he was the annoying gnat that descended to irritate and then depart. Perhaps return, who knows? But not to stay, not to get involved. The dinner party had convinced him that the turning over of the ants' nest was fun, but being in the ants' nest at the time was not. All the same, he'd have another look at Bocton first.

'Aren't you going to invite me to sit down?' he asked plaintively.

'I am not, dammit,' growled Alfred. 'The last time I invited you to sit down, you ran off with my wife.'

Albert sighed. 'If I might point out, Alfred, I did not drag darling Elizabeth away by force. It is rather difficult, as I have since discovered, to make Elizabeth do anything she does not wish to.'

'Don't you insult my wife, damn you! Best little woman in the world,' retorted Alfred heatedly. Then he recognised the incongruity of this statement. There was no need for Albert to comment.

'So she is living in Paris again?' he ruminated provocatively.

'You keep away from her,' roared Alfred.

'Believe me, I have every intention of doing so,' said Albert fervently, helping himself to snuff. 'I see you still have the old snuffbox that Queen Bess gave Nick.'

'Anything wrong with that?'

'Nothing. Nothing at all,' said Albert hastily.

'Why did you come?' asked Alfred bluntly. 'I don't see you have any interest in saving the old house, though it would give you great pleasure to see everyone else start up The Case again – provided you didn't have to pay.'

Albert raised his eyebrows. 'My dear Alfred,' he said sanctimoniously, 'Bocton is my home as much as yours. I have a son.' He paused provokingly. 'I felt it time he saw his English heritage and relations, though the latter cannot have impressed him greatly, I fear. He has a right to see what the future might hold for him if The Case were reopened.'

'On the scrounge, as usual!'

'As are you, Alfred,' retorted Albert politely. 'Robert informs me he is generous enough to give you the Dower House free of rent,' he added carelessly.

'That's enough. Remember, I'm your elder brother. Show some respect.'

'By all means,' Albert said, not a whit abashed, goading him.

Alfred's control broke. 'Don't sit there defying me, damn you! You haven't changed in twenty years. You're the same confounded jackanapes you were then. What do you want of me, eh? I don't have another wife for you to seduce.'

'You have two charming daughters.' Another pinch of snuff.

Alfred's eyes bulged. 'They're your nieces, Albert. Even you –'

He raised his eyebrows in mock surprise. 'How can you think that even of me, Alfred? However, I do have a son . . .'

* * *

90

Twenty-year-old Louis Stowerton had so far been distinctly disen-chanted with his heritage – rain, *mon dieu*, the *rain*. True, it made beautiful flowers but one could not live on flowers alone and this dampness was extremely disagreeable for the clothes. He examined his jacket ruefully. Until he had seen Mademoiselle Meg Stowerton, he had been *ennuyé, très ennuyé*. Now he thought he saw sport ahead. Let Father ramble round these dreary gardens and even drearier, not to mention dusty, house, talking of his youth. This tumble-down place was not to be compared with the châteaux of France, for elegance and style, and certainly not with the new villas of the Riviera, including their own.

Bocton had acquired a new charm, however, when he had persuaded Meg to take him round. 'You will show me this English paradise, will you not?' He had seen it twice before but this was different. Meg was captivated by his dark eyes, and his evident interest in her company, which far outweighed any interest that she had in Bocton. But with this temptation, even Bocton seemed attractive.

'And you, *ma belle cousine*, how does a rose like yourself dwell inside this dark and damp place?'

Meg was quite sharp enough to recognise a flirt when she saw one, especially one of her own age, and was now, she decided, fully prepared to enjoy the situation. She smiled mysteriously as they entered, rather without her intention, the Queen's Chamber.

'And what is this 'orrible old bed?' Louis enquired, taking her hand and pointing.

'That's Queen Elizabeth's bed,' Meg informed him, removing her hand. She would begin this game by pretending he were serious in his historic interest. 'She slept here on several occasions.'

'Ah. Then, *ma belle*, we will stand on this bed, and I will lift you up so that you can tell me what is in that dusty hole up there.'

Caught in a trap of her own making, she somewhat unwillingly allowed herself to be pulled on to the bed, and hoisted up in his arms.

'I can only see old beams, nothing interesting. Oh!' The feel of his arms around her was very strange, not to mention definitely indelicate, and she demanded to be set down. However handsome and delightful he was, she had to be careful. But as he handed her down from the bed, he seized her again, and kissed her, his arms tight around her, gently pressing an unmentionable part of her body closer until she struggled physically and verbally, pink in the face. He released her immediately.

'Ah, forgive me,' he twinkled. 'I forget you are English, and not so sophisticated as French ladies.'

'I am,' she cried indignantly. She was not going to be outdone by any French ladies.

'Then, *ma rose*, I will begin again.'

'No,' she said firmly, glancing at the old bed and realising the highly improper whereabouts of this interesting encounter. 'At least,' she dimpled, 'you will have to catch me first.' And gathering her muslin skirts in one hand she fled, before he could catch her, down the stairs and out into the gardens.

This was a game that Louis knew well. He deliberately let her outstrip him until – he calculated, the exact moment – when she reached the rose arbour, she would glance behind her to see where he was. She did so on cue to see him strolling casually towards her, laughing, until he had almost reached her. When she fled again, rather more slowly, he caught her easily and this time did not release her until her cheeks were considerably pinker than they had been before.

'What do you do with yourself all day here, Sophy?' asked Mabel brusquely, looking round the quiet parlour, bright with chintzes and embroidery, books and displayed china. Apart from the fact that it was brighter than most parlours, it was dull and uninteresting. Like Sophy.

'I live a quiet life, Mabel,' said Sophy guardedly. 'I have my charities.'

'Charities!' repeated Mabel in disgust. 'Village works! Teacakes and broth! Not much of a life for a woman.'

'No,' said Sophy, 'I mean my London charities.' Her voice rose a little. 'I visit London twice a month to help charities for unfortunate women.'

'Unfortunate women!' Mabel cackled. 'You're the one who's unfortunate, if you ask me, Sophy. How can a middle-aged virgin advise *them*?'

Sophy's eyes gleamed. If it had not been for the fact one had to forgive Mabel everything because she was George's widow, she might have made a very full answer. As it was she replied quietly: 'I am merely one pair of hands, Mabel. We all do what we can in this world, little or great. I should be as useless travelling through Albania, as you helping the unfortunates of London.'

Mabel shot a look at her. 'You're the best of the bunch,' she said unexpectedly. 'That's what George always said. "Good little Sophy", he called you. Trouble with being good is that no one thanks you for it. Much better to be bad, eh?' She cackled again.

'If you say so, Mabel,' replied Sophy thoughtfully.

'What am I going to do about this gavelkind case, Sophy?' her visitor asked forthrightly.

Sophy reflected on George. Kind, amiable, clumsy, the buffer of the family. That was how her brothers thought of him. What *would* George have done? It was not, she was beginning to realise, an easy question. She picked up her embroidery again, and bent her head over it. At last she said, 'I don't think you need my advice, Mabel. I think you know quite well what George would have done.'

'He'd have jumped in with both feet, eh?' Mabel grinned. 'And you think that's what I should do too, Sophy?'

'I don't know about should, Mabel. But I think you will.'

*　　*　　*

92

Messrs Foggett, Dodson and Pinpole were in conference. They felt they were standing on the edge of an abyss, yet they could not resist peering into it.

'We cannot consider starting *Stowerton, Stowerton, Stowerton v. Stowerton* until the question of *Stowerton and Stowerton* is resolved,' pointed out Foggett, blinking through his pince-nez nervously, and legalistically emphasing the 'and' in citing the latter case, usage having changed since the great and powerful days of Chancery.

'And what would be the grounds for reopening *Stowerton and Stowerton?*' enquired Dodson.

One whole office had been given over to huge piles of papers tied up in red ribbon brought down from their dusty dwelling-places in the attic where they had been since 1845 in the time of Mr Dodson's father.

'Might I suggest, Mr Dodson, with respect,' said Mr Foggett, 'that before we indulge ourselves in a reading of these papers, to enable us to determine that, it might be prudent to ascertain whether the Misses Stowerton have the funds to reopen their case?'

'But can we in conscience do that, as family solicitors to the whole Stowerton family, without exploring what kind of a case we have?' Dodson enquired anxiously. 'After all, there is the matter of Mr Jacob Stowerton, presumed dead. And indeed of proving that the Misses Stowerton are who they say they are.'

'They're loopy enough to be Stowertons,' said Pinpole.

'Mr Pinpole!' said Dodson, shocked at this unlawyerlike modern slip-shod speech.

'Only a Stowerton would even consider opening *any* gavelkind case in this year of 1880,' explained Mr Pinpole defiantly.

His partners began to wonder whether all this excitement were not too much for Mr Pinpole.

'All the same, I feel you should enquire, Mr Pinpole,' said Foggett gently, with all the unspoken might of senior partner.

'It is most exciting,' said Violet, trembling, looking up at the old house. 'Quite unlike anything in China, isn't it, Primrose?'

'Indubitably,' she agreed, trembling too.

'Where do you live in China?' asked Luke curiously.

Violet glanced at Primrose. 'We love England now,' she said firmly, 'don't we, Primrose?'

'Indubitably.'

It was like escorting two playful puppies around, thought Luke in amusement; he had been detailed by Mr Pinpole to break the bad news to them that law cases required money. Only puppies would have more sense.

'Isn't it lovely, Violet? I shall have this as my bedroom.' Primrose patted the Queen's bed lovingly.

'Oh, yes, Primrose. And I shall have the other wing.'

'Forgive me,' Luke said desperately, 'but have you any money?'

'Money?' they chorused, shocked at this intrusion into their dream.

'Mr Pinpole asked us that,' said Violet disapprovingly.

'Well?' Luke insisted implacably.

'When we win, we will,' Violet pointed out sullenly.

'But not before?'

'Not a great deal,' said Primrose hesitantly. 'Fortunately, dear Robert and Millicent look after us very well.'

'Do you have your fare back to China?'

'No,' said Violet, surprised. 'Why should we? We're not going back.'

Luke sighed, wondering why he'd been chosen for this assignment. 'In that case, ladies, you must realise that you cannot open your case again. You must wait to see if we open a new case against Robert, and hope for an ex gratia settlement. However, I have spoken to my uncle, Sir Robert. He is willing to grant you the loan of a cottage on the estate until the matter is resolved, and I will ensure you have sufficient income on which to live.' Quite how he was to explain this to his father, he hadn't yet worked out, but there seemed little alternative. Robert had been distinctly frosty, and only Luke's implied suggestion that Jeremiah would be only too glad to broadcast his brother's meanness had goaded him into agreement.

'Does that mean,' said Primrose rather crossly, and with scant respect for Luke's offer, 'that we wouldn't own Bocton?'

'I'm afraid so.'

'This is a great disappointment,' said Violet sternly. She glanced at Primrose. 'But we will stay here just the same,' she announced grandly. 'Does this mean that you *do* have money, Second Cousin Luke?'

'Why, yes, I –'

'Then you can pay for The Case for us,' said Violet triumphantly.

'Indubitably,' said Primrose in glee, clasping her hands. 'How clever you are, Violet.'

Katharine took her building manual into the orchard with her luncheon, a sandwich, after working in the garden all the morning. Her back was aching, and her hands were sore, for the old cotton gloves were ineffective against brambles and rose-thorns. She chewed her way through the sandwich, intent on finding out how to repair damaged beams and joints. She intended to be knowledgeable when she visited Hurstdene House. She needed to impress Mr Mayfield that she was serious about the future of Bocton and how to restore it. She sat down under an apple tree, leaning against the trunk, and began to read. But it had been a long morning and the sun was warm. Her eyes began to close and she drifted off into sleep. But there was a cough above her before she dozed.

'Could you spare a sandwich, I wonder?'

She turned, horrified, looking up to see Luke perched peacefully in the tree above her reading a book.

'What on earth are you doing up there?' she cried indignantly. 'Playing Robin Hood? You startled me.'

'I was waiting for you, Cousin Katharine.'

'Why?' she asked crossly, remembering Meg and her flowers. 'Meg isn't with me.'

'I am delighted to hear it. Then we shall be alone.' He began to swing himself down in a shower of late apple blossom just as she gasped, a memory returning to her out of the summer sky.

'It was you, wasn't it?' she said slowly, gazing up into the apple tree. 'You were the boy who climbed trees, when I couldn't.'

He laughed from his lofty perch. 'And you the little girl who looked so wistful in her petticoats and pantaloons below me. Wouldn't I let you? Oh, Katie May, small boys are crueller than men. They lordly rule over you, when grown men know they are at your feet.'

And so saying, he swung himself down to her side. 'See,' he announced, 'I am come to make amends, now we are alone.'

'Why do you want to be alone with me?' she asked innocently. 'To talk about Bocton?'

'To woo you, Katie May. To woo you in your ugly sun-bonnet and pretty print cotton dress.'

'I wish you would not jest,' she said, annoyed. 'You do it to annoy me, do you not?'

'Indeed I don't,' he retorted, hurt. 'Would I bring you these if I did not admire you above all women?' He flipped down a package from the tree where he had lodged it, and sat down beside her. 'This is for you.'

She opened it cautiously, then gasped. 'Why, these are –'

'Breeches, I know. I bought them for you.'

Her mouth fell open. 'For *me*. But you can't.'

'Why not?'

'It's not proper.'

'We're related, Cousin Katharine. Now you cannot pretend that those huge bloomers were a great success. A more unbecoming garment I have yet to see.'

'I did not intend them to be becoming,' she said, nettled. '*Or* to be seen,' she emphasised. 'They are practical.'

'These you will find much more practical.'

'No.'

He sighed. 'They will not fit me, and they are no use to Meg for she doesn't wear trousers, so we will throw them away.' He stood up, seized them and tossed them over the fence into the cherry tree orchard.

'Don't,' she cried involuntarily, then went pink as he laughed.

'Now you will have to find them yourself,' he told her, 'but not before you have given me a sandwich as my reward. I'm hungry.'

A vision of Meg clutching those flowers came to her. She swallowed. He was a flirt, was Luke. Well, he wasn't going to flirt with her. Perhaps he really liked Meg. They were well suited. She should promote her sister as a possible wife, perhaps. 'Meg is a wonderful person,' she began uncertainly.

'I am sure she is,' he replied politely.

'She is very lovely, is she not?'

95

'Wonderfully,' he agreed, munching the sandwich. 'I should add, however, Cousin Kate, that if you frequently eat cheese and onion sandwiches, I shall not be able to kiss you as often as you might desire.'

'I do not desire it,' she replied heatedly. 'Go and kiss Meg, if you must.'

'Why?'

'She is more attuned to your character.'

'And what is my character, Katie May?' picking up another sandwich.

Taken aback, she said without thinking: 'You do not take matters seriously.'

'And that is a bad thing?'

'Yes,' she said vehemently.

'Ah. And how have you deduced I do not take life seriously?'

'Serious people do not sit in apple trees,' she replied, saying the first thing that came into her head, goaded by the bright directness of his blue eyes.

'On the contrary, Cousin Kate, it takes a most serious person to sit in an apple tree. A comic sort of person would undoubtedly see such a performance as humiliating and demeaning. Only a serious person can sit there with dignity.'

'But you *mock* me,' she burst out as he took her hand.

'Do I mock you because you read books on building? Do I mock you because you have the courage to take a saw into your own hands to do the jobs that others won't? Do I mock you because you want to save Bocton, because you believe in it passionately? Now look at me and tell me.' He turned her defiant chin towards him.

'No,' she said unwillingly, uncertainly, 'but –'

'I take you seriously, Katie May.' He laid down the remains of the sandwich, and took both her hands. 'But do you still think, Cousin Kate, on a day like this, sitting under the apple blossom, that life must always be serious? Do you not think that seeing your hair flowing from under that ridiculous sunbonnet which hides the light in your eyes, and your face warm from the sun and with your feet peeping out from your gown, I might be forgiven – *we* might be forgiven – if we bid the sun stand still awhile and laugh with us?'

With one arm behind her, he turned her face to his with the other and kissed her, not on the cheek, but full on the lips. Then, as she did not struggle away, gently pushed her back on to the grass, leaning over her, coming down to her, kissing her again.

But the sunbonnet pushed forward, intervened, and he broke off to remove it, with a muttered choke of laughter. Belatedly she realised she had been allowing him to kiss her unprotestingly. Luke Stowerton, who cared not whom he kissed on a summer's day. She sat upright, furious with herself and shy of him. Perhaps that was how Mother felt – what had led her to pursue her will-o'-the-wisp chase of love. Luke put his arm round her.

'Close your eyes, Katie May. Do you not hear the song of the bee?'

'No,' she tried to say, but in answer he kissed her lightly again.

'If you will not close your eyes, then look at the blue sky, the green, green grass, and then tell me life is all melancholy, Katie May.'

'I did not say melancholy,' she tried to explain. 'I meant one must be serious about things that matter.'

'And do not kisses matter?'

'Not yours, Cousin Luke,' she said, her voice trembling slightly. 'They are too lightly given, to all who are foolish enough to heed your song.'

'And you are too wise, too serious, to listen to it?' he enquired, withdrawing from her, his face clouded.

'I –' She thought of the moment she had been swept away by his kisses, felt herself responding to him, wanting to respond to him. If it hadn't been for that sunbonnet . . . Then she remembered Meg, remembered Bocton, and all she must accomplish. How could a man from far away understand the burden that she had taken on herself and must see through to the end? And how could she trust the kisses of a summer's day when the dragons of doubt yet breathed at her back?

Chapter Six

Katharine stared out of the window trying to hide her rising excitement as the carriage bumped over the narrow dusty road to Headcorn, passing by farmhouses, with small children hopping up and down in curiosity at the gateways, oasthouses nestling in the green landscape, past hop-garden after hop-garden, string poles sticking barren into the air with the young plants growing at their feet. Mr Mayfield – Roderick, as she'd been instructed to call him – sat opposite her, intent, serious, and supremely confident in himself. Suddenly the excitement would not be hidden any longer.

'Kent – cherries, hops and women,' she cried delightedly as the carriage bumped past a large cherry orchard.

'I beg your pardon, Katharine?'

She flushed, fearing he had thought she was seeking compliments. 'Mr Dickens, you know. *The Pickwick Papers*.'

'Ah, I regret that my work leaves me little time for light novels. You must forgive me, Miss Stowerton.' An unexpected smile lit up his face, relieving the austerity of his countenance. He should smile more often, she thought to herself, then uneasily remembered that Luke had said the same of her.

Hurstdene Manor itself was at first a disappointment. Her instant reaction was that the dour Jacobean façade was uninteresting compared with Bocton, symmetrical without being pleasing, aged but without warmth. But Roderick spent a long time admiring it and pointing out its features before they entered the house itself. 'Of course,' he said regretfully, 'the classical approach is not in keeping with our age. Such a pity, would you not agree, Katharine?'

She did not, not wholeheartedly at any rate. Surely an age such as theirs, with the world opening up before them, science and industry making such advances, surely its hope and energy and promise should be expressed in exuberance, not restraint? Just as Bocton reflected its own age.

'Miss Stowerton.' Lady Headcorn's deep voice boomed out as she rose to greet her guest. She was as formidable as Katharine had feared, reading between the lines of Roderick's somewhat ecstatic description of his mother's qualities.

All in black save for the Brussels lace at neck and wrists, and the lace caps and mittens, the flounces of moiré that surrounded her dress served to heighten its severity not mitigate it. Her determined chin, jutting over the high-necked dress, seemed to pronounce consciousness of lineage without need of words.

I am His Highness' dog at Kew
Pray tell me, sir, whose dog are you?'

Horrified at her irreverent thoughts, Katharine hastily banished them, and dutifully greeted her hostess.

Her own carefully worked on white-spotted muslin, that she had hurried to finish despite Meg's demanding priority for her own wardrobe, seemed tawdry, and the deep blue taffeta underskirt had not the subtlety it bore at home. Lady Headcorn's cold eye on her apparel confirmed her worst fears and Katharine felt oddly nervous, as though she were on inspection instead of merely an afternoon guest. Almost as if I'd come to stay for good, she thought in amusement, thus regaining her self-confidence.

'Roderick,' the eagle face was turned to her son, 'no doubt you will entertain our guest? I look forward to conversing with you further at four of the clock, Miss Stowerton.' A royal command and a royal dismissal. Katharine almost bowed her head as she left.

Impressed though she was at the riches of Hurstdene in paintings and sculpture ('By Skildaw,' said Roderick offhandedly, stopping to admire a statue of a shepherdess busy tying her sandal) they were not to Katharine's taste. The impression was unwelcoming, and she smiled to herself, remembering Stowerton House where Millicent had insisted on covering the private anatomy of naked Greek heroes with white silk loincloths, when they were children. Her thoughts suddenly flicked to a day at Stowerton when she was about eight, and Philip, then a grown-up fourteen to her eight, had insisted on uncovering them all in the orangery and explaining in graphic, and incorrect, detail she later realised, the purpose to which these mysterious objects were put. Philip . . . he had been very quiet recently. Why? she wondered. It was not like him. He must be planning something. He and his father seemed to act in unison; Robert the spokesman, Philip the evil genius ever at his elbow, seen or unseen.

This dark house, however, was nothing like light and airy Stowerton. It seemed more like a museum than a home, and once again she compared it with the relaxed mellowness of Bocton. Or Bocton as it should be, she remembered with a pang.

'My mother keeps to her side of the house,' Roderick was explaining. 'I have my own rooms here. Let me take you to show you my excavations.'

'I would like to see the roof,' asked Katharine, 'if that is possible. To compare –'

'But I cannot take you upstairs, Katharine,' he looked surprised.

'Oh, there is damage there?'

'No, but it would not be fitting,' he explained, shocked. 'There are bedrooms up there, Miss Stowerton.' There was a note of reproof in his voice, underlined by the 'Miss Stowerton'. Meekly she followed him into the study where all one wall had been stripped. She gasped when she saw it, all disappointment forgotten now. The timber framing, its upright posts and braces were completely exposed, even the laths where

99

the old wattle and daub covering had fallen away. Graceful ornamented braces supported the huge horizontal beams, the main posts continuing to carry the eye upwards.

'It's – oh, Roderick, it's splendid. Will you leave it like that?'

'I shall cover it with the original daub mixture. I have had experiments carried out on the correct ingredients.'

'What are they?' She must know this for she would need it herself, perhaps.

'Lime and sand – and, ah, animal matter, with straw to bind them together.'

She remembered Luke's comment, understood, and was momentarily impatient with Roderick. This was important. Surely he could forget her sex for one moment?

'And what are the proportions of dung to lime and sand?' she pressed on firmly.

He blushed. Slightly daunted, she repeated the question.

'I don't know the proportions, Miss Stowerton. I did not mix it myself, naturally. Now let me show you . . .' The subject was closed. 'This end of the old house, I believe, would be a buttery with more sleeping accommodation overhead.'

'And where was the cooking done?' she asked, puzzled.

'I believe,' he said – how could he be so matter-of-fact about it? – 'in the middle of the open hall at first. But by the time this house was built, the fifteenth century, I think the house would be enlarged with a kitchen extension added. In later times ragstone extensions . . .' Katharine's imagination shot off and she ceased to listen for a moment. Would Bocton too have a kitchen wing? Why had she not thought of it? She mentally compared Hurstdene with the old manor house. Yes, of course, it would be hidden in the West Wing, which she had never thought of exploring, assuming it to be constructed as the East.

'Of course, it is possible that an earlier house, say thirteenth or fourteenth century, existed here and was merely adapted at a later stage to jetty out at both ends to give extra space, and a kitchen added. I confess, however, I see no reason, if building the house from scratch, that it should have been built in jetties –'

'Oh,' said Katharine brightly, 'Obadiah believes it is to do with strength and stress – to put the floorboards of the upper storey under tension and prevent sag.'

He pursed his lips at this unladylike interest in the mechanics of the building trade, but said nothing, merely suggesting in dry tones that they adjourn to the library.

The library was the nicest room in the house, she thought. Here the austerity of the leather chairs seemed welcoming, the smell of leather-bound books intoxicating. She automatically gravitated to the bookcase where the first book she saw was *Robinson on Gavelkind*. Her heart sank as she remembered the ordeal in front of her, wondered whether to tell Roderick about The Case and decided not. This was her own problem. If The Case went ahead, she could tell him then. *If* it went ahead . . .

'*Paulo maiora canamus*, Katharine,' he said kindly, as an olive branch.

But for once her mind was not on Latin. Not even Virgil.

'Brother Joseph,' commented Albert drily, drumming his fingers on Sophy's delicate occasional table, 'you seem deep in thought. Are you debating whether to stake your all and return to the old homestead, to the bosom of your loving family, to forsake those golden lands?'

'I haven't decided,' said Joseph brusquely. In fact he had. He was going to do it. Depending on how The Case turned out, perhaps he would come back to live, but certainly he would go ahead with it. There were scores to be settled.

The heirs of Nathaniel Stowerton gathered at Sophy's house, together with Mabel and Luke. Not Katharine. They needed to talk without her eager, hopeful presence. The time for decision was nearly here. The atmosphere was edgy, tense, and even Sophy with her soothing voice could not dispel it. Mabel was in the middle of the group, a solid bastion around whom the brothers warred. Even Alfred had forgotten the horses temporarily, intrigued by the prospect of what was to come. For Sophy had taken the bull by the horns and invited Robert too.

'Am I late?' he enquired rhetorically, having deliberately timed his arrival, his formal black cloth frock coat and grey striped trousers giving him, as usual, a spurious authority and establishing his position as head of the family. 'My regrets. The sooner we have a railway . . .' He smiled thinly at his own joke and took an upright chair, set somewhat apart, almost seeming the mediator rather than the putative defendant. Automatically he assumed control of the meeting, which the others present decided to cede to him. Having pondered the likely outcome of the meeting, Luke intended to play for time.

'Would it not be foolish to reopen this nonsensical gavelkind case?' Robert began without preamble. 'My view is that Father wished to keep his estates together and that we should honour his wishes.'

'But you're planning to sell them off,' observed Mabel brightly. 'Hardly keeping them together, is it?'

Robert ignored her. 'What need have any of you of it?' he continued as if she had not spoken. 'Joseph flourishes in Australia, Jeremiah in Colorado. Albert, you live comfortably in Cannes. Alfred –' he paused. 'Mabel,' he continued hurriedly, 'you would not wish to give up your travels and settle in one place.'

'By George, you're doing it again,' shouted Joseph bitterly. 'All these years later and still you want the whole cup for yourself. The only difference this time is that you've already snatched it.'

'My name was never on the cup either,' observed Albert mildly.

'You lost all right to be a member of this family when you walked out with Elizabeth,' said Sophy forthrightly.

'Sophy!' Albert was hurt. Had not she always mothered and protected him? Now even his sister was turning against him. 'Surely you should know that no monster is of quite the deepest dye?'

101

'Once black, always black,' muttered Alfred.

Sophy sighed. 'It seems to me the Stowertons need peace,' she observed.

'Precisely,' said Robert. 'I do plead with you all, for the sake of Father's memory, to drop this case.'

'I feel I owe it to George to look after his son's interests,' said Mabel. 'It's not as simple as you make out, Robert.'

Joseph stared at her, then said fiercely to Robert: 'Be hanged if you'll get away with it a second time.'

'Forget the damn' treasure trove,' said Alfred irritably.

'We can't,' said Albert quickly, smugly. 'No one can.'

'And whose fault is that?' declared Joseph. All eyes went to Robert.

'What do you say to that?' bellowed Mabel.

'Stop!' said Sophy sharply, but no one heeded her.

'I say,' said Robert slowly, 'that you're all against me, just as you used to be. All of you jealous. Because I'm the eldest, you feel aggrieved. Is it my fault when I was born? You manufacture this foolish excuse of the treasure trove. Stuff and nonsense! You're here out of jealousy and greed.'

'George, greedy?' cried Mabel. 'I won't hear his memory defiled.' She crossed her arms belligerently.

'Greed!' roared Alfred. 'That does it, Robert.'

But he took no notice. 'I *found* that cup – you *know* I did. You made up that story to spite me, Joseph. You have always been against me, all of you, despite what I've done for you. Always hated me. All of you against me. Well, Father knew whom to trust. You all conspired against me and now you have learnt your lesson.'

'You took that cup,' glared Joseph. 'Stole it. I found it. Leave it, you said, leave it and come back for it.'

'I did not,' said Robert in a clipped voice. *'Thief! Thief!'* echoed in his memory.

'It would have been just like you,' said Albert pleasantly.

'Who are you to talk?' Alfred shouted, turning on him. 'You were always watching, planning, waiting your moment. You're as bad as him. Worse. By God, the Stowertons have something to answer for in begetting you for the world.'

'Stop!' Sophy stood up, trembling, her voice cutting across them, stopping them at last as they turned to pay attention to her for the first time.

'Stop,' she told them again. 'Stop *now*. Go home, all of you. Forget this foolishness. Go back to your own lives and let us heal the wounds while yet we may.'

'Sophy!' cried Alfred. 'You were the one to encourage Katharine.' He was staggered that his meek sister could be so vehement, act so contrarily.

'I know,' she said more calmly. 'I thought – foolishly in the face of so much evidence to the contrary – that our coming together again could bind the wounds, make us a family again, bury the day of the

102

treasure trove and see it for what it was: an irrelevance. Now I know that I was wrong. It's not possible to go back. We must go on and ignore the past. Ignore the family.' She paused, looking at George's widow. 'Don't you agree, Mabel?'

Mabel gave a snort. 'You're a clever old thing, Sophy,' she said unexpectedly. 'I'll keep quiet – for the moment.' She grinned. 'Anyone going to tell that niece of ours?'

'I will.' Sophy knew it was her responsibility, but it was a hard one. For how could she explain just why she had reached this conclusion?

'Mr Dean!' Sophy stopped short, startled, in the parlour doorway at seeing Katharine engaged with her godfather.

He rose to his feet as startled as she, then said with concern, 'My dear Miss Stowerton, I fear you are not well. You look –'

'I am – all right, Mr Dean,' she smiled faintly.

'Let me escort you home.'

'I must talk to Katharine first.' She looked round. Alfred, of course, had disappeared.

'Then I will adjourn.'

'No, do stay, Mr Dean. You have been good to our family.' She coloured faintly. 'You know our affairs. Katharine, I have come to tell you that I have advised Mabel, Joseph and Albert to return home, not to participate in The Case. Alfred must please himself.'

Katharine stared at her unbelievingly, at this blow undercutting all her hopes. 'But why? Why?'

'It's the curse of the Stowertons,' said Sophy bitterly. 'My brothers all at loggerheads.'

'At loggerheads with Uncle Robert, perhaps, but –'

'No, it's more than that, and I'm not prepared to be part of it. Will you forgive me, my dear?' She looked at Katharine, weariness on her face.

Emotions battled within Katharine, the sick feeling that Bocton was slipping gradually beyond her reach for ever fought with her love for her aunt. She rose and ran to her, hugging her quickly. 'Nothing to forgive, dearest Aunt Sophy.'

Sophy began to cry. 'Mr Dean,' she managed to whisper, 'I will accept your offer to escort me home now.'

Joseph wandered round the gardens at Bocton, glancing back at the old house occasionally, as if feeling its pull, the pull of his Englishness. He belonged here. He could do much here, if he won. Perhaps even solve this family feud. He thought of Sophy's words, yet struggled against them. How could he let Robert get away with it? Win a different sort of cup. And how could he let his brother's name remain forever on the silver cup for future generations without fighting for the truth. Should he not stand firm, and ignore what Sophy said? Emily would understand his decision.

Australia had much, but it didn't have Bocton. He was caught up in old feuds again, summoned by ties of family, but ties bound up with hatreds and rivalries. If he could unwind them the family would be united for ever. Sophy was wrong. Don't turn your back. Fight for what's right, that's what George had always told him.

Full of an inexplicable anger, he walked up to the house, wandering round its walls curiously, as if for the first time, admiring it, loving it, romantic fool that he was. He read the inscription, taking it in for the first time. 'Grow rich in that which never taketh rust.'

Australia was rich, rich with promise. Its golden skies would never turn to rain. Emily was the future. The children too. Perhaps that was what he should do. That was where his riches lay. Bocton had served its purpose, given him a foundation, and now wiped the slate clean. Slowly, unwillingly, he began to think Sophy had been right. The feuds of the Stowertons could never be resolved. The family could never be united. He realised thankfully he had made his choice correctly many years ago. Bocton had no claim on him any more. It had given him what it had to offer, and it was for him to use it. He was free, because he chose to be free.

'Thanks, Bocton,' he said ridiculously, feeling as carefree as a boy again, looking for the last time at the mellow façade sad in its decay. But decay it must. He was rich in that which never taketh rust.

Albert too was thinking, though not on the same lines as Joseph. It had hardly taken Sophy's speech to convince him that The Case was something he would be well out of. Not that he had seriously thought of participating financially. He had been willing to put his name to The Case, not his francs. Now his primary object had been satisfied: curiosity. The return of the prodigal had ended in the hardly surprising discovery that he was a prodigal still. He grinned maliciously. He would look forward to telling Alfred his decision.

He salved his conscience over Bocton quite easily. So long, old house, he mentally saluted it. We all have to make our way in the world and you must make yours. Without me. He thought of the old inscription. Money, francs, never took rust. Nor women. Neither stayed long enough in his hands for them to do so. Tomorrow's pastures new were always more enticing. Strange it had taken Elizabeth to show him that.

His feeling for Bocton had been erased by its reality. When you are a long way away, conscience can prick; his had been easily allayed by seeing not the boyhood palace of his youth, but little more than a pile of bricks.

He sauntered into the Dower House. He was going to enjoy this.

'Pay?' Albert stared at Alfred and laughed. 'My dear brother, I couldn't pay to have this case reopened, devoted though I am to Katharine. I wish her and you well with it, but you know the rule. Once the black sheep, always the black sheep. You have told me that yourself. Even if I had money, which I don't for my wife has it all, I don't think I'd care to save Bocton. What has it ever done for me? I didn't even like Stowerton much, so why should I care for Bocton? I was only three, dear Alfred, when the treasure-trove race you seem so attached to came to a dramatic finish, and my later years here were devoted to gaining experience in the one field that has proved of lasting interest for me: the delights of the bed.'

'Out!' yelled Alfred, purple in the face.

'I would like to say that –'

'Out!'

'Very well, Alfred. I am sure you will approve when I say that on this occasion, however, I will endeavour to ensure that I do not remove your womenfolk with me.'

'What the devil do you mean – Katharine?' he asked with foreboding.

'Ah, *non*. The charming Miss Meg.'

'I must go, Louis,' said Meg regretfully. No response but a slight increase in activity. 'No really, I must.'

Louis unwound his arms from her at last, lay back with his hands behind his head and gazed in satisfaction at the blue sky above. Meg felt irrationally disappointed that he was prepared to let her go with comparatively little demur. Tomorrow, she consoled herself, she would consent to meet him again. Indeed, how could she not? A delicious tingling at his actions was coupled with a slight uneasiness, the latter quickly dispelled. The excitement of these secret meetings, secret from everyone, filled every day and night. Louis was so devoted to her, loved her so much, it was only natural she should love him back. True, he had been rather speedy in his demands. Yesterday he had made a determined effort to remove her drawers altogether and she had promptly stopped him, out of shock as much as propriety. He had laughed and tried again, and got quite cross when still she frustrated him. 'Ah, Meg, French ladies –'

'I am not,' she retorted on that occasion, 'a French lady. And all I can say is,' disapprovingly, 'that it doesn't seem very romantic to me.'

'Ah, but there you are wrong.' And he tried again. The results had been gratifying to both. However, she had resolved that there would be no repetition. Yet it was so delightful lying in the orchard with Louis, with his French endearments and appreciation of her charms, that today she had made little attempt to stop him, not only renewing the onslaught, but continuing it through to its natural conclusion.

Slowly now he unwound himself. 'Dearest Meg, I shall miss you,' he pronounced. 'Shall you think of me sometimes, *ma fleur*?' bending over her again and kissing her.

'What?' She pushed him aside and sat up very quickly. 'What do you mean, miss me? Where are you going?'

'Back to France. Tomorrow.'

She gazed at him, as impatiently she pushed aside his hands, still roving over her bosom. 'But when shall I see you again?'

'Ah, Meg, soon perhaps. Who knows? If you and your sister come to Cannes, we –'

'But don't you want to marry me?' she blurted out.

'Marry you?' He stared at her in surprise. '*Marry* you? My sweet Meg, we are too young for marriage. *I* am too young for marriage.'

'But why did you do – what you did?' she demanded, almost weeping.

His dark eyes held only amusement. He shrugged. 'The world is young and lovers play. But marriage, it is a serious thing.'

'But I only let you do it because I thought we were going to be married,' she wailed, busily rebuttoning and rearranging her clothes as she belatedly remembered maidenly modesty. 'Oh, Louis, I thought – I thought –'

'But, Meg,' he said simply, devastatingly, 'you should have known. Marriage is a matter of business, and you have no money.'

Katharine dropped the golden spotted muslin dress over her head, and shook her hair free of its confining bun, tying it back in curls instead. Her depression lifted slightly as she looked in the mirror and arranged another curl at her forehead. She wanted to look her best for Luke Stowerton; *needed* to look her best, she corrected, on this day of all days. True, this dress was hardly suitable for a meeting in Bocton, but she could always pretend that she intended to change into her bloomers – no, the breeches. It would please him to see she had retrieved them from the orchard.

She frowned. Why should she pretend so? And was it not dishonest of her deliberately to dress to appeal to him, when she intended to plead for Bocton – for money, to put it simply? It was enough that she had deliberately asked to meet him there, knowing of his interest in the house. The very thought of the house brought back her depression. It would be pulled down unless she could produce a miracle. And the only direction a miracle could come from would be Luke Stowerton – Gabriel Arch, she thought wrily. How ironic. She had not visited the house since Sophy's visit, in case it seemed to reproach her for her failure. But now it was imperative that Bocton should add its own arguments to hers on the all-important day.

Decision made, she quickly took off the sprigged muslin and put on her old everyday brown cotton dress, pushing her hair impatiently back into the bun. It was after all strictly a business meeting that called her back to Luke Stowerton, wasn't it? She snatched up the breeches, though she had no intention of wearing them. But he should see them lying there in Bocton and know that his present was not disregarded.

When she got there he had not yet arrived, and she sat in the entrance hall, huddled on the oak settle, uncomfortably aware that woodworm was steadily munching its way through it.

While she waited, she mulled over what Roderick had said to her, to take her mind off the coming difficult meeting. Kitchens. A whole wing perhaps added on at the rear or side of the mediaeval building. If Bocton had one its timber frame would still exist, blocked up like the great hall itself when they built the Tudor West Wing. If she could get into the roof of the West Wing, there might still be traces of smoke-blackened beams from all those centuries ago, as there was in the Great Hall.

Reluctantly she supposed she had better wait for Obadiah since he had told her on no account to go near the area on her own for it was dangerous.

Then she remembered the damage that the crashing tree might have caused to the remains, if any. Probably Nicholas Stowerton would have pulled the kitchen block down and built anew, but what if he hadn't? Of course, it would be where the ante-room off the hallway was. She jerked to her feet, as if pulled by a magnet, and ran into the West Wing, which was even mustier than the East because of the damaged roof. What now was mould and decay had once been the old ballroom, once echoing to the sound of music and laughter. The ballroom . . . But wouldn't that fit? A large mediaeval kitchen and storerooms – just as the old open hall had been adapted, so the kitchens had made a ballroom.

She stopped in the small ante-room. She and Obadiah had never investigated this room because they had thought that the mediaeval house could not possibly have run as far. The panelling was already beginning to rot, holes everywhere. It wouldn't take much to investigate behind it just as Obadiah had done.

Full of excitement, she quickly ran back to the East Wing study where she had left her tools, and snatched a hammer and chisel. Seeing her bloomers lying in a bag on the floor, and the old jacket she wore with them, she quickly stripped off the cotton dress and clambered into her working clothes, forgetting all about Luke Stowerton in her enthusiasm – and his breeches.

She began to tear at the panelling, wrenching away whole sections of rotten wood, holding her breath. It was harder than she had thought to tear it away and to her disappointment she found, as in the study, that behind the panelling was simply plaster. If the old frame existed it would be behind that, but the plaster laths would be attached to the old mediaeval wall – she must be careful not to damage the daub and fragile laths behind. Carefully she chiselled away at the plaster, pulling it away, prising out the laths to which it was fastened, until she had made a fair-sized hole. No posts yet – but they might be set at fairly wide intervals. She enlarged the hole, and peered in. A spider scuttled over her nose, making her scream. Bravely, and opening a shutter for more light, she looked in again. It was empty. Only brick lay behind.

'Oh, hell and Tommy,' she cried out frustratedly, tears of vexation beginning to form.

'I seem to see more of your backside than your even more beautiful front,' came Luke's voice behind her, as he walked up unnoticed. 'Especially in Bocton. Why –' He broke off as he saw the look on her face. 'Why are you crying?'

'I'm not.'

'What's this?' He ran a finger down her cheek, producing a smear in the dirt.

'I was looking for a kitchen.'

'Forgive me, but it seems an odd place to seek to boil a kettle,' he said solemnly.

107

'It's all very well for you to laugh,' she said angrily. 'Go away.'

'But you asked to see me, ma'am,' he said, hurt, as she scrambled unbecomingly to her feet in the bloomers.

'I'm sorry,' she muttered mutinously, deflated and annoyed now that she looked and felt her worst.

He sighed. 'First, Katie May, there is one thing I wish to know before you tell me why you are looking for a kitchen.'

'What?'

'Why are you wearing those *truly* unmentionables?'

'Because I want to,' she retorted belligerently.

'I saw displayed downstairs a fine pair of breeches,' he said pointedly. 'Go and put them on. I refuse to have a sensible talk with someone looking like Grimaldi.'

'I won't be ordered about.'

'Shall I come and help you?' he asked sweetly.

She took one look at his face and decided discretion to be the better part of valour. When she returned, self-conscious in this tight garment which hardly seemed designed to accommodate ladies' stays, he looked her up and down critically.

'Turn round.' Unwillingly she did so.

'*Now*,' he said approvingly, 'I have no objection at all to seeing your backside first. Especially,' he continued, as she opened her mouth to inform him that his opinion was of little interest to her, 'if you are determined to keep your hair in that bun.' He eyed it disapprovingly, but made no attempt to shake it free. 'Now what's this about a kitchen?'

'Are you really interested in kitchens?' she asked doubtfully.

'I am interested in *this* kitchen,' he qualified.

'Well, Roderick says that sometimes these hall houses with the jetty outside were merely improvements from earlier simpler houses – just as Nicholas Stowerton's red brick was an improvement to Thomas Stoorton's fifteenth-century house. And if it was, they sometimes added kitchen wings on the side. I thought I'd look to see if this had one,' she finished rather weakly.

'Hold on. You think you've got three houses here one inside the other?' he asked. 'Like a baby's set of boxes?'

'No. Roderick says they would have rebuilt part of it perhaps, and then added a kitchen block to get the smoke away from the main hall.'

'And why is it so important to you to know? More treasure?'

'I don't know,' she said, puzzled. 'I suppose –' Her eyes suddenly sparkled. 'It's like your gold and silver prospectors. What drives them on?'

Luke thought back to the silver mines of Leadville, to the craziness that drove men to strike claims so that the hillsides looked as if spotted with a million rabbit holes, each holding the promise of a fortune. At the moment in Leadville the promise was often fulfilled, but only on the bones of others, men who had come and died there and elsewhere looking for gold, who came and

108

who never gave up, crazed by the lure of a jack o' lantern that led them endlessly on.

'Money, Katie May. That's what drives them on.'

'Nothing else? Not the hunt itself?'

'Like your father's gambling, I guess.'

'*Gambling?*' She stared at him. 'But it's not like that at all!'

'I reckon it is. Tomorrow may be a better day. No wonder Sidney wrote "Grow rich in that which never taketh rust".'

'I think it's like Schliemann looking for Troy,' she said stoutly. 'Think how he must have felt when he swung the first pick at Hissarlik. Or Mycenae.'

He smiled at that. 'Are you going to crown me with a chamber pot when you discover your kitchen, as Heinrich crowned his wife with Helen's jewels?'

'I'll crown you with a hammer, if you like,' she said amicably. 'Now I want you to help me pull some more panelling down just to be sure. I was so certain . . .'

'Let's think about it first. Don't be in such a hurry. Look here.' He sketched out in the thick layer of dust on the oak sideboard, and looked around him thoughtfully. 'Now this was the old house and here the new wings. Right? Now if you were a mediaeval lady, building a new kitchen, where would you want it?'

She thought, impatient to be off and doing, but having to humour him. 'I'd want the fire as far away as possible,' she said dubiously.

'Right. You've got visitors. You've built a grand new house – and you don't want the kitchen on view, right? Yet it's got to be accessible.'

'I'd build it back a bit,' she said, suddenly interested. 'So that it abutted the back of the hall without interfering with the façade. Oh, Luke, is that it?' Her eyes sparkled.

'It *may* be,' he cautioned.

But she was already picking up the hammer and rushing back into the ballroom. The ballroom *must* be the old kitchen – a long room with the corridor down the side.

'Do you have another hammer?' he enquired.

'A shovel, you'll find a shovel,' she called, already attacking the plaster.

They worked in silence until –

'There's nothing there!' she cried indignantly. '*Nothing*. Oh, Luke.' She stared in dismay. 'I was wrong – and all we've got is a patchwork of holes. It looks worse than before.' She looked so woebegone that he laughed.

'Think some more, Dick Whittington. Don't you feel,' he said thoughtfully after a moment, 'that if you wanted a grand ballroom, it would have to be bigger than an old kitchen?'

'You mean . . .' She thought about it and her eyes widened. 'It would be *wider*. Oh, yes. So *that*,' pointing at the courtyard wall, 'is the old wall. *This*,' pointing at the outside wall, 'a new Tudor wall.'

With one accord they rushed to the inner wall, Luke beating her to it this time. Their efforts were rewarded as the plaster flew in all directions under Luke's shovel, and laths and nails were carefully removed.

And behind . . . 'Tudor beams,' she said with a sigh. 'Oh, Luke, it's here!'

He seized her hands and danced her round. 'Happy now?'

'Yes! Oh, yes. No!' Her face changed dramatically as she remembered what he had come for. 'It may be too late for Bocton,' she said stiffly.

'Because of the meeting the other day?'

'Yes,' she said awkwardly. 'You know what happened. Everyone's going home. I suppose you are too.'

'And that's why you wanted to see me?' A slight shadow crossed his face. 'You wondered what I was planning to do?' You have to watch the Stowertons, his father had told him. Even the best.

'Yes,' she blurted out. She had to be honest. 'It must look terrible to you, but I had to know.'

'I don't know what I'm going to do yet, Katharine. I'm sorry.' Absentmindedly he brushed a cobweb from her hair.

'But you must by now,' she blurted out. 'Look,' she gestured despairingly at the wall, 'you can't just go and let it all be knocked down. Not now. You'd be a kind of traitor. Just like William Stoorton. You *must* save it.'

'Must I?' he enquired politely. 'What you mean to ask me is, will I put up all the money?' She flushed angrily, but could not deny it. Tongue-tied, she turned from him.

'What about your new beau?' he enquired. 'Can't he save it?'

'Roderick is interested in Bocton of course.' She turned back angrily. 'But I can hardly ask him to pay.'

Luke burst out laughing. 'I agree with you there.'

'How dare you laugh at him?' she said. 'He's ten times the gentleman you'll ever be. He treats me like a –'

'A woman?' he asked with interest, his eyes running deliberately over the trim figure, albeit dust-and plaster-encrusted.

'A person,' she snapped.

'I didn't think he'd know how to treat you as a woman. Has he kissed you yet?'

'Of course not.'

'And he won't.'

'Why? What's wrong with me?' she asked indignantly.

'Nothing's wrong with you.' He hid a smile at the belligerent figure in front of him. 'It's what's wrong with *him*.'

'He's a gentleman,' she repeated furiously.

'And don't you think he knows how most gentlemen beget heirs?'

'Oh! I will not stay to hear you talk about him so.' And she turned her back on him, walking away, outraged.

'Delighted as I am to admire your backside once again, Katharine,' he called after her, 'don't you want to hear when and what I've decided about Bocton?'

She stopped, irresolute.

'I'll invite myself to dinner on Friday and tell you,' he announced blandly, infuriatingly.

Katharine had been alarmed to find Meg in floods of tears when she returned. She quite inexplicably refused to explain what ailed her, and only cheered up when she heard that Luke was coming to dinner on Friday. He arrived early and went into the study to talk to Alfred. Disappointed and on tenterhooks that he had not immediately sought her out, Katharine went to help Maggie in the kitchen, trying to concentrate on food and failing dismally.

'Did you bring in any lovage for the salad, Miss Katharine?'

'No, I'll go and pick some now.' Really, Bocton was obsessing her. She could think of nothing else, unable now even to remember ingredients for the evening meal. Contrite, Katharine hurried guiltily out and down the garden path, but stopped short when in the orchard she saw Luke, whom she had supposed to be still talking to Father, with Meg clasped in his arms. Tears were still trickling down her tear-stained face. Why was it, thought Katharine, fixing her annoyance on one aspect of the scene, that Meg still continued to look *pretty* when crying instead of red and blotchy like Katharine herself?

Luke's attention attracted, he turned and saw Katharine. She permitted herself one scornful stare and marched angrily back to the house. No wonder Luke had wanted to come here this evening! He had flattered her, Katharine, as the elder sister, merely because he assumed it was a way to Meg's heart. As in a way it probably was, she thought wrily. But this did not lessen her outrage and she sat silently fuming throughout dinner.

Luke, however, did not seem to notice, as Alfred talked incessantly about past and present Stowertons, laughing and joking, and regaling them with anecdotes of yet more and more Stowerton eccentricities. She was relieved when she and Meg could withdraw, leaving Alfred to produce the port on which he prided himself, and which accounted for more than its fair share of the household money.

Meg chattered on happily now, almost as if she were glad that Katharine had seen how Cousin Luke was attracted to her, so that conversely Katharine was now glad when the men joined them again. Eventually Luke rose to his feet. 'I should like to talk to you, Katharine, before I go. Will you walk with me? The air is still warm.'

She accompanied him stiffly out, aware of Meg's overt displeasure. The twilight air was full of scents and Luke sniffed appreciatively. 'In Colorado we smell only heat, cold, dust and money. The night is full of laughter from the saloons, not full of silence like this. Few birds sing in Leadville.'

She said nothing.

'Why are you so silent, Katie May?' he enquired. 'Are you cross with me for hugging Meg?'

'It's a matter of no importance to me whether you kiss Meg or not,' she retorted loftily. 'Though I think it's unfair of you to press

111

your advances on her. You forget how inexperienced she is, and how young.'

He cocked an amused eye. 'Press my advances? Oh, Katharine,' he said impatiently as they reached the river, surrounded by its watercress beds. 'Forget this foolishness. I want to talk about The Case.' She grew tense. 'I guess I'm still torn,' he continued, 'I don't know what to do. I love Bocton. I think it's terrible if it has to be sold, may be pulled down. But it's not my money, it's my father's, and even though he has more than all of us could spend in a lifetime, I can't with honour spend it for him if I don't feel it's right.'

'And what would make it right?' she asked, her heart sinking.

'I suppose,' he said carefully, 'to make it live again. Your father's behind it, but he has no stamina without you. It's you. The whole responsibility of The Case would be on us two. And what –' he hesitated – 'would I be fighting for? A mere symbol. I'd be in Colorado. Bocton is here. And there's nothing to keep me here, unless there's *someone*. Do you understand?' He took her hands and suddenly a late bird sang, but only for a moment.

'Meg,' she began stiffly, 'would make you –'

He dropped her hands with an exclamation of disgust. 'If that's your attitude, why do you object so much to my kissing her?' he asked coolly.

'Because I –' She thought wildly. There was no reason. No reason at all.

'Katharine, be careful,' he said urgently. 'You're letting this case blind you. Bocton isn't everything. Nor is The Case. You're putting it before your judgement, before your heart. Don't you –' She began to panic. His face was so close to hers that for a crazy moment she almost wanted him to come closer still, to feel his lips on hers again, forget about his character, about his kissing Meg . . . *Meg*!

'Roderick says,' she began wildly, 'that the house –'

'To hell with Roderick!' he said angrily.

'Why?' she said heatedly, glad for a reason to switch subjects. 'You and Meg. Roderick and I. Like to like.'

He stared at her aghast, then laughed bitterly. 'You're not thinking of marrying him, are you? Oh, Katharine. Roderick is not the sort of man to marry anyone, even you.'

'*Even* me, you say again,' she cried out.

'No, I didn't mean that,' he said, impatient at her naivety. 'He's not a man to marry *anyone*. Do you understand? He's not attracted to women.'

She stared at him blankly, not knowing what he meant, and came back to the question disastrously. 'What sort of man should I marry then?' she threw at him.

'Someone like me,' he said through gritted teeth, eyes bright with anger, gripping her by her shoulders.

'Like you!' tearing herself away, half laughing, half crying. 'I wouldn't –'

'Katharine,' he said softly, 'the moon is out now, the air is soft, the

112

roses in bloom. Can't you see?' he pleaded, changing track desperately. 'Oh, can't you see, my Katie May, where your path lies?'

But the night air deceives and whispers beguile and no light shone to show that path. Her mother had followed a path, a path that never ended. Now Meg too had set her foot upon it. She, Katharine, would not, *could* not. Anyway, he'd said 'someone like me'. Not me. *Like* me. Yet where were the words to speak on the edge of that great abyss that would draw her back to safety, as she tore herself away from him?

'But I am not Katie May,' she finally whispered. 'There *is* no Katie May,' the words forcing themselves out one by one. 'I am Katharine May Stowerton.'

Chapter Seven

'I regret, Miss Katharine, I have to impart unwelcome news.' Mr Pinpole looked as downcast as if he were the sufferer, not Katharine. Today, ominously, she noted there was no sign of Messrs Foggett and Dodson. 'Mr Luke has informed us,' Mr Pinpole averted his eyes in order not to witness her distress, 'that he cannot see his way to involving himself in a case for gavelkind against Sir Robert.'

Katharine had expected nothing else, but nevertheless to hear it put into words brought its reality home to her. There was nothing more she could do. Bocton would be sold, and with it centuries of history would go for nothing, together with her hopes and dreams.

'Such a pity,' continued Mr Pinpole wistfully, looking positively human, 'I was quite looking forward –' He realised the improper nature of this utterance for a solicitor and quickly broke off the sentence, continuing instead, 'I fear it was always a gamble, and like so many has not succeeded. The odds were too great, I believe is the phrase.'

Yes, she supposed a gamble was indeed what it had been. Had she, like her father, seen an impossible dream and pursued it irrespective of hard probability? She had always repudiated her father's way of life and yet for one wild moment she too had put hope before all else.

'It seems that you and I, Mr Pinpole, are the only ones left who wish to see Bocton saved,' she said sadly.

'I –' Mr Pinpole was at a loss, faced with such direct involvement. Did he wish to see Bocton saved? He had never asked himself such a question, but put like that, yes, he supposed he had wanted Miss Katharine to go ahead. He felt slightly ashamed of finding his heart capable of intervening in his profession. It did not seem right that Bocton should be sold merely for commercial reasons, not even through pressing financial need. 'Miss Violet and Miss Primrose would support you,' he said doubtfully, 'but their help can be little, merely adding evidence to yours that the land is subject to gavelkind. Alas, that does not answer the main problem.' He paused delicately, unwilling to mention the word money, though it shouted between them. 'Now that Mrs Mabel, Mr Joseph and Mr Albert have retired, and Mr Luke on behalf of his father has declined to contribute, I fear, Miss Katharine, that it is what I would term a dismal prospect.' He mopped his forehead agitatedly with a plum-coloured silk handkerchief. 'I must withdraw the injunction and we cannot proceed with the writ. Apart from throwing yourself on your uncle's mercy and asking him to spare the house itself, there is nothing to be done.'

'I'll never do that,' said Katharine mechanically, sick at heart, remembering the offer of ownership of Bocton she had so rashly, it now seemed, turned down. A gamble, her father had said then, and like so many gambles, see how it had turned out.

'I will communicate your decision to Sir Robert's solicitors,' said Pinpole glumly. 'May I add, Miss Stowerton, it was a brave effort,' rousing himself to something almost akin to fervour, 'why, yes, a brave effort.'

'Thank you,' said Katharine wrily. To be congratulated for failing was more humiliating than consoling.

The door was flung open and Mr Foggett almost fell into the room. 'Mr Pinpole – the most extraordinary communication,' he began excitedly. 'Pray excuse my unprofessionalism, Miss Stowerton, in front of a client, but since it concerns you, and may have relevance to your discussion, I feel certain you would wish to be informed. We have heard from Sir Robert's solicitors that Sir Robert has asked for a meeting to discuss a compromise.'

A compromise? Hope battled with suspicion in Katharine. Beware the Greeks bearing gifts. Uncle Robert must surely know the reason that Joseph, Mabel and Albert had returned home, and since Luke – her heart thudded painfully – was living under his roof, he must surely know his views too. Though perhaps Luke had not told him? A wild hope. Compromise . . . better than nothing, surely.

'Do you think we should do it?' she appealed to them. 'He must surely know what has happened?'

'Perhaps not,' observed Mr Foggett brightly. 'If I may say so, Miss Stowerton, your departed relations seemed to me either somewhat uncommunicative or downright mischievous. Perhaps they deliberately,' he coughed politely, 'left Sir Robert with the impression that The Case was to continue.'

Hope seized Katharine again like a rising fountain. 'In that case,' she said, almost laughing in her sudden excitement, 'let us wager on, gentlemen.'

She had been unable to sleep for the last few nights, forever seeing Luke's face and agonising over what had happened. Had she done right in so distancing herself from him, rejecting him? She had almost believed that he cared for her, but how could he when he paid so much attention to Meg? Her sister was endlessly chattering about him, about his attentions to her, how well they understood each other, how wonderfully he kissed. She shivered. She knew, oh how she knew! He was a philanderer, like Nick Stowerton himself, she told herself firmly – like Albert. Well, she was not going to be like her mother. Her heart would follow her head, not lead it.

After that evening, Meg had been furious, accusing her of taking Luke away from her. 'He's mine. He wants me, and you're trying to take him away. You want me to die an old maid,' she wept.

Katharine had tried in vain to comfort her, and was left with the sick realisation that she must have misunderstood Luke. He was just teasing her. Or if not teasing, had not seriously meant what he said. It was in his nature to pay court to women, especially on a May evening with the stars shining down and the roses in bloom. Luke was just a knight passing by on his charger, and she, Katharine, was not going to be beguiled by that. Her mother had followed love like a will o' the wisp. Not Katharine.

As a result, she thought bleakly, he had made his decision to abandon The Case and return to America. Perhaps he would take Meg with him. At least she would enjoy travelling. He must know that Katharine would never, never leave Bocton. She supposed he had toyed with the idea of being an English country squire, returning to the place where he was born, and now realised it would never work. She, Katharine, had been part of that fantasy of his. Yet why then did she still toss and turn at nights wondering if she had been right to spurn him? If he had been serious after all? Yet even if he were, rationally she had no other choice. The whole idea of marrying Luke Stowerton was ridiculous. Late at night, however, with the cool night air blowing gently through the window, she could remember only too well the touch of his lips and hands, the memory of his handsome face looking so earnestly at her that evening, and her whole body was inexplicably tense. She tried to tell herself she was an idiot, that many a girl had thought the same about many a man before. Beware the gypsy's warning, she tried to tell herself, morning in rhyming slang. But she was glad when the light came for then the beguiling temptations of the night could be stilled in the routine of the day.

Luke Stowerton sat in the library at Stowerton House, looking out over the fields of Kent, green now in full summer glory. Over there lay Bocton, hidden somewhere in its cloak of green woods, mysterious and unattainable. That was as it should be, for Bocton offered a promise, then snatched it away, just like the Stowertons themselves. Wherever his future lay it wasn't here; he had snatched at the chance it offered, but perhaps too greedily, and assuming Katharine felt as he did. But there were other places in the world, many others, unknown countries to visit. Perhaps he'd make it a condition of his staying at Leadville that he could travel half the year, go to all those places he'd read of at Yale: to Greece, to Rome, to see the ruined temples, Pompeii perhaps, retrace the steps of Scipio. Yes, there were other places – and other women.

Luke was surprised just how devastated he had been by Katharine's rejection of him. He had known from the moment he saw her crawling through that window backside first that he wanted her – for what he was not at first sure. Perhaps initially because here was a girl who cared for more than dresses and marriage – who cared about *something*, just as he did himself. That steadfast commitment was what he sought, for it had been lacking from his own life. Then it had been more than that. The look in her eyes when he put that flower at her bosom, the proud tilt of her head as she faced the impossible odds of The Case. Then more than that: when he kissed her there had been a warmth there, that told him of a passion beneath, as yet unawakened, but surely there. That passion at the moment seemed all for Bocton, but he was sure, so sure, he could divert it, share it. Now he found himself obsessed with the thought of her: the way she walked through the gardens, the grave earnestness of her hazel eyes, the way she moved her hands – no, not one individual thing, but Katharine. Katharine herself. How different she was to Meg. Meg kept chattering about Katharine's unattractiveness, but to Luke there was true beauty in her face. And so he had confidently gone a-wooing – to no end. Sure, his vanity was hurt – whose would not be? – but there was more. He was puzzled. He could not believe that she was not attracted to him. He felt it. Dammit, he *saw* it. Perhaps he had rushed her because of this ridiculous time limit on The Case, but to reject him outright was just plain inexplicable.

Even now he could not believe he was wrong. Perhaps it was that mother of hers had frightened her? He grinned despite his depression – he would like to know Elizabeth Stowerton better. But Katharine was sensible, surely? Or was she? For to turn away both him and the chance of saving Bocton was a blow he had not expected. True, though, he would not have wanted her to marry him just for the chance of saving the place. Now he couldn't go on with The Case, not without Katharine. It didn't make sense. If he were deceived in the one, then he was in the other. He must return and explain to his father.

The idea of returning to that grim household appalled him, but he'd leave for America next week, just as soon as this meeting was over. For after all, he too was a Stowerton – and a gambler. He was going to have one last throw of the dice. If only for Father's sake, he wanted to flush Robert out into the open. He had let his uncle think that he was going to throw Jeremiah's millions behind the case. He thought Father would thoroughly approve of that.

Robert still believed that *Stowerton v. Stowerton* was a practical reality. Only Pinpole and presumably Katharine and Alfred would know the truth. He was curious to see what would happen at the meeting. Better to draw the Indians' fire than let them sharpen their arrows in secret.

Alfred went to the meeting in Canterbury on 26 May protesting and groaning. 'But, my dear,' he pointed out plaintively, 'it had been planned for the first of June. I did not ask for it to be brought forward to Derby Day. I must at least be at hand to learn the results. Mr Fulton has promised to call in on his way home and communicate them.'

'This is more important, Father,' she told him firmly.

'I had fully intended to back Robert the Devil,' muttered Alfred defiantly, 'until you arranged this meeting. In deference to you, Katharine, I changed my plan. It hardly seems fitting to put my – our – money on such a horse. Despite,' he said regretfully, 'his good form. Shall it be Beaudesert? I then asked myself. No. True, he is favourite, but instead I have backed Bend Or. What do you think of that?' he asked triumphantly. 'Be bold, eh?'

'Yes, Father, I'm sure you did right,' replied Katharine patiently. 'Now please do take your gloves and hat, and let us go.'

'These are my best ones,' he said disgustedly. 'Tight.'

'You don't wish to give Uncle Robert any grounds for condescension, do you?' she pointed out.

'Hah! Robert the Devil,' declared her father more happily, sneaking *The Pink 'Un* under his coat.

To her surprise, Meg came too, and Katharine wondered at the sudden interest her sister was taking in Bocton and its future. It was only when they were actually on their way that she suddenly realised why. She had not told Meg that Luke had withdrawn from The Case and so she would naturally expect to see him there. She cast a glance at her sister's pretty face, peeping out from under her frivolous bonnet, and her heart sank. Meg was out to charm, but she would be disappointed. On reflection, Katharine was feminine enough to be just a little glad. Thank heavens that Luke would not be there, for to see him again in such a setting would be more than she could bear. It was ordeal enough anyway. She pulled her thoughts away from Luke Stowerton and steeled herself for the encounter. A compromise? Surely Uncle Robert was not going to suggest that she own Bocton again? Why should he? Hope flared within her and died; perhaps this meeting was merely a carrot to force them into the open, to make them admit there was no chance of The Case being reopened.

'Gutta percha,' she heard Alfred say.

'I'm sorry, Father, my thoughts were miles away. What did you say?'

'They've shod him according to the American style,' repeated Alfred.

'Who?' She was completely bewildered.

'Bend Or, of course,' said her father testily. 'Did you think I meant young Luke?'

Young Luke! He wasn't young, thought Meg. He must be at least twenty-seven, perhaps more. Still, he had lots of money, and all the attractions of the older man. He couldn't seriously be interested in Katharine, could he? She stole a look at her sister, hair scraped back as usual, frowsty old dark blue taffeta dress; she did not see the graceful line of Katharine's figure that the frumpy old dress emphasised, nor the way her profile stood out so classically, free from curls. All she saw was that she, Meg, had no competition so far as looks went. Should she go for Luke or Philip? One of them it had to be, but it wasn't a difficult decision for she couldn't abide the thought of Philip. Luke . . . she'd like living in America. It would be different. *Anywhere* would be different, more exciting than Bocton.

'A layer of gutta percha between the hoof and the shoe,' explained Alfred patiently. 'It lessens the impact of the hard ground apparently, and the going will be hard today. We'll beat Robert the Devil yet, won't we?'

'Oh, yes,' said Katharine, smiling. 'Yes, we will.' But she was not so sure.

Uncle Robert had already arrived, and was sitting flanked on either side by two portly solicitors, Mr Bean and Mr Meacham. Alfred eyed them interestedly, clearly mentally renaming them and about to impart his verdict to Katharine, but she shushed him into quietness. Philip and David sat together. David's presence somewhat surprised Katharine, though she was glad to see someone she suspected of being a sympathiser if not able to be an ally. She felt buoyed up by the wink he gave her, before turning his gaze on Meg with devoted, forlorn eyes.

'I am surprised that Luke is not here,' observed Robert drily.

'Detained,' said Mr Pinpole hurriedly. 'He'll be here shortly.' He wondered whether he could be disbarred for such a downright lie, and uneasily suppressed the thought. Mr Bean's eyes narrowed and a rapid conference took place in which Katharine could see Robert impatiently shaking his head.

Robert cleared his throat. 'We would like to know your intentions regarding The Case, Alfred –' ignoring Katharine '– in view of the fact that three of your possible supporters have gone home, and I notice that Miss Violet and Miss Primrose are not here today either.'

'Our plans are not yet finalised,' said Katharine quickly as Alfred opened his mouth to speak, earning Mr Pinpole's admiration. 'And the reason Aunt Violet and Aunt Primrose are not here is that my father is in a way senior partner in The Case, and it seemed that he should make the decision when we have heard your suggestions.'

Robert turned his attention to her. So he had merely been trying to gain the advantage by addressing Alfred only, she realised quickly as he began to speak. 'I am in a somewhat difficult position, Katharine.' Mr Meacham flinched, but Sir Robert quelled him with a glance. 'The London, Chatham and Dover Railway is once again approaching me as regards the Bocton estate, not to mention my own company. The matter must be settled one way or another quickly. If you wish to go ahead and lose money – not your own, of course – over this, then so be it. However, in the interests of speed, as well as economy, it occurs to me we might resolve our differences by settlement.'

The silence was broken by Alfred, who declared cheerfully, 'You liked playing the horses too, Robert, but yours were always Trojan ones. Watch him, Katharine.'

'Really, Alfred,' exploded Robert, 'if you have nothing serious to offer the discussion, I suggest you remain quiet. Katharine, I believe Philip spoke to you –' His glance went to the door, and he stopped, abruptly. Yet he seemed unsurprised to see it was Luke following hard on the heels of the clerk who announced him. Almost as though Luke wanted to observe their reactions, thought Katharine instantly, thrown by his arrival as Robert apparently was not. So he was expecting Luke whereas she was not. Did this mean Luke knew about this 'compromise'?

He caught Katharine's eye and she inclined her head stiffly. He bowed slightly, almost less than mere politeness dictated. So he had come to gloat, if not worse. Meg dimpled at him, the feathers on her hat bobbing, and Luke came across to kiss her hand. Katharine stared wretchedly, rigidly, in front of her. Had Luke proved a turncoat indeed by joining Robert's camp? she wondered dispiritedly.

'Katharine, I believe Philip spoke to you last year about our suggestion that you should own Bocton?' Robert continued smoothly.

'Yes,' she said guardedly, 'but –'

He cut across her. 'The offer is still open, Katharine. We will sell Charham and part of the Bocton grounds, and leave you ownership of Bocton.'

Luke stiffened. There *was* a plan here all right – and it was not at all what he expected. If Robert had made such an offer last year, why had not Katharine mentioned this to him?

'Why?' she asked bluntly, astounded, unable to think clearly so unexpected was this offer. 'Why should you do this?'

'For speed, niece,' answered Robert blandly.

'And why Katharine,' said Alfred belligerently, suddenly interested in the proceedings, 'and not me?' Something deuced odd here.

'My dear Alfred, let us face realities,' said Robert smoothly. 'You are hardly a first class businessman and Katharine is a remarkably sensible young lady. In her hands, Bocton would flourish. In yours, it would go to the dogs.'

'To the horses,' murmured Philip, sniggering.

Mr Pinpole sat stiffly, quite unable to take charge of the situation as he had naturally expected. He had always flattered himself he could see the way a case was developing, but this was a new and somewhat disagreeable tangent.

'Rather more than a compromise, would you not say?' commented Luke. Katharine had been offered ownership. Why, why, why, was it in their interests?

'There is one other condition,' Robert continued coolly, as if Luke had not spoken.

'Condition?' repeated Katharine warily, beginning to marshal her thoughts now and glad that she had not become over-excited at Robert's offer.

'We feel strongly, as do you, that Bocton is a family concern. That it should be kept within our close family. After all, I have been owner of it for many years, and my father before that for even longer.'

'But it would remain in the family,' Katharine pointed out, 'if I were to own it.'

'Not if you were to marry away from the family, perhaps move away from Bocton.'

Luke was very still. So that was it, he thought. Anything than that she should marry Jeremiah's son. Robert was cleverer than he had given him credit for. On the cup of life it would always be Robert's name engraved, not Jeremiah's. Robert had been ahead of him all the way. Well, now he saw the goal, perhaps two could play at the game. After all, he, Luke, now had the advantage of surprise – and the right cards might yet be in his hands, if he played them correctly.

'But I'd never, never move from Bocton,' Katharine cried, bewildered, outraged at the mere idea.

'Nevertheless, do you not feel it reasonable that we should ensure that ownership of Bocton remain closely in the family? In the circumstances, our condition is that you should marry Philip.'

The room spun round Katharine. Marry Philip? *Marry* him? The words did not at first make sense, and when they did a revulsion so strong seized her that she was unable to think coherently.

Luke drew in his breath sharply. Surely Katharine would see Robert's intention?

Still disbelieving, Katharine glanced at Philip who was smiling thinly, smugly, possessively. Marry Philip? She'd rather lose Bocton.

She rose to her feet with one explosive cry: '*No!*'

A burst of forced nervous laughter from Philip, a gasp from Meg, an expletive from David, and nothing from Luke, his brain still working furiously on this development. Katharine's 'no' hardly took him by surprise, but Robert's motives were clear.

So simple. Legally any property coming to the wife after marriage would automatically belong to the husband, and Robert would ensure that that little detail of timing was taken care of – Bocton would be back in their hands, still in time to sell to the railway company. With Katharine married to Luke, however, it would pass entirely from Robert's control – and into that of Jeremiah's family.

Philip, still flushed at the public rejection, came in with scarcely veiled venom: 'My dear Katharine, what reason can you possibly have for refusing such an offer? Surely you don't wish to remain an old maid, when we could work together to restore Bocton?'

'No,' she repeated helplessly, unable to think beyond the dreadful idea of marrying him. 'Not even for Bocton.'

'It does seem a sensible suggestion, Miss Stowerton,' ventured Mr Pinpole rashly. Even Alfred looked somewhat surprised at her vehemence. Were they mad? Katharine thought dazedly. *Philip?* How could they think in such terms? Meg she would expect to look delighted at the suggestion, but why did not Father support her, Katharine?

'Your reasons, Katharine?' Robert asked coldly, politely. 'What displeases you at the idea of marrying into my family?'

Trapped, she stared round at a room suddenly full of enemies. Luke – had he known about this? Suggested it even? What was she to say? They were waiting. The room was still. What to say? She fought rising nausea.

'My dear, it does sound a most sensible idea,' urged Alfred.

'I can't,' she said flatly, numbly.

'Why not?' Robert repeated again, beating her into a corner. Until, trapped, she shouted her reply. Where did the words come from? Did somewhere her mother laugh to hear? 'Because I'm going to marry *him!*' Her finger pointed straight at Luke Stowerton. 'We are already betrothed.'

Why, how, had she said it? No matter. The die was cast. Now he would deny it, and her humiliation would begin. A strangled cry from Meg was the only sound in that second of shock. Luke would repudiate her, quite rightly.

121

'You seem very quiet, Mr Stowerton,' said Philip silkily, eyes watchful. 'Is Katharine correct in what she says?'

'I thought she had made it quite clear,' he drawled, after interminably long seconds. He got up and walked behind her chair, where she sat paralysed with fright, placing his hand possessively on the back of it. 'Katharine has done me the honour of consenting to be my wife.'

He had a hard job to keep his face straight. So the ants were running – and in what directions! What a turn of events. Poor Robert. Without even seeing through his plans Katharine had scotched them. He was jubilant, he wanted to sing, raised to such heights. He would show her all the lands of the earth, they would travel together, to Paris, to Peking, and always, always return to Bocton, the magnet of their lives. And most of all, at nights after the long happy days he would hold her in his arms, loving her, adoring her calm face, kissing her beloved eyes, sharing her warmth. Katharine . . . But none of this showed in his face.

'I had not realised,' said Robert quietly, 'that you cared quite so much for Bocton, Katharine.' The emphasis on Bocton made his meaning quite clear.

Luke blenched, a muscle twitching, taking his meaning before Katharine himself, and despite himself, wondering. *Had* she done it just to save Bocton? No, he reasoned. If so, she would have accepted his offer the other night. She had done it because, whether or not she consciously realised it, she loved him. Triumphant again, he stared at Robert.

Katharine felt red suffusing her cheeks. *Had* she done it to save Bocton? The thought of The Case hadn't even been in her mind. But would Robert's words make a difference? She opened her mouth but no words came.

'You will regret this move, Katharine,' Philip burst out. 'You have made the wrong choice. Like mother, like daughter.'

With a roar Alfred was on his feet with surprising agility, seizing hold of Philip, shaking him to and fro by the back of his morning-coat collar like a puppy, while Meg flung herself into David's arms, suddenly for no reason he could fathom in floods of tears.

'A bear garden, a positive bear garden. These Stowertons,' moaned Mr Foggett. 'I must say, Mr Pinpole, I am somewhat relieved the gavelkind case has been dropped.'

Luke, escorting Katharine from the room, glanced back. 'Has it?' he said quietly.

'I owe you an apology, Luke,' Katharine blurted out stiffly. Meg had been silent on the way home, tight-lipped, while Alfred talked happily of the Derby, perhaps out of a tactful realisation that all was not well. Only now had she the chance to speak to Luke alone as he took her arm and firmly escorted her through the Dower House garden out into the orchard, and through into the main Bocton park. 'Why did you do it?' she cried when he did not answer.

'I needed some time with my fiancée,' said Luke blithely, purposely misunderstanding.

'You know what I mean. It was good of you to support me, but please do not feel you have to keep up the fiction.'

'Fiction?' He looked flabbergasted. 'What the hell – what do you mean, Katharine?' he asked slowly.

'You merely supported me as a jest, did you not?' she replied stiffly. 'In order to annoy Uncle Robert?'

'I never jest about marriage,' he said grimly. 'Far too expensive,' he added to lighten the tone. 'Do I take it,' he said with some effort, 'that you were not serious about our betrothal?'

'Serious?' She stared at him in amazement. 'I had not thought –' She broke off. Had he indeed been in earnest then that evening, when she had taken it as the impulse of a summer eve, lightly voiced and quickly forgotten? How could one ever tell with Luke?

Emotions battled within him, but none showed on his face as he said in an objective tone: 'I might point out, Katharine, that you are committed. Quite a number of people, including five lawyers, heard you state you were going to marry me. And so you are.'

'You mean you will hold me to it?' Terror battled with something else, a fluttering, then a surge, as the prospect of being married to Luke and all it would mean opened before her, emotions warring to be free.

'You are hardly flattering,' he said wryly. 'Do I take it that I am not preferable to Philip?'

'No, but I don't have to marry either of you. I spoke before I thought.'

'Oh, but you do.'

'Why?' she blurted out.

'My father would never forgive me if I passed up the chance of such revenge against Robert.'

'But I can't marry you just because you might change your mind and save Bocton,' she said indignantly.

'I hope, Katharine,' he said with a mock dignity that cost him dear, 'that there are more reasons for marrying me than just saving Bocton. I hoped you might be swept away by my wooing.'

The way he kissed . . . Then Meg's image swept before her. He kissed Meg too. Often.

'I can't,' she said wretchedly. 'I can't!' In her mind her mother made clucks of disapproval at such anti-romanticism.

'Katharine, you stated you were going to marry me. Marry me you shall, and Bocton shall be yours, if all the lawyers in the world have to fight The Case out. Or, rather, it shall be ours.'

'Ours,' she whispered, suddenly captivated, remembering what fun it had been discovering the old woodwork of the kitchen, envisaging what they could achieve together there in the future, a Bocton fully restored, lived in and loved again by a family.

'Katharine,' he began, then stopped. 'This is foolish,' he muttered. 'Come here.' He took her into his arms and kissed her.

'But Meg –' she managed to say between kisses.

'Will you forget Meg?' he said patiently. 'I owe her nothing.'

'I can't marry for Bocton.'

'If you refuse to, I'll sue you for breach of promise. Does that make you feel better, Katie May?'

'But that's for women against men.'

He sighed, freeing her. 'And you think men and women should have different rights?'

'No one can force me to marry you . . .'

'I thought you wanted Bocton.'

'That's a fine reason for marrying.'

'Will you marry me or not?' he said quietly, blue eyes dangerously bright.

'Is that a proposal?' she glared back ridiculously.

'Do you want roses and a band playing "Love's Old Sweet Song"?'

'Yes,' she said defiantly.

'Here then.' She found herself swept once more into his arms, not gently now, but brooking no denial, and his lips on hers warm and demanding, until she relaxed against him, enjoying the feel of his body against hers.

'Now,' he said breathlessly, loosening his hold a little, 'do you hear the music?'

'I – I think I do.'

He put his lips on hers again, and held her so close to him that she was hardly aware of his lifting her from her feet and sliding with her down on to the grass, for his hands never ceased to move over her body, or his lips to demand. 'I think the next time you had better wear breeches,' he murmured after a while.

'Why?' she asked hazily.

'You don't wear stays then to protect your breasts. Perhaps, on the other hand, I could not avail myself of the undoubted advantage of skirts.' Before she could protest, even had she wanted to, save for a fleeting thought that Aunt Sophy would doubtless deem this most improper, he was gently lifting her dress and she could feel his hands on her legs. But he was kissing her with such sweet passion that only belatedly did she realise that his hands were where no man's had ever been before, and more important that the involuntary cry of pleasure she gave had little to do with the kiss. Or had it? Perhaps . . . Suddenly she came to her senses, pushing his hands away so indignantly that he laughed, well satisfied, saying in exhilaration, 'After all, Katie May, we are betrothed.'

'You beast,' yelled Meg, tears streaming down her face. 'You've stolen him. You know he loved me. They both wanted me, Philip and Luke, and you schemed that they both proposed to *you*.' The last word was a long drawn-out wail.

'Meg, I'm sorry.' Katharine was stunned. 'I know you are attracted to him, but he loves me.' The words assumed a great significance for her, as for the first time she believed them to be true.

124

'Love *you*? Look at you. How *could* he love you? You're dowdy, an old maid!'

'Not quite,' Katharine protested, trying to keep her temper. 'Oh, darling –'

'You are, you are! It's *me* he desires. Only you stole him.' She had almost persuaded herself of this fact, after Louis' defection.

'How could I do that?' said Katharine, suddenly impatient with her sister. 'If he really loved you, of course I could not steal him, as you say.'

Meg glared at her, determined to prove her point, jealousy welling up inside her, side by side with fury at being thwarted. 'If only you knew,' she said mysteriously.

Katharine lost patience. 'Meg, if you have anything to tell me, tell me. Otherwise, be quiet. I know you're jealous that I'm to be married, but your turn will come.'

Meg stared at her. Katharine was not going to get away with it that easily. 'I'll tell you,' she said suddenly. 'Oh, I'll tell you all right. You remember that day I was so upset? It was then.'

Katharine remembered it very well

'What about it?' she asked.

Meg paused, inventing wildly. 'I'd been with Luke. I had told him I was expecting. Expecting *his* baby!' She tried to sound tragic and heroic, not triumphant, but it was hard.

'What?' The words did not make sense at first. Then they did. Katharine went white. 'I don't believe you,' she said flatly.

Meg saw she had won a point, and looked smug.

'You mean you actually made – let him –' Katharine stopped, sickened, revolted. This was Luke they were talking about. She wanted to say it was a pack of lies, but for the memory of Meg in Luke's arms, not once but more than once, her constant talk of him and his attraction to her. Could Meg have done it? Oh yes, she could. She was like Mother. But could Luke? No, not the Luke she knew. 'I don't believe you. You're jealous, Meg.'

'He did. I'll – I'll prove he made love to him. Really. Just as if we were man and wife.'

'How?' said Katharine scornfully.

'I'll tell you what happened,' said Meg suddenly. 'After he kissed me, and said he wanted to – I said I wouldn't, but he – went on kissing me, and suddenly we were lying down and I couldn't stop him. You know how persuasive he is, Katharine.'

Katharine stared at her unable to speak, unable to believe Meg, yet went on listening in sick horror.

'He couldn't get my stays off, but the next thing I knew his hands were under my skirt and chemise and he was unbuttoning my drawers and he was on top of me and I couldn't move him. Oh, Katharine, he kissed so sweetly. He made me do it. I didn't notice what he was doing – till he'd taken his unmentionables down. I thought it was just his hands under there and – oh, Katharine it hurt, and I cried, but it was lovely. We were truly lovers and he sang to me . . .' Her eyes went dreamy.

Katharine wanted to vomit, to shout that it couldn't have happened. Not Luke. But who else? Meg had seen no one else. She'd have told her if so. And there was no way she could have described it so graphically unless she had experienced it. But numb in horror and disbelief, Katharine went on questioning. 'Luke is an honourable man,' she said slowly, nausea rising in her. 'If what you say is true and he loves you, why does he not marry you?'

Meg stared at her piteously, tears beginning to cascade anew. Should she say she refused him? No, Katharine would not believe that. 'Oh, Katharine, he *wouldn't* marry me. He told me he wanted to travel, that he didn't want or even like children at all. They were an encumbrance and would grow up just like the other Stowertons, and he didn't intend to be there to witness it.' A triumphant finishing touch.

Katharine froze. This was too much. Not even Meg could have invented this.

'That's the only reason he wants to marry you,' said Meg tearfully. 'So that he's not forced to marry me, if I go to law or Father turns nasty. Stowertons don't like responsibility,' she added simply.

Katharine missed the note of triumph, wrapt in her misery. Was that indeed why Luke wanted to marry her? So that he couldn't be forced to marry Meg? Meg was almost worried when she saw Katharine's face, but told herself she would soon get over it. She ran to her and hugged her. 'Oh, Katharine, I'm so sorry. But it's right you should know the truth,' she explained piously.

'I'll go to him,' said Katharine numbly. 'I'll make him marry you.'

'No,' said Meg sharply. 'No.' She toned down her voice which had made Katharine look at her in surprise. 'Don't tell him I've told you, Katharine. Oh, please.'

'Why not?' asked Katharine, past querying now. 'You must want him to marry you if you are to carry his baby.' She forced the words out.

'Something might happen. I'm so ashamed anyway. I won't marry a man who doesn't want to marry me. I don't want to be forced into a loveless marriage,' with some hazy recollection of the circulating library romances that she had read.

'But what are you to do? I can't marry him – I can look after you, but I can't protect you from all the scandal.'

'I'll think of something. It might even be a mistake,' said Meg hopefully. 'It was my first time,' she said shyly, 'it might have made me late. But *enceinte* or not, it doesn't alter the situation.'

No, it didn't alter the situation that Luke Stowerton was unprincipled and a philanderer. Even now Katharine could not believe it of him, yet by next morning she had thought it out logically. It all fitted; there was no other explanation for his conduct. Yet even so, now that dawn had come, she found it grey.

Luke stared at Katharine in blank bewilderment. 'What is this nonsense? Are you *still* telling me you don't want to marry me?'

'Yes.' She faced him defiantly. They were in the park once more,

126

even though it was raining, for Katharine felt that to have walls around would suffocate her.

Were all the Stowertons mad? Luke thought. Had he made such a mistake in Katharine? No, he was sure not, and he'd back his conviction. 'Any particular reason?' he enquired politely, though he was shaking with suppressed anger.

'No,' she said dully. How could she explain? He must after all know that it had been lies and deceit.

'Then I must tell you that I will indeed bring an action against you,' he informed her matter-of-factly. 'You gave your word. I have started the gavelkind case with Mr Pinpole, I have informed my family of my imminent marriage, I have seen the vicar about our wedding. I am not prepared to be a laughing stock without fighting back, Katharine. Let us reduce it to basic essentials. Do you or do you not wish to own Bocton?'

'Yes, but –'

'So do I. So we will consider it a business partnership. You will marry me and I will save Bocton, no more nonsense. Come now,' he softened, 'it may not be too bad. Come.' Still holding the umbrella aloft, he pinioned her with his other arm and kissed her gently. But today there was no response. Careful, Luke, be careful, don't send her yet further away. He drew back from her, considering his next move.

'Very well, Katharine,' he said, suddenly changing tactics. '"Since there is no help, come let us kiss and part."' He planted a kiss on her lips and walked away.

'Part? Luke, where are you going?' she cried in bewilderment, for he seemed to be heading straight for the lake.

He made no answer and, in front of her disbelieving eyes, did not stop at the side of the lake but simply marched straight into it, shoes, socks, trousers, jacket, waistcoat, cap, umbrella and all.

'Luke,' she cried, sharply now on a note of fear, 'what on earth are you doing?'

Again silence, save for the swishing of the water as he marched in deeper, the water waist-high now; he was still holding the umbrella aloft however.

'Luke!' she cried in horror. 'Come *back*!' Panic made her immobile.

But he did not come back. Only his head was above the water now – and the arm holding the umbrella.

'Luke!' Suddenly her legs obeyed her, and she ran to the side of the lake, shouting. He couldn't be intending to – no, that was too ridiculous. It was a trick to gain her sympathy. But to her horror the head had disappeared now, only the umbrella and a hand to be seen. Then the hand too was gone, a few bubbles, and she was staring at the place where Luke had once been, crying out in alarm.

'Luke, Luke!' She rushed in herself, looking at the umbrella floating unheld on top of the water. He could climb out on to the island. He must, he *must*.

But he did not, and all was silence, only the whirl of the dragonflies

127

moving in that still place. It was as though Luke Stowerton had never been.

'Luke,' she wept, pushing her way further in, her skirts hampering her, wet and clinging. She was breast-high now, but still there was no sign of Luke Stowerton.

Dizzy with shock, she glanced back towards the bank. There, dripping wet, lolled Luke watching her. Relief made her forget the ridiculousness of the situation as, feeling like a drowned Lady of Shalott, she waded out, hampered by sodden clinging skirts. 'Luke, oh Luke, you *fool*! I thought you –'

'You reckoned I'd drowned myself for love of you?' he asked, grinning as she emerged. 'I swam round the island and came back the other way. Now will you marry me? I might not come back next time.' He took her by the hand and pulled her up the bank and into his arms.

'Very well,' she said, fighting back tears and laughter.

'And there was I thinking you'd decided to marry Philip after all, and consign me to the arms of Sister Meg,' he joked, holding her lovingly and wondering why she was suddenly so still.

How could she have forgotten? Katharine thought dully. Meg. Always Meg. Where she was now, Meg had been so many times before, and look what had happened. It was Meg he had wanted first. Not her, Katharine. Her lips he had kissed, her body he had wanted, explored – and then taken. A vision of them lying together, of the words of love that must have poured from him, of the love – or lust – he had forced on her . . . such a tide of jealousy swept over her that when it passed she shivered, and the wet clothes had little to do with it.

'I will marry you, Luke, but I will not share your bed.' How could she, after what he had done to Meg? And as he wanted her, Katharine, for Bocton's sake, he could not object.

'Not share –' His face flushed suddenly, and he said quietly, dangerously, 'What has gone wrong, Katharine, that you should demand such a thing?'

'It is a business arrangement to save Bocton,' she repeated steadily. 'You said so yourself. You will not wish to marry me now, will you?'

'And you will lose Bocton.' He held her gaze, fighting this night-marish octopus whose origins he could not guess.

'I can always marry Philip. It's not too late,' she said, close to tears.

'No,' he said abruptly, 'have it your way.' For the moment, he was thinking.

She wanted to tell him she was unfair, retract what she had said, that she had not been right to demand this of him, but the image of Meg came once again between their dripping, defiant figures.

'This is a most exciting. Very rewarding indeed.' Mr Pinpole beamed over the top of his rimless spectacles. 'I have obtained an optimistic

128

opinion from Mr Smithers-Drysdale, the eminent barrister. A most persuasive and lucid advocate.'

He'll have to be, thought Katharine, trying to keep a straight face as Mr Pinpole expounded the intricacies of what lay before them. She glanced at Luke, unable yet to believe that tomorrow he would be her husband. Every time she thought of it, she was swayed by tangled emotions that could not be deciphered. 'No point in waiting,' Luke had said. 'I assume you agree that in all the circumstances a quiet, speedy wedding is best? Before,' he had added meaningfully, 'we change our minds. We'll be married by special licence – it'll have to be very special since I live in America. They'll just have to take my word for it that I'm not a bigamist.'

A bigamist? she asked uneasily. With Meg so much in her mind, the jest was displeasing.

'They say that June weddings are propitious,' she answered, trying to be lighthearted, but he did not reply and she knew that the gulf between them lay unbridgeable for the moment. Yet how could she feel she was behaving unfairly towards him, in view of the way he had behaved towards Meg? Every day she was alternately throwing a tantrum or bursting into tears or both as she waited to know whether she was to have a baby. She never let Katharine forget her agony, so that it had taken precedence in Katharine's mind even over the matter of her own wedding. Or because of it, she thought ruefully. So strained was the atmosphere at home that to come to Canterbury to discuss the gavelkind case was a relief.

'It was not easy to obtain his services,' Mr Pinpole continued with pride, 'in view of the current move to the new Royal Courts of Justice, but fortunately the unusual nature of The Case and the fact that the preparation time is likely to be – um – longer than usual, has resulted in his agreement. The Case will be heard in the new Courts, of course, in the Strand. A pity perhaps, since the fact of our little problem being heard in Westminster Hall might have somewhat helped our cause. The sense of history. Generations of Stowertons taking the stand before the bench . . .'

'What do we do first, Mr Pinpole?' Luke's quiet voice broke in. His expression was unreadable as Katharine glanced at him uneasily.

'Naturally we have to get the acquiescence of your co-parceners, or rather Mr Jeremiah's, even though you do not require them to contribute money. I do not foresee difficulty here. In the event of a successful outcome they would in any case all inherit equally with your fathers, yet it would much strengthen our case if they could contribute a mere nominal sum towards the costs, so that all names might appear in the suit.'

'One penny,' said Luke, flatly.

Mr Pinpole stared at him, astounded.

'Even Albert would consider that worth his while,' said Luke grimly. 'I don't want any risks.'

'Very well,' said Mr Pinpole resignedly. 'One penny. Our first priority after that is to establish that since Nathaniel Stowerton's will pre-dated the Wills Act of 1837, only lands of which he stood in lawful seisin – er, possession – could pass by it, no matter what he later inherited by legal title. You see, Mr Luke, Miss Katharine,' he leant back contentedly in his chair, the tips of his fingers pressed together in front of him, as he proceeded to expound on the feudal basis of modern land law, 'the Wills Act changed the position, altering the focus to the testator's legal possessions at the time of death. How fortunate your grandfather made his will when he did, since we can prove with no difficulty that he inherited Bocton later than the date of the will.'

'Then I guess that part of The Case will be easy to win?' asked Luke, with some relief.

'No case is easy, Mr Luke,' Mr Pinpole pointed out cautiously. And certainly not, he might have added, where Stowertons are concerned. 'I suspect Sir Robert's lawyers might well try to establish that by the fact that his father was maintaining – to some extent – the Bocton grounds all the while *Stowerton and Stowerton* was being fought, that this proves his seisin or possession.

'Fortunately for us,' he beamed, 'Mr Dodson has lighted upon *Muggleton and Barnett*, 1857. Yes, quite a little find.' Pinpole sat back smugly, mentally thanking the absent Muggleton for his litigious bent of mind. 'Nevertheless, Sir Robert may well choose to contest our interpretation of the Wills Act, or on the other hand he may choose to concentrate his efforts upon the gavelkind issue itself.'

'And that's complicated?' asked Luke.

'Good gracious, yes, Mr Stowerton. We are then only just beginning in legal terms.' There was relish in his tone. 'Granted that we win our point over the Wills Act, that simply leaves the situation that Bocton and Charham are treated legally as if Sir Nathaniel had died intestate. It is for us then to prove that the lands are and have always been subject to gavelkind, in other words to the custom of Kent and not the common law of England, whereby the estates would pass to Sir Robert as eldest son, will or no will.'

Katharine had spent the last week instructing Luke on gavelkind and the Stowerton legends of the problems it had caused. He had been an apt pupil, partly out of genuine curiosity – and partly because it was a no-man's-land where they both might meet without trespassing on to more explosive subjects.

'From what Katharine tells me, Mr Pinpole,' he said, 'it all seems to hinge on Sir Nicholas Stowerton.' Some of the stories Katharine had told him raised a memory from far back. And Sir Nicholas, with his Midsummer service to the Queen of one red rose, was one of them.

'Ah, yes, it all goes back to Sir Nicholas,' said Pinpole. 'Four sons, and a most interesting legal situation as to whether one or all should inherit.'

'But didn't this Nicholas leave a will?' asked Luke, puzzled.

'At that time the custom of gavelkind could not be overruled by willing property elsewhere. His eldest son held that the tenure of the land had been changed by reason of Sir Nicholas's grandfather's treason, and the Queen's granting the lands to him in payment of a red rose each year. As no hint of Sir Nicholas's own wishes could be found, his sons fell to with a vengeance,' Pinpole explained.

'Sir Nicholas's father Philip had been born posthumously to William Stoorton's widow, Luke,' Katharine told him. 'She and her son were given shelter by distant cousins, the Stowertons, whose name Philip adopted. He died very young, shortly after his son was born. Nicholas, Luke, it all goes back to Nicholas,' she said wryly. Fair-haired Nick Stowerton, whom Luke so closely resembled.

'The country people assembled to hear the hue and cry, Nicholas. Your father, then an infant in my arms, was heard to squeal, and thus my dower was lost according to the Custom of Kent.' The old woman looked wearily at the fair-haired child playing by the hearth. Was he listening? Would her words be remembered, despite his tender years, whether consciously or not? It was right that he should know these things, for it was his birthright of which she spoke, for all it was long ago, for all that Cousin Stowerton had sheltered her and her baby son Philip when all others had gone. The need for vengeance remained.

Philip was born but six months after William her husband had been taken from her, and three after he had lost his head on Tower Hill. She had nothing to hang her head in shame for before the country people. Yet she had been turned from the house by the King's men; they had assembled the crowd to listen for the hue and the cry, in order to disbar her from her rightful home. She still called it her dower, for no charge of treason had been brought against William until the week he died, and only treason could render her dower forfeit – that or a charge of fornication, proven only by the child being heard to squeal within the dower house. The King would have all. The woman smiled grimly. One day, ah, one day, the Stowertons would be revenged on the upstart Tudors. And for that she must entrust this child here with her secret, painfully recorded with her gnarled fingers and stored in the plain wooden box that would be his after she herself had gone. The hue and the cry!

She gave a sharp cackle of laughter, and Nicholas, alarmed, ceased his playing. He gazed up at his grandmother in wonder. He did not forget. Dower or no, she knew well her right to live at Northwell Manor, which the King had taken from her. Yet it was a right she could speak of to none but Nicholas. 'Listen, my chick. Listen to me.' And she spoke urgently, and at length. When at last she had finished, he chuckled, smiling up at her with innocent blue eyes; he saw this pleased her, though as yet he understood not one word.

'Luke!' Katharine cried out, concerned. 'What's the matter?'

'A great deal, Katharine.' His face for once expressed his true feelings, unable to conceal his shock at the unbelievable news in the letters in his hand.

Three days ago they had been married by special licence, at Bocton Bugley church. Despite Sophy's offer of help she had refused to wear a full-trained white wedding dress, pleading the excuse of time and the small assembly of people that would be present. Seeing Sophy's

131

disapproving face, she had compromised on cream satin with a tiny hat swathed entirely in fresh flowers. She went through the ceremony almost in a daze, the reality only coming home to her when they entered Durrant's Hotel in London where they were to spend a few days on 'honeymoon'. To give us, he had phrased it carefully, time to be with each other. A strange honeymoon in separate rooms. And what would follow? He hardly knew. And now – he stared at the two letters in his hand – it did not matter, for whatever plans he might have would have to be abandoned for ever. He almost swayed as he began to take in the full implications of his father's letter, after having read the devastating contents of his mother's. The two of them added up to a life sentence.

'Everything has changed, Katharine. Everything,' he said, unable to keep the horror of it from his voice.

'The Case?' she cried in alarm at the despair in his voice.

He made a wry face. 'If only it were. No –' He hesitated then blurted out: 'These letters are from home. I have to return immediately.'

'When will you be back?' she asked blankly.

'I doubt if I will be, Katharine,' he answered helplessly.

'But – but The Case.' She was too proud to say 'our marriage'.

Noticing the omission, he shrugged: 'The Case will go on, without us on hand, that's all.'

'*Us?*' she picked up the word disbelievingly.

'As my wife you will naturally come with me.' Shock made him incapable of dressing up the words.

Her world spun round her as she stared at him, the friend suddenly become stranger.

'Go to America? Leave Bocton? Why?' she burst out, agonised, pitchforked into nightmare.

'I'll explain later,' he said wearily. He had not the strength to tell her that unless he returned and sacrificed his plans for his own life to run his father's business, there would be no case. It was Father's price, his blackmailing, hypocritical price. For Father, strict, upright, sanctimonious, Godfearing Jeremiah, had left Leadville, left his wife and daughters. Jeremiah had run away with one Daisy Petal Garden, a visiting artiste at a Leadville saloon.

Chapter Eight

Heat, stifling heat, beside which the sun of even the hottest English day seemed gentle; dirt, dust and the endless horror of travelling ever onwards.

Luke glanced at Katharine from time to time, trying to hide his concern, for he was unable to help her in her misery. 'It'll be cooler in the mountains,' he told her awkwardly. 'When we get to Pueblo and change to the Denver and Rio Grande line for Canyon City, we'll start climbing. Then you'll feel better.'

She stared at him blankly. Names, they were just names, in this vast emptiness of a country.

She'll feel better – at least until the stage gets going, he thought to himself tiredly. The last 126 miles to Leadville had to be done by stage coach, with everyone packed in together, miners, hobos, tourists – no first class and second class there. Travelling day and night it would take twenty-six hours to reach Leadville, twenty-six hours of hell. They'd rest up in Canyon for a day to build her strength. No longer – every hour counted. Any day now the new railroad would have reached Leadville, and the days of travelling by this perilous stage coach would be no more. Yet he couldn't delay this journey, not even for Katharine. He had to reach home as soon as possible, for fear of what he might find. His mother needed help, his sisters – and, heaven help him, the business. It was a month since Father had written to him, and a month in Leadville history was a long time for a town that had only existed for two years. A town where men had silver in their eyes now, not just stars, and blinded by it, had little compunction as to the way they got it. Marshal Duggan had kept things pretty well under control, but Martha had written him that the Marshal had gone now. What would be happening to Leadville? Luke had a pretty fair idea, from the work he'd done for the *Leadville Chronicle*, and it wasn't going to be good news.

Katharine was almost oblivious by now to her surroundings, the mere effort of survival taking all her strength. She had endured all the partings stoically, giving little hint that she felt her heart would break at leaving Bocton. Father was fooled by her composure, Meg ignored her, Aunt Sophy realised her torment but the pity in her eyes was almost more than Katharine could bear. Once on the steamer, sea-sickness had taken over from heartbreak, and she kept to her cabin for some days, tended by Luke and too ill to care that he was changing her nightclothes, sponging her face, removing bowls of vomit and bedpans. After four days she was able to stagger on to the deck,

133

breathing the air thankfully but still too weak to worry over what she, Katharine May Stowerton, was doing on the high ocean when Bocton lay far behind. As her strength grew, Luke kept more to his own cabin. Luke, her husband yet a stranger, ever since those letters had arrived from that far-off place, Colorado. Before that the days had been magic in his companionship as they laughed their way round London, visiting the theatre, the Tower of London, happy together. Yes, happy, she told herself defiantly, despite their odd marriage.

Not now. Luke had retreated into himself to a place where she could not reach him, even had she had the strength to try. After they landed in America he became even more remote, blending naturally into his surroundings, as she, without the protection of the anonymity of the steam-ship, felt self-conscious of her English accent. Her clothes seemed dowdy amidst the sophistication of New York, where they had rested a day before continuing the journey.

She had no qualms about the railway journey – or railroad as Luke called it – for railways must surely all be the same, she had reasoned. She had not taken into account that a journey of well over three days was unlike a journey from nearby Ashford to London. 'We change at Kansas on to the Atchison, Topeka and Sante Fé railroad – that will give you a break. But we will have a Pullman Palace car throughout with a sleeping car.' Yes, at least, he thought bitterly, money could achieve some things.

Katharine looked at him somewhat puzzled, not understanding why she should object to a railway journey. She soon discovered, as the train chugged endlessly on, through nearly 2,000 miles of plains and farming ground. The station, or depots as Luke called them, were miles apart, dusty small wayside halts with jostling farmers and their wives clambering on and off, shouting in their strange accents, and the occasional black face – but no one entered the Pullman carriages, and so they remained a world apart. Even through the unreality of a railway window, the sense of limitless space overwhelmed her, till she felt lost, a speck of humanity in a vastness she could never have imagined. Surely all this was a dream, and she would wake again and find herself in the cool woods of Bocton, not under harsh pitiless skies that left you exposed. To add to her misery, she fell sick through eating fruit brought at a depot, and for twelve hours was constantly moving between the sleeping car and lavatory, her misery making her oblivious to embarrassment each time she passed the black steward, who muttered something unintelligible but sympathetic. On her sixth time past him he proffered a glass of some milky substance.

'Missy, you takes this.' His face was alive with concern. Too weak to resist she did so, and it had a pleasant taste of honey and sourish milk and something else. Whatever it was, she began to feel better, and was able to join Luke in the day carriage.

'Kansas,' he said briefly. 'We'll be at Kansas City shortly.' She looked out. No sign of a city, just cattle, thousands of them, not fat and sleek like old Betty at home, but hardier, leaner, thousands and thousands as far as her eye could see. 'Getting to be the end of the round-up season,'

Luke explained. 'The cowboys begin rounding them up in April after the winter common grazing, to divide them up back to their owners.'

'Cowboys?' she asked. 'Like shepherds?'

He grinned at that. 'Something like,' he agreed.

At Pueblo they changed trains again, without a break, running from one to the other. 'We'll stop over at Canyon City,' he reassured her. 'It's a coal-mining city, but tourists go there too.'

'Coal?'

'Yup. *Everything*'s mined now in Colorado. It's just one big mine. First gold, now silver, and every darn' thing. Gemstones, lead, copper, coal, iron, zinc . . . you name it, Colorado and the Rockies have got it. It's as exciting underneath those mountains as it is on top.' Even as he spoke, he was surprised to find enthusiasm in his voice. It sure was beautiful country; it was the ethics of mining he wasn't so certain of. 'It's real rewarding,' he said.

She did not miss the wry note in his voice. 'For you?' she asked.

He gave her a cool look. 'I reckon I don't see my whole life bound up in it. I hope not.'

She fell quiet, not knowing the full reason for his bitterness. 'Why do tourists come, if it's just a coal-mining town?' she asked curiously.

'They come to see the Grand Canyon of the Arkansas River, about a dozen miles from town. And the springs of course. Iron springs.'

'Like Tunbridge Wells?'

At that he laughed outright, the first spontaneous reaction she'd heard him give since they'd landed. 'Not quite like Tunbridge Wells, I reckon,' remembering a visit he'd made there while in England, to the elegant eighteenth-century Pantiles. Yet Canyon sure had something, bursting with promise for the future.

But after Canyon came the most terrible part of their endless journey. The twenty-six hours to Leadville by 'Barlow and Sanderson', as Luke put it. Katharine had not understood that this was not another railway but a rugged stage coach, where she sat jammed in with would-be millionaire miners, in outlandish clothes, only the smell of tobacco smothering that of their sweat. Luggage was piled on top, often falling off, necessitating endless stops to rearrange it. In the heat, intensified by the fug inside the coach, her own thin lawn dress was wet with sweat too, the stays under her long bodice and straight skirt digging painfully into her. Tonight – if there was one, for perhaps this hell would go on and on – she'd forswear modesty and take them off, she vowed miserably. At first the journey was easy as the road was choked with traffic and they moved only slowly along the perilous mountain path.

'Over there,' Luke waved his hand to the right of the path, 'is Pike's Peak.'

'What's that?' she asked, forcing herself to show some kind of interest, despite her blistering headache from heat and altitude, and the jolting sickening fug of the coach. At least now that the ground was rising sharply the air was just a little cooler. If she could keep her face to the window the air would play on it.

135

'Pike's Peak or Bust,' Luke explained. 'That's the sign the wagons carried when they came east from the worn-out California fields in '59 in search of gold. Colorado wasn't a state, or even a territory, then, just a load of barren nothing, a barrier over the continent. Worth nothing.'

'Except to the Indians who lived there.'

She was startled at the response to her casual comment. All faces turned to look at her, with suddenly sour expressions, and Luke quickly continued: 'A hundred thousand people came from east and west in the gold rush. Most of them either turned back before they got here, or before they struck gold. But those that hung on struck lucky. It kind of started the Colorado mining craze off. Gold was sought everywhere. South-west of Denver, John Gregory panned for gold in a gulch near Central City, and, boy, did he strike paydirt. "I shall be rich", he cried, "and my wife shall be a lady".' And he was right. He made a fortune.'

There was a sudden stillness in the coach, all faces on Luke. Or were they? thought Katharine suddenly. Was not that look in their eyes turned towards some far-off dream of their own?

The stage coach obligingly stopped briefly at the Grand Canyon of the Arkansas River. Down at the bottom of this 2,000 foot gorge, the new railroad would be shortly running, invisible from their great height at the edge. The mighty river itself looked a mere ribbon from here. Katharine shivered, holding tightly to Luke's arm. 'It'll be some trip along there,' he said. 'The railroad would have been here sooner, but two companies were fighting over it.'

'Like over our railway?' she asked, forcing a smile.

'Yup, only more. They hired gunmen too. Shooting it out in the good oldfashioned way.'

'Trial by *bataille*. Like that gavelkind case Father used to re-enact with the coal scuttle on his head.'

'And the poker,' said Luke.

'You remember that, too?' asked Katharine wistfully. How far away and long ago.

At the look on her face, he wanted to take her into his arms and kiss her, as a husband should his wife. Until he remembered, they weren't husband and wife save in name. He said more harshly than he intended: 'Katharine, don't go talking about the Indians. You don't understand the situation. There's a lot of bad feeling. The wars weren't over that long ago, and the Indians treacherously attacked a post only last year. Killed a man, took hostages, *women* hostages,' he emphasised. 'War nearly broke out again. People feel strongly.'

'But don't the Indians have right on their side? Some at least?'

'That's enough, Katharine,' he said sharply, then as he saw her face, 'trust me.'

'Why?' she said, almost to herself, and he made no reply.

The stage coach jolted on behind slow-moving wagons, unable to overtake because of the narrow mountainous track. She slept fitfully then awoke with a scream as the coach overturned, throwing them into a jumbled pile. She was crushed beneath the weight of bodies till Luke

136

freed her, and got out, cursing the driver who merely grinned. She sat down at the wayside, trying not to look down, while the men set the coach upright again, then sobbed her fear and terror of the future in Luke's arms when at last they set off again.

'Easy now,' he calmed her. 'I remember your Good Queen Victoria is used to getting overturned in coaches. Remember the time she was suspended upside down by her crinoline?'

'I don't think,' Katharine managed to say, 'that Queen Victoria had a ravine like that by her side when the coach overturned.'

'Little lady's scared,' observed a fellow passenger, spitting thoughtfully.

'Sure,' agreed Luke. 'So was I, pal.'

At which the miner gave a toothless grin and resumed his tobacco chewing. The briefest of stops were allowed for refreshments and change of horses, only sufficient to tantalise as the coach wound on through towns that bore no relation to anything Katharine thought of by that name; these were mere collections of wooden cabins, clusters on hillsides, growing sparser as the altitude increased. She slept fitfully, opening her eyes to see bright blue birds on the hillsides, eagles circling over the peaks, threatening in their strangeness, and then, in the midst of them, a goldfinch perching on a tree. The occasional wild turkey roamed by the track on flatter ground. Around them spruce-covered mountainsides loomed upwards on all sides; further down the hillsides were covered with trees in greeny-grey leaves, shivering in the air currents.

'Aspen trees,' said Luke, 'forever weeping in shame at having made the Cross.'

She stared at him, hovering between sleep and wakefulness.

He laughed. 'I didn't make it up. It's an old Spanish legend. Spanish Mexico used to own all this land. Hold on, Katharine, we're nearly there.' He was surprised to find in himself a certain excitement, his forebodings momentarily forgotten.

Roused from fitful sleep, she sat up. Ahead of her was a vast conglomeration of low wooden cabins, and over them hung an ominous dark cloud of yellow and black smoke.

'From the smelters,' explained Luke apologetically. 'You'll hardly notice it except on very hot days.' He tried to smile reassuringly, but met her eye and turned away, angry at himself for feeling guilt at bringing her. What other course could he have taken? He had not foreseen this course of events, and now that it had happened there was nothing he could do to change it. It was only guilt made him turn from her, but she assumed he did not care.

Wooden shacks were everywhere, endless low buildings, the grim treeless hills enclosing the town, each one scarred by stakes, potholed where men had dug in vain, machinery proclaiming those that had been rewarded. There were more of the latter than the former in Leadville, however, such was the richness of the ore. Now the distance between the cabins widened out as the stage suddenly turned to sweep up a broad thoroughfare, packed with men and wagons, swarming with life, noise beating in upon them after the quiet of the mountains. The stage gathered speed in order to draw attention to its arrival; dust swirled in at the windows choking her, half obliterating the scene from her eyes. Men everywhere, dirty and unshaven; miners mixing with conventionally dressed shopkeepers and businessmen. Wooden verandahed sidewalks lined the streets. Banks jostled side by side with places called saloons, vibrating with noise.

'They're wearing guns,' Katharine said to Luke, horrified. *'Guns!'* As if to emphasise her words, the sound of a shot from a saloon echoed round the street.

'Only for self-defence,' he said hastily, but she turned to him doubtfully, fear for the future intensifying.

The coach drew to a halt as it turned the corner. 'Don't worry about the luggage,' said Luke. 'One of the helps will be here, waiting.' A shy-looking black boy of about fifteen edged towards them from the sidewalk.

'Sure glad to see you back, Mr Luke,' he muttered, head cast down.

'Where's the buggy, Charlie?' Luke frowned.

'Missis said you walk. But don't you worry now, I carry all this,' he said cheerfully.

Luke looked taken aback, but said reassuringly to Katharine, 'It's not far.' He took her arm and she was glad for otherwise she would have fallen. Travelling had at least provided some sort of breeze. Here everything was stifling hot, as though time itself were suspended in this haze of heat and smoke. Her head reeled dizzily.

'It'll take you a day or two to get used to the altitude,' Luke told her. 'Then you'll be fine,' he said without conviction. 'Cloud City, they call Leadville, and the thin air does strange things to folk. These hills you see around you don't look high, but they are, because the town itself is over two miles high. Take it easy now. You'll be fine,' he repeated, glancing at her sickly yellow colour and the drab shadows under her eyes. Concern made him helpless. 'We'll be there soon,' he said, as they slowly followed Charlie who set off at a spanking pace back along the wide avenue. He was almost invisible under the piles of luggage carried on shoulders and arms.

'We're at the far end of Chestnut Street, set back, away from the noise.'

Away from the noise – could any place escape it in Leadville? The shouting and yelling in the streets, from the saloons, and the sounds of waggons, loaded with ore, and coaches, throbbed through her head.

'Here,' said Luke at last. Katharine looked up, less at what he said than at the sound of his voice which held a note of uncertainty that she had not heard before. Dismay seized her. What she had taken to be an austere public building was the Stowerton home. *Her* home. This dark house almost hidden by looming trees, built of brick with cold grey stone pillars, *home?* Its bricks were not warm and mellow like Bocton's, but made the house seem the more austere.

Making a supreme effort, she stirred leaden limbs that seemed too heavy to place one before the other, and walked up the path beside Luke. Ahead of her she could see three figures waiting, lined up like the fates. Like gaolers, it seemed to her tired eyes, dressed almost identically in high-necked tight black dresses, virtually unrelieved by lace or frills. The most dominant of them was a grey-haired figure whose hostility seemed tangibly to envelop her as she mounted the steps.

Katharine looked up at what lay ahead of her and the last shreds of her stamina faded. She tried to force her lips into a smile, for the woman must surely be Luke's mother, was aware of the frosty lips moving, then nothing else, as she swayed and fainted.

The room was pleasantly cool as Katharine opened her eyes. Leaning over her was a young black girl desultorily waving a huge fan back and forth. She jumped as she saw Katharine stir and immediately one of the younger two women she had seen waiting for her on the steps got up from her seat by the window.

'Are you still sick?' she asked timidly.

Katharine struggled to sit up but the effort was too much and she sank back into the pillows, and into the oblivion of sleep. But not for long, for what seemed like the next instant she was awakened by a tap on her shoulder and a trayful of what looked like beef pie, oozing with fatty gravy, was set in front of her.

'I'm sorry, I cannot eat it,' she tried to say.

'The Lord shall not suffer waste in my house, daughter.'

From her weakened position, Katharine stared up at her mother-in-law who had now taken her daughter's place, as nurse or wardress.

'What ails you? Are you with child?' Katharine stared at her aghast, unable to believe this gorgon of a woman could be Luke's mother. Why had he not warned her? Perhaps it was his maternal grandmother – no, surely not. Luke had said his mother had come from England on her marriage. This must be she; perhaps she was younger than she looked in that severe purple bombazine. Katharine had a moment's sympathy for the absent Jeremiah.

'No,' she replied dully, too weak even to protest at this outrageous question from a stranger, however closely related now.

'Then eat,' Augusta commanded. 'The Lord provideth and shall not be mocked.'

'I cannot. I –'

'*Eat!*'

'Momma, she does not want to,' the girl tried to say, having come back into the room.

Her mother ignored her. 'Eat.'

Hypnotised by her dark cold eyes, Katharine tried to eat a mouthful, then felt herself retching and choking on the horrible stuff. Still the voice bade her eat.

Then mercifully Luke appeared. Hot and weary though he was, trying to acclimatise himself to Leadville after over three months away, he took in the situation at a glance. 'Take it away, Eliza,' he told the help quietly.

'She will never breed strong sons for the Lord, my son, if you pamper her so.'

'She is my wife, Mother,' he said grimly. 'Mary, tell the kitchen to prepare some barley broth for Katharine, something light.'

His mother stared at him, at a loss to understand her son. 'If she is your wife, why does she not share your bed?' she finally demanded scornfully.

'Katharine is ill, Mother,' he answered flatly. 'And here she shall remain until she recovers.'

Until she recovers? Katharine lay still, unable to hold back tears of weakness. What did Luke mean? She felt like some trapped animal, waiting to know her fate at the hands of her captors. Where, oh where, was Katharine May Stowerton with her famous determination? When I get well, she told herself, when I get well, I will . . . Then I will . . . But before she could decide a course of action, she drifted off once more into hot, feverish sleep.

It was a week before she recovered her strength enough to come downstairs. This was her first ordeal. Outside lay another, that of Leadville itself. Slowly she descended the ornately carved wooden staircase that bragged of great riches. This was one of the grandest houses in Leadville, the first built of brick, Mary had told her with pride, not realising that, to Katharine, Bocton's bricks laid three hundred years ago were all that could impress her. She hesitated as she saw the family waiting for her, the mother, the two sisters – and Luke. All, it seemed, ranged against her. With head held high, she advanced towards them.

Luke wiped his forehead, which was running with sweat in the July heat, and listened to the sounds of money. Money in the making, money changing hands, with the continuous magic of silver. Outside in the streets, travelling salesmen and tricksters were intent on depriving miners of their money as speedily as possible; inside the stores cash changed hands with lightning rapidity. In his Harrison Avenue offices, handling the accounts of his father's empire built in little over a year, Luke too lived and dealt in money. Money made by his miners, by the assay office, the sampling office, the smelter – and because Jeremiah was canny, from other interests too. A bank, a saloon, a freighting company, a hotel. Some said a whorehouse, too, but if so the books did not show it. 'Take risks – and care' was Jeremiah's business maxim. Paupers became rich men overnight, but could as quickly be paupers again if luck went against them.

Luke had walked back into the situation he feared. Through absence, they had lost out on buying up a claim next to Father's best mine, the Bosworth; Father had a hunch about that claim. Moreover, the railroad had now arrived in Leadville which was ecstatic greeting this new chapter in its history. Riding in on the first train had come General Ulysses Grant himself, and Leadville was putting on its brightest face to welcome him with celebrations of all sorts and a new play at the Tabor Opera House, Robertson's *Ours*. Katharine might have enjoyed that, he thought suddenly, but, being ill, she was missing this sight of the town *en fête*.

Only the freighters, of whom he was one, had not rejoiced at the coming of the railroad. Up till now, freighters had been the kings of Leadville; no matter how much silver you mined, it had to be smelted, here or elsewhere. If elsewhere, the ore had to be freighted out to the railheads or direct to the smelters. If smelted here, coal had to be freighted in for Leadville had none of its own. Jeremiah disliked vying with competition, so he had bought his own smelter, and his own freighting business. Now the railroad was here, and the freighting business would be decimated. Men would be thrown out of work, their livelihood gone, and it would be he, Luke, who had to do it.

And then there was Smith. Perhaps every company had its Humphrey Smith, efficient, keeping the business running on a daily basis. Yet Luke didn't like him. He was a smooth-talking New Englander, come west to make money. Father gave him a generous salary, but somehow Luke suspected this was not enough. A man to be watched.

Then there were the mines, the heart of Jeremiah's fortune, and most of them were on Fryer Hill. Luke grinned despite himself. Now he knew how the Bosworth had got its name; his father must have a sense of humour somewhere after all. It had been a lucky day for Jeremiah when, as a financier, he had personally grubstaked those two hunks that turned up one day at his bank. The Bosworth mine yielded silver at 550 oz to the ton average, rising to as high as 8,021, and in the first three months of operation produced $485,000. In February this year the ore mined had brought in $305,262, beating the previous month's record set by the Robert E. Lee.

'As much chance of finding silver down there as of finding Richard III's jewels,' Jeremiah had told Luke when the hunks first set off with their grubstake of a few hundred dollars. Luke didn't know what he meant, and Father would not explain. After the hunks reported back their first slender finds, Jeremiah backed his sudden hunch and bought out their 50% share for $20,000. They were delighted – and Jeremiah was even more delighted. He bought up as many neighbouring claims as he could. All save this last vital claim that lay next to the Bosworth. It had gone to a Chicago businessman called White, Smith told him. And he wouldn't sell.

Twenty years back placer gold had been found in California Creek that ran past the site where Leadville now stood, but the placer gold taken from the surface was quickly exhausted and the hunt for gold by lode mining expensive. Most miners moved on to easier territory, although some stayed, determined to dig till they struck gold, or die where they were. Die they did, ignoring the lumps of black rock they threw out of the way. No gold in them, so they were worthless. Two miners spared a thought for them, however. They examined the black

141

rock, and, curious, took it to an assay office far away lest news get out in the camp – then called Slabtown. The black rock proved to be carbonate of lead and, more than that, it came from a silver-bearing lode. The silver content was only 15 oz to the ton, but where that silver was, there would be more – perhaps higher grade. The silver rush began quietly, but by '77 and '78 miners and would-be miners were swarming into the site, cabins springing up, service stores appearing to cater for their needs, followed by saloons and dance halls, growing at such a rate it had to be organised into a town. So in January 1878 prominent citizens got together and, in gratitude for the foundation of its fortunes, called the new town Leadville.

The town thrust forward with determination. It organised balls and entertainment, employed and employers grew further apart, society established itself, setting its rules and regulations. Money was hardly a criterion for in Leadville during those first crazy years everyone had money. Churches were established, and a school; sports and races were organised. Everything to tempt miners to come into town from their hillside camps to spend their money as soon as they made it exploded into being: saloons, whorehouses, gambling dens. Book stores, playhouses, and newspapers sprang up.

Leadville had a fascination about it, a momentum and a robustness that Katharine could not yet appreciate. All she could see now, Luke realised wrily, were the black and sulphur fumes. How he hated the other side of the coin; the rush, the hypocrisy that money brought with it. Even now he could hardly believe what had happened. Father, of all people, to run off with a whore. For that's what Daisy Petal was, he had gathered, for all her artistic pretensions to be a singer. Had Father changed or had he always been like that, lust and passion pent up with no outlet? He had been converted to hell-fire doctrines when he met Mother in England, that much Luke knew. Perhaps that had been his escape from the frustrations of his doomed feud with Robert? He began to comprehend, if not to sympathise, how it might have come about. Perhaps Father had needs that Mother did not fulfil, could not . . .

Caught unawares at where this thought took him, Luke felt a stirring in his body that reawakened him to the hopelessness of his own position. What the hell was he to do? What *could* he do? He could not rape her, he would not plead. A girl looked up from the street, saw him staring, and winked, as if to provide an answer. Perhaps it had been for Father. But for himself?

It was hard to endure the almost patent mockery of the town over his father's fall from grace, if not from grandeur. Jeremiah had been respected but hardly popular. His departure with Daisy Petal had been greeted with rapture by his foes, who saw a speedy end to his empire. That hadn't and wouldn't happen, as Luke traded on sympathy for his mother and sisters and his own popularity – for he was known for his writings for the *Leadville Chronicle*, exposing hard conditions and fraudulent dealings in the town.

Also a new scandal was creeping through Leadville, making Jeremiah yesterday's news. There were murmurs that Horace Tabor, erstwhile

142

mayor, present Lieutenant-Governor of Colorado, and the most popular (and richest) man in Leadville, was caught in the toils of one Elizabeth McCourt Doe, who had come to Leadville following her divorce to look after her future. 'Baby Doe' McCourt was after silver, so the stories went – and in particular the Silver King himself, Horace Tabor.

In desperation Katharine left the house despite Augusta's strict injction against going out alone. She had to be alone for a moment or two; she was stifled between the three of them. The smoky fumes of the smelters were easier to bear than Augusta's frosty disapproval, and Luke's sisters' slavish obedience to their mother's every whim. There were shops here she could walk round, and she could find Luke's office. Surely she could go there alone? It was only a few minutes' walk away, in Harrison Avenue, and that was at right-angles to Chestnut Street. She would find him, try to talk to him away from the house. She walked out on to Chestnut Street. She was gradually beginning to get used to the noise of Leadville, which continued twenty-four hours a day, in the streets in the daytime, and in the saloons and gambling dens at night. Noise without cease. At Bocton there was silence, save for the call of a nightingale or the shriek of an owl, the only light that from the moon. Here there was perpetual noise, and the harsh glare of electric lights from the saloons.

People crying out in loud broad accents, brawling and singing, overwhelmed her, and she began to feel dizzy again through the sheer pace of life humming around her. Wagonloads of ore trundled by throwing up dust faster than the squirt wagons could keep it down, and men swarmed everywhere. Most of the women were in pairs, she noticed uneasily, or in groups. Used as they were to strangers, the men fell silent as she walked past them, almost clearing a path for her, murmuring to one another. But one drunk lurching from a saloon fell across her path.

'Looking for a job? Down State Street, lady, that's where you want.'

She pushed by impatiently not knowing quite what he meant, though the general meaning was clear. Other men pulled him away. A lady was a lady, whether alone or not. She heard the word 'Stowerton' and a laugh. She took it to be about her, but in fact it was a snigger about Jeremiah. It was quickly shushed. The Stowertons were still a force to be reckoned with now that young Luke was back, and the new wife out from England must be treated respectfully.

Katharine turned into Harrison Avenue, stepping on to the wooden sidewalk, past a crockery store and a bookstore. Ignoring the temptation to linger, conscious of eyes on her, she hurried on past a clothing house, outside which she stumbled, missed a step when the level of the wooden sidewalk dropped six inches between stores and tumbled over. Feeling more foolish than hurt, as she quickly rearranged her skirts, she got to her feet shakily, helped by a better dressed man than the rest, with shifty eyes.

'You hurt, ma'am?' he asked unctuously.

'No, I –' She was conscious of a gathering audience. She rubbed her eyes, which were stinging from smoke fumes. 'Could you tell me – my husband's office?' she blurted out.

'Why surely, ma'am. Not far at all.' It was only after they had set off that she realised she had not told him who her husband was. She did not need to. The man was Humphrey Smith, manager of the Stowerton empire.

'What on earth are you doing here, Katharine?' Luke greeted her none too warmly. He cast a grim eye on her companion, but managed to thank him before he disappeared smugly into a neighbouring office. 'Are you hurt?' seeing her examine grazed wrists.

'No, I came out to see Leadville.'

'And now you've seen it,' he said abruptly. 'What possessed you to come on your own without Mary or Martha, or at least one of the helps? Didn't my mother tell you –'

'I *wanted* to come alone. Anyway, no one accosted me. Everyone was polite.' She skipped over the drunk.

'They would be. Women get treated well here. When they deserve it.'

She took this as a reproof, which it was not intended to be, and answered angrily: 'Am I not permitted to talk to my husband alone? We're *never* alone.'

'We're hardly alone here,' he said quietly, and she dropped her voice.

'At the house your sisters and your mother are always around. I never see you,' she began desperately.

'You can move into our bedroom,' he remarked devastatingly, looking straight at her. 'You're well now, Katharine,' trying to keep his voice steady.

She gulped, taken aback. 'I thought we agreed –'

'That was Bocton, not here.' He forced himself to appeal to her. 'You have to do this,' he said reasonably. 'Do you expect me to be shamed in front of my mother and my sisters?'

So that was all he cared about. He didn't want her for herself, only to preserve his pride before his mother and sisters. Was this the happy companion of London, the man who had cared for her so tenderly on the way over? How could she share a bedroom with this grim-eyed stranger? Would he not expect . . .

As if reading her thoughts, he tried to say lightly: 'I'll endeavour to keep a naked sword between us.' Now even she could see despair in his eyes, was tempted to run to him, but her pride held her back. This smoky heat, the dizziness. He didn't want her. Not as he had Meg. He had told her so. So what did it matter?

'Very well,' she said dully.

He sighed. 'I'll take you home,' was all he said.

Home? Home was Bocton, not here. Tears stung at her eyes, but she would not let them fall.

144

'Is there nowhere I can go,' she asked desperately, 'while you are working? No work that I can do?'

At that he smiled, though without warmth. 'I fear Leadville would consider it strange indeed if you entered the building trade.'

'I'm serious,' she said angrily.

He flushed. 'Do what other women do,' he answered shortly. 'Be company for my sisters, help at the church with charity work. There are teas, I believe,' he said vaguely. 'The women meet. Dances. Do what women do in England.' He knew it was a weak response. Katharine was not 'other women'. 'There are nice places near Leadville,' he added consolingly. 'Green places. Woods and valleys. I could take you on a picnic.'

'A picnic?' She began to laugh wildly. 'That would be nice,' she said, trying to keep sarcasm from her voice and failing.

'Dammit, Katharine,' he burst out, 'I could take you to Denver, to Colorado Springs, to Manitou – but what's the use? You have to find the answer yourself. Now, let's get back home.'

'Very well,' she said listlessly, as they stepped out into the hot glare of the street once more, the noise doubling, seemingly mockingly, as they did so. Clothing stores, gun stores, offices, banks, saloons, coaches, wagons, dust from the ground and smoke from the air. All these met her eye. 'Which way I fly am hell,' she thought, remembering her Milton bitterly. 'Myself am Hell.' She nearly stumbled again, in the depth of despair. As Luke held her upright, her attention was drawn to a building on the other side of the road, tall, imposing, built of brick.

'What's that?' she asked, pointing.

'What? Oh, the new Tabor Opera House,' he answered.

'Opera House?' she repeated, dumbfounded. '*Opera* House?' She began to laugh hysterically. 'Like Covent Garden?' Faces turned to look at them.

Luke quickly shushed her. 'No, not quite like Covent Garden, I guess. It means more than straight opera here. They have shows, plays, travelling concerts, all sorts of things. Most mining towns have them. This is the biggest and grandest, I reckon, but there are a few others in town too. The Tabor has shows coming from all over – New York, London, France. Are you interested?' He looked at her with sudden hope. 'I'll take you some night. It's not,' he hesitated, 'not quite what you'd call a London audience, but it's better here than at the others in town.'

Katharine had ceased to listen. The idea of the Opera House held her like a magnet, a sign that she was not entirely in an alien land. It signified in some small measure that there was a means of escape.

'It was built by Horace Tabor, Father's big rival,' Luke was telling her.

'Who?' she asked.

'Made his money in Leadville. Nowadays he lives mostly in Denver since he's lieutenant-governor, but spends time here as well. Lives in West Fifth Street. He had a house on Harrison here, but upped and

145

moved it so he could build the Opera House. He and his wife didn't have two dollars between them before they came to Leadville. They first arrived in Denver in the '59 rush, in a wagon complete with their baby. His wife – another Augusta incidentally –' (he didn't mention there were other similarities between the two women, such as their bitterness) '– kept them going in Denver by taking in boarders and laundry while he ran a store. He tried his hand at grubstaking, not very successfully. Not till they came here at the beginning of the rush. There wasn't a town here then of course, so they set up a post office and bank, and Horace went on grubstaking. One day he grubstaked Rische and Hook with food and shovels to dig at what's now the Little Pittsburg – and that was that. They never looked back. The Tabor Opera House is the biggest and best in Leadville and maybe in the whole of Colorado, and Augusta no longer takes in lodgers.'

A group of about five men burst from a saloon, thrown out by the owner; they picked themselves up, and re-started the fight.

'Gambling,' said Luke succinctly, 'probably caught cheating.'

She glanced into the packed building. Gambling? In a trice she was back at Bocton seeing Father, in his smoking jacket with the patched elbows, reading the *Pink 'Un*.

'On horses?' she asked unsteadily.

'Cards. Travelling card sharpers go round the mining towns. Had a couple here two years back, Doc Holliday and Bat Masterson. They left. We've been pretty lucky since. Not too many shootings.'

An Opera House in the midst of this wildness? She shivered. Its very incongruity would draw her if nothing else.

Meg was unhappier than she had ever been in her life before. She found herself unexpectedly missing Katharine, for the simple reason that she was totally unused to and unfit for housekeeping, and relations between herself and her father had therefore deteriorated sharply. Having offended Maggie to the point where she left in tears for her father's cottage, she was forced to go cap in hand to beg her to return, in order that they might at least eat.

Sophy wisely avoided calling at the Dower House, determined that Meg should learn, if only by bitter experience.

The main reason for Meg's distress, however, had nothing to do with housekeeping or her sister's absence. It had to do with the fact that, having blithely lied to Katharine about expecting a baby, Meg was now some weeks later forced to realise that it was indeed all too likely to be true. Panic took over. To whom could she go? Father? Even Meg realised this was impossible. Aunt Sophy? Meg shrank from this step. She had never been close to Sophy, not like Katharine, and though her aunt would undoubtedly help, Meg was not at all sure, even in the midst of her panic, that she wanted Aunt Sophy's kind of help. It was likely to be generous but essentially unsympathetic. Only one person could be relied upon to understand her: Mother.

Immediately she had fastened on this one indisputable fact, everything became simpler. After all, Mother was living in Paris. Mother could write to Louis and explain and he would then most certainly marry Meg. However, Meg had a cautious side too: hand in hand with her romantic imaginings, fuelled by the works of Lady Wittisham, went a niggling but ineradicable thought: What if he doesn't? However, that too was simple. Mother would know what to do. The only problem to be resolved was how best to reach Mother. She would write to say she wanted to come on a visit. Father need not know till after it was done. Full of enthusiasm at this straightforward plan, she closeted herself in her bedroom, completely forgetting that it was her turn to dig the potatoes. Maggie, with a grim sigh, left her other chores to undertake the task herself. She looked at Katharine's carefully tended gardens, and wept for her out there in a foreign land. Who would tend the gardens now? Maggie decided that she would. She could get her younger brother to help; he wanted to be a farmer and it was high time he started. Whether Miss Katharine came back to Bocton or not, she would like to know that her gardens were not being forgotten.

Up in her room Meg was busily scribbling an artlessly worded letter, which with rare devotion to daily exercise she took into a neighbouring village to post lest Mr Brown at the post office saw the address and word reached Father. Meg then dismissed the matter from her mind – in which she now considered the other small problem solved.

Katharine woke up, remembered where she was and glanced at the other side of the huge bed. Luke had already gone. Instantly she suffered again from the mixed emotions of the night before. Had she been disappointed that after kissing her on the forehead, he had merely climbed into bed on her other side, turning away from her? No need of naked swords here, she thought wrily. That was what she had wanted, wasn't it? She had lain awake from some time, stiff and tense from the strangeness of having him so close, lying in the same bed. They might have been in different continents, so much lay unspoken between them. Every nerve had been aware of his presence. She had finally drifted off to sleep then woken again, disturbed by the sound of breathing at her side; she had turned to look at him, his face smooth in sleep, a lock of his fair hair fallen over his eyes, one arm thrown out over the thin sheet that covered them. How vulnerable he looked, how young.

For a moment she wanted to take him in her arms, to hold him; then he opened his eyes and stared straight at her without a sign of recognition. He held her glance for a moment with no condemnation in his eyes, no desire – just a blank look. Then he turned from her and soon deep rhythmic breathing proclaimed that he was asleep again. Had she wanted him to turn to her, insist on her love, to take her in his arms as he had that day at Bocton, overriding her objections? To love her – *as he had Meg*. The sickening thought thudded in upon her, killing all doubt in her mind.

Mechanically she got up, washing in the water that had been brought some time previously. Water was precious here, Luke had told her. It had to be paid for, expensively. It wasn't like England where it flowed disregarded, this precious asset. 'You'll have enough,' he said offhandedly. 'Water flows towards money, they say here, and in Leadville there's money.'

And much of it in this house. The house itself proclaimed money, outside and in, but only the house. Mary and Martha wore no diamonds as other Leadville girls, had no New York fashions; the Stowerton table bore little sign of the elegant fare their income could have afforded – the food was strictly of the Pilgrim Fathers' simplicity. Simplicity would have been acceptable, thought Katharine, as she ploughed through yet another tough mutton chop, if this wasn't just plain badly cooked. Perhaps she could plant some herbs, some fruit. There must be fruit in Colorado? But her flame of interest was quickly extinguished as she saw Augusta's eye on her, as if reading her thoughts.

'We take no heed for food in this house, daughter,' she explained almost kindly for her. 'The Lord provideth.'

'Amen,' said Martha quickly.

Martha was the leader of the two, insofar as there could be one under Augusta's strict eye, Katharine realised. Mary looked to her elder sister for guidance in how to behave to this strange person in their midst. Leadville was used to foreigners; almost every nationality was represented, so far had news of the silver had spread. 'There's even a group of miners from Cornwall. That's in England.'

'Yes, but Cornwall is a long way from Kent,' Katharine had replied.

'How far?' Mary wanted to know.

'About,' she calculated, 'three hundred miles.'

They seemed surprised. 'It's two thousand to New York,' they pointed out, 'and we've been *there*.'

Impossible to explain that everything seemed on a different scale here, that landscape changed in ten miles in England more than in perhaps ten times that distance in America. There were so many other differences too.

'What do you do all day?' she asked Mary, seeing her sitting in the parlour empty-handed; not even sewing or reading a magazine. 'Do you never think of making a garden here?'

'Garden?' Mary looked puzzled. 'There's no room in Leadville for gardens.'

'There's at least two hundred feet at the rear,' said Katharine, puzzled. 'Just barren earth.'

'Oh, you mean the back yard. You think we should plant some trees there?'

'Grass, flowers, herbs.'

They absorbed the idea slowly. 'We could get the help to do it,' said Martha.

'No, yourselves,' said Katharine desperately. 'Us. We'll do it together.'

'Flowers are but vanity, Katharine,' Augusta's reproving voice thundered from the doorway.

'Herbs are not,' she said defiantly. 'We can use them in our food.'

Augusta dismissed this. 'Ornaments.'

'Medicine,' said Katharine firmly. 'Herbs are the basis of medicine.'

Augusta looked horrified. 'Black culture,' she said. 'Not in a home devoted to the Lord. If you seek work, do the Lord's work, Katharine. Spread the gospel.'

'You are right,' said Katharine demurely, provokingly. 'I shall go to the mines tomorrow to do just that.'

'The mines? You must never, never –'

'Where else would you have me preach, Mother? In State Street?'

'No!' Augusta's face turned white at this effrontery.

'You mean the men are dangerous?'

'Not to respectable women,' said Martha with a gasp, seeing her mother on the verge of an explosion.

'Then why should I not go?'

'This is a law-abiding house,' replied Augusta tonelessly, eyes glittering. 'You would be taken as a daughter of Satan. All Englishwomen are known for their loose ways. And now you lead my daughters into immoral ways.'

'But are you not English yourself? Did you not meet Uncle Jeremiah in Kent?'

A deep red flush that might have been embarrassment at mention of her errant husband, or might have been anger, suffused her cheeks.

'I am an American, daughter,' she said vehemently.

'I am not your daughter,' said Katharine quietly, desperately, hemmed into a corner by her own impetuosity, praying Luke would never hear about this, wondering how he had existed in this prison if Uncle Jeremiah too was like Augusta. How could Luke with his light-hearted ways, his love of travel, of writing, be a child of this household? For the first time since arriving in Leadville she began to think about him rather than herself. He was forced to run the mine; whatever he had intended to do with his life had been put behind him now. He was forced into a situation over which he had no control, as she was herself. Yet this was not her family, but his. And I am his wife, her conscience reminded her.

'Why did you come back, Luke?' she asked him in despair that evening, hoping for a common bridge. But again her effort was doomed.

'I had no choice,' he said shortly. 'And you, Katharine, must do your best to conform.'

She flushed. 'Conform?' she asked incredulously. 'Bible reading three times a day? Visiting worthy ladies as dull as –' She bit off 'your sisters', but the inference was clear. 'Can I do no *good* here?'

Luke sighed. 'You can do most good by keeping out of trouble.'

'You cannot order me to –'

'I can,' he said quietly. 'And I do.' Had she not promised, she recollected dazedly as he hurled this at her, to love, honour and obey? Could she truthfully answer she did anything of those things for this silent, grim man, who bore little resemblance now to Gabriel Arch?

149

Luke changed his tone, almost pleading. 'You will pay due respect to my mother while we are in her house, and do your best to make my sisters' lives more interesting within – I repeat, *within* – the bounds of the accepted behaviour of Leadville ladies.'

'The ones in State Street?' she enquired, icily sweet.

He glared at her. 'Many of them have a better idea of womanly qualities than you, Katharine.'

She gasped. 'So you know them, like your father?' she shot at him, not really meaning it, but lashing out furiously.

'Could you blame me?' he flashed back and, as she reddened, 'Katharine, I ask little of you save that you conform to what is expected of you as my wife – save in one respect, naturally,' he added ironically. 'And just keep *quiet*.'

The carriage drew up at the door and French perfume mingled with that of the late roses, bedraggled and unkempt without Katharine's restraining care, as Elizabeth Stowerton picked her dainty way along the brick path to the front door of the Dower House. Meg, looking from the parlour window, had beaten Maggie to it; she opened the door and threw herself into her mother's arms.

'You've come, you've come!' she sobbed.

'Darling,' said Elizabeth Stowerton reprovingly. She understood her daughter very well, despite her short acquaintance with her, and knew that something besides love for her mother had been behind Meg's letter. Elizabeth Stowerton, beneath the surface vagueness, was an astute woman. She simply patted her daughter comfortingly.

'And now,' she enquired briskly, 'where is dearest Alfred?'

Dearest Alfred, having heard the familiar voice with horror, was busily fleeing through the French windows down the garden path in the hope of reaching the orchard and losing himself on the Bocton estate before he had to wrestle with what was undoubtedly going to be a problem.

'Alfred!' Elizabeth's voice penetrated the evening air, its husky cadences sending a shiver through him. 'Do come here.'

Caught, he obediently turned to face her as she strode down the path, skirts flapping. 'I thought it would be nice, Alfred, if I took Meg back to Paris with me on a little holiday.'

'No,' he cried without thinking. Then he considered again how trying life was under Meg's management. Perhaps if she had a few weeks away, he might manage very well with just Maggie looking after him. 'What an excellent idea,' he decreed thankfully. 'Er – who will pay?' he enquired delicately.

'I will, naturally, Alfred,' said Elizabeth. 'Klaus is so generous,' she added meaningfully.

'So was I,' he said hurt.

'Only when you won,' Elizabeth reminded him. 'That *was* a drawback, you know, Alfred.'

'I'd have won more often if you hadn't gone,' he said sulkily, remembering for once the starlit nights with Elizabeth in his arms, her husky laughter and enchanting ways; then remembering the temperament, the flashing eyes, the whole house revolving around Elizabeth.

'Oh, come, Alfred,' she patted his cheek. 'You wouldn't want me back, would you?'

'No,' he said regretfully. 'No.'

'Good. Then why don't you give me a divorce?'

'Blast you, Elizabeth,' he yelled, falling into her trap. '*No*! No divorces.'

She sighed. 'Oh, very well.'

The Château des Roses was on the outskirts of Paris near St Germain. Meg thought it quite wonderful. The baron was charming, they had lots of rich friends, and dances galore, with Meg admired as the beautiful English rose. She almost forgot why she had come. If this was the upshot of an immoral life, she reasoned, then it certainly had its recommendations.

Elizabeth, however, was not to be put off. 'Tell me, my daughter,' she asked innocently in the midst of a session with Madame Nerissa the milliner, 'why you wished to come.'

'To see you, Mother.' Meg idly twisted her head one way and another to see the effect in the mirror.

'Are you pregnant?' enquired Elizabeth.

Madame Nerissa's hands trembled for a moment.

'Really, Mother!' Meg was more outraged at the use of the forbidden word than at having the initiative wrested from her.

'You're not?'

Meg cast an agonised look at the milliner.

'What is the matter, darling? Madame Nerissa is almost an old family friend.' The hand trembled again. This was news to Madame Nerissa.

'Yes, I think I am expecting,' whispered Meg uncertainly.

'Oh?' Elizabeth pulled a face. 'Don't you think, Meg dearest, you had better tell me all about it?' she suggested resignedly. 'After all, that is what mothers are for.'

Somewhat shamefaced, Meg told her.

Elizabeth's face was a picture. 'Louis? Albert's son?' she shrieked.

'Mother, you're laughing,' said Meg indignantly. 'How could you! I'm so unhappy,' she pouted.

'I'm sorry, darling, it's just so funny. What would your father say? And poor, *poor* Albert.'

Meg tried to maintain her own seriousness, but failed, and joined her mother in laughing. Suddenly she stopped, as she remembered her problem was all too real. 'But, Mother,' she wailed, 'what am I to do? He wouldn't marry me when he'd just ruined me, so why should he now? He's a profligate, a rake, a degenerate.'

'Oh, not a degenerate, my dear. Hardly that!' Elizabeth snorted with indignant laughter.

'It's no use your saying he'll have to marry me, because he won't –
I'll be ruined.'

'Do you love him?' Elizabeth enquired romantically.

Meg thought quickly of Louis, and of the answer most likely to
appeal to her mother. 'Yes,' she said soulfully.

Elizabeth smiled mysteriously. 'Then I think I have a little plan.'
And she proceeded to explain it to Meg, whose eyes grew rounder and
rounder.

Appalled at the depths to which relations had sunk between herself
and Luke, Katharine did her best to bring about an uneasy truce with
Augusta and improve relations with Mary and Martha. But the latter
was hard work. Any conversation other than that relating to everyday
living met with little response and gradually Katharine came to live
her daily life on their terms. No more was said about a garden. She
endeavoured to help in charity work, visiting the families of sick and
injured miners, carefully chaperoned. The endless round of Bible
readings and afternoon visits continued, until Katharine mutinously
thought that if she had been Jeremiah she would have left much sooner.
She wished him well with Daisy Petal Garden, wherever they might
be, and however 'unfortunate' a woman Daisy Petal was. Though with
Uncle Jeremiah's millions to spend, unfortunate, many might say, was
hardly the word.

Luke endeavoured to study the zig-zag graphs of the yield of Bosworth
and the other Stowerton mines. Figures, figures . . . trying to make
sense of them, work out if there were a pattern to them, if downward
turns were ominous or merely routine. No use. Today the figures
merely danced before his eyes.

He buried his head in his hands. No rest at home, no rest in the
office. No haven. No wife. No Katharine. How could he blame her?
Seeing her here amid his family, she was a symbol of what he and
his sisters had missed all their lives; her presence, unbeknown to
her, threw it into sharp relief. With her glowing chestnut hair,
and her light, bright dresses, she was a candle by whose light
the rest of the household seemed cast into even greater darkness
than before. And, he was forced to realise, he was blaming her
for it. He could not continue like this, sleeping in the same bed,
distanced by misunderstanding, by abstinence. Yet how in present
conditions could he woo her back to him – if his she had ever been,
he thought bitterly. The wooing of Katie May – how long ago that
seemed, and yet it was not even three months. Was he really that
man who had laughed and wooed in the Bocton gardens? It was he
who had changed, not she. The tragedy was that she remained the
girl he'd first seen crawling in that window backside first. She was
more honest than he, for she had not changed, and perhaps could not
do so, to adapt to these new demands on her. The wooing of Katie
May . . .

*   *   *

Katharine watched Luke at supper, concerned. He said little, was very pale and seemed to avoid her eye. Finally, in between trying to cope with tough fried chicken, she spoke out. 'You look worried, Luke. Is something worrying you at the mines?'

He looked at her, startled at this unexpected – and unusual – enquiry. Mine discussions were usually reserved for Augusta and himself after supper. Katharine had always refused to join in as an unwanted third, as she put it. Even now, Augusta began to speak, to block her daughter-in-law's encroachment onto her territory.

'Yes,' he said, cutting across his mother, 'the smelter is failing. Now the railroad is here, so much more ore is being shipped out instead of being smelted here. We're not competitive.'

'Can you not lower your prices,' Katharine asked hesitantly, 'to attract more trade?'

'We could,' agreed Luke, 'but even that might not solve it, since production is still down after the strike.' That was something else he'd missed in the summer – the miners' strike, a bitter hardfought wrangle that ought to have been foreseen and forestalled, for it was no true strike but one planned on deliberately planted false rumours. Bosworth had suffered though not as badly as most mines since they paid their miners at the top rate, but it had not been easy to gear up the mines again to produce at full capacity. Other mines had fared less well, and much bitterness lingered on.

Luke looked away again and began talking to Augusta. Katharine thought it yet another reproof, but it was not. Luke could not bear to look at her any longer. This evening she seemed so determined to flout the darkness of the house in an unusually low off-the-shoulder chiffon cream bodice over a brocade skirt of the same colour, her chestnut hair in curls, against her skin the garnet necklace he had bought for her on their honeymoon. Honeymoon . . .

In their bedroom that evening, Luke stood at the window gazing out over the dark of Leadville, shivering slightly in his short nightshirt. He did not turn to look at Katharine as she slipped the lawn and lace nightdress over her head and climbed into bed, exclaiming, as she always did, at the puritan hardness of the mattress. He did not join her.

'Luke,' she eventually asked, puzzled, 'are you still worrying about the smelter?'

At that his shoulders shook slightly and he turned. 'No,' he said simply, but still did not move, watching her in the dim light of the oil lamp, her skin warm from its soft glow. What she read in his eyes made her tremble slightly, not in retreat but that it had come so unexpectedly, the moment she had instinctively guessed would face her shortly. Now that it had come, she found herself relieved, unable to remember now quite how this had come about in the first place, and wanting only to be over this first immense step.

'Katharine, I –'

He had not called her Katie May. Had she been wrong about what he was trying to ask? She swung her legs from the bed again, and saw his eyes fall on her bare legs and feet. 'I should never have asked it of you,' she said softly. 'I never wanted to, not myself.'

Luke did not ask himself what she meant; he forgot her words, if he even heard them; he only realised that miraculously, astoundingly, without his pleading, without his wooing, she was coming to him. He took her in his arms, kissed again the lips for which he'd hungered for so many weeks, and as she began to relax in his arms, gently, firmly, removed the nightdress then the nightshirt that lay between them.

Chapter Nine

What had she expected? To recapture that bliss she had felt in his arms on a summer's day in the orchard? Was it only weeks ago? Now it had gone for ever, extinguished by the knowledge that it had not been for her alone. It had been for Meg too, perhaps for any woman he lightly took, for pleasure and not for love. Last night Luke had not told her he loved her; he had been considerate, gentle, patient. In the height of passion he had called out her name over and over; after he had withdrawn he had held her close, but still said nothing. As his face brushed hers, she felt the wetness of a tear, but whether it was his, or hers, she could not tell.

Katharine lay awake staring into the dark of the night long after he had fallen asleep, aware that of Luke himself she knew no more. It had brought them but a little way closer together. Perhaps it was the effect of living in this terrible house?

She asked him diffidently the following evening if they could not have a home of their own? He answered her briefly, impatiently. 'What's the point?' unable to explain even to himself that to provide a home of their own, which would be simple enough, however much his mother might protest, would seem to him a capitulation to the stark truth that he might have to stay here for ever, running his father's business. By living in his mother's home he could manage to survive, treating it as a temporary measure till another solution could be found.

Now another problem confronted him. Suppose Katharine should conceive? This was no place for children. 'We'll make sure we have no baby here,' he told her. He meant it to be consoling, knowing she felt as he did about the house, yet she did not see it as such. In a moment she was back at Bocton hearing Meg's tearful whining voice: 'He doesn't like children. That's why he won't marry me. He doesn't want the responsibility.'

'Yes,' she replied now to Luke, sick at heart. 'That would be best.'

Was there no way out? he wondered desperately, seeing her stricken look but not understanding the reason. Was he being unfair to her, denying her children, if she wanted them now? Perhaps it was the answer, for her at least. No. When he and Katharine had children they would be born not in this cold mansion, not in the hurly-burly of Leadville's silver craze. After all, they wouldn't be here for very long. Father would find some other solution, or he would himself.

It was not long, however, before bleakly he faced the truth. At the moment there was little chance of escape. He knew it the moment he walked through the door of their splendid Denver house on Broadway and saw Father with Daisy Petal Garden.

Father? Was this really Jeremiah Stowerton? Was there not a lightness about his face, a lack of shadow in his deep dark eyes that made him at first glance almost unrecognisable? Sitting by his side, rising hesitantly, almost shy, was presumably Daisy Petal. But where was the scarlet whore of Babylon his mother had depicted? Certainly not in this almost demure-looking girl. Luke's first reaction was envy, envy at the evident ease and pleasure they had in each other's company. Father stood protectively partly behind her, not touching, but both of them every inch aware of the other's presence. She was much shorter than he, slightly plump, full-figured, and with a softness of face and figure that made her look defenceless. Yet how could she be? Was she not a travelling singer? The colour of her bright blue dress spoke of the stage, but its modest lines did not. And her face was almost plain by comparison with Katharine's.

'I'm delighted to meet you, Miss Garden,' Luke said warmly, spontaneously.

At once her face lit up and he saw the attraction Daisy Petal held for Father – for any man, come to that. A roguish smile, eyes sparkling, a turn of the head as she glanced happily at Jeremiah . . . that first intrigued, then captivated.

'Didn't I say, Jer, if he was your son, I guess I'd like him?' she announced in a New York accent. 'I'm mighty glad to meet you, Mr Stowerton. Now, I reckon you boys would like to talk, so I'll be moving home, Jer.' She hesitated, then gave her hand to Luke as regally as a queen. He kissed it.

'Don't you –' He stopped.

'Live here?' she helped him. 'Bless you, no. Jer wouldn't have it. My reputation, he said, didn't you, Jer? Not till . . .' She clapped her hand over her mouth and went red.

'Daisy Petal,' reproved Jeremiah indulgently.

'I'm awful sorry, Jer. I didn't mean to.'

Not till what? thought Luke, puzzled. Then he realised with sinking heart what she had been going to say: not till they were married.

'Does Mother know your plans?' he asked abruptly once Daisy Petal had left.

Jeremiah fidgeted with his albert watch chain. His very silence told Luke what he wanted to know.

'She'll never agree,' Luke continued flatly, 'and you have no grounds. Do you – do you have to marry her?' aware that he was being crude.

'No, I don't have to, Luke,' said Jeremiah placidly. 'But I'm going to.' He clasped his hands behind his back. 'You wouldn't understand – or perhaps you would, being married yourself now. It's mighty different than a jelly-roll on Saturday night.'

Luke stared at his father in disbelief. *Father?* Moralistic, upright

Father to use such words? And not, it occurred to him, as though they were anything new. There was a thought here to be grappled with, but not now, not when he needed to get to know this stranger before him.

'You're thinking I've lost my senses, forgotten my God-fearing ways, aren't you, Luke?' Jeremiah smiled grimly, reading his thoughts. 'Well, I ain't. Not altogether. They're just showing up in different colours, that's the way of it.'

'They're certainly different,' said Luke slowly. 'But God-fearing? You haven't asked me how Mother is. You don't answer her letters.'

'Don't open them,' said Jeremiah succinctly. 'No point.' Luke began to speak, but Jeremiah cut across him: 'And before you go telling me, Luke, that she stood by me in the early days, worked her fingers to the bone until we struck it rich, you can tell her she'll never lack for money, not from me.'

'Is that all?' said Luke scornfully. 'Only money?'

'Ain't no such thing as "only money", not where wives are concerned, Luke. Daisy Petal now, she's different. But most of 'em, "only money" is what they want.'

Luke went white. Katharine? Not her. Then he remembered Bocton and The Case. She wanted money for both.

'Does the girl know why you came back?' Jeremiah asked him bluntly.

'No,' replied Luke coldly.

Jeremiah cackled, a sound so strange coming from him that Luke was taken aback. 'Only way I could do it, boy. I had to have you back. Couldn't stay on in Leadville myself – town wouldn't hold both Augusta and Daisy Petal.' He paused. 'You make sure you're winning, Luke. No other way with the Stowertons.'

'Like you and Robert? Did you win – or are you still fighting?' Luke continued, angry at this intrusion into his affairs.

Jeremiah's eyes flickered, his face darkened. 'You'll win that case, Luke, won't you?'

'I've got the documents for you to sign your assent,' he said, pulling them out of his case.

Jeremiah stared at them. 'Will we win it?' he asked abruptly.

'The solicitors think we have a good chance.'

'Millicent. How was Millicent? Fat, I'll be bound. Always on the plump side.'

'She's well,' said Luke, puzzled.

'Married Robert and not me,' said Jeremiah briefly. 'Make sure you win that case. I'd like to get even with Robert. That would show him, eh? Gavelkind!' He cackled again. 'Out here you buy, you sell, you build a house. Next day you have it picked up and move it somewhere else. It's not for ever. Not like Bocton. Land here's for digging in, not camping on.' He paused. 'It's good to see you, Luke. Maybe we didn't talk enough in the past. You'll be at our wedding?'

'There won't be a wedding, Father. Mother will never agree to a divorce, never.'

157

'She'll have to. She won't get no money otherwise,' said Jeremiah forthrightly.

'But you said you'd never leave her without money.'

'So I won't, if she sees reason.'

'And if not? If she won't divorce you?' Luke asked with foreboding.

Jeremiah looked at him, calculating. 'You'd have to support her, Luke. Go into business on your own account, buy up claims. Now's the time. Can't go wrong. Everything you touch is silver.'

Enmeshed in a trap, Luke fought the tentacles being wound around him. Buy mines of his own? Become an owner, not a manager? Never. But the alternative was to persuade his mother to be divorced, so that Father would continue her allowance. But how could he in honour do so?

'I can't do it,' he said angrily. 'But I'm not going into the mining business on my own account.'

His father shrugged blandly, confidently. 'I'll still ask her for the divorce, and if she refuses she can starve.'

'I'll stop running your business,' Luke flung at him.

'Then these papers go unsigned,' said Jeremiah.

The Case. The damned Case. A split second decision to be made. One on which the rest of his life – and Katharine's – depended.

'Do it,' Luke threw at him, calculating.

Jeremiah's eyes narrowed, staring at the papers, saying nothing.

'I thought so,' said Luke, not triumphantly, for there was precious little triumph here. 'It's still you and Robert, isn't it?'

There was no answer, no need of one. For Luke was right. Still the old need for revenge, as sharp as ever. With an exclamation of fury, Jeremiah picked up his pen, dipped it in the inkstand and signed. 'I won't give up Daisy Petal, Luke,' he said grimly. 'No matter what. Divorce or no, I won't be returning to your mother. A man needs a woman,' he said, almost to himself. 'A woman he can trust.'

The words echoed unceasingly in Luke's mind on his way back from Denver by the new railroad. A roundabout journey, but worth it for the comfort compared with the stage-coach as well as for the spectacular scenery at the foot of the Canyon by the Arkansas River. But on his return journey he had little thought for the wonders of nature. A woman to trust . . . Katharine, he thought, he *knew*, was his woman to trust – and yet they were further apart now than ever. He just did not understand what had gone wrong, and back in Leadville he was too depressed, too tired to try. But somehow he must force himself to bridge the gap between them. He had thought there was only the one way. So he had buried his pride, demanded of Katharine what he had thought never to ask, yet found himself still dissatisfied.

This wasn't how I meant it to be, he tried to say to her. There's more. But the words would not come, could not come. How he meant it to be was part of a dream that could not now come true. Perhaps, when this crazy headlong rush for silver was over, they would find somewhere in the vast promise of America as lovely as Bocton; perhaps even return to Bocton itself; or travel the rest of the world – one day, when he was not chained, a Prometheus to his rock.

Meanwhile he made few demands on Katharine; only on occasions when he could stand the loneliness no more did he turn to her, with quick muttered words almost of apology that made him as miserable as she, as Meg's quick-silver loveliness invaded their bed in her imagination. Only occasionally with his hands on her body did Katharine sense the yearning inside him, but before she could respond it was gone again and he was in his far-off land where she could not reach him – or he return to her.

Luke seemed to Katharine, as August wore on, more remote than ever, preoccupied after his return from Denver and with little time for her. He greeted impatiently her request to see the Bosworth mine. 'It won't be like Bocton,' he told her drily.

'I'd like to see it,' she reiterated stubbornly. Why she hardly knew, except that if this were Luke's daily life, she might in some way get closer to him by understanding what went on.

As the trap reached the camp, however, she knew it was a false hope. Barren hillsides, cabins, mine workings, dust and more dust; groups of men, dirty, bearded, uninterested even in the unexpected arrival of a woman, only bedazzled by one thing – silver. After the bitter strike that summer, Luke explained, the men were only now getting fully back to work. In Leadville all miners did well – only eight hours a day for three dollars, not the more usual ten-hour day, and Bosworth paid three dollars fifty.

'Why is it called Fryer Hill?' Katharine asked brightly, determined not to reveal how different this reality was to what she had imagined.

'After George Fryer who first found carbonates here when he sank a shaft at the New Discovery claim. North of Stray Horse Gulch, that is.'

She laughed. 'Stray Horse Gulch! What a name.'

'No different from your Burnt Mills and Waterditch Farms, I guess,' he said. 'People name places after what happens there. Like Bocton and Bugley – didn't you say that was after some Saxon woman?'

'Bucge, yes.'

'There you are then. No different from Fryer.'

'Bocton is older. It's history.'

'So is this, Katharine,' he said quietly. 'This is history in the making.'

But to her it was a collection of dusty, dilapidated wooden huts and mining equipment, and try as she would she could see no romance here. Nothing worth fighting for.

'That mine down there,' Luke pointed, 'that's the Chrysolite – used to be the richest mine till this year. Now it's dropped and given way to the Robert E. Lee and Bosworth. The Chrysolite, the Little Eva and Kit Carson are all Tabor mines. And he owned the Little Pittsburg over there.' He pointed. 'But he's sold out. Just in time. It's worked out.

The Carboniferous was his too – these are all the mines that won Tabor his fortune. Fryer Hill has the richest ore deposits in Leadville, and all because a grocery store owner grubstaked those German shoemakers I told you about, who hadn't a dime between them.'

'Grubstaked?' she asked, remembering what had puzzled her.

'Paid for their tools and upkeep while they were digging in return for a share of the profits – if any. In this case the share was a third. Tabor's outlay was seventeen dollars. They had to dig only twenty-six feet before they struck mineral, and the first wagonload sold for two hundred dollars. That was the Little Pittsburg. Only weeks later the mine was bringing in eight thousand dollars a week, and Tabor was the richest man in Colorado. Up to April this year he'd made over two and a quarter million dollars in turnover from the Chrysolite and the surrounding mines.'

'But not Bosworth?'

'No. And Tabor missed out on one. Father got down here from Denver, and bought up the claim before Tabor realised it. He took a chance, you see, because Bosworth is on the side of the hill furthest away from the deposits that were already producing richly. He had a bonanza. As well as the carbonates, there's a seam of grey sand with chlorides and horn silver. The ore is high grade, still averaging five hundred and nine ounces of silver to the ton. When you think most mines produce well under a hundred, that's quite something.'

'And it's just the Bosworth your father has?'

'No. He bought up all surrounding claims, just like Tabor. Big Hat, Silver Queen, White Rose. But he's missed one: the Manhattan claim. Belonged to a Canadian immigrant; he couldn't dig, but wouldn't sell. Now he has. But not to us.'

'Why not?'

Luke shrugged. 'I was away. Father had left.' He didn't add: And I suspect there's more to the story.

'Is it important?'

He smiled wrily. 'How do you rate important? In Leadville terms at the moment, yes. Father thinks that's where the next big strike will be. The silver on Fryer Hill is unusual in that it comes in pockets as well as in veins. At first Father thought the Bosworth ore was in a pocket, but now he's convinced it's an exceptionally wide lode. The ore body is over eighty feet thick in some places. On Fryer the lodes, unusually, are more or less horizontal instead of vertical – and that means the Bosworth lode could run into the Manhattan claim.'

'Can't you buy it from them?'

'Nope. They're sitting on it too. Not mining it, not yet. But the new owner won't sell. I reckon he's a front for someone else.'

She looked at him curiously. 'You hate this, don't you?' she said in some surprise, annoyed with herself for having been so absorbed in her own feelings, she had not considered his.

He shrugged. 'Once this was a wooded hillside with aspens, raccoons, birds – sure, it's got to happen to support the civilised

160

world, but it sickens me to see it, because I see no sign that mankind's the better for all this progress.'

'Is that why you want the Bocton Case to continue?' she asked with sudden insight.

He looked at her in surprise, as if he'd almost forgotten her. 'Yes,' he said slowly, 'I suppose it is. I couldn't bear to think of Bocton being a mass of brickworks and railroad sidings. This hillside is littered with broken dreams, Katharine, but they're forgotten amid the riches. Only the pickings will be remembered, not the men who ran out of money, died miserable and in poverty, those who did not dig deep enough, those who were cheated out of their rights.' He said no more as he helped her down from the trap on to the rough ground. The heat on this unsheltered hillside was overpowering, smoke from the engine room chimneys filling the air, piles of black ore and sand as far as she could see.

'Can we go down the mine?' she asked, more out of desire to escape this heat than to see the Bosworth.

He looked at her doubtfully.

'I haven't got my breeches,' she tried to joke, 'so I can't help to mine silver, but I'd like to see it.'

'You relieve my mind,' he said, laughing suddenly. 'I thought you wanted to be added to the wage bill. Three dollars fifty a day for you would break me.'

'At least it would be my money,' she said wistfully, thinking of her lost school. Rather to her surprise, he said nothing as he ushered her into the small iron cage.

Down into the blackness, hearing Luke's steady breathing at her side, feeling his nearness. A moment's panic at the dark all around. And finally, jolting to a halt at the first landing, the cage steadied by unknown, unseen hands, and a few lamps dimly showing. She clutched at Luke, sorry now that she had suggested it, shivering in the unexpected cold.

'This is Jonathan Trevanick, Katharine, my mine manager.'

'Pleased to meet you, Mrs Stowerton.' The man's soft burr came out of the dim light.

'You're Cornish?' she asked. 'I heard there were some Cornish miners here.'

''Es. There be a group of us, left the tin mines for silver.' He said no more, but led her a little way along the tunnel, or drift as he called it, explaining how massive timbers in square sets supported the roof and walls of the cavity around them from which the ore had been mined. This lode was so thick, so rich, that there were many sets one above the other, sometimes rising up as high as 80 feet to the top of the workings. Katharine shivered at the thought of men working in this dark, damp place.

'Don't they mind?' she asked Trevanick hesitantly.

He smiled at her, and said simply, 'When they gets silver in their eyes, Mrs Stowerton, they gets rubber in their joints.'

He showed her the rail lines that took the ore to the shaft for

161

hoisting, and she gazed curiously at the dark glistening ore, running with water.

'There's the lode, Mrs Stowerton.'

A curious note of reverence entered his voice as he pointed out the silver-bearing vein. To her eye it was just black rock and it was hard to imagine that within it lay silver, the precious metal that ruled the life of Leadville.

'Some do reckon there be one lode under another if you goes deep enough 'ere, separated by porphyry. But I do reckon it be just the same lode put out of kilter, displaced if you likes.' He seemed to be talking more to himself than her, stroking the ore almost as if it were a sweetheart, something to be cherished and loved, Katharine thought curiously.

''Tis a bonanza mine, Mrs Stowerton. Rich in silver, 'tis. We'm lucky to be 'ere.'

'Will you stay here for good?' she asked. 'Not return to Cornwall?'

'There be no future in mining there,' he said shortly, perhaps thinking of the moors and cliffs of home.

'But Leadville is not home, is it?' she said softly.

'Home be a mine, Mrs Stowerton. It gets in your blood. And it don't matter where the mine is. All miners speak the same language, be it Cornish or Eskimo, I reckons. This be home, now, and nothing will change that.'

Nothing will change it. Nothing could change home for her either. But her home was Bocton.

It was less than a month she'd been here, yet it seemed more like six. Each way Katharine tried to turn, it seemed to her in her dulled state she found it blocked either by her mother-in-law or less obviously by her sisters-in-law. Even by Luke himself.

'If I could get my mother's consent, would you like to help with the keeping of the books for the office?'

Pride battled with enthusiasm even at this limited prospect of work. 'Why do I have to have your mother's consent?' she asked vehemently. 'You are the mine manager.'

'And you are living under her roof.'

'But surely I would work at your offices?'

'It's not an office designed for women,' he replied shortly. 'You must work from home.'

'*Why?*' she burst out again. 'I don't see –'

'The clerks in the office,' he said impatiently, 'would not wish to be constrained by the presence of a woman, particularly you, Katharine.'

'Then why not that empty office at the side of yours?'

'There are not the facilities,' he said wearily.

'What on earth do you mean? Oh, *Luke*. Very well, when I wish to pee, I'll run home.' She knew she was behaving like a naughty child, and felt the more reproved when he merely said: 'I would prefer that you remained at home.'

'In that case,' she said haughtily, 'I will choose my own employment.'

He compressed his lips, knowing full well that to forbid her to look for something to occupy her time outside the home would bring a confrontation he had not the energy left to face.

Very well, Katharine thought to herself mutinously, if I am to stay at home I can at least interest myself in the household. Tired beyond measure at the boring plainness of the food they ate, she descended to the kitchens, to the great amazement of the staff, and in place of the planned beefsteak pudding, the dinner table was graced by Mrs Acton's recipe for Veal Sydney, Sussex pond pudding and syllabub. The storm that followed this bid for independence took place almost unbeknown to her, as Luke battled it out with his mother. For once his sympathies were entirely with Katharine, even if not with her methods.

'The girl must learn her place, my son. It is not to mingle with the helps like a common servant girl. Nor to waste time on fancy food.'

'She needs activity, Mother. And I see no reason that –'

'She can employ herself sewing for the needy.'

'She does not enjoy sewing, Mother.'

'What she enjoys is of no account. Sewing is the Lord's work. I shall so inform her.'

'You will not, Mother,' he said in deadly calm tones. '*I* will talk to Katharine, but you will not. Nor will you force her to do sewing if she does not wish to.'

Augusta stared at him, and for the moment held her peace.

Katharine's one avenue of escape was her daily walks with Martha and Mary to the stores. She soon found it easy to steer them into gazing into the clothing stores while she disappeared into one of the several book stores in Leadville. One in particular she liked for its very randomness of stock. Charles Dickens jostled Buffalo Bill dime novels, guide books for 'get rich quick' hopefuls with Bibles and hymn-books.

'Hoping for a bonanza, ma'am?' asked the owner cheerfully, seeing her studying one of the mining guides. 'Not a word of truth in 'em, of course.'

She laughed. 'Then why do you sell them?' she asked.

''Tis the best bit of the dream, ma'am. The dream that a silver bonanza is right round the corner. You lay down a hundred dollars, the books say, and you make a quarter of a million in a month. Mind you, in Leadville you 'most always can. You don't need no book.' He waved a hand to distant hills covered with huts and mine workings, where spruces once stood. 'All those dreams come true, and they rush down here and spend the results. Gambling houses, saloons, State Street women – begging your pardon, Mrs Stowerton.'

'You know who I am?' she asked, surprised.

'Reckon just 'bout everyone knows who you are,' he said drily. 'Mr Luke's new wife from England.' He didn't add that quite a few felt sorry for her. Pretty soon she'd look like Miss Martha and Miss

Mary. He paused, wondering how to put it delicately. 'Like Leadville, do you?'

Katharine flushed, then seeing the genuine interest on his plump face said carefully: 'It's an unusual and exciting town.' If you happen to like noise, smoke and gambling, she mentally added.

'It's unusual all right. Why, there's theatres, concerts, churches, schools – all in jus' two years. You been to the Opera House yet? Tabor's, I mean. The others ain't no place for a lady. Mighty generous man is Horace Tabor. Trouble is, he's generous in other ways too. With the ladies.'

'Oh?' Katharine was intrigued.

''Course, I shouldn't be telling you, but seeing the whole town knows anyways, he's a-courting a new young lady right now. They call her Baby Doe.'

'Baby Doe? I don't believe you,' Katharine laughed.

'Sure is, ma'am. Horace is like a young kid in love again. Augusta, she stays up in the Denver house mostly now, 'cept when they entertained General Grant and his lady last month. But Horace, he stayed on. You know the passageway from the Opera House high up over the street to the Clarendon Hotel? Horace uses it to visit Baby Doe in the hotel. That's where she lives. Folks do say,' added the bookseller wickedly, 'that's why Jeremiah took off with Daisy Petal, so's Tabor wouldn't be one up on him. Now I shouldn't be saying that about your family and all, but he was never one for letting Tabor get away with anything. What Tabor did, Jeremiah wanted too. And Daisy Petal Garden was the next best thing to Baby Doe. That's what the town says,' he concluded hastily, in case he had gone too far. But Katharine was fascinated, not offended.

What Robert had, Jeremiah wanted. She was back in a flash to Bocton, the treasure trove and the enmity between two brothers. Was this the reason that Jeremiah had so willingly entered the gavelkind case? Revenge against Robert, a need for revenge so great that he pursued it even from three thousand miles away?

'Oh, yes,' the bookseller was saying happily, 'there's plenty in Leadville for those who open their eyes, Mrs Stowerton.'

She smiled at him. 'Thank you, Mr –'

'Pemberthy, ma'am, failed prospector,' he confessed cheerily. 'Most folks call me Joe.'

All thoughts of Jeremiah and the Tabors flew out of her mind, however, when she got home, finding Luke for once already there. He eyed her speculatively, wondering why she looked unusually animated, but said nothing. Charlie had collected the mail daily from the Post Office, queuing patiently in the long lines that collected and by now adept at paying for the privilege of creeping higher and higher up the queue. When Luke gave the letter to Katharine, she recognised the sprawling childish writing immediately, and with sinking heart knew Meg would never have bothered to write unless there was bad news – a feeling that intensified when she saw the letter had a French stamp on it. She opened it with trembling hands.

'What is it, Katharine?' asked Luke quickly, seeing her face turn white.

'It's Meg,' she gulped. 'She –' She could not continue, and he took the letter from her hands. It was as he had expected, short and to the point.

Dearest Katharine,
I hope you are well. Do not be upset when you hear this for I know I will be very happy. I am leaving with Louis for Rome. I know this will be a surprise to you, but he loves me very much. We met again in Paris while I was on a visit to Mama. We will be married in Rome.
With love,
Meg.

Katharine's face was ashen. 'He won't marry her, not that young man. Has she gone mad?' Words began to tumble out of her, until she recollected to whom she was speaking, and began to realise Meg's dilemma. She had been driven to it. She had lost Luke, the man she really loved, and out of desperation, out of a need for a father for her child, fallen into the arms of the first man she met. Louis, of all people! Albert's son. Poor, poor, Father – and she was helpless, thousands of miles away.

'He'll never marry her. She doesn't realise. What on earth was Father doing letting her go to Paris?'

Luke took her hands compassionately. 'Katharine, it will be all right. I will make *sure* it is all right.' Should he tell her? Some of it, perhaps. It would make her feel happier, and she should know in any case that her sister was as much to blame as Louis. 'Katharine, this is not exactly news to me. I had a letter from your mother.'

'*You what?* From my *mother?*' She was bewildered and hurt. Why should Luke have a letter from Elizabeth, her own mother, who never bothered to write to her? 'What did it say?' she asked stiffly.

Luke edited its contents for her. 'She told me that Meg had run away with Louis.'

'Why did she write to you and not to me?' Katharine demanded.

'Because she wanted me to break it to you. I guess she never thought Meg would inform you herself.'

'But Louis will never marry her.' And the baby, what about the baby? she was thinking. Luke's baby.

'He will,' said Luke quietly. He hesitated. 'There is to be a baby, you see,' he said finally.

She stared at him dumbly. He was going to let this happen to his baby – his responsibility – no doubt glad that Meg was to marry another.

'I know,' she said stiffly. So the nightmare had come true. Meg was certain now about the baby, and Luke was callously palming her off on Louis.

165

'Elizabeth thought I ought to add my weight to persuade Louis to marry her,' Luke explained more fully than he had meant. 'I am prepared to settle money on him to do so.'

'Yes,' she managed to say, though humbly. 'Yes.' So that was why Mother had written to Luke. 'You couldn't do anything else.'

'No,' said Luke, puzzled by her attitude. No gratitude? No thanks? Surely she must now realise that Meg was a coquette, and be grateful that Luke had saved her from the results of her folly. Yet Katharine seemed more remote than ever. He grew even more worried as the weeks went by. Katharine, despite her bright face and polite interest in his affairs, seemed to be living in a world of her own. Finally he dismissed it, deciding that the girl he had thought was warmhearted and passionate, and with whom he could share a life of happiness, was incapable of love, at least for a man. He'd find more genuine warmth among Mollie May's girls on Fifth Street. Katharine cared only for Bocton. And there wasn't a damn' thing he could do to alter it.

Katharine took to making longer and longer visits to the book store, listening with increasing interest to Joe's tales of prospecting at Pike's Peak, the colourful characters who had passed through Leadville, the thousands of fascinating stories that lay beneath the surface appearance of this rumbustious town. Finally, diffidently, she asked Joe whether there were not some way in which she could assist him. Taken aback, he murmured of Mrs Augusta, an objection which Katharine brushed aside. Against his better judgement at first, he allowed her to pack and unpack books, then to make the occasional sale if she happened to be in the front. Such was the increase in business when news got out that a lady was helping mind the store that he rapidly forgot his fear of Mrs Augusta. But the news did not take long to reach Katharine's mother-in-law, relayed primly by a shocked Martha.

Luke came home in the midst of the wrangle that followed. Once again he took Katharine's side. 'I see no harm in it, Mother. Joe Pemberthy is a respectable man. Neither Katharine nor her reputation can come to harm in a bookshop during a day's work.'

'She,' Augusta turned frosty eyes on Katharine, 'is *trading* there, son. Selling wares.'

'Bibles, Mother-in-law,' Katharine pointed out, a glint in her eye.

'And the literature of the Devil,' said Augusta firmly. 'A Stowerton to lower herself to trade!'

'And what else are mining and selling silver?' Katharine retorted.

Augusta turned white, for once bereft of words. 'The Lord –' she began, but Luke cut her off in tones of finality.

'Katharine has my permission, Mother, to work in Pemberton's store.'

The look Augusta gave her did not bode well for the future, but Katharine did not care. It was freedom: stiltedly she thanked Luke afterwards, bleakly realising that his gesture had been made more to keep her quiet than from conviction of any right of hers in the matter.

166

He did not forget his promise to take her to the Opera House, though despite all he had explained she was still slightly puzzled as to why an Opera House should be featuring *Julius Caesar*. Directly they entered the doors, she caught her breath. This was indeed no ordinary play-house, and was a world away from most of Leadville's buildings; it was solidly built, with grand, red-carpeted staircase, white and gold balustrades, and cast-iron seats with red plush upholstery as elegant as any she had seen in London. Not that visits to London theatres had been very frequent from Bocton – only the occasional theatre or opera tickets sent by Godfather, with hotel accommodation tactfully arranged for them. Here, in the Tabor Opera House, she could almost imagine herself at the Theatre Royal in the Haymarket. That is, if she closed her eyes to the audience around her. Noisier than any London pit, full of movement as day-time miners laughed and joked with comrades in other parts of the theatre, hats waving in the air as at last the painted drop curtain, covered by a picture, so Luke told her, of Tabor himself, rose.

The audience was restless to begin with, and she had to struggle to hear the words. Only when Caesar was murdered did interest pick up, disapproving and audible comments being made about lynchings. 'Friends, Romans, countrymen,' from Mark Antony stirred their interest.

'Guess it's the Marshal,' was one audible comment.

'Marshal Duggan?'

'He ain't marshal no more.'

'What's he up there for then?'

Animated discussion continued until the sudden lowering of the lights extinguished the gas jets altogether, plunging the whole house into darkness. Katharine giggled, as a small boy was seen on stage busily relighting the footlight jets, and she joined in the cheer that followed.

The rest of the play was well received, chiefly on account of the fighting. But it was the ghost scene that drew the loudest cheers after the apparition had disappeared. When the transparent figure first floated across the stage, it threatened to start a stampede as stalwart miners decided they must have drunk too much rye whiskey and headed for the exits. Only the sound of the ghost speaking and being identified as the swell who came into Pap Wyman's saloon last night reassured them into staying put.

As the curtain dropped, furious applause began, with shouts of 'Author' growing so loud and insistent that Brutus stepped forward to explain somewhat nervously: 'The author, William Shakespeare, is dead, gentlemen.'

'Who shot him?' enquired a stentorian voice from the rear.

But Katharine was oblivious to the uproar from the audience. For suddenly, unbelievably, a whole new avenue of possibility had opened up. She had been spellbound by the play, despite the noisy surroundings, and fascinated by the scenery, painted on canvas backdrops, simply but evocatively. The Forum, the Plains of

Philippi, Brutus's Orchard. An idea had come, so simple she wondered she had not thought of it long since. Luke wondered at her sudden abstraction, the sudden happiness that lit her face.

At first Joe was disapproving. He had told her that he spent some free time down at the Opera House working behind the scenes. Why should she not work there too, to help him? 'Back in England, Joe, I did *all* the household repairs, both on our house and an old manor house.' How far away it seemed, how long ago. 'I'm good at carpentry and painting. I could paint scenery at least.'

He looked doubtful.

'Oh, Joe!' Her eye fell on a shelf pulling away from the wall high up. 'Here,' she said firmly, 'let me show you.'

Before he could stop her, she had seized the ladder and his tool bag and was efficiently refixing the shelf, as he stood remonstrating below. Then she came down the ladder triumphantly, a finale somewhat ruined by her catching her heel in her hem.

He steadied her.

'Back home I wear breeches,' she said, laughing.

'I have a kind of feeling Mr Luke's not going to like this,' he said.

'Oh, no,' she contradicted him, sure of her ground. 'My husband always encouraged me in restoring the manor house. And to wear breeches.'

'He did?' said Joe, scratching his ear thoughtfully. 'Well, I'll be darned. If that's so, I guess I could do with some help down there at Tabor's.'

'Oh!' cried Katharine, her eyes sparkling for the first time since her arrival in Leadville. 'Oh, thank you.' She flung her arms round him in excitement.

'Careful, Mrs Stowerton,' he grunted, pink in the face. 'I got a reputation to think of. I'm a married man. And what's that ma-in-law of yours going to say if she sees you a-hugging me?'

'She'd be delighted,' replied Katharine ruefully. 'It would confirm all her worst suspicions.'

Luke opened the latest letter from Mr Pinpole, almost dreading the contents. He didn't want to be reminded of Bocton, of The Case, of anything save the duty of getting on with this drudgery, in the hope that events might reach a stage where he could plan some kind of escape for Katharine and himself.

Stowerton v. Stowerton was progressing satisfactorily, was the gist of his letter. 'Sir Robert's lawyers, while conceding that the Wills Act of 1837 only applies to wills made after 1 January 1838 or subsequently republished (as was not done in the case of Sir Nathaniel's will), nevertheless contend that since the will contained a clause disposing of all the testator's property not especially appropriated by other parts of the will, Bocton and Charham necessarily come under that, and are now therefore Sir Robert's lawful property. If personalty were at issue, no doubt the law would be on his side (*Cambridge and Rous 1802*).

168

However, we need have little fear, I think, that it would apply in the case of a devise of real estate. If prior to the Act a testator had devised a fee simple to A, for example, and made a residuary devise in favour of B and A . . .' Luke skipped a few paragraphs. '. . . necessity of proving the lands comes from a pre-Conquest tenure of ancient socage.' He grinned, but there was little humour in it. So Pinpole was confident? Good. As to the details, such words as ancient socage, devise, fee simple, seemed to have little to do with the wagonload after wagonload of silver ore rumbling past his office window.

Bocton's trees would be changing colour now. He was sorry not to have seen that. Perhaps – a sudden idea came to him – he'd take Katharine on a trip, to see the wonderful aspen trees changing colour from green to soft gold and flaming red. Yes, they needed time together. A vacation. Perhaps they could spend Christmas in Denver to escape the grimness of Christmas in his own home.

Filled with sudden delight by how excited she would be, he left the office and went in search of her at the book store.

'Morning, Joe,' he said cordially.

'Morning, Mr Luke.' Joe tactfully made himself scarce.

'I've had a letter from Pinpole,' he told her. Katharine looked up eagerly, and he handed it over. She read it twice.

'That's quite good, isn't it?' she asked carefully.

'Looks that way.'

She sighed. 'It's a long way away. I wish –' She stopped.

'Katharine, let's go away,' he broke in.

Hope flared in her eyes.

'Just for a few days, that is,' he amended, seeing she misunderstood. 'Say at the end of September, or October. And maybe Christmas too.' He broke off at the alarm in her eyes. 'What's the matter?'

'Oh, Luke, I can't,' she cried apologetically. 'Not now.'

Chapter Ten

'Why?' Luke enquired blankly, completely taken aback. What possible reason could Katharine have for not wishing to escape from the smoke of Leadville for a few days. Did she so dislike him? Was she ill? With child? No, the last surely was not possible. What reason then?'

'I am needed at the performances for the next few weeks,' she blurted out defensively.

'Performances? What in heaven's name are you talking about?'

'I am assisting at the Opera House,' she told him miserably. She had not known what his reaction might be, but had guessed and had been nervous of telling him earlier. Yet why should she be? she tried to reason. This was Luke, her husband, not some fierce gaoler, although that, she realised, was more and more what it felt like – as though he, his mother and sisters were ranged against her in a disapproving barrier between her and any kind of life for her in Leadville.

'Selling programmes?' Luke asked, his face darkening. What trouble was Katharine going to cause in the house now? He couldn't entirely blame her, but he dreaded the thought of summoning the energy to deal with it.

'No, I am a backstage hand,' she told him, torn between pride and apprehension.

'A *what*?' he asked blankly.

'Painting scenery and helping with the props.'

'How long has this been going on?' he cut across her peremptorily, cursing all the long evenings he had spent at the office and wishing he'd paid more attention to his mother's complaint that Katharine had refused to accompany them on evening visits to the church.

'I began in earnest only this week. So you see, Luke, it would look very bad if I took time off right away.'

'It will not look bad, as you put it, for you will not be continuing this ridiculous farce,' he told her grimly. The words rang false even in his own ears, especially knowing exactly what her reaction would be, but he was too tired to consider his words more carefully.

She flared up immediately. 'Who are you to forbid me to go *anywhere*?' she cried without thinking.

'I'm beginning to wonder,' he replied bitterly. 'Katharine,' softening slightly, 'do you not see that what you could do in Bocton Bugley cannot be done in Leadville? For pity's sake, have some sense. My mother and my sisters are amongst the town's most prominent citizens, so how can my wife flout convention in this manner?' He immediately realised the incongruity of what he'd said, but too late.

170

'Convention?' Katharine shouted, before she could stop. 'Your father is no more conventional than my mother. You think that my working at a task I like is worse than –'

'Katharine!' His voice was whiplash sharp, and she had the grace to blush.

'I'm sorry, Luke,' she said more quietly. 'I shouldn't have mentioned your father. I know it upsets you. But now that I have, how can you justify it? What's the point of convention if it merely provides superficial rules and not moral ones?'

'Katharine, I'm not going to enter into philosophical discussions on society,' he retorted angrily. 'We're living under my mother's roof – and, oh God, I want some peace and quiet, not quarrelling women all day long.' He slumped back in his chair, covering his face with his hands.

Katharine gulped, but continued bravely, 'Luke, please see my point of view. You are trying to stop me from doing something I'm really interested in, much more so than in keeping books. You don't really need my help with that. You knew what I was like when you married me. You *liked* me for it. I ran the household, restored Bocton, did all the repairs at the Dower House and managed the gardens. What is there for me to do here? Nothing at all, save this. Oh, Luke,' she appealed to him, 'please don't let's quarrel. If only you could share it with me. It's a different world there behind the scenes. It's hot under the gas lights, and the wings are small and stuffy, the paint runs on the actors' faces. You can smell their sweat, and yet once they tread the boards it's magic. A transformation – just like in pantomimes. And they are good plays. They're performing Robertson's *Ours*, and Shakespeare of course.'

'Rather wasted on an audience chiefly of miners.'

'Why?' she flashed back. 'Shakespeare wrote for everyone.'

'As I recall, Shakespeare did not employ women scene-shifters,' Luke commented drily.

'I'm not a scene-shifter – I paint scenery, help with the props, and just make myself useful.'

'A pity you cannot employ that last talent in the house and give some companionship to my sisters.' He knew he was being unfair, but it seemed to him he had to make a bid for control in a world in which everything seemed to be slipping away.

'I have nothing in common with your sisters, Luke,' she tried to say evenly.

'You don't try.'

'And little wonder. My daughters are brought up in the fear of the Lord.' Augusta had entered without their hearing, and was standing over them as if in judgement in black silk robes. She wore black more and more Katharine had noticed, as if to emphasise a kind of widowhood. Luke rose automatically, as if to stand between his mother and his wife, but she continued coolly, 'It is hardly surprising they do not wish to sort with one who performs in a den of sin, clad in unmentionables.'

'Unmentionables?' Luke turned wearily to Katharine.

She could not meet his gaze. 'I have to,' she said defiantly. 'And, anyway, how do *you* know?' she hurled at her mother-in-law. 'Have you been snooping round our room?' This was ignored. 'I have to wear them,' Katharine said again, faced with two stony expressions. 'I am constantly going up and down ladders, and perching on high platforms. It would be dangerous as well as indecent to wear skirts. Besides, it was you who bought them for me, Luke,' switching tactics.

'That was at Bocton,' he said quietly. 'Another time, another place.' Could she not see that Bocton lay thousands of miles away on the map and still further in spirit? It seemed almost a dream now of which the only reality was Katharine, part of a youth that had vanished, a promise that had evaporated, leaving only this day-to-day struggle for existence behind it.

Augusta quickly followed up her advantage. 'The Lord abhors houses of abomination,' she informed her son smugly, ignoring her daughter-in-law.

'There is more humanity in one night backstage at the Opera House than in a year at your chapel,' Katharine flared back. Hellfire and gloom was what it preached, so unlike the Norman church at Bocton, with its peacefulness, timelessness. She found the chapel claustrophobic and forbidding and had told her mother-in-law that in future she would attend the Catholic church. This had precipitated another formidable quarrel. To her mother-in-law's furious prophecies of both immediate and eternal retribution, she had retorted that she understood freedom to worship as one pleased was a tenet of the American constitution, which had silenced Augusta but hardly endeared her daughter-in-law to her. The confrontations left Katharine weak and exhausted, feeling she was fighting an uphill battle – and one she had to win quickly if there was to be a future for her here. Now instead of a battle on churches, it was a conflict over trousers. The incongruity struck her with grim humour. No wonder Jeremiah found Daisy Petal more congenial company and had left.

As if reading her thoughts, Augusta burst out: 'Have not whores brought troubles enough on this household?'

'Mother!' Luke's voice held a note that stopped even Augusta in her tracks. 'You will treat Katharine with respect while she is under your roof.'

'Respect!' She looked Katharine up and down scornfully.

'Or we will leave Leadville,' said Luke quietly.

Katharine held her breath at this unexpected intervention. If only they could, if only! Always before Luke had taken Augusta's side; it was a bluff on his part now but his mother could not know that.

Augusta cast her eyes upwards. 'The Lord who send trials to test Thy Loyal Servant, grant me strength to endure them.'

'Katharine will continue to work at the Opera House,' Luke said tonelessly.

Afterwards Katharine tried stiltedly to express her thanks to him, knowing she could not have resisted them both, but he waved them aside. She realised bleakly that it was not from any conviction that she was right, but that again it was less effort to support his wife than his mother. She felt like a rag doll pulled between the two of them, forbidden to have a will of her own, the puppet of her husband's forbearance and her mother-in-law's anger.

She had in fact spoken more confidently than she felt about her work in the Opera House. To begin with, it had been an ordeal. The other backstage workers were curious, even resentful of a woman amongst them, especially Mrs Luke Stowerton, and did not take her seriously, even when she had shown how adept she was at painting and carpentry. Her breeches, when she bravely wore them, brought forth barely concealed sniggers and even guffaws, with talk of Calamity Jane. Fortunately much was put down to the fact that she was English and all English ladies were well known to be eccentric; on this basis she began to win a qualified acceptance, if on a trial basis only.

The stage manager, an anxious young man called Matt, deemed it politic to confine Katharine to painting canvas scenery backdrops and flats at first. Watching her repairing the scenery for Act III of *Ours*, he then had the happy thought of keeping her out of the firing line by asking her to paint a new backdrop for the first act. Hitherto they had been making do with the stock backdrop of a forest scene, but Robertson's text demanded an English tree-lined avenue with falling leaves. Taking advantage of her nationality, he set her to work and no one was more surprised than he when at the end of a week Katharine had produced an evocative avenue of limes, culled from her memory of the wide avenue of nearby Chilston Park at Boughton Malherbe.

'And I've had an idea,' she told him excitedly, 'you could get the impression of three dimensions by putting aspen leaves together and holding them in place with very fine net.' Matt scratched his head, eyeing her dubiously and wondering quite what he had let himself in for. 'That's if you like the idea, Matt,' she added meekly.

'You know, Katharine,' commented Joe afterwards, 'that's a mighty fine avenue you painted there. Only one thing wrong with it, and I reckon Matt don't like to tell you. It's *too* detailed. Remember stage craft is illusion, Katharine. You got to indicate, not imitate. Otherwise you gonna draw the audience's attention to those trees of yours and not the actors. See what I mean?' She didn't and was upset at the criticism. But after he had patiently shown her what he meant in detail, and she had looked at it from the auditorium circle, she began to realise what he was after. Yet how to achieve that effect? Next time she tried she did better, when Matt asked her to represent D'Alroy's Mayfair lodgings for a forthcoming production of the same author's *Caste*. This time she used colour on flats and backdrop to indicate opulence and lavishness rather than detailed representations of Chippendale chairs.

Gradually she began unasked to carry out small repairs, nails here and there, until it became accepted to call on Mrs Stowerton, then Katharine, then Kate, for anything that needed doing. Kate would do it. Sometimes, in fact, she did it too well.

'What the devil took – pardon me, Kate, what took you so long?'

Matt came up to inspect the flats for the new production and whistled. 'Hey, now, we don't need this here scenery to last till the twentieth century.'

'But I thought you wanted it strong,' she said, dismayed.

'Sure, and that's fine joinery work, but all we needs for stage carpentry is a couple of short stays and nails, Kate, *nails*.' He went away laughing, till her ears burned as the story of Kate 'Chippendale' went round the theatre. But, oddly, it marked the point from which she was accepted. From then on she took her part in helping with the props unnoticed, sitting up high on a flown platform, patiently dropping leaves throughout Act I of the play, as stipulated in the text.

The heat of the gas flares from the hung battens together with the heat rising from the footlights exhausted her, and each night she sank into bed, too tired even to converse. Rather than leaving it to a help, Luke took to coming to the theatre unasked to escort her silently home. Finally he rebelled, and glad of the excuse, she cut her Opera House attendance down to three times a week, even though it meant enduring endless evenings of silent dinners, afterwards sitting in the parlour with Augusta reading her Bible, Martha and Mary obediently playing music of sorts on the piano, and Luke quietly reading. Seldom did they talk, for the past was forbidden territory and the present raised too many problems. How miserably this dull life in the Stowerton household compared with the theatre's bright bustle, endless excitements, and thousand and one small emergencies, as something could not be found, pieces of scenery collapsed, and always the thrill of watching as the curtain rose. Helping to control the roller which prevented the drop curtain from swinging was one of her jobs and she loved seeing the front row of the audience, a blur of white faces waiting expectantly, and herself enjoying the tension of the magic moment when the cast ceased to be a group of actors and submerged into their characters.

Sometimes Horace Tabor himself on a visit from Denver was seated in the ornate Tabor box, at the side of the stage. 'Here to see Baby Doe' was the knowing talk, with bets wagered as to how often the walkway from the Opera House where he had his own private apartments to the Clarendon Hotel across the street would be in use this month. The more charitable claimed it had been provided for the sake of the hotel employees who took vacant rooms high up in the Opera House to board in. Whichever it was, his wife Augusta never accompanied him now to the theatre.

Further back in the audience were the rougher patrons who never hesitated to make their views known, whether it be on Shakespeare or some variety artiste. If they approved, showers of silver and gold coins might descend on to the stage in a spontaneous show of appreciation. If they disapproved the means of expression was more vocal, though hardly more restrained.

As Katharine began to feel part of it all, she lost her nervousness and revelled in the unity that held actors and stage hands together while the show was on. After it came the relaxation, the relief that another show had successfully taken place – or if it had been less than perfect, then it was at least over. Tomorrow was another day, another performance, another chance. At such times she watched the cast again, still gripped by the unity of the evening, exalted by the parts they had played, still inhabiting their own world. They would climb the steps from the small dressing rooms, dressed in their outdoor clothes, their minds still in Arden or Elsinore.

Katharine listened fascinated to as much of the performance as her duties would permit, always at the beginning and the end, when she stood ready for the curtain, and throughout whenever she could, the words holding her spellbound. The stage began to intoxicate her as liquor in the Silver Dollar saloon or cards in the gambling houses did the miners. Occasionally Luke would come to the show, and they would discuss it afterwards. They rarely agreed, for they saw it from different viewpoints, he objectively, she from passionate involvement with the effort poured into it on the stage management side and by the actors, with their hopes and fears. With her hair tucked in a cap and wearing breeches, she occasioned little comment during a performance from her colleagues, and the actors maintained an Olympian aloofness, well used to men in drag or women in trousers.

Luke, seeing her happiness, tried to feel glad for her absorption, and though the evenings ticked slowly by for him, he did not remonstrate again, even when she spoke of worlds he did not know and did not want to enter, even vicariously. They were worlds he longed to know more of, yet he feared to involve himself lest they cause him to deviate from the path in front of him. Realising his abstraction but not its cause, she fell silent on the subject. So another avenue lay blocked between them and no more was said about going to view the colours of the changing aspen trees.

Only once did he grow angry, when she had to work on Mary's birthday – she had genuinely forgotten – and, guilty, she burst out the more vehemently in her own defence. 'You're treating me as some kind of companion. I'm *not* her companion. Not like Mary.' He stared at her blankly thinking she meant his sister, until he remembered *Ours*, the play that was running at the moment, a modern one with modern ideas, and realised with sinking heart she was identifying herself with it. '"It is amazing to be a companion . . ."' she quoted bitterly. '"To know that you're kept in the room to save another woman from rising to ring a bell or to hand her the scissors." And that's just what I feel like in your house, Luke.' Not home, for home was Bocton.

He flushed, but was determined not to become embroiled in another quarrel. 'Better battle than a discontented woman,' he said lightly. 'There now, two can quote from the same play, you know.'

'You don't take me seriously,' she cried, annoyed at his flippancy. 'Why did you marry me if you didn't like me this way?'

Luke stared at her, anger slowly devouring him. 'No!' he said devastatingly. 'Why did *you* marry *me*? You remember Chalcot in your beloved play? Who overheard his fiancée saying, "I don't care very much about *him*, but then he's so very rich." Isn't that why you married me?'

'No,' burst out Katharine, aghast. 'No, that's *not* true. I would never have married for money.'

'But for Bocton, you would,' he said quietly. 'And you needed money for The Case.'

'No.' She stopped. How could she deny it entirely? The Case had seemed important at the time. Would she have married him without it? Yes – no, but because of Meg, not the money. Seeing her hesitate, he shrugged.

'But you didn't care for me,' she began slowly. 'It was –' The word 'Meg' was on her lips, but before she could say it he'd intervened.

'Bocton,' he finished for her. 'Of course. A business proposition, didn't we say? On both sides. You for love of it, and me so that my father could take his revenge on his older brother.' Surely she would not believe him? Did she know him so little? Or was it he who had misjudged her so badly? Sickened when she made no reply, he glanced out of the window into the hubbub of Leadville. Somewhere there must be peace after toil, somewhere an escape. Katharine had found hers. Where was his?

As new companies arrived, Katharine seized on them to talk to. Surprised at first to find a woman backstage, most soon succumbed to chatting avidly of their experiences in New York, London, or Europe. The more she listened to their tales, becoming immersed vicariously in their lives, the more Martha and Mary withdrew from her at home, convinced their mother's story of the whore of Babylon was correct. But Katharine did not care; she left the house early and returned late. Because of the shining glory of the Opera House, she was reconciled to Leadville itself, finding in its noisy bustling enthusiasm for the future all the romance and excitement that she had missed before. Here dreams were fulfilled in real life as in the theatre.

Luke played no part in this. Happy herself, or as happy as she could be away from Bocton, she tried to reach him, but could not for he was caught in a caul of others' making, and at last she gave up trying. When he made love to her, it was impersonal, with words that meant little, actions that widened the gulf rather than bridging it. And afterwards, when she lay awake far into the night, sick at heart, Meg was constantly in her mind.

Meg lay in bed and contemplated the lace-trimmed sheets and her own position. The latter was not altogether satisfactory. In Paris Louis had been most attentive and only too eager for a *vacance* in Montreux with Meg. A most delightful week in August had followed with romantic excursions to the pretty village of Glion and its surrounding mountains, and to the castle of Chillon, so romantically situated on the lake just outside Montreux. Meg had never read Lord Byron's poem on the Prisoner of Chillon, but she knew all about Lord Byron and told Louis he reminded her of him, with his dark saturnine looks. Louis, too, had heard of Milord Byron and thought that sweet Meg was much more accurate than she knew, as

176

he contemplated the line of ladies who would undoubtedly have agreed with the comparison.

There had been only one point of difference between them. Louis had been under the impression that Meg was to return to Paris to rejoin her mama; Meg was firmly of the opinion, following Elizabeth's instructions, that she was staying put, if not in Montreux at the Hotel Cygne, then at least firmly clamped to Louis' side elsewhere. Matters had reached a head last night.

'You do love me, don't you, Louis?'

By now swept off his feet by Meg's charms, he fervently agreed that he did. It was true. The only problem was, he thought regretfully, he seemed to have the capacity for loving many women at the same time.

She sighed happily. 'I just needed to be sure, because – oh, Louis, you remember the orchard at Bocton and what happened?'

'*Chérie*, how could I forget?' he asked fondly, racking his memory. Wasn't that when he'd at last persuaded her that love such as theirs should know no bounds?

'Well, you see, we shall remember it for ever. Oh, Louis, I am to have a little baby in February.'

'*Quoi?*' His face darkened and he stood up abruptly. This problem he had faced before *naturellement*, but not with the likes of Meg, his own cousin. 'But it was only once. You must be mistaken,' he said, alarmed.

'Oh, no. And now I know you love me,' she said artlessly, 'I felt I could tell you and we can be married.'

Louis looked out of the windows of the Hotel Cygne towards the lake. Suddenly he felt trapped as surely as that old prisoner in Chillon. True, Meg was pretty; true, he enjoyed being with her, who would not? They were young and in love. But marriage and a baby were different matters.

'*Chérie*,' he said automatically, fondly, 'our baby.' He was desperately thinking.

'I knew you'd be pleased,' said Meg happily. It had all been much easier than she had expected, although Louis was not quite so ecstatic as she had hoped and had not yet committed himself over marriage. But today he would, she thought, plucking at the lace trim on the sheets.

Unfortunately here she was mistaken. Louis, having left, like the gentleman he was, sufficient funds on the washstand for Meg to reach Paris once more, had departed.

The day before, Alfred Stowerton had stared perplexed at a letter in his hand. He almost hadn't opened it, seeing Elizabeth's flowing hand and fearing yet more talk of divorce. Now that he had, he wished he hadn't. Daughters. They were second only to wives in causing trouble. Meg had skipped the coop and gone off with that fellow's son. Dizzy with shock, he found himself quite distracted, planning his strategy for the Newmarket October meeting. He was filled with a rage he had not known since Elizabeth disappeared with that fellow. This had to be her doing. Albert's doing. Had he not taunted Alfred by saying he might take Meg away? He hadn't taken the fellow seriously. Mistake. Always take Albert seriously. Only for a second, to think wistfully of his *Sporting Times*, did Alfred hesitate. Then he slammed his panama on his hand and stalked purposefully across the grounds of Bocton to see Sophy.

'Whatever's the matter, Alfred?' She came rushing down from upstairs after being called by her companion, and was alarmed to find him in the hallway, panting heavily and considerably redder in the face than whisky would explain.

'Look,' he fumed, handing her the letter without further ado.

Sophy read Elizabeth's bold handwriting without her spectacles and her face grew pale. She thought rapidly.

'I know what I'm going to do,' snarled Alfred. 'I'm going over there to bring the girl back, ruined or not. What's Elizabeth thinking of to keep so loose a rein on her?'

'Suppose she doesn't want to come back?' asked Sophy practically.

'I'm not going to have a daughter of mine marrying that fellow's son and that's as flat as the Lincoln Handicap.'

'Alfred, dear, have you thought that they may be obliged to get married?' Sophy asked gently.

Alfred had not, but he considered the matter, then his eyes bulged. 'You mean that fellow and I could be joint grandfathers? No – I'm going today. *Today*,' he barked.

'But you don't know where they are,' Sophy pointed out, deeply troubled.

'I'm going to see that blasted fellow,' he declared. 'He's behind all this. You'll see. He'll know where they are, if they don't turn out to have been at Cannes all the time.'

Sophy blenched at the thought. 'Alfred dear, I really think you should see Elizabeth first.'

'No.'

'Then I shall come with you.'

'I don't want you to,' he said baldly. 'I'm quite capable of murdering Albert on my own.'

'That's precisely what I'm afraid of,' said Sophy calmly. 'Just give me an hour to make arrangements.'

It was an hour too long, for when she arrived at the Dower House, Alfred had already departed. 'He said, miss,' said Maggie, eyes agog at this emergency, 'that he can handle it alone.'

Sophy groaned, then asked delicately, 'Maggie, did he mention money at all? Does he have funds for travelling to France? I don't recall talk of recent winnings.'

'Oh, yes, ma'am,' said Maggie proudly, 'he borrowed from me.'

'Did he?' said Sophy firmly. 'Did he, indeed? Then I shall repay you. Now.' She returned to the Lodge, quite determined that there was no way in which she could allow Alfred to face Albert alone. Disaster might follow – so far as Meg was concerned. Alfred and Albert could fend for themselves, but she wasn't so sure about Meg;

she was a secretive girl, and she'd been looking very peaky before she went to Paris. Upset at Katharine's going, Alfred had dismissed it. Certainly, but only because she now had to run the house, had been Sophy's caustic reaction to this. What if, however . . . Yes, she was glad she had sent that telegram to London. However, she sighed, she supposed she would need a chaperone.

She knocked on the door of her companion's quarters. 'Matilda,' she called quietly, 'please pack a bag. We leave for France by steamer as soon as I have a reply to a telegraph.'

Albert hummed happily to himself. He had told Louise it would be all right, and he'd been proved correct. The lad had merely been amusing himself and now he was back. All was well, and there was no need to enquire further. Doubtless, as a gentleman, Louis would have seen that the girl, whoever she was, was not left destitute, and the escapade could be considered all part of his education. Louise had been somewhat reassured by his return, but was still rather cool to the boy. Nevertheless, Albert's thoughts began to turn to whether he would visit the gambling room of the Cercle Nautique in Cannes or whether he should summon the carriage and travel to Nice on the same mission. Perhaps Cannes would suffice. The season, after all, would soon begin and Cannes was definitely becoming most fashionable now that the railway had reached it, and Russians were vying with the English for social pre-eminence. First, he would visit his tailor in the Rue d'Antibes, then he would take luncheon at the Faisan Doré, then accompany Louise to play croquet at the Villa Eleanore, then dinner with the Duc de Vallombrosa at the Château des Tours. A most satisfactory day. That should take care of Wednesday very nicely. He yawned and readjusted his cravat. Really, life was very pleasant. A self-satisfied smile on his face, he descended the staircase, noticing that as usual Louise had not yet made her appearance. Ah, well, after last night . . . Complacently he recollected his virility.

Unfortunately his plans for Wednesday were to be seriously disrupted. He blinked. Could his eyes be deceiving him? In the light and airy morning room, amid the potted palms, paced brother Alfred. A certain unease crept up Albert's spine, but try as he might he could not see that he had done anything with which to reproach himself. Not recently that is. It must be about that damn' case, but surely he'd signed all the papers necessary?

'How very pleasant to see you, Alfred,' he said cordially, advancing with outstretched hand. 'Have you yet taken *le petit déjeuner*?'

'You damned hypocrite,' snarled his loving brother, in exchange for this welcome. 'Don't deny it. It was your idea, wasn't it?' He grasped Albert by the carefully tied cravat, shaking him to and fro. Taken by surprise Albert lost his balance, falling ignominiously to his knees, so that the cravat became a suffocating dog collar. It was thus that Louis saw them and quickly backed out again, correctly perceiving that this might have something to do with his own recent exploits. He cannoned into his mother, apologised and vanished. Somewhat surprised, Louise entered the morning room, and beheld a most unfortunate scene.

'*Mon cher,*' she remarked after an infinitesimal pause, 'would you introduce me to your friend?'

Alfred stopped his shaking, albeit reluctantly, and, coughing, Albert clambered unsteadily to his feet. 'Allow me to introduce my beloved brother Alfred,' he said with as much aplomb as he could manage. 'Alfred, my wife, Madame Louise Stowerton, Comtesse de Fréjus.'

Alfred's manners were impeccable and the bow he gave on being introduced grandly ignored the events of the past few minutes.

'*Enchantée, monsieur,*' Louise said blandly, offering her exquisite hand. She turned to Albert. 'As your business doubtless does not concern me,' she announced thoughtfully, 'I will perhaps retire.'

'It concerns your son, Madame,' said Alfred, who had no intention of letting Albert off any hooks at all.

'Louis?' asked his mother sharply.

'Where are they?' Alfred was beginning to lose patience. Two startled faces greeted him. 'Don't pretend you don't know what I'm talking about.'

'Where are what, Alfred?' asked Albert blankly.

'Not what. *Who*,' he said testily, infuriated by the fellow's prevarication.

'Who?'

'Damn you, Albert! It's your doing. Your son and my daughter Meg. Where are they?'

Albert's face slowly changed. Louis and Meg? Shock ran through him as he rapidly reviewed the probabilities, and all the connotations. He took a pinch of snuff automatically, but Alfred assumed it an insult.

'Damn you, Albert, where are they?'

'One moment, Monsieur,' said Louise coldly. 'You claim my son and your daughter are together?'

'I regret, Madame, I know they are. Your husband has helped himself to my family *again*. First my wife and now my daughter.'

Louise's eyes narrowed. There were things not spoken of in this household and this was definitely one. 'But I regret, Monsieur, that you are mistaken. My son is at home, and your daughter is not with him.'

'Not –' Alfred's face went white, even more worried now. 'This true, Albert?' he asked gruffly.

He hesitated. 'Louis is here,' he confirmed.

'Bring him here.'

'I –' Albert prevaricated, but there was no need. Fleeing from the house, Louis had met two new arrivals who promptly sized up the situation correctly. He was returned, sandwiched between the two of them.

'What the devil are you doing here, Sophy?' Alfred exploded wearily, while Albert sank down on a sofa, totally bewildered. 'And, furthermore, what are *you* doing here, Dean?'

'Somebody had to come to sort out this situation, Alfred,' said Sophy firmly, 'and I fear you and Albert are hardly best placed to bring matters to a happy conclusion. Mr Dean,' she hesitated, 'who has always had the interests of our family at heart,' she said diplomatically as Alfred glared at him, 'is so qualified on the other hand. He has so frequently been employed in that capacity in the past. Besides, I needed an escort.'

'Hardly fitting, is it, eloping like this?' Alfred said grumpily.

'Stowerton,' said Dean mildly, 'you go too far. Eloping indeed! Naturally Miss Stowerton has her companion with her. She is at the Hôtel du Plage if you wish to check.' Alfred had the grace to mutter an apology to Sophy.

'Would someone kindly introduce me,' requested Louise sweetly. 'Delighted as I am to welcome you all.' She had quickly summed up Sophy's modest dark green home-made cotton travelling attire with a practised French eye. She smiled cordially, having compared it unfavourably with her own clinging deep blue Lily Langtry jersey dress. 'I am enchanted to meet Albert's sister. And another brother?' she added, with some interest, for Dean was a good-looking man. Here Albert was at a loss and Sophy obliged.

'Delighted as I am to meet your family, Albert – at long last – I hardly expected to greet so many at One time,' Louise announced with a thin smile. 'However, it seems to me we should discuss the matter at issue. *Mon fils*,' she turned to her son firmly, 'what have you to say to these accusations?'

'Young man,' barked Alfred, suddenly remembering why he was there, 'what have you done with my daughter?'

Louis opened then shut his mouth like a fish. However, he was not Albert's son for nothing and he speedily recovered.

'*Cher oncle*, I met Meg in Paris – as I told you, Father –' he added virtuously, 'at the Château des Roses, the home of Madame Elizabeth Stowerton.' Louise's eyes narrowed. There were matters to be investigated here later. 'We had a delightful few days of companionship and then I left. Meg is therefore still at her mother's home, so far as I know.'

'Then why do I get a letter from Elizabeth saying Meg's run off with you?' There was real anxiety in Alfred's voice now.

Louis went white. 'I really cannot imagine. Perhaps you misunderstood. We had a day at Fontainebleau . . .' His voice trailed off.

'Where is my daughter?' thundered Alfred, pressing home his advantage.

Louis was saved from answering, but not in the manner he would have chosen. Through the door, in a wave of perfume and red and pink rustling silk, came two more Stowertons, the last two to expect a welcome in this household.

'Elizabeth,' croaked Alfred resignedly, before turning his attention to his errant daughter with a mixture of relief and anger.

'Good morning, Alfred,' boomed Elizabeth firmly. 'Darling,' she beamed at Albert, ignoring – even if she had noticed – Louise, now languidly reclining.

'Do please introduce me to your friend, Albert,' Louise remained in her chair, poised and composed but with a distinctly acid note in her voice. Soignée the Lily Langtry dress might be, and unfashionable the flowing silks of this upstart intruder, but Louise was well aware when competition worth her mettle entered the scene. Especially *this* competition.

'Louis!' Meg threw herself into his arms, sobbing loudly. 'How could you run away from me, leaving me all alone?'

He looked uncomfortably over her shoulder avoiding everyone's eye – except that of Elizabeth who beamed happily at him, as an angler at an unwary trout.

'Mrs Stowerton,' Joe was too nervous of Luke not to observe the formalities in the bookshop at least, 'I reckon there's trouble brewing for that husband of yours.'

'Trouble, Joe?' Katharine looked puzzled.

'You know there was a miners' strike here back in June? State troops called in and all. Real humdinger.'

'What did they strike for? More money?'

'Nope. Someone had a damn' fool notion of keeping back part of their pay 'case they got sick and needed it.'

'But isn't that a good thing?'

'Not to them, it ain't. They wants their money and says it's up to them how they spend it. Well, they went back to work but it kinda rumbles on. Now, they're mighty good miners up at the Bosworth – or were – but I heard they're getting dissatisfied again.'

Katharine mentioned it to Luke that evening, but he dismissed it impatiently. 'It's only two months since the strike. Takes time to settle down.' The implication was she should keep out of mine affairs. She smarted at yet another reproof, but wisely said nothing.

One day, however, when she was delivering some food for a sick miner, she remembered Joe's words. Outside the miner's shack was a familiar figure coming from the hut, the man who had escorted her to Luke's office the first day she arrived. Luke's manager, Smith.

'Morning, Mrs Stowerton.' Did he look disconcerted? Why should he? It was part of his duty perhaps to visit sick miners. Only when she entered to see half a dozen other miners there, who fell immediately silent, did she think it strange. The conversation stopped abruptly, not because she was a woman, she was sure, but because she was Luke Stowerton's wife.

She tried to talk to Luke again, but he merely said, 'They won't strike. They know I'd dismiss the lot of them. With winter coming on, jobs are harder to find.'

'They're experienced men.'

He lifted his eyebrows as if questioning her claim to knowledge-ability. 'It won't come to that. There's nowhere else would pay as well.'

Nothing further happened, and busy at the Opera House she dismissed it from her mind. Her hesitant criticism of Smith did bring a response, however. Luke considered it, then again dismissed it. 'Why should it be in his interests to stir up trouble?' he answered, and to that she had no reply.

The battle of Cannes raged for three days. As it approached its dénouement, Elizabeth and Louise were firm friends and Albert heartily wished he'd never heard of women at all. Louis was sulking and Meg weeping. Nothing had been resolved, and only in Sophy's presence did the pace of battle lessen.

How do I know the baby is mine? was the gist of Louis' case.

It was this that had turned Louise from defensive mother into Meg's unexpected ally. 'Mon fils,' she had pointed out firmly, 'I am quite sure that your father will have instructed you long since on whether others had preceded you, and the common sense you have inherited from me should convince you that Meg is hardly likely to have consoled herself after your departure with anyone else, if only because there was apparently no one around.'

'I have no money to be married,' Louis pointed out sulkily, falling back on his reserve position.

'Don't look to me, dear boy,' murmured his father.

Another wail from Meg. 'But I want to be married. I *have* to be married.'

'And so you shall, darling,' soothed Elizabeth. 'It's quite all right, Louis. I have heard from that nice nephew of mine, Luke. Katharine's husband.'

Meg suddenly stopped crying.

'He's prepared to give a dowry as Meg is Katharine's sister. If, of course, Louis marries Meg.'

'How much?' enquired Louis practically.

'Five hundred thousand francs, and a small income thereafter.'

There was a short startled pause, then Louis smiled and took Meg's hand. 'Forgive me, dearest,' he said contritely. 'It was the shock. Of course we must marry.'

At the back of his mind was something his father had said yesterday. 'Marriage, *mon fils*, is not the end of diversion. It merely establishes a secure base from which to operate. But it is for you, *mon fils*, to ensure it *is* secure. Keep her happy.'

Meg's baby was born at the end of February, a boy, healthily sized for a 'five and half' month child. Elizabeth suggested it might be a nice gesture to call him Louis-Luc to which Meg and Louis were quite agreeable. It hadn't proved nearly so boring to be married as Louis had feared. They had a delightful *bijou* residence in the Bois de Boulogne, and Meg was very charming. If her housekeeping was not all that could be desired, no matter, for their housekeeper was most efficient. The Baron kept an excellent stable which suited Louis well, and since Elizabeth constantly entertained he found many distractions while Meg awaited the baby. Charmed with the novelty of her own little baby (and nurse) Meg's restlessness did not begin for at least a month after the birth.

The winter in Leadville bore no resemblance to that in Kent. Snow and frost bit hard into the ground, piled up everywhere around. Snow at Bocton had been fun, turning trees into fairytale castles and the ground to a white carpet. Here, as the cold intensified, work continued, the miners huddling from the cold streets into saloons and gambling houses. Katharine hurried to the Opera House swathed in a heavy coat and hood, scarves and muff, rushing in to escape from the bitingly sharp cold. The Opera House with its packed hive of action was a release before the ordeal of a return journey to a house that was never warm. Christmas had been a muted festival. News of Meg's marriage to Louis had alarmed as much as relieved Katharine: to marry after such a short acquaintance seemed foolhardy, if unavoidable – and did Louis know the truth about Meg's condition? She tried to put it out of her mind by throwing herself into work.

But the long winter and excitement of the Opera House did not improve her physical health. There were deep shadows under her eyes, and when Luke announced early in April that he intended to take her away for a week, she did not protest.

'To Denver?' she asked with a flicker of interest.

'No, not there.' He could hardly not take her to meet his father – and Daisy Petal – if they went to Denver. Of Katharine's reaction to her he would have no doubt, but it would lay her open to yet more recriminations from his mother. She did not dare attack him, but Katharine was more at Augusta's mercy. He banged his fist down on the table making Katharine jump in surprise. He grinned apologetically. 'I'm sorry, I guess I was thinking of something at the mines.'

'You nearly always are,' she said.

He shot a look at her. 'And you of the Opera House,' he retorted.

'Yes,' she said bleakly, 'yes.'

'We've made a fine mess of it between us, haven't we?' he said flatly. Was it an appeal or a statement?

'It doesn't have to be, does it?' she asked in sudden hope, as though the spring buds swelling on the trees might signal some kind of answer.

'No,' he said slowly. 'No, I guess it doesn't. We can make of it what we like.' And as if this were admitting too much, he hastily continued: 'We're going to Georgetown.'

She looked puzzled. Georgetown was much nearer than Denver. 'But, Luke, isn't that another mining town?' she asked hesitantly. More miners, more smoke, more noise.

'Yup. Sure is. Silver too. But I promise not to talk contracts, lodes, ore prices or carbonates. Georgetown has been around longer than Leadville and has some pretty nice country round about it. Lakes, mountains, waterfalls – *and* it has something else.'

'What's that?' she asked with curiosity.

'Wait and see,' he told her, suddenly lighthearted.

Leadville's best clothing store only succeeded in making Katharine look like a slightly less severe version of Martha and Mary in her view. Expensive, ornate and straight from New York the clothes might be, but they were too ornate for Katharine's taste, no inch left uncovered with frills and tucks. At least this Georgetown might have better shops, she thought, without a great deal of hope, and slightly wondering at the fact that she, Katharine Stowerton, should suddenly have developed any interest in her appearance. It was not wishing to be compared with Martha and Mary, she told herself firmly. That Luke had taken to commenting on what she wore did not enter into it.

'They're building the Colorado Central railroad out towards Leadville from Georgetown, but I'm afraid it's the stage again for us this time,' he apologised. 'Only fifty miles or so.'

This time, however, the coach was less of a boneshaker than on the ride from Canyon. All the same, comfort was not a high priority.

'This surprise of yours had better be worth it,' she said grimly, clinging to a strap.

'It will be,' he assured her.

As Luke had warned her, Georgetown, though built more solidly than Leadville, was uninteresting in itself. But when at last they reached the hotel, her interest was quickly aroused. A two-storied building, glass-fronted, with the unlikely name of the Hôtel de Paris above it. 'Here?' she asked, intrigued.

'Yes,' Luke replied. 'It's not long been open, and is run by a young Frenchman, Louis Dupuy. You'll meet him. The glass front is because it used to be Delmonico's bakery. It's more of a restaurant at the moment than a hotel, but it does have some rooms, and people are coming from all over to visit it. He's a fine French cook. I thought we'd save the expense of going to Paris,' he joked, then wished he hadn't, as the thought of just how far away it was lay between them.

The rooms were small and the furniture heavy, but the dining room made up for that. Superbly floored and panelled, it possessed a centrepiece of a beautiful fountain in the middle, just like the pictures she had seen of French restaurants. Katharine laughed in sheer pleasure when she saw it.

'It's like seeing the Opera House in the midst of Leadville,' she said.

'Wait till you see the menu, if you think that's something.' He handed it to her. Sweetbreads Eugénie, pheasant, strawberry Charlotte *avec coulis de cassis, coq au vin*. She laughed again. 'I'll wake up and find myself back at Hank's Diner.'

'America's a surprising place,' rejoined Luke. 'There's room for anything. When a place is new, there are no precedents, no rules to follow. You build what you like. People are open to anything. Try something out. If it doesn't work, there's a dozen other ideas to take its place. But I reckon Louis has this working all right. There's a library here, too. I came to see it when he had just opened.'

'A library?' she asked doubtfully.

'I know what you're thinking: dime novels. But it's not like that. He's very learned, is Dupuy. His library contains erudite volumes on philosophy, science, classics.'

'Classics?' she echoed, suddenly alert.

'Even Virgil,' he joked.

'Then you, my pious Aeneas,' she retorted happily, 'can introduce me. In the Opera House, behind the scenes, Latin is rarely spoken.'

'Alas that Roderick is not here.'

'Roderick?' She looked blank. 'Oh, Mayfield,' she said, surprised. 'Do you know, I'd quite forgotten?' Worlds away, and would she change one man for the other? Never. Suddenly excited, she knew she would enjoy the next few days, and entered with enthusiasm on all his suggestions for excursions. There were indeed silver mines, but they were dominated by the huge peaks that towered over them.

'The dome of the continent, they call these,' said Luke as they set out one day. 'Gray and Irwin peaks. Over fourteen thousand feet high. And we're going right up to the top.'

'On a rope?' she enquired sweetly.

'Not quite. There are bridle paths up. Remember, we're some way up already here,' he said encouragingly. 'Around ten thousand, I guess. Not quite so high as Cloud City, Leadville.'

The ascent was hard going in such thin air, but the view when they arrived at the summit compensated.

'Silent upon a peak in Darien,' she quoted, for here above the timberline there was no sound even of birds, only an eagle circling.

'I feel just like Stout Cortez,' he grumbled, flinging himself down exhausted on flat rock. 'You're supposed to be able to see way over one hundred miles from here. I'll leave them to you to count.'

She looked out over seemingly never-ending plains, mountains, and more mountains, and below them on one side green valleys as far as the eye could see.

'If we come up here in the summer we could take a trip to Middle Park. Now that's something,' he said longingly, lolling back, hands behind his head. 'Rivers, prairies, mountains, animals, birds – it has everything, but it means a day in the saddle to get there, and camping out. Worth it, though, for the animals.'

'Aren't there any on this mountain?'

'Nothing much up here. Only the pika – look, there's one!' The small rabbit-like creature, almost invisible against the rocks, uttered a shrill bark of alarm and rushed for cover at the movement. 'Down below, there's only bears – grizzlies – oh, and lions of course. Bobcats . . . nothing too much.' He tried to keep a straight face as he saw her expression, but failed.

'But we walked up!' And, it struck her, they had yet to walk down. 'Oh,' as she heard him laugh, 'you're joking.'

'No, honey, I am not. But they won't come near our path. Not in daylight, anyway.'

'Then let's go right *now*,' she said firmly.

*   *   *

186

Sleeping side by side in the huge mahogany bed that night, tired after the long walk, she felt closer to Luke in spirit than she had since their marriage, almost able to imagine them at Bocton again. Luke was sleeping peacefully, for Monsieur Dupuy had excelled himself at dinner with a *pot-au-feu* and *tarte tatin*. Perversely, tonight, as if awakening after a long winter, she wanted his arms round her, but he slept on oblivious. Her body tense, she took a long time to fall asleep, staring out at the stars in the dark sky. Tomorrow, there was always tomorrow . . .

The air was pure up here, on the rowing boat out on Green Lake. Hot for April, the sun danced on the water. Katharine took off her jacket, as did Luke, rolling up his shirt sleeves. She noticed as if for the first time the fine golden hairs on his arms, the freckles at his wrist. Suddenly he glanced up, catching her watching him intently, and wondered what she could be thinking that she looked at him so. He smiled slightly, and she felt an answering tug of her heart.

'I was thinking I could give you perch for lunch, caught by my own hand, and cooked on our own fire like the old pioneers, but the perch are spawning so I guess we'll just have to put up with Louis's picnic,' he said when they got back to land.

'That won't be hard,' she said greedily, unpacking goats' cheeses, thinly sliced ham, and pâtés, together with freshly baked bread.

They had found a sheltered spot and the sun was pleasantly warm on their faces. After eating, Luke began to doze. Restless, she picked up a book to read. Then she laid it aside, and sat back to observe the signs of returning spring. A ground squirrel squatted on its hindlegs a few yards away, a chicadee sang in a tree hole above her head, a blue heron fished in the lake oblivious to the spawning season, a kingfisher watched and waited its moment. She thought of Bocton and the spring there. The wood anemones would be out, and violets, and wild daffodils. Her garden at Bocton – who would care for it now?

She felt tears prick her eyes, but then the pangs of loss were assuaged by the thought that if it wasn't for Luke, Bocton could have been razed to the ground by now. In gratitude she picked a sprig of spruce, and waved it back and forth as if in salute to her sleeping husband. He had taken off his tie in deference to the sudden spring, and she bent over him, thoughtfully tickling his nose with the spruce. He sniffed in his sleep, brushed it away, and then awoke, his eyes full on her. Turning pink at being discovered watching him so closely, she stuck the sprig of spruce in the neck of his shirt in embarrassment.

'What's that for?' he asked lazily, staring up at her, resting his hands behind his head.

'To adorn the bosom of the fair,' she answered. Whence had it come, that reply? Out of a past that was dead, gone for ever.

A glint. A sudden flame in his blue eyes. 'It scratches.'

'So did the Sweet William,' she said lightly, her voice trembling for no reason, it seemed.

'Then why didn't you complain?' he countered, apparently lazily, but with every nerve tense.

'I –' She stopped, for to this she had no answer.

In a trice he had sat up, gripped her by her arms and was kneeling at her side.

'Katharine, *why* did you not complain? Tell me.' Insistent, gentle, demanding, his blue eyes daring her. So easy to lie, so hard to speak the simple truth. Yet when had she ever evaded difficulties?

'I suppose because I liked it,' holding his gaze, despite her pounding heart.

'The Sweet William?' he enquired gently, mockingly.

'No, you.' On a helter-skelter now. No stopping.

'Liked?' holding her inexorably.

'Loved,' she answered, crossly.

His grip relaxed.

'Oh, Katie May,' he whispered. 'Oh, Katie May.' He took her hand, sitting down by her side again, and said no more, for there was no more to say. But that night he watched her from the bed, as she brushed her long chestnut hair with measured strokes. Self-conscious, as she sat before the old wooden dressing table with its gilt mirror held up by two cupids, she was aware of his gaze first on her hair, then on the rise and fall of her breast under the thin lawn nightdress.

'You've miscounted.' His voice came unsteadily, huskily. 'You've already passed a hundred.'

'Yes,' she said, and laid down the hairbrush and turned round to face him.

He swung off the bed and came to her, pulling her to her feet and into his arms. She thought the kiss would never end, as though all the poisonous anguish of the last months were being sucked from her by the sweetness and the fierceness of his desire. He held her so close to him that she wanted to pull away, feeling his desire grow yet more insistent, yet wanted to be closer still, afraid and unafraid, until at last she lost all power of thought as he swept her off her feet and held her aloft for a moment until she laughed aloud in happiness at the joy on his face and at the promise of what was to come. He laid her down on the bed, and began with loving hands to undo the lace ribbon at the neck of her nightdress. 'And now, my heart,' as he bent over her in love, and spoke with husky voice, 'shall truly begin the wooing of Katie May.'

She stirred sleepily in the morning, opened her eyes, closed them again and then remembered. She glanced across to the other side of the bed, irrationally disappointed to see it empty. Yet Luke was not far away. At the sound of her stirring, he came across, bent over and kissed her. He said nothing, obviously waiting for her to speak first.

'What shall we do today?' she asked inanely, smiling languorously, confidently up at him.

'How about what we did last night?'

Their last two days at Georgetown passed in a mist of happiness. Later she remembered animatedly discussing with him whether it was preferable to be attacked by a black bear or a grizzly. She remembered the minute crayfish caught under a rock near the

Devil's Gateway, and Luke's indignant face as, having cleaned them assiduously, he then burnt them to uneatable fragments on the fire he had so carefully built.

'I didn't know you could build fires,' she said.

'Certainly I can. Old Grimmer taught me, the same day as I chased you round the old maze and left you in it.'

'I don't remember —' she began. Then her eyes opened wide in indignation. 'Yes, I do,' she cried. 'How *could* you?' She aimed a blow at him. 'I was only three.'

'I'll make it up to you,' he said penitently. And deep in the night, with a sky like velvet outside, he did, till she cried out in pleasure, holding him to her as though she would never let him go. Ah, yes, she remembered that, for surely nothing could erase it now.

Yet as the stage coach rattled up Chestnut Street, she felt panic sweeping over her, caught again the pall of life under Augusta's roof. 'Luke,' she said questioningly, turning to him, her eyes full of fear.

Catching her mood, for he felt it himself, he replied soberly, 'It will be all right if we stand together.'

But how short that time was to be. Among the letters awaiting them was one for Katharine from Meg.

'I have a dear little baby boy,' she told her sister casually. 'We've called him Louis, and of course Luc.'

Of course, *of course*. After all, she tried to reason, it was Luke's baby, whether Louis knew it or not. And never would Meg let her forget it. Even far away in America. She heard again Meg's voice: 'He's mine. It's me he really loves.'

'There's a letter here from Pinpole,' said Luke, tossing it over to her. 'They're still arguing over the wills part of The Case, but Pinpole doesn't think it will come to court, and that it's more to hold us up than from conviction in their argument. He's sure they're saving their real ammunition for the arguments over gavelkind. So he's preparing our case for that. Full steam ahead, like the Colorado Central railroad, it seems. All roads lead to Leadville, even Boc — what's the matter, Katharine?' he asked in concern, seeing her white face.

'Nothing, nothing.' She tried to be casual. 'It's Meg. She's had her baby.'

'Splendid.' Luke picked up Pinpole's letter again to study it in more detail and then realised he was being somewhat offhand. 'Boy or girl?'

'Boy. They've called him Louis-Luc,' she said flatly.

'Luke. That's nice of them.' He continued reading the letter.

Didn't he care? she thought, bewildered. Perhaps not. Not even for his child. Meg was someone else's responsibility now. In another country, another time. Paid off in full with thirty pieces of silver. *He doesn't like children. He doesn't want the responsibility*, she heard Meg say again.

'Suppose we had a child?' Her voice rose out of nowhere.

He looked up sharply. 'No, Katharine,' he said gently. 'Not here. I've tried to explain how I feel.'

189

'Yes, you've tried to explain.' Or was it an excuse because he didn't want children? This last week – the memory hurt now, the wooing was all – but the living after, ah, that was different.

'Suppose I want one?' she said quietly.

He stared out of the window, unable to face her. Over there was Bosworth, the black magnet that kept him chained to Leadville. How could he raise a family here? Condemn a child to the life he had led in this house? He would want a child to know the happiness of green fields, of mountains, not the smoke of a mining town.

'Wait,' he said desperately.

'But –'

'No!' His face changed. Unable to face her, unable to bear the ensuing battle, he left for the office to face whatever awaited him there. It was not good. As he walked down the street he felt the animosity directed at him from groups of men he recognised. When he reached the office, he found out why. The Bosworth miners were on strike.

Wretched with misery, Katharine went to the book store where Joe greeted her as though she'd been away six months, not a week.

'Anything happened, Joe?' she asked dispiritedly.

'Sure has, Mrs Stowerton. They'll be mighty glad you're back. The opera company's come to town, and they changed the programme. We got no scenery drops for 'em. We ain't had much call for ships before.'

'Ships?' she repeated, bewildered.

'*HMS Pinafore*,' he announced with relish. 'And *The Bohemian Girl*. "I am the Ruler of the Queen's Navee",' he suddenly boomed out happily.

When she went to the Opera House later that day, she could hear there was already a rehearsal in progress. A new atmosphere, a new excitement. She felt her interest quickening as she heard a tenor voice ring out from the stage singing: '. . . And told his tale/In his own melodious way/He sang "Ah well a day".'

She stopped a moment to listen before entering, as the sound lifted into the smoke-filled Leadville sky. Then she pushed open the door and went in.

Chapter Eleven

'But what are they striking *for*, Smith?' Luke demanded, bewilderment mixed with rage as he burst into the office. Smith was unconcernedly studying yield pay sheets. He looked up lazily.

'Wahl,' he drawled, 'Mr Stowerton,' pushing his hat back on his head and leaning back in his chair, 'more money seems to be at the root of it, I guess.'

'More money? But they get three dollars-fifty a day,' said Luke, astounded. 'That's half a dollar more than most other mines are paying. I'll talk to them. There's some misunderstanding.'

'I don't advise that, Mr Stowerton. Things are very ugly at the moment. The yield was down.'

'But that was last year. It's all over with,' said Luke impatiently.

'Sure, but the way they see it is this. They don't have no confidence that Bosworth is going to last for ever. Not now the Little Pittsburg ore has given out *and* the Chrysolite's stock is down. If Tabor's mines can run dry, so can Stowerton's. And their jobs with it.'

'But that's plum crazy. That means we're back to where we were a year ago. Sure, one ore body gave out in the Little Pittsburg, but they've found a new deposit and it's still trading.'

Yet Luke knew as well as Smith that the old confidence had never returned. When he had come back to Leadville last July, the strike had already finished, but he'd heard plenty about it. The miners had returned to work on the same terms as before the strike, having won nothing. Resentment festered and confidence in a bright future ahead had been shaken irrevocably, especially when share prices in Little Pittsburg and Chrysolite remained low. Yet the Robert E. Lee, the richest mine on Fryer Hill, had no problems. This was the mine that held the fabulous record of two tons of ore producing 11,839 oz of silver per ton at a time when 200 was reckoned a bonanza, beating even the Bosworth's yield. If the Robert E. Lee still flourished, then the expectation should be that the others would also. Including Bosworth – and the Manhattan claim lying tantalisingly unworked.

'Rumours about Bosworth, the same as there was about Little Pittsburg. If you get on the wrong side of them,' Smith pointed out dispassionately, 'the union can call them all out again.'

'Rumours,' said Luke disgustedly. 'That's what started the strike last year. The rumours were started by the union itself. Why else did the leaders all leave town doublequick afterwards?'

'Seems they're back,' said Smith shortly, 'now the summer's coming.

Leave it and you'll see, Mr Stowerton. The men will drift back to work when they run out of money.'

Luke didn't altogether trust Smith, yet what he said made sense. No point in letting the men think they had you on the run. And after all, what had he, Smith, to gain from a prolonged strike? The less profit the mines made, the less he himself made.

'I'll give it two weeks,' he told him, 'and see what happens.'

The intimidation of working miners and the violence of last year had sown seeds for the future, making deeper the rift between men and management, and he didn't want to exacerbate it. Sullen miners would be all too ready to believe that the bonanza on Fryer Hill was now exhausted. Luke still found the strike puzzling, however, since Bosworth men were among the highest paid miners in Leadville. They must know how well off they were? He decided to visit the mine straightaway. He found it desolate amid the din and clatter elsewhere on Fryer Hill. A skeleton crew was working the Bosworth under Jonathan Trevanick, but to his relief Luke found the mine manager in the office adjoining the shaft house. The news was not good.

'There's summat going on, Mr Stowerton,' Jonathan said grimly. 'That Manhattan claim's about to be worked. The shaft is now equipped with a windlass and a shafthouse is being built. I heard tell that the Manhattan's aiming to pay four dollars a day,' he added, with a sidelong look at Luke.

'That's crazy, Jonathan. And why only a windlass? That means they are banking on striking silver between fifty and a hundred feet. Yet they must know Bosworth's shaft is much deeper than that – that we need steam hoisting?'

Jeremiah was convinced that Bosworth's rich lode dipped eastwards and ran into the Manhattan. If Father was right, the Manhattan would never get to it with only a windlass. Father must be right, he reasoned; they were under-capitalised. Then why not sell? Why risk starting operations? It would not look good if they then had to sell with no trace of silver down to 100 feet. Promise was worth more than half-explored claims.

As if picking up Luke's thoughts, Jonathan said, 'Seems to me they're fitting it up for the look of the thing, more than anything else.'

'No, they're banking on not having to go too deep.'

'If they can't afford no machinery, how come they can run to four dollars a day?'

There was no answer, for Luke had none to give. He stared out at the enigma of the Manhattan.

'Two weeks,' said Luke slowly. 'That's all *we* can afford.'

Jonathan looked startled. 'Money, Mr Luke?'

'No,' said Luke. 'Time.' The men wandering round the Manhattan claim were strangers, newcomers to Leadville. But there weren't enough there to mine in earnest. For that they'd need old hands . . .

The days went by, and nothing happened. The striking Bosworth miners swaggered in houses, drank in saloons, which in itself was odd,

192

Luke thought. Miners were not known for their savings. Earn it, spend it, was their usual way of life. The State Street brothels flourished, and the miners had an insolence in their step as they passed the offices of the Stowerton empire. Inside Luke sweated and waited. 'Just for a handful of silver . . .' Browning's poem came into his mind. Men fought over it, killed for it, it beckoned and enchanted until it wove a filigree net around you, coiling you in it, strangling, choking, temptress turned murderess. Yesterday a young journalist from the *Chronicle* had come to see him, enthusiasm and intelligence in his face, determined to ferret out the truth. A year ago Luke might have been that young man. Now he was firmly entrenched on the other side of the fence.

Katharine hummed as she hurried down the street to the post office to pick up the Opera House mail, hoisting her dress well clear of the roadway covered in dust and dung. The tunes of *Pinafore* never seemed to leave her head with their catchy light-hearted rhythms, so right for spring and the promise of the summer ahead. The Opera House was a livelier place than when plays were being performed. Then intensity had reigned, whether comedy or tragedy was being performed. Now singers bathed the theatre in song. She did not care for all the cast, however. In particular she disliked the tenor. However captivating and handsome he was on stage with his tall figure, dark hair and liquid brown eyes, she thought him vain and conceited; he jested offstage in a way she thought patronising, and had a lazy habit of expecting stage hands to obey his every bidding immediately. Perversely it annoyed her that this included her. I am Mrs Luke Stowerton, she had an impulse to say. She could not, for had she not demanded, and wished for, equality? She was a stage hand and that was that.

At the post office she found more of a milling crowd than a queue, the first people already being given their mail. She squeezed inside the door of Tabor's palatial building, but there was a sudden commotion in the street as a group of miners decided to push their way into the post office, colliding with the first few satisfied customers trying to emerge. One smartly dressed man staggered off balance at her side, his mail knocked from his hand. Instinctively she bent to pick it up, handing it back to him – and then recognising him. It was Herbert Smith, Luke's manager.

He thanked her stiffly as he took in who she was, and she almost recoiled at the dislike in his eyes, as he quickly grabbed his letters and hurried outside. The encounter troubled her, and for a moment she could not think why. Then she did. Why should Luke's manager collect mail addressed to the New York Mining Company? She'd never heard of such a company. She began to wonder.

The following day Luke unexpectedly began a family discussion on the future of the mine. Although he had told her that his mother had a good head for business, she smarted at the way the discussion was aimed at Augusta and not at herself. It was unreasonable of her, she knew, but she felt that Luke's refusal to discuss mine matters with her blocked off a line of communication between them that should have remained open.

'Dismiss them,' ordained Augusta in lordly fashion.

'That would be unwise, Mother. It might precipitate action that would endanger Trevanick's men.'

'If you dismiss them, then you know where you are. At your absurd rates, men are easy to come by.'

'And risk setting off another miners' strike in Leadville just when it is beginning to recover from the last one?'

'It would remind them that they gained nothing from last year's strike,' she said scornfully.

'No, and they haven't forgotten that,' Luke said shortly. 'The profits for the managers grow greater, but their share remains the same. I am tempted to an increase.'

'If you do, you'll have every mine manager in Leadville your enemy,' said Augusta unemotionally, 'and the men will merely think you a fool.'

In the flickering light of the oil lamps – Jeremiah had refused to patronise Tabor's gas plant – Mary and Martha sat silently, knowing their opinions were not sought by either side.

'Luke, are you sure that man Smith is telling you everything?' Katharine began slowly. She would have preferred to wait till they were alone, but felt bound to raise it now, since the subject was under discussion.

'What more is there to tell?' He turned to her, almost unwillingly.

'He was picking up mail addressed to the New York Mining Company.'

'Who?' asked Luke blankly. 'I've never heard of them.'

'Mr Smith is a Chapel man,' said Augusta warningly. 'A God-fearing man. I will not hear the word of the devil spread about him.'

'It is hardly the word of the devil to report a fact,' said Katharine caustically.

'Katharine,' Luke said sharply, but she smarted at the injustice.

'Will you allow her to speak to your mother in such terms?' Augusta asked tonelessly as she sat back smugly.

'We are discussing the future of the mine, Katharine. Nothing else at the moment,' Luke tried to deflect further conflict.

'Very well. Then I ask again. Why should Mr Smith collect mail for a company not even registered in Leadville?' Luke looked up sharply. 'I checked with the claims office,' she explained. He frowned. 'Could you not use the telephone to see if it is registered in Denver?' she suggested.

'The invention of the devil,' muttered Augusta.

'No, Mother-in-law, Alexander Graham Bell,' said Katharine sweetly, keeping her eyes on Luke. 'You could ask your father to check.'

A split second for reaction to this mention of the unmentionable, and Augusta stood up. 'That name is not spoken in this house.'

'But as Luke pointed out, this is a business meeting,' Katharine said

194

calmly. 'I'm sorry, Mother-in-Law, if it pains you, but Uncle Jeremiah is the owner of Bosworth.'

Luke tried to ignore the tension between the two of them and concentrate on the mine. 'Yes,' he said finally, 'I will do that. There's precious little else I can do after all,' he said bitterly. However, the telephone was still rare in Leadville, and the Stowerton household, hardly surprisingly, did not possess one. He pushed back his chair. 'I'll do it now. Smith will have left for the day, and I'll have the office to myself.' He was thankful to escape the house, rather than seeing any real need to follow up this will o' the wisp thread.

The next day, unable to wait until she saw Luke in the evening, Katharine went to his office in the afternoon, having noticed Smith leave shortly before. The usual group of miners was hanging about outside. There were muttered comments as she passed; one thoughtfully spat on the ground in front of her; none removed his hat. What had happened to change them? she thought, bewildered. These were men she knew, men she had visited when sick.

'You're right, Katharine.' Luke looked up as she entered, almost as though he had been expecting her. 'There was something odd. The New York Mining Company now owns Manhattan. It's registered in New York. Father is leaving to come here right away. Smith's tied up with this strike somehow, that's for sure, and Father has a way with the men. They know him better than me.'

'Now ain't it a pity he'll be too late?' Smith was lolling against the outside doorpost, having arrived unnoticed. He smirked, and tipped his hat exaggeratedly. 'Your men have just signed for Manhattan at four dollars, Stowerton. Just too bad you didn't talk to 'em earlier. They was waiting for it. Not that it would have worked, I reckon. They figure the Bosworth's had its day.'

'And I wonder who told them that?' Luke commented wearily.

'Now would I do anything that underhand, Mr Stowerton?' Smith's voice rose plaintively. 'I do own just about all the shares in the Manhattan, as you'll no doubt discover, but we mine owners should stick together. And I thank you, Mrs Stowerton, for bringing my plans forward a little. No harm done, as it happens.' He swept off his hat and made an ironic bow.

Luke stood up, hands trembling, as blind rage gripped him. He took two paces forward, tried to check himself and failed. His right fist shot out in a punch to Smith's jaw.

Smith staggered back, losing his balance and collapsing on the floor. He got up quickly, eyes narrowing.

'Now that, Mr Stowerton, *was* an unwise move. I can see you're sore about the situation,' he said softly, 'but suppose I call my boys in here? I wouldn't give much for your chances – or hers,' he leered. 'Still, I reckon I can wait till I see Daddy. Daddy won't like what you've done, Mr Stowerton. I won't bother to take my wages this week. Reckon you'll need them.'

Luke slumped in his chair after Smith had left.

'Can you get more miners?' Katharine asked worriedly.

'Easily. We pay well. But what I don't like is miners that know our ore body working the next door claim. There's trouble in that. Claim limits are clear enough above ground, everyone can see them, but below ground it's a different matter. There have been ugly scenes when rival claim miners meet. And with Smith's poisonous tongue it's like leaving a flank of your army unprotected when the enemy's advancing. If only we could get hold of that mine.' He crashed a fist on the table. 'Father is sure the seam from Bosworth runs horizontally to the Manhattan and reckons it's getting richer the further east it goes. It could be the richest bonanza in Leadville.'

'You're getting the fever,' she said half-jokingly. 'You've got silver in your eyes. The richest vein yet, indeed. You're getting like my father and the horses.'

'Don't forget he sometimes won, Katharine,' he replied quietly.

'But more often lost,' she came back quickly in sudden alarm.

Luke ignored this, continuing disjointedly: 'Jonathan Trevanick will stay with us, and so will his men. I can make up the rest easily enough.' He grimaced. 'Four dollars a day and an eight-hour shift indeed! No wonder Smith seduced them. Easy enough to start a rumour that Bosworth ore is running low just like the Chrysolite, and there's a bonanza next door. That's the trouble with Fryer. It's unpredictable. You think a patch is just barren rock, like the Triangle Mine over there. You dig it and discover a pocket worth a king's ransom. Several kings. Yet you can dig where a seam ought to lie and find nothing,' he said bitterly.

'Take care, Luke,' she said soberly. 'One gambler in the family is enough.'

He took her hands. 'Never fear,' he said, 'never fear.' But his eyes were not on her but at the yield chart, and fear she did.

The rehearsal ended early that evening and, tired from concentrating on her prompt book, she decided to hurry home without waiting for Luke who, judging from the light burning in his office as she passed, was working late hours. The usual buzz of noise came at her from all sides, the sense of pulsing entertainment going on behind closed doors, as miners from the Manhattan celebrated their good fortune, and the stories of the four dollar mine circulated – along with tales of the failing Bosworth – and how the new mine had deposits to beat even the Robert E. Lee.

She was glad as she turned into Chestnut Street, hurrying past the Grand Hotel and stores, past saloons, until the tall dark trees guarding the Stowerton boundaries came into view. She was not far from their home, the only dim lamp thirty yards off and the street deserted this far along, when from behind a hand grabbed her, pulling her to an alcove, stifling her scream. It was Smith, she knew instantly, as he hissed in her ear, 'I thought I recognised you passing by, Mrs Stowerton. no need to scream, I ain't going to harm you.' He released her, blocking her way, and his eyes ran up and down her lasciviously, making her shiver, calculating her chances of dashing past him to gain the security of their property, where he would never dare follow her.

'Just thought I'd like to thank you personally for interrupting my plans. No harm done, of course, but you couldn't have known that. You and that stupid husband of yours.' He grabbed her wrist as she tried to move past him. 'Oh yes, Herbert Smith don't forget who his friends are. Nor his foes neither.' He pulled her to him again in one rough movement. 'Tasty little piece, ain't you?' as she struggled against him. 'Let's see now if you English misses are as prim as you seem.' He stopped her scream with his thick lips and steaming breath, one hand pushing aside her cloak and fastening over her breast. He was choking, revolting her for a moment, until as suddenly she was free as he was yanked away from her from behind. Luke?

'Friend of yours, Kate?'

Not Luke, she thought dazedly, almost staggering in the dark as Smith lurched triumphantly away. She tried to express her thanks stiltedly. Her heart sank. It was Daniel Pearson, the tenor at the opera house.

He looked at her quizzically. 'Not at all, Kate. I take it that was not your husband?'

'Of course not,' she cried, indignant that he could think so.

'Then I had better offer you my escort home.'

'Thank you,' she said stiffly. 'It is only a short way now. There is no need.'

'I believe there is,' he insisted. 'I cannot feel this is any place for an English lady to be walking unescorted after dark. What can your husband be thinking of?'

'It's not his fault,' she said defiantly. 'It's mine. I didn't wait for him.'

'Then you must certainly allow me.' He offered his arm which, feeling rather like a naughty child, she took – just as Luke came up behind them, seeing them step out together into the street.

'Might I enquire who you are, sir?'

'This is Daniel Pearson, Luke,' Katharine said quickly. 'He has only just offered me his escort.'

'Then, Mr Pearson, you will kindly desist from escorting my wife anywhere ever again.'

'Luke, you don't understand,' she said, horrified. 'It was my fault. I was coming home alone and your manager, Mr Smith, followed me and –' Her voice faltered.

'I arrived and he saw the error of his ways,' said Pearson cheerfully.

Luke's face changed. 'Then I offer you my gratitude and my apologies, Mr Pearson,' he said stiffly. 'I had not understood, and I am indeed grateful to you.' But the look on his face boded ill for Katharine.

The quarrel had been sharp but short, and tension still simmered between them at breakfast the next day. It was a Saturday and thus the whole family breakfasted together, unlike other working days. Augusta still kept to her spartan diet in mute protest at a battle lost over the food. Her muffin was taken without confection.

A commotion in the entrance hall then a raised irritable voice were the first indications that this was not going to be a normal Saturday. With an appalled glance at his mother, Luke quickly rose and went to the door, just as Jeremiah swept through it, throwing hat and coat at the help.

There could be no doubt as to who it was. It must be her uncle. She would meet Jeremiah at last. Katharine stared fascinated, a piece of muffin halfway to her mouth, at this tall man with craggy face and dark brooding eyes.

'I thought you would come to the office, Father,' said Luke, embarrassed, his eyes on his mother.

'Why?' asked Jeremiah testily. 'My house, isn't it? Good morning, Augusta.' His wife sat expressionless, immobile, her daughters frozen at their breakfast, until they could work out what was expected of them in this unexpected situation. Augusta spoke slowly, deliberately, addressing not her husband, but her son.

'You knew of this visitation, Luke?'

'Yes, Mother. It was necessary because of business, but I did not know Father was coming to this house, or I would have warned you lest it cause you pain.'

'Pain!' she snorted, rising to her feet. 'It will cause no pain, for I have nothing to say to him. Come, Martha, Mary.' She moved towards the door, not even glancing to see if they followed.

'Wait!' Jeremiah's voice rang out, and through years of habit Martha and Mary stopped in their tracks. 'Don't be a damn fool, woman.'

Katharine tried not to laugh at hearing Augusta so addressed.

'The future of the mine concerns you as much as me. More, because it provides the money you live on. How else do you think you're going to get your money. No mine, no smelter, no roof!'

'It's not my concern,' she began, involuntarily addressing Jeremiah as she began to consider her position more carefully.

Seeing his advantage he pressed it home. 'Come, Augusta, you've a good head on you. Time you used it instead of spreading my bad name all round town.'

'I speak only the truth,' she said haughtily.

'And what is truth?' he asked wrily. 'Come, Augusta, sit down and finish your breakfast.' He glared at the table. 'Call this breakfast? Don't I pay you enough to eat decently?'

'The Lord provideth –' she began.

'Some good food, and I'll make sure I'll eat it. Luke, we'll take our luncheon at the Clarendon, and dinner.' His eyes went to Katharine, belatedly realising Luke's wife's presence. 'Luncheon anyway,' he amended hastily. 'Alfred's girl, eh?' He ran his eye over her critically.

'I'm so glad to meet you, Uncle Jeremiah,' she said sincerely.

He grinned, an expression that made his face almost unrecognisable to his family. 'Handful, my brother Alfred. Got a good head on you, have you? Need to to have kept my brother in order, I'll be bound. Who's doing it now? Sophy, I suppose. How *is* Mouse?' he asked wistfully. 'That's what I used to call her.'

'Aunt Sophy's well.'

'Don't underestimate her, your aunt. Never so surprised in my life as when Mouse told that curate to pack up his suit and go.'

'But I thought he jilted her,' replied Katharine, intrigued.

'No,' he replied with scorn. 'That's what everyone thought. Not true. She didn't want to marry him. Preferred spinsterhood. Always surprised me. Dark horse, Sophy. Like me, eh?' He chuckled, smoothing his dark hair. Augusta regarded him with as much distaste as if Moses had danced a jig on her dining table. 'Now, coffee, if you please. Can you manage that, Augusta?'

'Before you sit at my table, Jeremiah,' his wife retorted, 'you will answer one question. Is that *person* accompanying you?'

'Daisy Petal, you mean? No, too much of a shock.'

'It is good of you to appreciate my feelings,' said Augusta, gratified.

'Not yours,' Jeremiah took a bite of muffin and grimaced. 'Too much of a shock for her,' he added devastatingly.

Luncheon at the Clarendon Hotel was a vast improvement on the Stowerton residence, and Jeremiah at last proclaimed himself satisfied after a trout and steak.

'Now, my boy, not doing too good a job, are you?'

Knowing this to be his father's usual method of flushing argument into the open, Luke kept a grip on himself. 'Smith was your man,' he pointed out.

'Mind you,' said Jeremiah, grandly ignoring this, 'I don't blame you. You don't know how to handle the men like I do, and things have always been difficult up on Fryer's. I'm going to take a look to see what's happening at the Bosworth and Manhattan.'

When their buggy arrived at Fryer's, Jeremiah sniffed the air appreciatively. Luke looked at him in surprise. 'You can't be admiring the fresh air here, Father, not after Denver, surely?' Smoke dust, the acrid smell of coal and steam, was making the May sky overcast and yellow-grey.

'Why not? Nothing like it,' said Jeremiah with relish. 'I know what you're thinking, lad, but you're wrong. What I smell here isn't smoke. It's silver – and I'm never wrong about that. I can dowse it out; my nose twitches over silver and it's twitching now. I tell you, I *know* Bosworth's ore runs right along into Manhattan.'

'We can't find anyone who knows what the Manhattan thinks it's got. Not even the miners.' Luke had paid enough spies but when he had disentangled rumour from fact, had been left with nothing. 'And according to what Trevanick says, the lode is petering out on the boundary adjoining Manhattan. It happens. Happens all the time. It could be running the other way, away from Manhattan, or even not be a lode at all, but an extra large pocket.'

Jeremiah snorted. 'Get off your backside, boy, and learn to get a nose.'

'I have one,' retorted Luke quietly. 'And it's smelling something wrong. Look at that windlass. Where's the steam-hoisting equipment, or even a whim and horse which would see them down to two hundred feet?'

Jeremiah dismissed his doubts impatiently, as Luke had feared. 'Undercapitalised. Wait till they hit silver,' he said with relish. 'Then they'll seek capital or sell out – and I'll be right here when they do. I'll give them the biggest grubstake ever.'

Silver fever, thought Luke dazedly, that's what Katharine called it. Silver fever.

Jeremiah seemed to take a perverse satisfaction in haunting the house at every opportunity, although sleeping at the Clarendon. It was almost, thought Luke, as if he intended to provoke Augusta into divorcing him. He must have forgotten what Mother was like if he really thought that would work. But the everlasting silence and wall of disapproval in the household began to affect even Jeremiah.

'Next time,' he told Luke grimly, 'I'm bringing Daisy Petal. Trouble is, she's more of a lady than your mother, she'd come off worst. I'd back Augusta in the ring in a fight against Tom Sayers with one hand tied behind her back.'

When he wasn't talking about silver, Jeremiah occupied himself with endless discussions of the gavelkind case. He had struck up a rapport with Katharine, at first delighted at her work at the Opera House (for its annoyance value to Augusta), then in talking to her about Bocton. Never his brothers, or even Stowerton House, she noticed. Bocton, always Bocton. Nothing loth, however, she talked for hours about it, until suddenly he would stop her almost angrily. 'That's enough,' he would say, unable to bear more, yet always he would come back to it. He pressed Luke for details of The Case.

'The pleadings are still going back and forth,' explained Luke reluctantly. He didn't want even to think of Bocton. 'Statement of claim, defence, reply – it's never-ending. It's all over the question of what happened to the tenure of the land when Sir Nicholas received it from Queen Elizabeth. Even his sons couldn't resolve it, so it's hardly surprising, I suppose, that Pinpole's having difficulty.'

'And what about the other matter – the question of the Wills Act?' Jeremiah pressed on.

'Nothing much further. They've got as far as the Interrogations, which is where one side or the other has to answer questions on oath and Pinpole is still hoping that Robert will admit – concede – this part of the case entirely and simply leave the Gavelkind issue. Nothing so far though.'

Jeremiah struck his fist on the table. 'If you want a thing done well, do it yourself.'

Luke flushed angrily, seeing this as recrimination against himself for not taking a closer part in the proceedings, and noticing this, Katharine flared up on his behalf.

'Then why didn't you? You were the only brother who didn't come.'

Jeremiah cackled. 'I like this wife of yours, Luke.'

'No doubt,' said Augusta, tartly. She had been so silent they had forgotten her presence. The inference was plain. He who liked one whore could like another.

'Didn't you want to see your brothers again?' Katharine asked daringly.

Jeremiah eyed her belligerently. 'I'll tell you,' he said at last. 'Didn't trust myself. I'd have liked to have seen Alfred and Sophy again, and that little monster Albert. And of course George.' He paused. 'Luke tells me he's dead,' he said with an effort.

'Yes,' said Katharine. 'I'm afraid he died on the Gold Coast, in the Ashanti War.'

He sighed. 'Best of the lot, George. Always came between me and Robert if he could.' He pronounced the name with difficulty.

'The day of the treasure trove,' she said flatly.

'You heard about that? Yes, that was in my mind, I confess. I always hated Robert, always, at least as far back as I can rightly remember. He hated me too. You remember, don't you, Augusta?' Silence, and he resumed. 'I was getting to be a rival, bigger than him, and he didn't like that. And in families, you get one bad egg and it turns the rest off.' He thought back to the day of the treasure trove. Nearly forty years ago now. The vicious fight. Father standing over them like Jehovah. What was he saying? He couldn't hear it over the years. He only remembered Robert and longing to get at him again, fight him, conquer him for ever. Now Father's words came back to him, declaimed like a funeral oration: 'There will be no more treasure troves.' No more silver cups. 'Grow rich in that which never taketh rust'. He remembered the Sidney tag on Bocton's brickwork. The poet had meant everlasting values, to pile up treasures in the next world, but for him it meant something different. Silver didn't rust. It tarnished but never rusted. His eyes gleamed. Silver, you could trust. That – and Daisy Petal.

Monday was the first night of *HMS Pinafore*, and Jeremiah and Luke escorted Martha and Mary – Martha tried hard to restrain herself from displaying excitement, but Mary had no such qualms; both were aware that they were there to annoy their mother, but had been unable to resist sitting in the box right by the stage opposite the Tabor box itself. Martha consoled herself by partly drawing the lace curtains on the audience side so that they could not be seen. Mary took peeks at herself in the ornately mirrored walls of the box. Annoyed, Jeremiah wrenched back the curtains. He was there to be seen.

Both girls were relieved that they would not have to see Katharine until after the performance, so that they would not view her sinful trousers, and be able to answer Mama truthfully. Martha, in particular, disliked Katharine because she stood out against their mother. This was something Martha would have liked to have done, but dared not. It was far easier to accept her mother's verdict on Katharine, and weaker Mary followed her sister's lead.

Behind the scenes, Katharine had all her metaphorical fingers crossed. The tension tonight was different to other first nights at which she had helped, perhaps because it was an all-musical performance. There was in fact more excitement than tension, as though everyone knew they were going to enjoy themselves and intended to without pretence. Katharine made encouraging signs to Daniel Pearson as he came up the steps from below dressed as Ralph, to take his place in the wings ready for his entrance. She had revised her earlier opinion of him. He wasn't arrogant and, if vanity there was, it was offset by self-deprecating humour at the absurdity of life on the boards. They had had several long talks together about England and, starved of news, she encouraged him to talk and he listened to her tales of Kent – though not of Bocton, for that was too great a hurt to speak of.

Luke had not had the time or inclination for much conversation since they had been back from holiday. Knowing it pained him for her to talk of Bocton, taking it as a reproach, she desisted, keeping her longings bottled up inside. Now she had a new audience to listen to her love of England's green fields, and one who surprisingly understood. She was equally surprised to find that when Daniel dropped his light banter he was as passionately interested as was she in the plays and operas put on at the Tabor, as well as having a general interest in literature.

'I am afraid you will find the audiences not quite like London,' she had tried to warn him. 'They do throw and shout things if they are not satisfied. Or fight.'

'Fight?' he asked, amused. 'Not when I sing, they won't.'

At first it seemed the performance was headed straight for disaster. On the second line of the opera the footlights blew out, plunging the cast into total darkness and the performance halted until the boy ran on stage to relight them. Then restlessness pervaded the audience, after they had got over their initial surprise at seeing the stage set as a ship, the backdrop rigging and masts, with a bridge built in front. The songs were enjoyed, but the plot was beyond most of the audience. Voluble discussions could be heard as to just why the captain's daughter should not marry a simple sailor. A heated argument broke out as to whether Josephine should or should not marry Ralph. The shoulds won and a deputation was making its way to the stage to put its point forcibly to the captain, when Daniel saved the evening by simply strolling on and singing Ralph's solo all over again. Muttering approval, the men returned to their seats, and were silent except for more excitement when Sir Joseph appeared to claim Josephine for his own. Fortunately the rhythm of his song, 'I am the Ruler of the Queen's Navee', had them stamping their feet and in such good humour they forgot the oddities of the plot and waited patiently for more songs. The ending, when Josephine and Ralph were united, they took as a tribute to their own powers of persuasion, a forest of hats being thrown in the air.

In their box the Stowertons watched and listened – when they could

– with approval. Particularly Mary, whose eyes were fixed on the handsome figure of Daniel Pearson. Her eyes grew dreamy as she leaned over the edge of the box, hoping he might glance up and see who applauded with such enthusiasm, admiring perhaps then her daring bright green low-cut evening dress and even, blushing at the thought, what lay beneath. She twitched her lace fichu to one side.

'He is very handsome,' she whispered to Katharine afterwards. Other than this incontrovertible statement, she remained silent on the way home. She was in love.

'There's a silver-bearing lode there somewhere,' said Jeremiah for the umpteenth time, brooding. 'I wouldn't put it past Smith to have routed the Bosworth drifts the wrong way – to support the rumour Bosworth is failing, and to give the Manhattan a better chance of mining into our land unopposed. Yes,' he declared, banging his fist on the desk, 'that's where Trevanick got this notion the lode was petering out.'

Luke sighed. 'The smelter is my main worry at the moment. I can't feed it. We'll have to shut down two of the furnaces.'

'No!' thundered Jeremiah. 'No true lode ever gives out. Bosworth will still be producing in a hundred years.'

'But at what rate, Father? Suppose we've been wrong and Bosworth isn't on a vein, but is merely a pocket deposit which is being worked out?'

Jeremiah glowered at him. 'Losing your nerve, boy? *I'm* not worried.'

It had started as a single shout in the street that they disregarded, then a murmur which swelled into a roar. They went to the window, curious – and saw outside the assay office waving hats, dancing, cheering. And Smith, top-hatted, frock-coated – and triumphant.

'Come on, Luke,' said Jeremiah grimly, stalking out of the office. He caught hold of the nearest onlooker, demanding to know what was happening.

'The new Manhattan. They've struck silver, only twenty-five feet down. Six hundred ounces to the ton.'

'That's not our seam,' said Luke. 'Not at twenty-five feet.' But his father did not hear him.

'A bonanza,' Jeremiah shouted, pounding his fist on the door, his face darkening. Smith had won, *Robert*, damn him, had won. The blood rushed to his face. No one was going to get the better of Jeremiah Stowerton. He'd been right. He had a nose for silver, had always said so. This time it had twitched as usual, and he'd been right. He needed this mine. He needed it because he knew it was going to be the best.

'Buy it!' He turned on Luke. 'Sell everything except Bosworth itself, and *buy*. Sell the houses, if you have to, the smelter, the mines on Carbonate Hill. Damn it, sell your *mother* if you have to, but buy it,' he roared.

'No,' cried Luke angrily. 'It's too risky. Too much at stake. We should wait –'

'Find out how much the hunk wants, and buy it. Ten to one that's what they're counting on, because they don't have the resources to capitalise it. We have.'

'It's too big a gamble.'

'Buy it!' screamed Jeremiah. 'It's my money. Put everything up for sale, and buy it. Whatever Smith's price is.'

'No.' Luke stood firm. 'Not yet. Wait till it's truly proven.'

'I don't need you, boy.' Jeremiah was beside himself. 'I'll buy it, and there ain't nothing you can do.'

Silver mania, the silver in his eyes. The silver cup – and Jeremiah's name was going to be on it, not Robert's.

Chapter Twelve

Smith was not hard to find. He was in the Clarendon Hotel, his boots resting nonchalantly on the red plush cushions of the chair opposite, puffing on a cigar, and surrounded by a crowd of smirking sycophants. A bottle of rye stood on the table at his side. If he'd sat down to describe a picture of cheap triumph, he couldn't have done it better, thought Luke savagely, hating every moment of what appeared – to him – capitulation. Jeremiah had no such qualms, striding in, eyes gleaming, silver-bound, regardless of the circumstances.

'Well, now, Mr Stowerton – and Mr Luke too – mighty glad to see you. Have a drink now, won't you?' Smith waved the bottle towards them.

Jeremiah ignored it and the pleasantries. 'How much?'

'I reckon I paid over the odds for this 'ere bottle, Mr Stowerton,' Smith drawled. 'Clarendon don't 'xactly keep low prices.'

'How much?' repeated Jeremiah, not put off in the slightest. 'Don't beat about the bush, Smith. You've had your price worked out some while. I need to know. *Now.*'

'So do all these gentlemen.' Smith waved a lordly hand.

Luke had already summed them up. Grubstakers? Partners? Bankmen? Whoever they were, they weren't buyers, of that he was sure. So why were they here? Something didn't smell right.

'Your price, man,' Jeremiah barked.

'Well, now, seeing as it's you, my old employer, and you got two ladies to support in a manner of speaking, I reckon four and half million should see it through. No, I'll say five. Sounds fairer that way. No sense my giving it away, now is there?'

'Five million?' Jeremiah's eyes bulged. 'You think you got the Robert E. Lee there?'

'Only three years' takings at the rate we found today.'

'Takings, not profits. You ain't even capitalised. No machinery.'

Smith shrugged. 'Don't look as though that's going to be necessary, does it, now we found silver so close to the surface. I'm not aiming to work Manhattan again, Mr Stowerton. So if you want it now, you capitalise.'

'Four,' said Jeremiah jerkily.

'Father, let's talk it over,' put in Luke sharply.

'Time's past for jawing, Luke. I want that mine, and now. What do you say, Smith?'

'I kinda recall my asking price was five million, Stowerton.'

'That's right. It was.' Jeremiah's eyes narrowed. 'I don't hear no other takers, though. Four-fifty, like you said.'

'I'll match that, Smith,' said one of the men.

Luke glanced at him. That hunk couldn't raise four-fifty cents, but Jeremiah was past caution.

'Seventy-five,' he jerked out hoarsely.

Smith didn't even bother to look at the other 'bidders', but got up slowly and stuck out his hand. 'Reckon I can't turn that down. We'll shake hands on that, Stowerton.' Eagerly Jeremiah's hand shot out.

'Too much you think, Luke, eh?' Jeremiah paced up and down in the office later, hands clenched behind his back, not from tension but excitement. He had no regrets, but Luke had nothing but sheer despair.

He lifted his hands helplessly and let them fall heavily on the desk. 'We can't meet it,' he told his father bluntly. 'It's out of the question at a time when Fryer Hill's credibility is wavering.'

'I'll talk to the bank. Horace Tabor himself if necessary.' Jeremiah brushed this aside.

'It will need more than talk,' said Luke bitterly. 'They'll want to see returns. And all we can show them is a falling output from Bosworth, underworked smelters and –'

'Sell the gambling houses, the hotel, the house, the lot. Even,' Jeremiah's eyes gleamed in what could have been mischief, 'the whorehouse if you have to. We'll get 'em back when the mine starts producing. But put this deal together now. Do it, Luke, and I'll make you part owner, majority share,' he emphasised, 'of the Manhattan.'

Luke hardly took this latter promise in, so shaken was he. So there had been a whorehouse. The last illusion vanished. He had been brought up in an 'upright' homestead, sacrificing his childhood on the altar of conformity, while Father had owned a whorehouse, and his mother had been corseted in a religion that hid no inner humanity. Father, whose uprightness had merely masked frustration. How right he, Luke, had been to try to escape, to find some other life than here. At Bocton, for example. His heart sank. That too must go now. How could they continue to pay for The Case? They'd have to withdraw, but how was he going to break the news to Katharine? She'd understand, of course, when he told her what had happened; she understood that the lure of silver led men to crazy actions. Silver-crazed. Thank heaven for Katharine, now his one sure rock.

Katharine struggled to move the large sheet of glass, regretting that she'd proudly refused offers of help the night before.

'Can I assist you, Kate?'

She looked up, red in the face from exertion, to see Daniel Pearson standing before her, and was suddenly conscious of the picture she must present in unbecoming breeches, hair falling from its constricting bun, perspiration running down her face.

'No, thank you.'

'Why not?' He took one end of the glass and immediately the strain was lifted. 'You see how simple it is?'

'You are in the cast,' she said awkwardly. 'You should not be doing this.'

'You think I am incapable of moving without lines writ down for me, that my hands are of use only to illustrate a line, and that I move only as a puppet to my master's bidding?'

'You should not be seen so much talking to me. It will not be well thought of.'

'I would think very well of it.'

The more she tried to explain that cast and staff did not usually mix, the more ridiculous it sounded, so at least she yielded, accepting his help.

'This is the glass for Pepper's ghost. We're putting it into the wings – there's no pit in front of the stage where it should ideally be placed,' she explained to him, suddenly wondering what Daniel was doing here on a day when there was no performance of the opera.

'Ah, for the variety concert this evening.' The Opera House occasionally interspersed special evenings of entertainment by individual visiting artistes on Saturday evenings in between regular performances. 'Now let me see what else you have in your magician's world.' He ferreted around in the small props area. 'Thunder sheet, old lightning flare – you should try those new tubes with a spirit lamp at the end – silk and cylinder for wind, artillery, volley machines, and, yes,' he cried triumphantly, slightly mockingly, 'I do believe . . .'

'The rain machine,' she said defensively.

He laughed aloud. 'You still use these? There are new ways of doing it, you know, other than just a few pebbles in a cylinder. Have you heard of the spectacular way they do it in Paris? A sheet of gauze is lowered, with silver strips on it to shimmer.'

'No doubt. But this still works,' she broke in crossly. 'It is the illusion that matters, not how it is achieved.'

'Ah, yes, the illusion.' He paused. 'Have you ever been to the pantomime?'

'Once, when I was very small,' she said, swept back to that magical time accompanied by Father – and Mother, who in her furs and delicious perfume made everything an adventure, from the ride on the train to buying the tickets. Everything done on a grand scale, so that the performance itself merely topped an excitement that rose headily as the day went on. 'It was *Sleeping Beauty*. I remember the Harlequinade, the transformation scene, with different coloured mists – crimson, green, blue – and the fairies floating on wires.'

'Ah, yes, but now they have a huge *parallèle* with the girls floating outwards as invisible spokes are let out, like an umbrella; it is worked from below on a windlass, and achieves a magical effect. It is a wonderful machine, and to hear the audience's cries of delight is truly magnificent. Yet I tell you, Kate, for all that spectacle, all that fantastic, wonderful scene, for me it does not compare with the excitement of being on the boards here, and sensing the sudden stillness

207

of the miners in the audience, and knowing you have struck home to them. Everything is relative, and all is illusion, though illusion too is real. And talking of relatives, Kate,' he continued without a break, in the same conversational tone, 'tell me how it is, if you please, that Mrs Katharine Stowerton, wife of Mr Luke Stowerton, one of the most prominent businessmen in Leadville – ah, yes, I have ears to hear – fills her time by working at an Opera House? How is it she does not attend morning At Homes, arrange flowers and sew fine seams, gossip the hours away . . . all matters that the matrons of Leadville excel in? Have you acting in your blood? And does your husband not object?'

'My husband understands me well,' she said defensively. 'He knows how much I enjoy this. I do not have acting in my blood. Only hammers and nails.' Her eyes fell away from him. 'I am not used to visiting,' she confessed, 'or flower arranging.' She felt a sudden fear for her garden at Bocton that no one tended now.

'Were I your husband I should chain you to my side.'

'Were I your wife, Mr Pearson, you would find that *most* uncomfortable.'

He laughed aloud. 'Then tell me why you use hammer and nails so well. Why you have them in your blood. Come, tell.'

'You sound like Mr Carroll's poem about the old man sitting on the gate,' she observed mildly.

'Is it so secret?' he asked mildly.

She flushed, feeling wrong-footed. 'I'm sorry. Of course it's not. I live – lived on an old estate, our family home. The manor had not been inhabited for sixty years and it needed much work done. Also my father is more learned than practical and thus it fell to me to carry out our own household repairs.'

'This seems to me a rather short story,' he said thoughtfully, seeing the lost look in her eyes. 'But let it suffice. What is the name of this manor?'

'Bocton,' she replied, as if the word choked her. 'Bocton.'

'Then you will tell me more of Bocton, sweet Kate, anon.'

Four and three-quarter million. The figures seemed to brand themselves into Luke's brain. How to raise it, without selling everything they had? He had been almost silent at dinner, and afterwards, for this was one problem he could not share with his mother. Only possibly with Katharine. Yet somehow he could not. He wanted escape, a time when he could be free of the burden that had fallen like an albatross around his neck, and even to talk of it would bring it back again.

As soon as he was once more behind his desk, it would assume its glaring, monstrous reality again. He knew, and Father knew, that without selling everything there was only one way that money could be raised – on credit from the banks. Easy enough to raise, but it depended on one factor: on Manhattan's yield being good enough to repay the loan. Father had said there was silver, and silver there had proved to be. So why was he so uneasy about the Manhattan?

Or was it just that four and three-quarter million dollars blinkered and suffocated him? He couldn't burden Katharine with this; it was something he must worry through alone. Tomorrow he'd think more clearly, make all the decisions his brain had refused to contemplate today. What to sell, what to keep . . .

'Your husband has not arrived, Kate?' Daniel suddenly appeared at her side, as after the performance she stood at the front entrance, looking down Harrison Avenue.

'He has a business meeting this evening. He told one of the helps to come to escort me home, but no one has. Yet,' she added quickly.

'I suppose,' he sighed dolefully, 'that means I shall have to escort you home again.'

'There is no need,' she began heatedly, then saw his eyes twinkling, and smiled. 'That would be kind,' she said, relieved.

'Did my singing enrapture you tonight?' he enquired politely, taking her arm.

'I was most enraptured, Daniel. As always,' she answered solemnly.

'Good,' he said, pleased.

'You're very vain, aren't you?' she rejoined severely, though in truth she was growing used to his theatrical façade.

'Alas, it is the fate of us poor actors. A dream, a passion . . . And all for nothing.'

Katharine wrinkled her brow, then crowed with triumph. 'What's Hecuba to you or you to Hecuba that you should weep for her?' she capped. 'That's *Hamlet*, isn't it?'

'It isn't often,' he remarked, steering her round a group of staggering miners, 'that one meets a stage hand as erudite as you. Or as beautiful.'

She stiffened, withdrawing her arm, until she suddenly tumbled and laughingly he clutched it again. 'Do you really disapprove of my calling you beautiful, Kate?'

'I am not Kate, nor am I beautiful, outside the theatre,' she said firmly.

'You mean that you wish to be called beautiful inside the theatre? I shall certainly obey you. Like Cinderella, does your glory depart once you step outside? Ah no, my Kate, that is for actors and actresses, ennobled and beautified by the parts they play, not for stage hands. Their beauty glows on with an eternal light.'

'Shall we discuss the new opera?' she asked politely.

'By all means, dearest Kate.' And he promptly began to talk of *The Bohemian Girl*.

When somewhat to her relief they arrived at her home, he released her arm, sweeping off his hat and bowing low in farewell. 'You surely do not mind,' about to leave and changing his mind, 'that I call you beautiful?' He spoke seriously. 'After all, the Mona Lisa is beautiful, the Venus de Milo is beautiful, but I cannot call them mine. Much as I would desire it.' And he was gone before she could protest once more.

Feeling her cheeks redden, she hurried up the path; the front door was open and Mary stood there, staring fixedly at Daniel's dark figure on the far side of the street till it passed from her view. Was it Katharine's imagination or did her gaze fall reproachfully on Katharine herself? Mary let her enter and closed the door, but caught her sleeve before she could escape.

'Was that Mr Pearson?' she asked abruptly, in a low voice, glancing round nervously in case her mother might be about.

'Yes,' said Katharine guardedly.

'I should like to go to the opera again,' said Mary surprisingly, almost conspiratorially. 'I found it – very edifying.'

Edifying was hardly the word Katharine would use for *Pinafore*. 'Who would escort you, and what would your mama say?' she replied weakly. She realised now what the attraction was, and it was neither Mr Gilbert nor Mr Sullivan.

'You could,' said Mary firmly.

'I could not attend the performance. I have to work. And even if I did not, two women could not go alone,' she said, beginning to feel she had adopted her mother-in-law's mantle. Then she had an idea. 'The first night of *The Bohemian Girl* will take place next week. Perhaps Luke would escort you to that.'

'Will the same cast perform it?' Mary asked offhandedly.

'Yes,' Katharine said, her fears confirmed, and then rashly: 'Mr Pearson will certainly sing.'

'I should like to come very much,' Mary said grandly, ignoring the last remark. 'I shall ask Luke to take me, but I should also like to see *HMS Pinafore* again. I shall ask Luke to take me to that too.'

'Will he not think it strange?' Katharine asked helplessly.

'I shall say,' said Mary loftily, 'that Mr Pearson asked me to go.'

Taken aback, Katharine was about to remonstrate, but Mary forestalled her. 'If you say anything,' she cried shrilly, descending from her lofty pedestal, 'I'll think you as horrid as Martha does.'

'Thank you,' replied Katharine drily. What could she do? Mary was over twenty-one, however inexperienced. How could she tell her whom to love and whom not to? Yet suppose this forlorn love, for forlorn it must be, did not burn itself out? Daniel was probably married, and even were he not, the idea of a union between them was impossible. Nevertheless, Katharine became uneasily aware that as well as Mary's own unhappiness, she herself could be caught in a difficult position between being seen to encourage Mary on the one hand and having privately to point out to the girl the hopelessness of the situation. Perhaps she should speak to Daniel, but before there was cause he might think it singularly forward of her. In the end, undecided, she did nothing.

Luke was dreading his first visit to the Manhattan. It might have a new owner, but it had old miners, ex-Bosworth miners, no doubt embittered at the turn of events, and worried about their future now that they were back under Stowerton ownership. Luke cursed his father for having gone back to Denver, leaving him to cope with the mess here. Running mines was more than a matter of negotiating money. It was dust, dirt, hard feelings and ruthless men. He called them together outside the shack that had been dignified by the word office by Smith.

'You will have heard,' he began simply, 'that the Manhattan is part of Bosworth now, and most of you know Bosworth well enough. I guess that makes you the best men for this job. The men still at Bosworth are getting three dollars fifty and glad of it. You took four dollars to join Smith at the Manhattan. Now I can't have two rates of pay. I can drop you all to three dollars fifty or raise Bosworth to match you. What would you do if you were standing where I am?'

'Lower it, Mr Stowerton,' one said sullenly at last.

'As we've paid over the odds for this mine, Smith not being as generous to us as he was to you, that's what good sense tells me to do. But I'm not going to.' A ripple of interest ran round the men. 'I reckon it's not your fault the mine was sold. So I'm going to raise Bosworth to match you – as long as the Manhattan silver holds out. And as long as our funds do, and provided nothing goes wrong with this deposit.'

'Reckon that'll see us through our lifetimes, Mr Luke,' said Jonathan Trevanick afterwards. 'Good silver like this don't usually give out.'

'I hope not,' said Luke grimly. 'Jonathan, you're in charge of the Manhattan. Take as many of your best men as you need. But don't ever forget these were Smith's puppets. Watch them, I don't trust them, not till they've proved they're worth it. I want you in charge every minute – as overseer you'd get five dollars elsewhere. I'll double it.'

'Luke, we're going panning for gold,' Katharine burst out excitedly when at last they were alone in their bedroom one night. 'All the cast and the staff, everyone, we're going to have an outing because the opera has been so successful. Mr Tabor's paying for the buggies and for the picnics. We're going to one of the disused claims up on the California Gulch,' she ran on enthusiastically. 'Oh, do come. You'd enjoy having an afternoon away.'

'Don't you think I see quite enough of mines here, Katharine?' he said lightly, trying to hide his impatience. 'You go.'

'But this is different, Luke,' she pleaded. 'It's gold – and it will be such fun.'

'It isn't possible at the moment, Katharine. I wouldn't be able to enjoy it. Not until this new mine is producing. Just be patient till then, and we'll go away again. Denver perhaps.' He took her hands gently, placatingly, but her disappointment remained; she withdrew her hands, and he let her do so.

'By the way,' he added absently, 'Mary says she wants to go to *Pinafore* again. I told her you'd arrange it. Take her on an evening when you're not working, could you? You can get one of the helps to take you there, and escort you home.'

'Do you think it's wise, Luke?' she asked hesitantly.

'Wise?' His face darkened. 'I thought you would be willing to do this at least for my sister. I will tell Mother, if that's what your excuse is.'

'It's not an excuse,' she replied angrily, feeling like a traitor. 'She wants to see Daniel Pearson sing again and I'm not sure it's a good thing.'

'Whyever not? Just do it, Katharine.'

'Very well,' she agreed shortly, smarting from the injustice, but reflecting that perhaps she was making too much of it. When the visit took place, however, her forebodings returned, as Mary, starry-eyed, insisted on meeting Mr Pearson afterwards. When she did so, she was tongue-tied – except when in politeness, as conversation turned to the gold-panning expedition the following day, he invited her too. She would be delighted, she said quickly, and after their return home insisted Katharine help her select her prettiest gown for the great adventure. Their views differed, and the old-fashioned full-skirted bright pink brocade dress did little to flatter Mary's drab skin and dull brown hair. But she could not be persuaded into the dark green cotton of Katharine's choice, and when Mary descended the stairs, matching pink hat perched atop her head, Katharine's heart bled for her.

The gulch was a desolate sight; Leadville's hills were at least populated. Here, well outside the city, the old placer workings had been abandoned for years, and the hillsides were only just beginning to show signs of recovering their vegetation. Despite this, Katharine's first impression was of stark grey hillsides, abandoned wooden flumes of sluice boxes running into the gulch, houses mere dilapidated wooden shacks, rusted pans buried half deep in the murky gulch, the water not so swift-flowing as it had been then, in the days of the gold rush at California Gulch, long before a place called Leadville had sprung into existence. Her initial reaction was dismay that it looked so similar to Fryer Hill, and Daniel must have read her face for he came up to her, putting his hand under her arm. 'Gold is in the eye of the beholder,' he whispered.

Before she could reply, Mary had followed him jealously. 'You two are always whispering,' she said petulantly. 'Will you show me how to pan for gold, Mr Pearson?'

'I'd be delighted, but I gather we're in luck. One of the old-timers has come along to show us.'

Ambling on an old packhorse towards them was an old man, clad in a mixture of buckskins and dilapidated modern wear, an ancient stetson crammed on his head and a filthy red scarf at his neck. 'That's just how I'd play it,' commented Daniel admiringly.

Katharine watched fascinated as without a word the old miner hitched a thumb at the group to join him, and by sign language, grunts and demonstration showed them how the old sluice boxes running down from hillside to gulch worked; the dirt hosed down through the sluices to the gulch, leaving the heavier material, the gold, clinging to the riffles at the bottom of the boxes.

'Is that what we're going to do?' Mary asked him eagerly, clinging to Daniel's arm on the pretence of the hillside being slippery.

212

He didn't bother to answer, merely stared round at the group contemplatively and spat out some tobacco. Then he jerked a finger at Katharine. 'You,' he said simply. 'Here.' With the strangest feeling, she went to him, as the rest of the group gathered round the sluice boxes to experiment. Only Daniel hovered uneasily, then having engaged Mary's interest on the sluicing, wandered down to the gulch following Katharine and the old man. The old man looked her up and down, not curiously, not provokingly, just interestedly, then picked up two of the many old pans lying around. He stood by the water's edge, gazing into it. Then he pointed. 'There,' he grunted simply. 'Sit.' He grinned at her suddenly, a toothless grin that lit up his face. Even as she obediently sat on the stream bank, glad she had forsworn too much femininity today and was wearing dark brown cotton, a strange feeling of unreality came over her. Had she not been here before? Had this not happened before? No, it wasn't that. It was . . .

'Lovely, lovely,' he crooned, as he waded into the water and began to scrape with a sharp stone all the material around and in a crack in the rockbed into the pan. A sidelong look at her, as hesitantly she waded in after him, following his pointing finger towards another crevice in the streambed nearby. He examined the contents of her pan carefully, bending over it lovingly. 'Sit,' he ordered again and, wading out, skirts clinging wetly to her, she sat again on the bank.

He plunged his pan into the swift-flowing water, and indicated she should do likewise. She followed his movement, grunts indicating when she did right or wrong, swirling the pan, throwing out rocks and pebbles, then dipping, swirling and tipping the pan under the water so that gravel and sand floated away. The process seemed to go on endlessly, till he indicated she should stop. By this time there was very little matter left in the pan.

'Water, ma'am.' His voice rose, as they trickled a little fresh clean water over the bottom of the pan. 'There now,' he murmured gently, lovingly, as he swirled it round. 'There now.' An almost caressing note in his rough voice – or was it so rough? Daniel still hovered behind them, watching, sensing something strange, but unable to detect what. 'There now, my lovely, my handsome,' the old man crooned to the pan, as bright specks began to appear, caught in a half-moon in the bottom ridge of the pan.

'It's gold,' cried Katharine in a high voice she hardly recognised, gazing hypnotised into her own pan.

'There now, of course. A Stowerton to find it. Stowerton, Stowerton, Stowerton . . .'

'How did –?' She jerked up her head, as Daniel moved quickly forward. Katharine looked at the old man's face, grizzled untidy hair, long straggly unkempt beard and weather-browned lined face. But she saw only his blue eyes, as blue as Luke's, as those of old Nicholas himself.

'You're a Stowerton, too,' she whispered.

'Me?' The old man looked frightened, edging away, but her hand shot out and grasped him by the grimy sleeve.

213

'Aren't you? *Aren't you?*'

'Mebbe. Mebbe once.' He gave his toothless grin once more. 'Grow rich in that which never taketh rust . . .' he cackled.

'Katharine,' said Daniel sharply, trying to intervene, standing behind them now.

'I'm all right, Daniel, please.'

'A Stowerton, Stowerton, Stowerton,' cackled the miner. 'Like the lovely lady.'

'Who –?' Katharine began, but then she knew. 'You're Uncle Jacob, aren't you?' she told him flatly. 'You're not dead at all.'

'Maybe I am,' muttered the old man.

'But how did you get here, where do you live?' The questions began to pour out of her.

'Gold,' was his only answer, if answer it was, and that impatiently. He moved away before she could stop him, ignoring her for the rest of the visit.

'Daniel, fill a pan for me.' Mary had rushed up, realising his absence, followed by Lottie, his leading lady, who had already been experimenting. Dazed, Katharine stood up to join them, and Mary darted a look at her as though it were some triumph as Daniel obediently found an old pan.

'Oh dear,' Lottie was crying ruefully, looking at the contents of her pan, 'I thought I was going to look like Helen of Troy.'

'You already do, darling,' shouted Daniel wading out of the water.

'Do you think so?' she said happily, and totally ignoring Mary: 'Come here, darling, and find me some more gold.'

Daniel gave Mary her pan, who gazed at it as though it held Mycenae's treasures themselves, and went to help Lottie. Katharine turned to the old man, her thoughts more ordered now. He had gone, but in the distance she could hear the clip-clop of a horse's hooves on the rough track.

'I have invited Daniel for dinner tomorrow evening,' Mary whispered to Katharine, 'and asked him to sing.'

'On a Sunday? Mary, what will your mother say?' asked Katharine, dismayed, trying to concentrate on her and not on Uncle Jacob. How could she have been so foolish as to let him leave without finding out more?

'Nothing,' said Mary triumphantly. 'I've asked him to sing hymns.'

Katharine repressed a thought of what Daniel must be thinking, as Mary said accusingly, 'You don't want him to come, do you? You want him all for yourself. Well, it's me he's coming to see, not you. You're trying to keep him away from me because you're jealous.'

Katharine, still shocked from meeting Jacob, caught only the last words. Jealous! She strove to keep her feelings under control. 'Mary, he's a singer, very charming, he'll move on. He's only here for a few short weeks, then he'll go, to another town, another company. And, after all, he might be married.'

'He's not. I asked him,' Mary said defiantly.

So she was in love with him, and there was nothing Katharine could do about it. She remembered Mary's words with some unease. Was she jealous? No, that was ridiculous. Quite ridiculous.

'I've bad news, Mr Luke.' Jonathan appeared in the Harrison Avenue office, twisting his hat nervously in his hands.

'What?' Luke looked up resignedly from the endless juggling of figures necessary to make this purchase practical. Always paying some creditor, some interest on a loan, selling this, selling that. The Manhattan had to start producing in earnest at well over the rate of its early promise – for there were limits to the amount of juggling he could perform.

'Men have reported no more silver,' Jonathan blurted out.

Luke stared at him in bewilderment. 'They've only been digging a few hours. They've just hit a barren patch, that's all. You should be used to that,' he told him impatiently.

'I don't think so, Mr Luke. Best come and see.'

It had to be a mistake, unlike Jonathan though that was. He knew the mines like no one else in Leadville. When Luke arrived, the miners were grouped round, curious eyes being cast from the surrounding territory. The windlass was idle, and there was complete silence as Luke walked up to inspect the heap of ore brought up so far. 'We won't know for sure till we gets more confirmed by the assay office. But it look to me jes' like yesterday's load, and day afore that's. And that 'twas barren. We're down to a hundred feet now. Nothing. 'Tis a long way for a barren patch to go.'

Luke's face hardened. 'Go on digging,' he said hoarsely. 'Bring in a horse-drawn whim from one of the other mines.'

Shrugging, the miners went back to work, and Luke strode into the makeshift office. Some office – a rickety table and two chairs, waiting, waiting for news. At the end of the shift, Jonathan came to report. One look at his face was enough. 'Still nothing, Mr Luke.' He didn't need telling.

'Keep on digging tomorrow.' Sharply.

'Sunday tomorrow, Mr Luke.'

Another twenty-four hours to wait before this nightmare could be resolved. How to wait? How to endure?

'What's the matter with everyone, Katharine?' he asked impatiently when he returned home. The whole household seemed to be rushing around, a sense of coiled tension pervading the house, which seemed even to extend to his mother.

'I think it may be because Mr Pearson's coming to dinner tomorrow evening. Luke, I've something so exciting to tell you.'

'Pearson? To dinner? *Here*?' Luke was dumbfounded. No one had received this honour, if honour it was, since Father had left. 'And why Pearson? Why on earth did you invite him?' To have to be polite to strangers this Sunday of all Sundays was insupportable.

'Me?' she asked, puzzled. 'It was Mary invited him. I did warn you,

Luke. But she did not ask her mother first.' Katharine could not bring herself to call Augusta 'Mother', even for Luke.

He grunted. 'That's all I need. A thunderstorm tomorrow evening, tearing the house apart.'

'Oh, Luke, it won't be so bad. Now she's got over the shock, I think your mother is secretly looking forward to it. And Mary and Martha deserve some interest here. They have no kind of life.'

'They'll have no kind of home either soon,' he remarked incautiously.

'What do you mean, Luke?'

'Nothing,' he said quickly. He couldn't bear to discuss it, nor bring this doom hanging over him into the bedroom. He made a lame excuse and, seeing Katharine still unconvinced, came to her, holding her fiercely, that desire and possession might force everything from him. He made love to her so urgently, so desperately, that all was driven from her mind, and it was only much later as he lay in slumber beside her she remembered. Torn between conscience and a desire to wake him to tell him what had happened, she compromised and breathed into his ear so low he would not wake, 'Uncle Jacob's come back,' and when an impatient twitch suggested a reaction, she kissed his forehead and slept.

'This is delightful,' murmured Daniel valiantly, breaking an awkward silence. 'What do you call it?'

'Chicken gumbo,' said Mary brightly.

'Barbecued squirrel,' said Martha simultaneously, maliciously.

Her voice being the louder drowned Mary's and Daniel went pale, gazing at his plate in some distress until Katharine quickly reassured him, trying not to laugh and doing her best to keep the conversation on neutral ground. Augusta presided, a silent Buddha, and Luke remained abstracted by his own thoughts, only occasionally forcing himself to be polite to his guest. At last Augusta spoke of the matter uppermost in her mind.

'I did not see you at chapel, Mr Pearson?'

'No, Mrs Stowerton,' he replied meekly. 'I am strictly Church of England, and I could not find one here.'

This nonplussed Augusta, who could only say: 'I trust the songs my daughter tells me you are to sing for us are suitable for Sunday, Mr Pearson?'

'I think you will be satisfied, Mrs Stowerton,' he gravely replied.

'Anything you sing, Mr Pearson, would be . . . would be . . . lovely,' said Mary fervently, and seeing the ardour in her daughter's eyes, Augusta promptly rose to lead a majestic procession of daughters and Katharine to the parlour, leaving Daniel and Luke to the bottle of port that had remained untouched since Jeremiah's departure.

But Augusta's expectations of an evening of quiet religious observation were immediately doomed, when Daniel and Luke rejoined them.

'Now tell me, Mrs Luke,' Daniel's innocent eyes gazed at her, 'what you and that miner talked of so earnestly yesterday?'

216

An imp of mischief took hold of Katharine, who had been disappointed by Luke's reaction to her news earlier that day.

'Nothing very much,' she said offhandedly. 'He turned out to be Luke's and my long-lost great-uncle – and Mary and Martha's, of course.'

'You didn't tell me!' Mary's mouth fell unbecomingly open, after her shrill cry.

'Indeed,' said Daniel rallying. 'Your brother – er, uncle, Mrs Stowerton,' turning to Augusta politely.

'I have no idea who this person might be.' Augusta glared, 'But I am *not* related to any miners. My daughter-in-law is jesting, Mr Pearson, and I apologise for her ill-manners.'

'I am not jesting, Mother-in-law,' said Katharine firmly. 'He is Uncle Jeremiah's uncle. He disappeared after the last gavelkind case was dropped and was presumed dead.'

'What a lark!' said Daniel enthusiastically. 'What's he been doing? Where does he live?'

'I don't know,' said Katharine. 'He wouldn't speak to me again, and then slipped away while I was talking to Mary. We must find him,' she appealed to Luke, 'for it could affect The Case, could it not? The gavelkind case.'

'Ah, *Jarndyce and Jarndyce*,' said Daniel.

Luke went white. Now of all times to talk of this.

'How could you be easily deceived, Katharine? The man was crazed,' he said impatiently. 'Did he tell you he was Jacob – or you he?'

'I mentioned the name first.' Katharine was scarlet.

'There then. The lure of silver and gold sends these old miners out of their minds. He'd agree with anything you said.'

'It was Uncle Jacob,' she shouted. 'He looked like Jeremiah.'

'This is Sunday,' thundered Augusta. 'No talk of that name. No talk of the lure of Mammon. Of poor wretches who followed the lust of gold and not the love of the Lord.'

'And haven't you all done the same?' said Katharine. 'Only you are worse. You live on the wares of Mammon –'

'Throw out the Lifeline,' Daniel's soaring voice drowned her last word, as he stood up and leapt manfully into the breach with the old Temperance song, 'Throw out the Lifeline, Someone is drifting away.'

Katharine swallowed, regaining control, as the song continued, the mellifluous voice absorbing even Augusta's attention.

'Will you do me the honour of playing for me now, Miss Mary?' Daniel asked meekly, as he finished the last chorus. 'I thought I'd go on to "Come Home, Father" next,' he whispered in Katharine's ear, as he passed her to give the music to Mary. He had vanished before, horror-stricken, she could determine whether or not he was serious. Fortunately he was not, and struck up mournfully with 'Ring the Bell Softly, There's crepe on the door', and she began to relax despite noticing a distinct note of melodramatic parody. Besides herself, only Luke seemed to be aware of it, however, judging by his compressed

217

lips. By the time Daniel had rendered 'The Death of Nelson' she had
an insane desire to giggle. Daniel fixed a stern eye on her, and launched
into 'The Gypsy's Warning'. 'Do not trust him, gentle lady, though
his voice be low and sweet'. For herself Katharine had no fears, but
for Mary, valiantly tinkling inefficiently at the piano, she had many.

Luke had hardly expected anything else, yet the assay office's confirmation that the ore was devoid of silver stifled and oppressed him.
Surely no mere barren patch could go on this long? But what choice
did he have?

'Go on digging, Jonathan,' he ordered in as even a voice as he could
manage. Use of a horse-drawn whim meant they could go down to
around two hundred feet if need be without the major expense of
installing steam-hoisting equipment.

'No barren patch would go this deep, Mr Luke,' Trevanick
grunted.

Luke stared at him. 'You've known all along, haven't you?' he said
abruptly.

Misinterpreting, Trevanick showed a rare flash of anger. 'I'm not
one of Smith's men, Mr Luke.'

'I'm sorry, I didn't mean that. I meant you suspected what Smith
had done, when you saw that first batch of ore we brought up.'

Trevanick glanced at him. 'Reckon I did, Mr Luke,' he said slowly.
'Couldn't believe it, though. Or maybe I could, of Smith.'

'A salted mine,' said Luke heavily. He flung back his head and swore
long and softly. He felt dizzy with the enormity of what had happened.
They'd paid getting on for five million dollars for a barren mine. Smith
had merely dug a shaft, salted the mine with a good grade ore, in order
to lure Jeremiah into purchasing. The oldest trick in the book – and one
that only a fool with silver in his eyes would fall for, because he wanted
to fall for it. The Manhattan was barren. He found himself clutching
at the desk for physical support, then slumped down in his chair.

What to do? The men were digging on, time ticking away, time that
had to be paid for, that he had no money to pay for. He couldn't dig for
ever. The whim would only take them to two hundred feet, what then?
More money. More machinery. And all for nothing probably. There
was no proof that Bosworth's seam ran through to Manhattan ground.
All the indications were to the contrary, and growing more positive
daily. Bosworth miners reported thinner ore body on the drifts, on
the Manhattan side.

Luke's head swam with the horror of his situation. Yet he found his
thoughts concentrating not on mining but the gavelkind case. Bocton
– and Katharine. She would never give up Bocton. How could he give
up this fight? Yes, but his problem was not the same, was it? The
Manhattan was a matter of fact, not honour. Already the news would
be reaching the Denver Stock Exchange; they had precious little time
to restore confidence if that was the way they chose to go. Father had
been so sure that Manhattan held silver, and his instinct had never
let him down before. But did he want this mine *too* much? Had his

instinct been swamped by desire? If there were no ore in Manhattan it suggested that Bosworth's silver might only be a pocket, not a vein, and that too could be nearly exhausted. And yet, and yet, suppose it *did* run through? Just suppose the old story about Chicken Bill Lovell came true again – the fellow who had salted his own mine in order to sell out, and a day later the true vein was revealed only a few feet down, and the new owner made a fortune. If Manhattan had a vein, however, it was more than a few feet down.

Jonathan Trevanick didn't believe it existed. He shook his head dubiously when Luke suggested it. 'Fryer Hill has always been known for pockets, not veins. Bosworth's ore body is thinning out. It's in a pocket. We can go deeper in Bosworth, but there's no vein running through that'll guarantee silver in Manhattan. I told you that, Mr Luke.'

'I'm not going to be beaten by a swindler,' declared Luke. 'There's silver there somewhere. There must be.'

'Reckon you're fooling yourself, Mr Luke,' said Trevanick uneasily, watching the abstracted look on Luke's face. A look he'd seen on Jeremiah's face often. 'Save what you can, that's my advice.'

'No!' Luke strode outside where the miners were waiting for orders. 'Keep on digging,' he ordered peremptorily. 'We'll bring in steam-hoisting machinery, if need be, but keep on. Double pay for a week when you hit silver.' How he would pay them, he didn't know. What he did know was that business depended on confidence, and that at the moment he was the only person who had any at all. And that was precious litle.

'Dig!' he yelled at the men, still standing stock still. '*Dig, damn you!*'

Katharine flew to him, as soon as Luke entered the door that evening. 'There's a letter from Mr Pinpole, Luke. What do you think? Uncle Robert's solicitors have admitted!'

'Admitted what, Katharine?' he asked dully, putting an arm round her.

'They've – oh, look!' She dragged him by the hand into the morning room and thrust the letter into his hands. 'They've admitted,' she seized it again when she saw he was not reading it, 'they've at last conceded completely the point about the Wills Act, so we do not have to prove it. Now,' she went on triumphantly, 'we can concentrate on the gavelkind issue. They've put forward all the claims we expected on that. Remember they have to prove the land is not subject to gavelkind, not the other way about, so they have to have a strong case. And they have produced nothing new. Look – the disgavelling statute, the treason case. So Mr Pinpole is optimistic.' She stopped. 'Luke, what's the matter?' she asked quietly.

'We can't go on with it, Katharine,' he answered bluntly.

'With what?' blankly.

'With The Case.' He looked away from her to avoid seeing her distress.

Shock hit her like a blast of water. 'What's happened? Why not?'

'It's the Manhattan,' he told her heavily. 'It has no silver in it. Smith salted it – he planted silver in it to make us think the ore was silver-bearing. He's got nearly five million dollars, *we've* got a glory hole – just a hole in the ground, and nothing but debts. By the end of the week we could have nothing. Not even,' he lowered his voice, 'this house. Salting mines is as bad as you can get. Smith has left town and there will be sympathy for us, but sympathy doesn't pay bills. Leadville has seen plenty of fortunes come and go, it's too familiar a story.'

'But what about Bocton?' she asked stupidly as she tried to take this in.

'Don't you understand what I've been telling you?' he asked impatiently. 'The Case will have to be withdrawn. We have no money to pay for it.'

'I understand, Luke,' she said dully, as the world crashed around her ears.

Work, she must throw herself into work in order to glaze over the shock, forget everything, forget her hopes for a miraculous day when she and Luke might return to Bocton, that this was merely an interlude in her life. She had clung to it as to a life raft, and now the raft had been swept from her clutching fingers. The Opera House offered escape from the nightmare situation at home, trying to appear normal to avoid arousing Augusta's antennae that something was wrong. She tried to offer comfort to Luke; but it was stilted for it was tainted by an unreasoning resentment that Bocton and their future had been subjugated to the demands of Jeremiah, of Augusta – and of mining. Even to herself she tried not to let her real fear escape: that the business of mining was becoming a euphemism for the lure of silver. In any case, Luke seemed to shrug off any attempt at comfort, or support, preferring to stare into their bleak future alone.

'Dearest Kate, I beg a favour.' Daniel appeared, as she was arranging the properties for *The Bohemian Girl* which had proved a great success in Leadville, for its story of kidnapped heiresses and gypsies was more immediately exciting to Leadville audiences than that of *Pinafore*.

'I am not "dearest Kate",' she answered crossly. He was only joking, she knew, but this week she could not take jokes.

'I need someone with whom to rehearse, please, on the stage.'

'Why not Lottie?' she asked suspiciously.

'Lottie is not here,' he said plaintively. 'And you are, Kate.'

'I'm busy,' she said firmly.

'Then if I help you finish your task, will you stand in for Lottie on stage?'

'Very well,' she said resignedly. 'Unless you expect me to sing "I dwelt in marble halls".'

'I don't want *you* to sing, *I* want to sing,' he said simply.

Despite herself, she found it fascinating to be on the stage itself. Even with just the one dim rehearsal gas-light, the stage was a different world; though the seats were empty, she imagined them full, the audience's anticipatory excitement reaching out to the players. To her.

'Read Lottie's lines, Kate, after I've finished my song of love.' He sang the air to her sweetly, mellifluously, gazing into her eyes so that she stood woodenly, self-consciously, close to him.

'Whatever may be our future lot,' she began reading stiltedly, 'nothing should persuade you that I can ever cease to think of – ever cease to love you.'

'Not like that, Kate. You must convince me that you are madly in love with me, or I shall not give the correct responses. Like this.' He flung an arm out melodramatically. 'My heart is overpowered with happiness. Yet alas! 'tis but of short duration, for I must leave you now for ever.'

She looked at him suspiciously, but endeavoured to obey him and, entering into the spirit, she threw herself with gusto into the lines. 'Oh no, no! Say not so,' she cried. 'I cannot live without you.'

'And will you then forsake your home, your kindred, all! and follow me?' he replied passionately, seizing her in his arms and kissing her lightly, then rather more forcefully, until she indignantly pushed him away.

'That is not in the script, dear Kate,' he said hurt, but with eyes twinkling.

'It is in mine,' she said firmly.

'Alas, dear Kate, forgive me. We poor players . . . I quite forgot it was you in the passion of the words. Until I touched your lips and then . . . I was overcome. I admit it.' He fell to one knee, smiting his chest in contrition. 'I confess, I love you, dearest Kate.'

'Daniel,' she began weakly, then, suddenly amused, she responded in melodramatic vein. 'Away, wicked Sir Daniel. Knowest thou not my husband might return at any moment?'

'Then I must make haste. One kiss and I'll descend.' He leapt to his feet and seized her again, until she struggled free.

'No,' she cried fearfully, seeing his eyes change, no longer teasing, held close to him, his lips on hers, and feeling herself respond, her lips began to part, and her body came alive as it had not done this long, long day. Feeling her respond, his kiss grew triumphantly gentler, his hands slipping down to caress her body, behind her holding her closer and closer until she felt herself reacting and, recalled to her senses, broke away.

'Forgive me, Kate,' he said huskily, clutching her hand as she turned away.

'You know very well you are only fooling, Daniel,' she said unsteadily.

'Am I?' His face was serious.

'You know you are.' He had to be. He was a travelling singer who would be leaving in a few weeks. A midsummer madness. 'You are a bird of passage,' she stated wildly, 'who passes the time before returning to a winter warmth.'

221

'And you,' he said softly, 'are a prim English rose who will not shake her petals free.'

'My petals, Daniel, belong to another,' she retorted firmly. Belong – what an odd word. Did she indeed belong to Luke? 'To my husband.'

'I am aware of that,' he said sadly. 'The severe and sober Mr Stowerton.'

Severe? Sober? Shock ran through her. Was that how Daniel saw Luke? But Luke wasn't like that. He was the man she had refused to marry because he was never serious. Like Daniel himself. That was the Luke Stowerton she had married. And now, what had happened? For whatever reason, she was in the arms of another man who wooed with quicksilver charm, with summer magic – and for a moment she had responded. Hoist with her petard. Who *was* Katharine Stowerton and what did she desire?

'Anything yet?' Luke strode up to Trevanick in a fever of impatience. Confidence. He had to look confident. Even Father was telephoning him daily, telling him to give up, fall back on Bosworth before they lost everything. So far he'd refused. But for how much longer?

Jonathan shook his head. 'Down to one hundred and eighty feet now, sir.'

'It's got to be down there somewhere,' muttered Luke, grey-faced. 'The lodes dip eastwards. It *must* be there.'

'No, sir. And even if it were, the men are leaving.'

'*What*? But I'm paying them four dollars twenty now, and promised double when they strike mineral.'

'For how long, sir? They know there's no silver down there, and then they've no jobs. Some of them are already looking elsewhere, going over to Carbonate again; it'll mean lower wages, but at least there's silver there. The "Silver Fool" they call the Manhattan.'

'Me, you mean,' said Luke ruefully. 'The fool who won't give up.'

'If we go further, sir, we'll need steam-hoisting machinery. You have to decide.'

'I *know* it's there.' Luke's face was furrowed, lined, his blue eyes staring as if the mine were transparent and he could *see* the silver waiting. Now he knew what Jeremiah meant by 'knowing' silver. He too *knew* it. He too had a nose for it. Or did he? Perhaps it was not wishing to admit he was wrong? No, it was more than that. He *knew*.

'You're putting wishes before facts, sir.'

'Let the men go,' said Luke abruptly, decisively. 'Anyone who wants. The lot preferably, except for your twelve best workers. Get the steam hoists over from the White Rose mine, from Bosworth itself if necessary. I'll stop production there. Or buy more. Whichever is quickest.'

Trevanick stared at him aghast.

'I know it seems crazy,' admitted Luke, 'but it buys us time.'

'For what, sir?' asked Jonathan woodenly.

'It's a gamble.' He began to work out the reasoning behind his impulse. He had to keep Trevanick with him, believing in him. 'If you and your best men go on digging, at the same time as the others are leaving, they're going to think we know something they don't, remembering my double pay offer. That will keep our stock up for a bit, Jonathan.'

'And when we're forced to give up because there's no silver?'

'Then we've lost nothing. If we give up now, we're done for anyway. Let's gamble.'

'Will you not escort Mary to the concert as she wishes?' pleaded Katharine. They had managed (thanks to Daniel) to return to their old easy companionship.

Daniel pulled a face. 'I would rather escort you. It would be kinder of me not to take Mary,' he added. 'I will do it only if you come too.'

'Very well,' she said resignedly.

'It is not you making the sacrifice,' he pointed out agreeably. 'It's me. How can I tell you how bewitching your eyes are, how entrancing your figure, if Mary is there to listen?'

'It seems to me,' Katharine remarked, 'that it's just as well she *will* be there.'

The days passed, the tedious, expensive, difficult business of transferring and installing machinery continued, and then came the depressing task of watching grimly every day as ore came up in the cages into the shaft house. They erected a building round the ore dumps so that the curious should not see that the hoists unloaded what still seemed barren ore. Indeed, it had the opposite effect. Word was now going round that something so extraordinary was happening at Manhattan that no one was to know. Only Trevanick and his small band of hand-picked men knew the truth. Nothing had changed. Two-fifty feet, three hundred, three-twenty. And nothing had changed.

'Come down, sir. We're at three-ninety now, well past the level of Bosworth's lode. Nothing. We'll need water pumps after this.'

Luke usually hated going down in the cage into the mine itself with all the claustrophobic hopes and fears it aroused, but today it seemed different. Today he must decide. On either side cross cuts, only a lamp at the shaft end, showing the limit of the failed efforts. Here a drift went off to the left, water seeping in, running everywhere.

'Can't go no further down, sir. Ain't safe without pumps.'

Jonathan wriggled with his lamp along past miners, only their faces illuminated by the dim light.

'I reckon this drift is seventy feet under where the Bosworth vein runs. We should have hit it well before now, dip or no dip.'

'Suppose,' Luke said, his neck aching uncomfortably, 'as well as the eastward dip, it bends to left or right.'

Jonathan shrugged. 'Never heard of that, Mr Luke.'

'We've nothing to lose,' he said steadily, more steadily than he felt. There was silver here somewhere. He *knew* it. He could *smell* it. 'Strike off to the left,' he said peremptorily, irrationally.

Gloomily, the men half-heartedly resumed with their picks, hacking, chipping. Suddenly fevered because there was nowhere to go from here, Luke picked up a pick and swung it himself, chunks of rock coming away under the desperation of his swing.

'Careful, Mr Luke. Careful there,' as a black nugget crashed down into the drift.

Jonathan swung his lantern incuriously, then closer, and closer, as Luke went on manically. The men stopped work to watch him as his shoulders worked, swinging the pick, sweat soaking his shirt even in the cool clammy air.

'Mr Luke!' Jonathan's voice behind him stopped him at last. 'Look! That's the gangue. It's quartz. *Quartz!*' His soft burr ended almost in a shriek.

Luke swung the pick almost calmly now, bringing away a last small piece of ore. 'It's the matrix,' he said flatly, staring at it unbelievingly. 'The quartz matrix of a gold and silver-bearing lode.' He tried to temper the quick rise in his heart, to steel himself to face another failure.

'This bain't the Bosworth vein,' said Jonathan as the men behind him started cheering. 'Mr Luke, this . . .' He stopped, almost choking. 'I do think this is a fissure vein, like Bosworth's. But it's a new vein, the Manhattan lode!'

Steady. Steady, thought Luke. They called the Manhattan the 'Silver Fool'. But all he could think of was the quickening of his heart, the lurch and then the all-powering sweep of emotion as he realised he'd been right. He could *smell* silver.

'Don't tell me you don't want my company,' Daniel said happily. 'You know you do,' seeing Katharine's look of hesitation as he came to the Opera House one morning again at a time when there were unlikely to be others around.

'What I want is immaterial, Daniel. You're not supposed to be here,' she said steadily.

'Practising,' he said promptly, 'for tonight's performance. Can't you take pity on me? After all, I shall be gone in two weeks.'

'What?' She gazed at him in surprise.

'The time is passing, Kate. Our season ends in July, and I must leave with the company.'

'I shall miss you,' she said inadequately, picking up the brush again to steady her hand.

'And I you,' he said bitterly, removing the brush and taking her hands. 'Katharine, I know are you are not happy here.' He hesitated. 'Or fully in your marriage.' Her head went up proudly. 'Katharine, I love you. It was just a jest at first. You were so different, so proud, I wanted to tease you. Now,' he shrugged, 'I love you. I know you won't leave your husband, and I wouldn't ask you – for anything else,' he said jerkily. 'But I wanted you to know that I love you.'

'Thank you,' she said stiffly, ridiculously, so ridiculously that they both laughed awkwardly.

'But just in case,' he said lightly, 'you change your mind, I shall be here next summer.'

Next summer. A whole year and she would still be in Leadville. The June day suddenly seemed bleak. She opened her mouth to speak, but was prevented by the uproar which had broken out in Harrison Avenue, unusual even for Leadville, and they rushed to the doorway to see what was happening. Men were running from all directions, converging on the assay office.

'It's Luke,' she gasped, seeing him on the sidewalk being mobbed by a group of men.

'Katharine, don't!' Daniel pulled her back.

'But they're attacking him.' Crows swarming round to pick the bones of dying Stowertons. The worst had happened. The news had broken of the Manhattan mine's failure. She moaned and started to run to him, but again Daniel pulled her back as more and more crowds gathered and Luke vanished from sight.

'They're not attacking him,' Daniel cried. 'Listen, they're cheering. Cheering *Luke*.' Then she heard the chant. 'Silver, silver, silver . . . Silver for a Stowerton.'

Luke saw her standing across the way with Daniel, and forced his way through the mob, eyes blazing with triumph. 'We've struck it! Silver, Katharine, silver! Nine hundred ounces to the ton. High grade ore. I've done it, Katharine. It's a new vein and there's plenty, plenty more.' He pulled her fiercely into his arms. 'The Case can go ahead now. We've found it. Look!' Clutched in one hand was a piece of glistening black ore. 'Isn't it beautiful?'

She shuddered, not looking at the sample, only his eyes. The eyes of a stranger, and the look she had seen before, the blank, abstracted gaze fixed on some unseen far horizon.

'You've got it too, Luke,' she cried in horror. 'You want *your* name on the silver cup. The curse of the Stowertons.' She laughed bitterly. '*Silver!*'

'I'll be back,' said Daniel quietly to himself, as he left them alone.

Luke looked at her uncomprehendingly. 'Don't you understand, Katharine? The Case can go ahead. We've struck it at last. *Silver*.'

Chapter Thirteen

Her second winter in Leadville seemed to Katharine even harsher than the first, both in its weather and in her alienation. Every day seemed dominated by the one word: silver. The price of silver, the yield of silver, the prospects of silver – and the rewards of silver. And here, she realised with sinking heart, she could not hold herself above it. Bocton was to be one of the rewards of silver, for it was thanks to the Manhattan ore that the gavelkind case could still be brought. The winter cold in Leadville's thin air invigorated, but froze her to the core, biting at her cheeks. Swathed in heavy coats and beaver fur muff, hat and boots, she would run the gauntlet of house to theatre or bookstore, arriving with pink cheeks but unable to feel fingers and toes despite all the protective clothing.

Deep snow lay piled in heaps at the sides of the road, and the hillsides were a mountain of white broken only by the stark ugly dots of mining works. Sometimes overnight after a heavy fall even these would disappear, camouflaged against their background, only as the day went on to make their dark presence seen again, as if to remind the city beneath them that they and they alone owned Leadville.

During the winter Katharine and Luke paid two visits to Denver. It was a city of dash and verve, and a beautiful one, with a pride in itself as one with a rich future in store. It was the hub of the richest mining country in the world, not just for silver and gold but other minerals, and its pride in its achievement was obvious. Ostensibly they were on holiday, but although Luke escorted her to the Opera House, built like Leadville's by Tabor, and walked through the parks and along its broad boulevards, listening politely while she talked of the differences between the Denver and the Leadville Opera Houses, it was obvious to her that business, and not pleasure, had been his main purpose in coming. It occurred to her that Luke was turning into a younger version of the formidable Jeremiah, while Jeremiah himself grew daily more like the Luke she had known. Impatiently she tried to forget the fantastic notion, but it refused to budge.

This time Katharine met Daisy Petal as well as Uncle Jeremiah, and was charmed to find her not at all as she had expected; despite Luke's conviction that she would like her, or perhaps because of it, she had been prepared to find a mercenary schemer. Instead they talked happily of the stage, albeit from different standpoints; Daisy Petal's knowledge was confined to the hubbub of music hall life and burlesque, Katharine's to the practical side and to the love of the plays themselves. Yet the love of theatre was in both, and gave them a shared

226

interest which led to Katharine's cautiously agreeing to go shopping with Daisy Petal in Larimer Street.

'Now why not this?' said Daisy Petal, holding out a foot-high effusion of golden felt with ribbons and feathers to match. After the small hats of recent fashion it was startling indeed.

Katharine giggled. 'I'd just look ridiculous.'

'Maybe that's how Luke would like you to look.'

'Ridiculous?'

'No. Kinda exotic,' said Daisy Petal, standing back and considering the effect of golden hat on chestnut hair.

'Luke wouldn't notice if I wore nothing but the hat,' Katharine said absently, as she laid it aside a trifle regretfully. Exotic? Her? On an impulse she picked it up again and self-consciously handed it to the milliner for purchase.

'Oh, I reckon you're wrong there,' said Daisy Petal, smiling, obviously at some memory of her own. 'Men always do.'

Luke, loosening her hair, arranging the curls on her shoulders, on the pillow . . . But so long ago, it seemed.

'Doesn't he mind you working at the Opera House?' Daisy Petal continued straightforwardly, her frankness blunting the sting of her curiosity.

'No,' said Katharine shortly.

But Daisy Petal was not to be put off. 'Are you sure? He looks sick to me.'

'That isn't because of my work at the Opera House,' began Katharine stiltedly; then responding to the kind and genuine interest in the girl's face, added bitterly, 'That's silver, Daisy Petal. Silver, not physical illness. You must know. Isn't Uncle Jeremiah the same?'

Daisy Petal laughed. 'Sure, but I tease him 'bout it,' she said, 'so it's no problem.'

'But how?' asked Katharine impressed.

'Well,' Daisy Petal looked at Katharine, clearly wondering whether to speak out or not, 'in bed, you know. They may not seem to take much notice, but they do. Afterwards, I mean,' she added hastily.

In bed? Teasing? Katharine had a wistful memory of a man in an orchard, a man with fair hair and the light of the devil in his blue eyes, the eyes of Nicholas Stowerton himself. Teasing, mocking, loving . . . Now the love that was between them in bed was based on shared need, an attempt to lay a bridge to the other that, once crossed, provided no answer, for they still sought something that fluttered tantalisingly but seemed forever beyond their reach.

'It sure is hard to fight silver,' Daisy Petal was saying, 'but you can find a way somehow – if you really want to, that is. Do you?'

'Did Luke tell you, Uncle Jeremiah, that I'd met your Uncle Jacob?' Katharine said, apparently casually but burning to know, at a loss to understand why neither seemed interested in the mysterious Jacob.

Jeremiah shot a look at her as he puffed on the cigar lovingly cut

227

for him by Daisy Petal. 'He told me you'd been hoodwinked by some old hobo,' he said agreeably.

'I wasn't,' said Katharine impatiently. 'He *was* a Stowerton. You could see it in his eyes.'

'Crazy, was he?' Jeremiah retorted amicably.

'Yes,' admitted Katharine. 'But don't you think we ought to try to find him? Suppose I'm right and it is your uncle, impoverished, sick in his mind . . .'

'How do you know he's impoverished?'

'He certainly looked it.'

Jeremiah gave a short laugh. 'Listen, niece, if that was Jacob, he's been out here since the gold rush, 'fifty-nine, probably 'forty-nine as well. Like me. How do you know he's not sitting on a crock of gold bigger than the rainbow itself? Mining gets in their blood, you know. It's a fever. They can't bear to leave the smell of gold, even if it's only in their heads, and even if they have enough to buy up all New York. 'Sides,' he switched tack, 'it was back in June you saw him, and you ain't heard sight nor sound of him since. He'll have moved on. And if he's a Stowerton, he'd have been down to Leadville to tell us about it long since. 'Specially Jacob. That man's a bloodhound where money's concerned – and then he's a leech,' he added.

'I've made a few enquiries,' admitted Katharine, 'but no one seems to know where he came from that afternoon. I thought he had been paid to come to show us how to pan for gold, but it turns out he was just wandering around when we came by.'

'Just as I said,' Jeremiah put in complacently. 'It was one of the hobos from the old California Gulch gold rush, come back to try and find the lost mine.'

'What lost mine?' asked Katharine, intrigued.

'Any lost mine. All these fellows have a story – how they stumbled on a gold mine, nuggets fairly throwing themselves at them, till they walked away, or the snows came, or took a wrong turn and the mine ain't never been seen again since. 'Specially California Gulch. Why, if all the lost gold mines were laid together, there wouldn't be a square inch of land that side of Leadville didn't have a bonanza on it.'

'But suppose it is Jacob, don't you want to see him again?' asked Katharine, determined not to be side-tracked.

'He disappeared when I was knee-high to a grasshopper,' Jeremiah snorted dismissively.

'A very tall grasshopper. You were about eighteen,' Katharine pointed out scathingly.

He grinned, unperturbed. 'Perhaps I remember the old rascal at that. I mean what I said, niece. If you think I'm money-crazed, you should have met your Uncle Jacob. He could sniff out a dime at forty paces. He never got over having to abandon The Case, you know, running out of money. He shot himself, that's my view. He's dead all right.'

'Unless he came to seek a fortune and start it up again,' observed Katharine.

Jeremiah gave her a hard stare and laid down his cigar. 'Katharine, you haven't done so badly out of a fortune,' he said mildly. 'Luke tell you I made over the Manhattan to him now, all but five per cent? And we're doing our best to get you back Bocton, aren't we?'

'Yes,' she admitted honestly. 'I know. But that doesn't stop me seeing the dangers of money.'

He gave a bark of laughter. 'More dangers being without it, than with it. How's The Case going?'

'The solicitors have put our case – a reply, Mr Pinpole calls it – that the lands *are* subject to gavelkind, and are refuting Uncle Robert's claim. They're showing the disgavelling statute passed under Cromwell was illegal, of course, because only the monarch personally can disgavel, and now they're going back to the treason case, demolishing Robert's arguments. And so it goes on. I don't understand why it takes so long.'

'A question clients have been asking ever since justice was invented,' said Luke drily, coming into the room. 'Never fear, Katharine, the wheels of justice grind slowly but they grind exceeding small.'

Slowly indeed. 'And just suppose Jacob comes back if you win, eh?' said Jeremiah. 'Thought of what that might mean?'

'No,' admitted Katharine, puzzled.

'Guess you should before you start hunting all over for him and reminding him of Bocton.'

It was eighteen months now since she'd seen her family, eighteen months since she had seen Bocton. And how she missed both. For all the worries she had had then, they seemed in retrospect halcyon days, the winters gentle compared with the harsh thin air of Leadville, overlaid with smoke that gave her a perpetual cough. It had been so bad this winter that she was firmly banished by the stage manager from working at performances. This meant more evenings to be endured at home, endless hours of Augusta, Martha and Mary, a life ordained and ruled by her mother-in-law. Mary was still writing love letter after love letter to Daniel, Katharine noticed, but there was never a reply, or one that she knew of at least, until one day she saw, with an odd lurch of her stomach, familiar handwriting on a letter to her sister-in-law in Charlie's bundle of mail. So Daniel *was* replying to her. A pang of what could have been childish jealousy was firmly dispelled, as Katharine told herself that her concern was merely for Mary. Yet in her more rational moments she acknowledged it for what it was – and laughed at herself for day-dreaming.

'Daniel says he will be back in May,' announced Mary importantly. 'I have received a letter from him. He is looking forward to seeing me again.' She was unable to hide the tremor of excitement in her voice.

So it was true Daniel was to return. He hadn't changed his mind. Happiness at the thought of seeing him again was tempered with the anti-climax of relief – it was relief, was it not? – at the fact that if he were writing to Mary, he could no longer be imagining himself in love with her, Katharine. Yet this too gave cause for concern. She had knocked on Mary's door one day and entered after an absent-minded 'Come in', to find her sister-in-law obviously startled and bundling a

229

collection of objects into a drawer. This would have meant little had it not been for the blush on Mary's cheek and the fact that Katharine recognised one of the items. It was Daniel's red silk kerchief that he had worn in *The Bohemian Girl*.

The letter from Daniel, brief though it was, spurred Mary on to increasing interest in the Opera House, leading to a fresh assault on the armed truce that prevailed between Katharine and Augusta. It broke out violently and unexpectedly one evening, when on a rare occasion all were there together. Sudden wealth had led to Luke's spending more time at his office in the evenings, not less, but this evening he was at home since Katharine was there working on a ledger.

'Mama, I intend to go to help Katharine at the Opera House this week,' Mary announced blithely. 'She says I may, don't you, Katharine?' she added blandly, as two accusing faces, Martha's and Augusta's, turned to stare.

Caught by this flagrant lie, not wishing to deny it for Mary's sake, Katharine blurted out something to the effect that if Mary wished it she thought it might be arranged.

Augusta laid down her embroidery deliberately. 'And the chapel cushions, Mary? I had feared Katharine would be a bad influence on you, and, see, I am right. It is of course quite out of the question for you to *work* –' she made it sound a sin '– at this place. Attending the performance is bad enough. I trust you know, Luke, that a degenerate has recently appeared there?'

He looked puzzled.

'I think your mother refers,' said Katharine demurely, 'to the recent visit of Mr Oscar Wilde. He is a young Irish writer who dresses somewhat flamboyantly. Your mother does not approve.'

'I remember him. Trevanick took him down the Manhattan. The men gave him a meal down there, so he reported, and a whole bottle of whiskey. Then they brought him down to Pap Wyman's saloon where he was highly amused at that sign Pap keeps on the piano: "Please don't shoot the pianist. He's doing his best". Trevanick says Wilde commented that it was the best piece of art criticism he'd ever read.'

Katharine tried to smile, but could not. She was well aware that Luke was talking for talking's sake, hoping even now that the storm could be averted by such transparent means.

'A degenerate,' repeated Augusta coldly. 'No daughter of mine shall attend such a place.'

Katharine's fingers tightened on the edge of the ledger.

'Why is it all right for Katharine and not me?' cried Mary furiously.

'It is not "all right" for Katharine, as you put it, Mary. If Luke wishes his wife to be a laughing stock, her reputation tarnished –'

Katharine glanced at Luke to see if he was coming to her defence but he remained silent, apparently absorbed once more in his Denver newspaper. 'My reputation, Mother-in-Law, is no more tarnished than yours. Women have a right to work without such slurs.'

'*My* reputation?' The enormity of the comparison slowly dawned on Augusta. '*Mine* tarnished? You compare yourself with *me*? How is mine tarnished, pray?'

'By the gossip and malicious stories you spread about your husband,' said Katharine evenly.

'Katharine!' Luke was reluctantly forced to be aware of what was happening. 'You'll apologise for that.'

'I am not a child, Luke,' said Katharine, flaring at him. 'And I will not continue to live like this, hated by those around me.'

'You are overtired,' he said mechanically, in a desperate, silent appeal for her to yield once again.

'You have seduced my sister into wicked ways,' shouted Martha, glad of an opportunity to spew out her outrage at another's freedom. '*You* have filled her head with this nonsense.'

'I have not.' But there was no heart in Katharine's denial, for she knew no one would believe her. She could not tell them it was all Mary's doing, though she would get no thanks for her restraint. Mary used her, but did not like her the more for it.

'I *will* go to work there! I will,' cried Mary excitedly, lest the main point of this battle be lost.

Augusta stood up, indicating discussion was at an end. 'You shall not, or else you can follow this whore wherever she goes. For she will not remain here, contaminating my roof.'

There was dead silence. Even Mary and Martha were quiet, appalled that it had gone so far. Katharine was past caring. Let Luke do what he would, she could no longer live under her mother-in-law's roof. But she needed his support. Oh, how she needed it.

Luke put aside his newspaper. 'Very well,' he said shortly, almost uninterestedly. 'We shall both leave this house, Mother. Tomorrow.'

He had stood by her. Oh, the relief. Katharine stole a look at him, but no love showed on Luke's face, no passionate indignation on her behalf. He had acted thus, she realised dully, not for her sake, or because he wished to be alone with her, but because he could not stand the constant tension in the household. It disturbed his concentration on business.

Augusta was silent, aware that by her own doing she had brought about what she feared most – the loss of her son.

Mary, wide-eyed at what she had begun, ran to Katharine, hugging her. 'I'm sorry. Please don't leave me behind, Katharine. Please.'

'What else can I do?' she said listlessly. 'You wouldn't enjoy working at the Opera House, you know. It's hard work and you are not used to it.'

'I can paint water-colours,' said Mary defiantly. '*And* play the piano.'

'We have nowhere to live yet,' said Katharine, desperately hoping for Luke's help over his sister. He gave it.

'Mary.' He took her hand. 'Think carefully about this. You are better here, with Mother, for all the restrictions.'

Sullenly, she acquiesced, yet they went to bed that night with the sound of her sobbing reaching them through the walls.

231

'Why on earth does this have to happen now mining is getting into its stride again for the spring?' grunted Luke irritably, as they lay, unable to sleep, in bed. At least he was not reproaching her for what had happened, thought Katharine wrily.

'There's never a right time so far as the silver mines are concerned.' Her matter-of-fact voice came out of the darkness.

'What's that supposed to mean?'

'You're wedded to the silver mines, Luke, not me. It doesn't much matter where we live, provided it's not here.'

A silence, no denial. 'Don't you see I'm trying to get away from it?' he said at last, unconvincingly.

'No, Luke, I don't see that. I see you trapped like a fly in a spider's web. The mine is running now, producing silver beyond anybody's wildest hopes. If you walked out tomorrow we could live for the rest of our lives on what you've made this last few months. *And* restore Bocton,' she could not resist adding.

'I promise you we won't be here for ever, Katharine. I want –' His voice halted, as if pleading for her understanding when *he* did not understand himself. 'We'll move into the suite at the Stowerton Palace Hotel,' he continued.

Her heart plummeted, her fears as to his motives in moving confirmed. 'We could have a house of our own,' she ventured.

'No. It'll make our departure the sooner if we live in the hotel.'

With this compromise, she was forced to be content. Anything was worth it to get away from Augusta. As the wagons with their possessions moved away from Chestnut Street, the last thing she saw was Mary's reproachful face, yet as Katharine turned to the front again, already something that might have been hope stirred within her.

At first she revelled in her freedom without Augusta's oppressive presence, yet without household responsibilities, gradually it began to pall. Far from seeing more of Luke and growing closer to him, she saw him less since as well as the evenings he worked in the office, he often visited his mother to talk over business matters – he claimed – and to hearten Mary and Martha. Tired of being alone and bored in their suite, she began to spend more and more time at the bookshop and at the Opera House, relying on them for the companionship she lacked from Luke. When he was with her he was often abstracted, and only relaxed on the rare occasions when, with the coming of spring, they drove into the countryside or to the mountains for fresh air. Then, and then only, did he become more like the man she thought she knew, although even then his eyes still bore that haunted look. And still, even then, he talked of silver.

'Luke,' she broke in one day, deliberately startling him, 'when can we visit England?'

'Perhaps soon. Just a few more months,' he said eventually. 'I've got this legal case to see through over a rival claim next to the White Rose mine.' He seemed almost frightened at the idea of tearing himself away, she thought bitterly, as though Leadville and not she was his security. One bright spot lay ahead. It was spring, and very shortly Daniel would return. At least she would hear the sound of laughter again – and it struck her as strange indeed that it should be she, not Luke, who now reached out for that precious gift.

'I bid you good morrow, Kate,' came his soft voice, making her jump and her paintbrush throw a streak of blue paint over the white river on the wooden flat.

'Daniel!' she cried, delighted. 'What on earth are you doing here? The company isn't due for another week.'

'I am aware of that. I thought instead of spending my holiday in New York, I would come to enjoy the delights of Leadville, especially one.' He eyed her critically. 'I see being rich has made you put on weight.' He pantomimed an appreciative ogling of her hips, which were clad in her working trousers.

She was highly indignant. 'I've lost weight if anything.'

'Indeed? I must see whether you still fit my arms,' he said, advancing meaningfully on her. She neatly dodged round the side-scene, but found him looming again in front, having vaulted over it. He backed her into the corner and then his lips were warm on hers. 'Just a welcoming kiss. You can't deny me that.'

'Daniel,' she said heatedly, if rather belatedly, 'no!'

'No what?'

'No, thank you,' she said, pushing him firmly away.

He laughed, then said, concerned, 'Kate, you should look after yourself. You look tired. Your lovely eyes have the tiniest of crow's feet round them, and black shadows under them. You are not happy, are you?'

'I am,' she said defiantly.

'To see me, Kate?'

'Glad,' she amended, smiling and offering her hand in armistice.

'Ah, not your hand, Kate. Your heart, if you please, and then your body,' he added offhandedly, laughing.

'Daniel,' she said crossly, 'I'm sure you will recall that I am married.'

'And a millionairess, so the talk is. The Manhattan Mine. You are fortunate, though your husband is less so.'

'Why?'

'He has all the riches he needs and does not seem to heed them.'

'He does,' she said defensively, picking up his meaning and resenting it. 'We have moved into the Stowerton Palace Hotel so that I do not have to endure my mother-in-law any longer.'

'That is a basis for a good family life? And why no little Stowertons?'

'Daniel, you go too far.' She tried to walk past him, away, away, from awkward questions, away from temptation, lest he see from her face how much she longed to throw herself into his arms and pour out all the frustration that life in Augusta's house had brought. Now, seeing him once more, she realised just how much she had missed his companionship. That was all, wasn't it?

233

'Ah, you cannot have it both ways. Kate,' he went on inexorably, holding her closer to prevent her trying to escape from his tightening embrace. 'If I am not lover then I am friend, and it is the duty of friends to ask questions like these. And if not friend, why then, you must permit me to be lover.'

'Friend then,' she said, glaring. Why did he have to look just as she remembered him, not like the stranger she'd half hoped would return? Why did that sense of familiarity and content have to reappear quite so instantly? 'Daniel, I –' she tried to continue awkwardly, not knowing what to say.

'I absolve you, Kate,' he interrupted gently. 'But only because I am so very, very glad to see you.'

'And I you,' she replied fervently. 'And I you.' This time she did not resist as he took her into his arms and kissed her, only drawing away as she felt his hand warm on her thigh through the thin material of her pantaloons. But it was not aversion to his touch that made her do so.

Katharine plucked at her new blue satin dress nervously. Where was Luke? Surely he would not be late this night of all nights? At last he arrived, two hours after she had expected him, taking off his hat and sinking into a chair.

'Where have you been, Luke?' She tried not to make it sound like an accusation. 'This is our wedding anniversary.' The words sounded hollow even to herself. A wedding that had been no wedding, and a marriage that was proving . . . She broke off this terrible train of thought with difficulty.

'I have been home. I'm sorry to be late.'

'This is supposed to be your home,' she remarked bitterly.

Luke glanced round. It was a hotel suite, not a home. It was his choice and there was no help for it. Yet it was not a home like Bocton could be. What had brought that once more into his mind? Now that the hearing was drawing near, he found he was beginning to dream of Bocton. Of a house they could make their own, with children to make mellow walls ring with laughter. But he could not speak of it, lest it did not happen. Always he made an excuse to himself, some reason why he could not leave Leadville.

'Does our marriage mean nothing to you that you prefer your mother to me?' she cried, tears of vexation beginning to run down her cheeks.

'Today was different,' he said angrily.

'It always is.'

'My father is asking her for a divorce, and threatening to cut off her income if she does not agree,' he said flatly, averting his eyes from her accusing face.

'Perhaps Mary had better come to work in the Opera House after all to help support the family,' Katharine said flippantly, knowing how it would anger him.

'I am sorry you do not appreciate my mother's situation,' he said stiffly.

234

'Which she at least partly brought about, and has done everything to worsen,' Katharine pointed out.

'Are not all marital discords the fault of both those concerned?' he retorted. 'Do you think yourself blameless in this regard?' he added icily.

'You too, Luke,' she cried, gasping at this unexpected attack.

'Perhaps.'

The chasm lay between them, but they turned back, each to their own side, for there was no bridge unless one of them made it, and neither was willing.

'I am sorry about your mother,' she said stiffly. 'Will she agree to divorce your father?'

'I am trying to persuade her,' he said heavily, 'that it would be in her interests to do so.'

'I pity your father. Life will not be easy. Nor for you.'

'For me?' he queried, puzzled and annoyed.

'Unless your mother is stopped she will make the name of Stowerton even more of a laughing stock than it was when your father left, just as Mrs Tabor did that of Horace. She will be just like Augusta Tabor, with less cause. The scandal should keep Leadville amused for many a year.'

'And how will that affect *me*?' he enquired angrily. 'Even if your prejudiced predictions are correct?'

'You have to do business in this town, Luke. It will not be easy. Could you not sell up?' she pleaded once again. 'Could we not go to live in Denver, to England even? We could so easily afford to. The Case will be heard later this year, so Mr Pinpole says.'

For a moment Luke wavered. Katharine was right. Away from the mines, away from the Opera House, freed from endless business discussions and problems. Yet surely he had to see his mother through the divorce? And, besides, the Manhattan needed a few more months yet to ensure the silver was going to hold at the same high grade. He could not sell out till then and hope for a good price. Whereas if he waited a little . . .

'When the divorce is through and my mother is settled,' he said placatingly, 'then perhaps we could do that. But I need to protect our interests for a little while yet,' he said vaguely. 'No, we must stay.'

To combat her unhappiness, Katharine threw herself wholeheartedly into long hours of working at the Opera House, preparing scenery and props for *The Beggar's Opera*. She seemed to find herself thrown constantly into Daniel's company. Somehow he seemed always to be there, busily employed on his own tasks, but nevertheless there. Practice, he explained soberly to her, from the Olympian heights of the true artiste, was best done on the stage itself – daring her to contradict him. She kept silent, for if she were to contradict, as one day she did, it would leave her open to his quizzical mocking of her 'vanity'. After all, he would say, for what other purpose could he be there? It was strange, she went so far as to remark, that he needed no accompanist for his practice. Not at all, he retorted. He had a remarkably fine ear. One note played by himself on the piano was all he required.

So she worked as his magnificent voice floated round her, laying down her brush to listen:

> Youth's the season made for joy
> Love is then our duty . . .

Silence. A note on the piano. Then:

> My heart was so free it roved like a bee
> Till Katie my passion requited . . .

'Daniel!' She stormed on to the stage, paintbrush in hand.

'Mrs Stowerton, I am rehearsing.' A pained look.

'I thought I heard you call my name,' she said meaningfully.

'Good gracious, no. Now if you will excuse me?'

> Roses and lilies her cheeks disclose
> But her ripe lips are more sweet than those,
> Press her, caress her . . .

She fled, defeated.

Daniel had infiltrated himself easily into Leadville society, ever the target of invitations to the numerous balls, parties, concerts, teas and fêtes at which the youth of the town, as well as its leaders, disported themselves. Mary made it her business to call on Katharine regularly with artless enquiries as to which of the events he would be attending. As the weeks went by, she set her heart on a forthcoming Ball. Despite her faithful attendance at almost every performance, and her eager accosting of Daniel afterwards, two invitations to tea were all she had achieved – and both times there were others present.

She poured out her distress to Katharine who listened uneasily, trying gently to dissuade her from hope, but with little success.

'Dearest Kate, I shall escort you to the Fourth of July Ball,' Daniel announced one day, as he took her home to the suite.

'You know very well, Daniel, that I have to go with Luke.'

He laughed. '*Have to*? Ah, Kate, those words betray so much.'

'You know I didn't mean . . . oh, Daniel, why don't you take Mary? She would enjoy it so much.'

'Very well. If you insist,' he sighed.

Having suggested it, Katharine promptly regretted it, since Mary was beside herself with anticipation and self-importance. She watched, concerned, as Daniel danced with Mary until Luke complained: 'Why are you watching her so intently? Or is it Pearson?' he asked idly, with sudden awakening curiosity.

'Don't be foolish,' she snapped, but was aware that she was going red, and quickly fanned herself.

Yet when Daniel came to claim his dance from Katharine, Luke's face wore a frown as he himself took Mary on to the floor for the waltz-quadrille. He saw Katharine's face turned upwards to Daniel's, laughing, and it disturbed him. He didn't think of himself as a jealous man, knowing he had no cause for Katharine would never betray him; what troubled him was that she should laugh with others, and not with him. Never with him.

'I think he is fond of me, Katharine,' said Mary excitedly, her round face over-red from dancing, 'but I do not think Daniel is quite ready to commit himself to marriage. What do you think?'

'Could you not find someone else, Mary? That young owner of the Ethel mine, for example? He seems to like you.'

'He is very dull compared with Daniel,' said Mary firmly. 'Besides, he is much better suited to Martha.'

'I am sorry, Katharine, but I have to go to Denver,' said Luke more brutally than he had intended, through guilt.

'But you promised you would be here. It is my birthday,' she cried, dismayed.

'I am sorry. We'll celebrate it when we come back. We could go to the Inter-Lake at Twin Peaks,' knowing she'd always wanted to go to this secluded retreat.

'Of course,' she replied woodenly. Then she could not be restrained. 'And what of your other promises, Luke?' she asked in a low voice. 'You said we would go to England, you said we would restore Bocton, live there perhaps. What of them? Will you have to put them off for business too?'

Luke went white. 'You're overtired, Katharine,' he tried to say.

'Yes, I'm overtired,' she replied. 'Tired of living in a vacuum waiting for a day that never comes, while you chase moonbeams of silver.'

'I had some idea,' he threw at her, 'that part of a wife's duty was to support and comfort her husband.'

'I had some idea that it was supposed to be mutual. It's my birthday,' she reiterated childishly. 'Stay with me, *please*.'

'I can't. I can't. You must be reasonable, Katharine,' half pleading, half furious.

'Stay with me.'

'No.'

So much for promises, so much for dreams. Even if they won The Case, Bocton too would merely become part of the silver empire, she thought despairingly. Sold for silver, probably, the proceeds divided up between them all. Their dream of Bocton as a home had been a whim, a passing fancy, as unreal as their marriage itself.

'May I come in?' Daniel glanced down the empty stairs behind them, as she stood at the door of their suite.

'No, Daniel.' It was a struggle. Her pride would not let her tell him it was her birthday. 'My husband will be back –'

'He is away,' he said gently, and she flushed, having been caught in a lie.

'Yes,' she said, 'but still no.'

He took her hands. 'Katharine, it was the last night of the season tonight, and tomorrow we leave for Europe. Next year we will not return, *I* will not return. You are not happy, and I want to take you with me.'

'You know I can't, Daniel,' she said wretchedly.

'Because of the scandal?'

'No,' she said, amazed he should think so. 'Because I am married.'

'But what kind of life is it for you here?' he cried. 'Think, for God's sake, Katharine. You'll be here for the rest of your life.' He pulled her to him, holding her close. 'I've tried not to put pressure on you, or to embarrass you, but I want you. I love you. If I thought that husband of yours cared for you as you deserve, I swear I'd go, but he doesn't. We would be happy together, wouldn't we? Youth's a season made for joy. If he'd divorce you, we could marry.'

'Daniel, stop!' she cried, overwhelmed. Here for ever, a life sentence. Against . . .

'Don't answer now, Katharine,' he said quickly, seeing indecision on her face. 'I'll come for your answer tomorrow at two. We leave at six.'

'It will still be the same.'

'Hush,' he whispered, closing her mouth with his lips against the words, the sweetness of his kiss driving all else from her mind save the thought that her last refuge was being taken from her. He hurried down the stairs as though unless he did so he might yet rush back and plead for admittance.

Hidden from his sight on the next landing, Mary stood rigid, her face ashen, her eyes too blank for tears, her hopes and illusions in tatters, and only one thought in her mind: revenge.

Katharine watched the minutes ticking by. Daniel would come exactly at two, that she knew, but the waiting was unbearable. She could not go with him, but the fact that she would never see him again was throbbing in her mind as relentlessly as the ticking clock. She opened the door promptly at two. He smiled nervously, carefully laying down his stick and hat, then closing the door, took her in his arms.

'Daniel, I cannot come with you,' she said gently.

'I expected you to say that,' he said with some effort. 'Do you feel anything for me?' he asked lightly.

'As a friend,' she said steadily.

'No more.' He led her, an arm round her waist, into the reception room. 'Yes, I know you do. There is no point in your denying it. You would not allow me to kiss you if you did not care.'

All the things that Daniel could offer her and Luke could not, would not – how did one define love? Was the magic spell he spun about her love? His devotion, tenderness?

'I don't own the Manhattan mine,' he said ruefully, 'but I'm hardly a pauper. We could rove the world together. I'll even take you to your beloved Bocton.'

She was Elizabeth Stowerton's daughter, and now, thrown before her, was the chance to do as her mother had. Follow her heart, and not her head. Yet where was her heart?

'I can't leave Luke,' she cried out. She could not reason this out. She just knew it to be true.

He sighed. 'Then we must part. I won't return.'

Never to see Daniel again? Never hear his voice, singing, laughing? She felt as if she were being torn in two.

'But I can't come,' she repeated dully.

'Then you must tell me at least I haven't been wrong. Tell me you feel love for me.'

Seeing her silent, he knew his victory, and came to her triumphant in this at least, enfolding her in his arms. 'Give me one kiss to remember, the kiss of a lover, not a friend.'

No,' she said sharply, but he would not be gainsaid and, kissing her lightly, then more demandingly, bore her gently down with him on to the sofa, his arms tightly round her, his hands warm through her teagown, tantalising, seeking, caressing, till she was entranced into the magic he was creating, unaware of his slipping her teagown from her shoulders, caressing them, and, unable to reach her breasts, pulling up the chiffon of her skirts until his hands were so close she was aware, fully aware, of where they were, and began to struggle. Then pleasure took over, and her restraining hands fell away, creeping round his back, holding him to her. As she felt him removing her clothes, she rallied all her strength, pushing him away, aware of how near the brink they were, turning her head from him. He sat up, head in his hands, breathing heavily, till he regained his control. Then, with an attempt at his old bravado, he stood up unsteadily, pulling her after him, smoothing her tumbled hair and dress – and taking her once again into his arms.

'Katharine,' he murmured as the door opened and Luke stood there, and behind him Mary, triumphant, glittering with hatred now love was lost to her.

Luke said nothing, but the blue of his eyes blazed in pinpoints of anger, his face looking suddenly grey. He merely looked from one to other, waiting.

She wanted to run to him, not to excuse herself but to take him in her arms, comfort him and banish the hurt that his face betrayed to those who knew it well. But horror kept her still.

It was Daniel who spoke first, pulling himself together and walking up to Luke. 'Your wife has nothing to reproach herself with. I have, for forcing my attentions on her. I will not apologise. I would do it again, for you are not worthy of her.'

Then Luke spoke. Not to Daniel, but to Katharine. 'Is this sweet disorder in the dress –' his eyes flicked over her tumbled gown and hair '– one of preparation or reconstruction?' he enquired.

Katharine began to say something, but Daniel forestalled her. 'I have told you, Mr Stowerton,' he said angrily, 'she is not to blame.'

Luke turned to him at last. 'Get out,' he said quietly, flinging down his hat and stick.

'No. Not until I see Katharine is –'

'Get out, damn you!'

'Only if she comes with me,' said Daniel firmly. 'I will not see her hurt.'

Luke's face went white. 'Hurt? You think I'm going to tear her limb from limb? She's not worth it. Do you wish to go with him, Katharine?'

The world spun round her and she clutched at a chair for support, but fell. She looked at Daniel, who came back, taking her by the hand. 'Come.'

Mary threw herself across the room, moaning and sobbing. 'You shall not, you shall not. He's mine,' clutching and clawing at Daniel.

But in two strides Luke was there, removing her desperate hands, pushing her on to a chair, then whirling on Daniel, twisting him away from Katharine, and in one blow sending him crashing to the floor. Dazed, he clambered to his feet, ignored Luke and turned again in appeal to Katharine.

'Please, Daniel, I cannot come,' she managed to say through numbed lips.

'So *now* will you get out?' said Luke pleasantly. 'And leave me alone with my wife.'

Katharine watched, devoid of feeling, of tears, of emotion, as Luke quietly and efficiently tended to Mary's hysterics with smelling salts and cold water. Then when she was sufficiently calm he rose, without a word or backward glance at Katharine, and took her back to Chestnut Street. It was as though she did not exist, Katharine thought numbly, a mere pawn between two men, removed from play, capable of nothing more than sitting and waiting until he chose to return.

The clock ticked on, its sound filling the room in the silence. When he came back – if he came back? Surely he must. Or would he stay under Augusta's roof? Even now she could pack, join Daniel, be free of this nightmare for ever. But she sat as if chained in the chair, watching the door.

She sat there for four hours before he returned. She raised her head as he came in. 'You have been at your mother's?' she asked without curiosity. Of course, of course. Poor Mary, outraged Augusta, the prodigal son weeping on their bosoms.

'At the office,' he said briefly. His temporary refuge, her punishment. Never, never would she know the effort it had taken to enter it, deal with letters, problems, figures, when his whole being cried out with outrage and bitter hurt, when all he wanted to do was face her and demand: 'Why?' Except he could not trust himself not to break down. Years of pent-up emotion would flood out, weakening him, and that he could not afford.

'The office?' she cried in horror, beginning to laugh, wildly, hysterically.

He raised his eyebrows. 'It is a Thursday. You seem surprised.' He strolled to the cabinet and poured himself a whiskey. Neat. '*Are* you lovers?' he enquired conversationally.

'No,' she answered with no conviction in her voice. What made a lover?

'Can I believe that?'

'Yes. Because I'm here and not with him.'

'I'm honoured.' He gave a faint ironic bow. 'But do I want you? That is the question.'

She came out of her apathy, out of the stupor that had engulfed her, emotionally and physically. 'We are bound by marriage. You said I had a duty, loyalty to you. Does that not apply to you?'

He shrugged. 'I did not know then you had taken a lover.' A lover . . . oh, Katharine. Her chestnut hair on the pillow, her eyes gazing lovingly up at another, other hands upon her. He felt his stomach heave, and took a gulp of whiskey to keep it calm. Never, never let her know how much it meant, how much she meant. For knowledge was power, and never would he let her have power to harm him again.

'Even if I had a lover,' she blazed, 'at least he would be human. Not like yours. Silver is your mistress, Luke.'

'If she is, she is my only one.'

'Is she?' Katharine blazed. 'Is she? You who can kiss and woo with your lips while tumbling with another? How can I believe *you*, when you did that once with my own sister?'

'Not that again, Katharine – surely you cannot still believe I was making love to Meg?'

'How can I not when she has your baby to prove it?'

'My baby?' Anger went from his face, to be replaced by complete bewilderment. 'Katharine, are you quite out of your mind? Meg's married to Louis.'

'But the baby was yours. She told me so,' she said, as though it no longer had power to hurt.

His face was white with shock. 'And you believed her?' he said flatly, making it seem another betrayal of hers.

'Meg wouldn't lie about something like that,' she said defiantly.

'You believed her and not me?' he said slowly, incredulously.

'She was my sister,' she said. 'Of course. Besides,' uncertainly, 'you gave her the allowance, didn't you? And the boy is named for you.'

'So I did. So it is.' He flung back his head and laughed. Not true laughter, but bitter, forced mirth at the oddities of life.

'So I slept with Meg,' he continued calmly, 'made her pregnant and then married you? Why? might I ask.'

'Because you do not like children,' she said. 'You know you don't. It would have interfered with your life. As it does now,' she added. 'You married me in order not to have to marry her.'

'Meg said this?' he said in a strange voice.

'Yes. Why else do you think I,' her face flushed, 'regarded our marriage as a business arrangement, and would not share your bed?'

Luke stared at her, his face drained of expression and emotion. 'I thought I had rushed you, taken advantage of your love for Bocton, and that you would come to me, given time,' he said slowly. 'Because I thought also that you loved me. But it was all for Bocton. Would

241

it interest you to know, Katharine,' he continued after a moment, 'that it was Louis with whom little Meg copulated so happily in the orchard? That it was Louis who left her blithely, and that she turned to me to annoy you? Did it occur to you to ask me? To trust me? Be loyal to me?'

'Meg was my sister,' she faltered. 'I hardly knew you. You were never serious. Discuss? How could we discuss? Are you telling me the baby is Louis's own child? That all this has been for nothing?'

He shrugged. 'Only you can decide where your loyalty lies, Katharine, and you made that quite clear this afternoon. Perhaps you were thinking to start the family I would not give you?'

'No!' One heartrending cry that pierced him through. They stared at each other in silence.

'And if I believe you, Luke, could we not start again?' she said haltingly at last.

He looked at her unseeingly, all his emotions welling up; there had been too many betrayals, too little shared love. He had not the energy. 'That was in another country,' he said, almost to himself. And besides the wench is dead. Died this afternoon, tumbling in the arms of another man. 'It's too late,' he said quietly. 'Too late.'

She lifted her head proudly, as despair engulfed her. 'You are sure?'

'Quite sure.' His hands were unsteady as he turned to pour himself another drink.

'Then I had better follow Daniel,' she said at last. Tell me not to go, please, please, for whatever reason. Just a sign.

'Yes,' he said, as though it were of little interest. His rock split asunder and his dreams, his life, dissolved into the silver dust of Leadville.

Chapter Fourteen

'Darling!'

Elizabeth Stowerton floated into her morning room and stopped short, completely taken aback and for once showing it. When her maid had announced that her daughter had come to see her, she had braced herself for yet another tearful encounter with Meg. To see Katharine was both a most delightful surprise and more than a little ominous, judging from Katharine's strained expression.

Nothing of this was apparent on Elizabeth's face, however, as she rustled forward aflame in crimson moiré, to greet her daughter. Her face wore a happy smile, with no hint that this might be rather more than an unexpected filial call.

Katharine embraced her, apparently trying to achieve gaiety and nonchalance. She failed in both, as her self-composure fled and she burst into tears in her mother's arms.

'Darling,' said Elizabeth inadequately, now seriously alarmed. 'Darling.' Luke was dead? Ruined? Another woman? A miscarriage? Incurable disease?

After a few moments she gently disengaged herself. 'Perhaps,' she said thoughtfully, ringing the bell for Briggs, 'we had better take coffee. Several cups. And chocolate biscuits. From Rumpelmayer's,' she added brightly. 'then you can tell me all about it.' Meanwhile her brain was working furiously.

How had she got here? Katharine dimly remembered a black pit stretching for two days, in which she gathered travelling clothes at random; quietly listened while Luke explained that he had arranged for her to travel to New York with an elderly couple from Denver, and from New York to Paris with someone else. Everything was settled.

'It *is* Paris, I believe you said?' he had enquired politely, as of a stranger.

She had nodded, incapable of speech, not believing even now that he would not ask her to stay. She was his wife. Why did he make so little effort? There was only one answer. He no longer wanted her, let alone loved her. She was alone.

Luke had escorted her to the railway train, but did not stay until the train departed. She watched his tall rigid figure, his fair hair curling out under his hat, walking out of her life. As he had chosen, not she. Only when she was on board the steamer for France did feeling begin to return to her, and she tried to dull the pain by telling herself that a new life, an exciting life, lay ahead. A life with Daniel. A life a part of which at least she could spend at Bocton – or could she? She supposed

243

Luke might well halt The Case now. Odd, that she could think of that possibility almost calmly, set beside this greater calamity. No, she would not think of it. She must think of Daniel in whose arms she could forget, and learn to live and love again. For Daniel she came second to none, and nothing.

First, she decided, she would visit Mother, to give herself breathing space. Only lying awake in her bunk one night did it occur to her again with wry amusement that she, Katharine May Stowerton, was doing what her mother had done so many times: following her heart and not her head. Her heart? Yes surely, for, she told herself, she had married Luke for 'business reasons', for Bocton, or so he had accused her. Now love had come at last and made its power known. Having thus reasoned out an answer that temporarily satisfied, she fell asleep at last, to the words echoing through her dreams: 'I will love you all the day . . . over the hills and faraway . . . Over the seas and faraway.' Her body tensed as she heard Daniel's siren-like voice, in her imagination, seducing, felt his hands on her, owning her, holding her safe, and she longed to be with him, so that finally the die would be cast. He did not know she was coming, for there was no way to tell him before she arrived in Paris and obtained his address. For some reason she was glad of this, despite her longing. It gave her time to cross with care the bridge between the old life and the new.

'Delightful though it is to see you, Katharine,' said Elizabeth gently, 'I feel you should tell me why you are here. Is it Luke? Is he not with you?'

'No,' Katharine said calmly, having prepared her answer to this obvious question. 'He thought I needed a change from Leadville. That the air was not agreeing with me, I was working too hard.'

'One excuse would have been enough, darling,' said Elizabeth mildly.

Katharine looked at her miserably. How could she have hoped to deceive her mother for long? 'Luke and I have separated,' she stated flatly. 'I hoped I might stay here for a few days before – just for a few days.'

Separated? This was worse than Elizabeth imagined. She concentrated. 'That nice young man?' she said briskly and somewhat crossly. 'Katharine, what can you be thinking of? And I thought you were so sensible. Really, you are worse than Meg.'

'Meg –' Katharine began, then changed her mind. No, she would not embark on that now.

'Tell me *why*,' demanded Elizabeth.

'Luke is not the man I thought I had married,' Katharine replied stiffly.

'Who is, darling, who is?' said her mother sadly.

At the beginning of September Paris came to life again after the sleepy summer, like the court of the Sleeping Beauty after the spell had been lifted. The *rentrée* had begun, as shops rolled up shutters, removed bars from doors, and filled their windows with colourful displays. Boulevards were crowded once more with coaches and smartly dressed Parisians. Elegance such as Katharine could never have imagined pervaded the scene. Her Leadville clothes, however expensive, seemed frumpy and dull, and even in her emotional turmoil she was aware of it. Fortunately her mother took one look at her wardrobe, and insisted on her ordering a completely new one. She marched her off firmly to a 'little woman I know', who measured and tutted, threw her hands in the air and got to work; then she imported her hairdresser who threw his hands in the air with equal distress, and advanced with scissors. A week later Katharine looked in the mirror doubtfully. Elegantly draped pannier dresses, cuirasse bodices, severely tailored walking dresses, flimsy evening bodices with slender straps for sleeves – a new style for a new life. A new life about to begin.

Steadily she climbed the staircase. Fashionable though the Avenue Montaigne might be, these stairs stretched on for ever. Then suddenly she was there, only a door between her and the future. On the other side was Daniel – or at least his chambers. What if he were out? Suppose he had visitors? Suppose the look on his face was not delight but horror? She braced herself, telling herself not to be foolish.

She knocked, the sound deafening in her ears. Interminable seconds passed before the door opened and Daniel stood there, unshaven in red dressing gown although it was about twelve o'clock. His face expressed not horror but blank astonishment, his eyes rapidly flicking over the new Katharine, her chestnut hair arranged in a chignon high on her head and a fringe of curls wisping over her forehead beneath the small hat.

'Katharine,' he said at last. Simply 'Katharine', still holding the door, not moving. Why didn't he invite her in? Had he forgotten so soon? In her imagination he had let out one glad cry and seized her in his arms. Nervously, she almost turned away.

'You are alone,' he asked, in an almost unrecognisable voice, so different from his usual confident actor's tones.

'Yes.'

Then, and only then, did he move. He came to her, took her hand and led her into a small, overcrowded, untidy parlour, taking her light shawl, sitting her on the sofa as though she had paid a social visit to an At Home.

'I must dress,' he muttered, running his hand over the stubble and disappearing into an adjoining room. Ten interminable minutes later he returned, dressed now in lounge jacket and matching trousers; more self-possessed, he sat down by her side and, removing her gloves, took her hand again. 'What has happened, Katharine?' he asked.

'I have left Luke and come to you,' she said calmly, strangely at peace now that it was finally decided, finding comfort in his warm hand.

'Because of what happened?' he asked sharply. 'You must have left Leadville almost immediately.'

'Partly,' she replied, pride making her reluctant to dwell on it. 'But it would have happened anyway,' she added quickly, lest Daniel think himself to blame. Because he was still so obviously shaken, she cried out, 'Don't you want me?'

'Oh, yes,' he said immediately, reassuringly. He sounded more his usual self as he spoke, yet his body was tense. 'I want you. I love you, Katharine, I told you that.'

'Then what is troubling you?' she asked, sensing his withdrawal.

'You,' he answered simply. 'I am a vain man, Kate, and just as proud as your husband.' He kissed the hand he held. 'You think that you love me. But you did not love me enough to come with me when I asked, and we actors need to be constantly reassured. We are demanding creatures. And to love me, Kate, you have to love my life. Look!' He pulled her to her feet almost angrily, waving his free hand at the crowded room, then marching across and throwing open the door to his bedroom, where the bed was unmade, possessions left carelessly hither and thither; programmes, letters, bills, scripts everywhere.

'This is my life,' he continued. 'That of a travelling player. I speak like a player. I live like a player. I *am* a player. These small rooms are in the Avenue Montaigne. They are my own. It is very fashionable, but I live on the sixth floor, and save for the servants no one lives higher. I can change my way of life. My voice and reputation are good. I could work in one country only. But if your husband will not divorce you, we cannot live in England or America, and if he does, we cannot do so either, such is society's hypocrisy. So it must be Europe. And how would you live, my English Kate, cut off from all you love best?'

'Save you,' she said stoutly.

'A wilted rose without its nourishment,' he managed to say, lightly, emotion taking refuge behind words, then he burst out, 'Ah, Kate. I could offer but barren soil.'

'I will take it.'

'But I will not. I tell you, Kate, I am a proud and vain man. I will know before I take you to my heart, *before* I take you in my arms, that you love me as though you had never loved before, and as I need. We actors are strange fellows, and this you must learn, if you would come to me.'

Katharine fidgeted nervously as they waited for the curtain to rise. Her mother and Klaus gossiped happily about the audience from the lofty heights of their box. It was a most fashionable audience, for only the highest could afford to ignore the current wave of Anglophobia and attend a performance not only of an English opera, but played and sung in English. This was Daniel's first night and he had strictly forbidden Katharine to come alone for her reputation's sake. She had been forced to ask her mother to accompany her. Elizabeth had had every intention of doing so from the moment Katharine had first oh-so-casually mentioned English opera.

'Look, Klaus dearest,' Elizabeth held her glasses fixed to her eyes, 'there's that strange Duchess of Malfi – or do I mean Moltava? Isn't that dear Ivan Romanovitch? What a pity Meg is not here, she would have enjoyed it so.'

246

'*Meine Liebe*, your daughter is even more expensive as a guest than you are. I am thankful she is not,' announced Klaus. So was Katharine. She had not yet met Meg, who had left for a few days' holiday on the day Katharine arrived. She frequently did, observed Elizabeth, with a sidelong look at her elder daughter.

How strange to see the opera from this side of the footlights and not from the wings. And how different this theatre was to Leadville's, and how different an audience. Katharine imagined enviously the excitement and bustle behind the scenes, appalled to remember now that she had left the Tabor Opera House without a word. She had left Joe, left everyone. Left Luke. Her heart thudded painfully at the forbidden train of thought. She dragged her mind back to the present, seeing Daniel now holding the audience spellbound as his powerful voice and stage presence enchanted them in a universal language. Perhaps it was her imagination that he looked towards her box as he sang: 'All the night we'd kiss and play . . .' It would be most unprofessional if so, she told herself, yet she felt his spell anew. Involuntarily she leant forward, an action not lost on Elizabeth, who had been wondering quite why Katharine was so eager to attend this performance. She picked up her opera glasses and studied the cast with even closer interest.

'Klaus,' she remarked sweetly during the interval, 'you may obtain us some champagne. I have a few words to say to my daughter.' Klaus obediently left.

'Katharine.' Elizabeth studied her a moment – really, she was turning out almost as much of a handful as Meg. Perhaps more. 'Are you in love with that delightful young man?'

Katharine was taken aback; she had forgotten just how sharp her mother's eye was.

'Yes,' she said defiantly, plucking at the flowers on her dress, sent by Daniel.

'Is this a new acquaintance?'

'No.'

'Have you been to bed with him?'

Katharine turned scarlet. 'No.'

'Hum.' Elizabeth relaxed a little.

'But I'm going to go with him, Mother, when he leaves Paris for Rome.' She raised her eyes innocently. 'Like you, Mother.'

Elizabeth's mouth twitched. Definitely more trouble than Meg. 'A most charming place, Rome,' she said agreeably. 'I am so glad you will see it.'

Katharine was disconcerted. 'Aren't you going to try to dissuade me?'

'*Me?* My dear Katharine, you are a grown woman and – ah, as you suggest – I am hardly in a position to criticise.'

Katharine was not satisfied. 'You always told us love is all. We should follow our hearts.'

'And so you should,' Elizabeth cried enthusiastically. 'Oh, thank you, darling.' She turned her attention to Klaus, followed by two footmen and glasses of champagne. Seeing Katharine's mutinous face, he promptly vanished again. 'Once you decide where your heart lies, of course,' she added. 'My dear, he is quite charming. I think we shall take dinner with him after the opera.' It was a royal command.

'Mother, no, you know you'll terrify him,' pleaded Katharine, feeling eighteen again, not twenty-six.

'Nonsense,' said Elizabeth briskly. 'I get on very well with young men. Don't worry at all, my darling.'

Being Elizabeth, she got her way. Katharine tried to warn Daniel, but he merely patted her hand reassuringly. They took dinner at Voisin's, talking animatedly of the opera, capping each other's stories of the capital cities of Europe, until Katharine relaxed, sure now that her mother was merely summing Daniel up quietly. She should have known better.

'My daughter tells me you are planning to bed her and take her to Rome as your mistress, Mr Pearson,' she commented conversationally.

Daniel almost choked over the chicken *suprême*, catapulted out of his false security. Then his poise quickly reasserted itself. 'She will also doubtless have told you, Mrs Stowerton, that I care for her very deeply and would do nothing to harm her or her reputation.'

'Quite frankly, Mr Pearson, I don't quite see how you can avoid doing so,' Elizabeth continued in friendly manner. 'I do see Katharine's point of view, of course. I might even have considered running away with you myself, had I not met darling Klaus.' He cast a fond eye at her and continued battling with his partridge. 'And as I have some experience of elopement,' she said a trifle complacently, 'that is no small compliment. However, I do hope you'll both be very happy – if you go, that is. Life is so unpredictable.'

Steel clashed with steel. So, thought Daniel, the knives are out for all to see.

'If you can persuade her otherwise, Mrs Stowerton, then do so,' he said sincerely. 'I would not wish Katharine to come with me unless it is with her whole heart.'

Elizabeth gave him a long considering look, while Katharine sat numbly, feeling like a pawn trapped between the two of them. Then Elizabeth flashed Daniel her charming smile. 'Oh, I'm not going to dissuade her. I couldn't,' she said, shocked. 'My daughter is very headstrong. I wonder where she gets it from? No, you must spend all the time you wish together. Paris is a city for lovers, is it not, Klaus? I give you my blessing – now I know you care for her reputation, Mr Pearson.' Slight, unmistakable emphasis. 'And pray do not omit to try the Charlotte Romanov. It is quite a speciality here.'

Meg was prettier than ever, until one noticed the petulant droop to her mouth. Katharine had deliberately called on her at her pretty house in St Germain without Mother, for she wished to see Meg alone. It was a wise decision. The Meg she had known had had a defencelessness about her, an artlessness, that had made Katharine feel protective towards her. This new Meg was different. Plumper now after two children, she was even more restless and dissatisfied. The babies were relegated to the nursery, Katharine being allowed only a cursory visit before Meg announced she was bored. Katharine was relieved, for it saved her gazing at Louis-Luc's light brown curly hair and eyes so unlike Louis's, saved her from wondering yet.

Having Louis as a husband was exciting, Meg confessed, when she threw herself down on a sofa, unmindful of the bustle on her expensive brocade dress. Now that Jean-Albert had been born, she had hoped to be seeing more of Louis. She had not. She also managed to convey the impression that there was an absence of excitement about Louis's return to the marital relationship that made her suspect he had found more than companionship elsewhere during her confinements. She was setting about winning him back, but it was proving remarkably difficult. He was charmingly attentive to her, and affectionate – yet all was not well, she complained, making no mention of her own social sallies.

'Why did you lie to me about Luke?' Katharine taxed her bluntly.

'Did I?' asked Meg, startled. She had quite forgotten and was taken aback by Katharine's forthrightness. What on earth did she mean?

'You told me you were expecting a baby by Luke, and that he would not marry you, and so you then married Louis. Was the baby Louis's all along?' she appealed to her sister. Disastrously, for Meg liked power being placed in her hands.

'Did you ask Luke whether it was his?' she replied carelessly.

'He denies it.'

Meg looked up innocently. 'That's natural, isn't it, in the circumstances?'

Katharine looked at her. She didn't believe her. Why had she never noticed Meg's slyness before, seen that the pretty face and eyes held more than a touch of meanness? No use in questioning further. She would never get the truth from Meg. Only prevarication. She alone could decide where truth lay and she believed Luke. Too late, though. She should have seen through Meg immediately, then matters might have been different between Luke and herself. Yet how could she claim it was all Meg's fault? It was she, Katharine, who had believed too readily, yet still married Luke. And now it was too late. For there was Daniel.

The mellow September sunlight danced on the water, as Daniel rowed the boat slowly along the Loing river. Katharine leaned back lazily, smiling up at him.

'Are you laughing at my rowing?' he enquired.

'No, I'm merely smiling for happiness,' she answered. And at that moment it was true.

'Good.'

'The woods here remind me of Bocton,' she said lazily, closing her eyes in the September warmth.

'Take me there,' he demanded. 'Take me now. Describe it.'

She closed her eyes and imagined herself there. 'The cobnuts will just be ready,' she said, 'and the apples ripening in our orchard. The woods will just be beginning to smell of damp, mist in the morning, and the leaves turning yellow. The gardens are falling asleep again, and the house –'

'Yes, tell me of the house.' His voice drifted over to her.

'The house is red brick and stone. There's – oh, it's hopeless, I can't describe it. You will have to see it.'

'Yes,' he said, 'I shall.'

She opened her eyes again as the boat rocked, and a large yellow leaf fell on her upturned face. Then he was leaning over her, tickling her nose with the errant leaf.

'I'm tired of rowing,' he complained. 'It's too much for my beautifully expressive hands. How can I embrace my love on stage with blisters on my hands? Come to that, how can I embrace my love off-stage?'

She laughed. 'Don't be nonsensical. You're as strong as an ox, and almost as handsome.'

'Dear Kate, so complimentary. I would have you know half the women in Europe sigh over my dark, handsome looks. Why, one wrote a poem just about my left eye.'

'Why not the other one?'

'Because,' he said, busily tying the boat to a tree stump on the bank and making it rock perilously, 'she was not poet enough to do justice to the wonders of the other.'

Katharine giggled.

'There you go, laughing at me again. I tell you, Kate,' helping her out of the boat on to the grass bank, 'I shall give you every opportunity to observe my eyes from very close quarters, and you shall see that they are no laughing matter.' He took her in his arms and kissed her. He had done so often before, but this time it was different for the falling leaves made them conscious that the time for decision was nearly here. He pulled her down beside him on to the rug, but did not kiss her again.

'We could,' he remarked, chewing a piece of grass, suddenly happy again, 'forget that I am a highly respectable singer with the opera and you a matron of considerable years, and pretend we are but a lover and his lass. We can pretend, can we not?' He lay by her, partly on her, kissing her more urgently than before. 'The days are passing, Kate, and we must decide,' he whispered softly. His hand was light on her breast, and seemed to burn even through the clothing; then he ran it further down, beyond her stays, harder now until she gasped, closing her eyes in the warmth. She felt his lips brush her face, and opened them again to see by a trick of the sunlight not dark hair but fair. For an instant, a fleeting second, she thought it was Luke.

'Katharine?' said Daniel gently, questioningly.

'*Katie May,*' *said Luke softly.* '*Oh, Katie May.*'

'Kate, dearest Kate, you must decide. Only you know if you love me enough.'

'*It takes a most serious person to sit in an apple tree . . .*' That fair-haired boy so long ago. She had stretched up her arms and longed for him to take her with him up into the leafy magic of his kingdom. And then one day he had done so. Where was that kingdom now?

'And if you say yes, I shall love you, Kate. Now. I shall take off these clothes that hide you from me and love you, that you shall never leave me again.'

'*Oh, can't you see, my Katie May, where your path lies?*'

'Kate?' questioningly, gently caressing. 'Let it be now.'

'*And now shall the wooing of Katie May begin.*'

Yet she had shut him out, listened and not heard, loved and not known him. The ache in her was not for Daniel but for Luke. The hand that caressed, that aroused, was Daniel's, but it was Luke to whom she responded.

'You are too strongly whalebound against attack,' Daniel whispered, his mouth against hers, his hands impatiently caressing, holding her so warmly that the thin barrier of her dress was no proof against his gentle urging.

Ah, Luke, Luke . . . The path was clear now, stretching out before her into an unknown, perhaps empty future, but a path she could never leave.

She took Daniel's hand and brought it to her lips, kissed it, and sat up. She took both his hands as he turned his face away slightly, guessing what she should say, unable to face it. He read her answer in her eyes without her saying anything.

'A wandering minstrel,' he said lightly. 'A thing of shreds and patches. Yet we could dance together, you and I, along the highway of life, and be happy. But your thoughts would turn to Bocton, and my road would take you the farther from it.'

'Yes,' she said, grateful that the name Luke remained unspoken.

'Do you love me at all, Kate?'

'Yes,' she said. Part of me, she should have added. The part of her that was Elizabeth Stowerton, chasing dreams like butterflies.

'Then tell me, Kate,' he said bitterly, 'would it have made any difference if I'd bedded you when first you came to me? As you are honest, Kate, tell me.'

She stared straight in his face, but because she loved him she lied. 'No, Daniel.' In truth, she did not know. Had she done so, might she have set her foot upon a path that could have no turning?

He smiled faintly, relieved.

'What will you do, Daniel?' she asked hesitantly.

'Oh, I shall survive,' he said with an effort. 'I shall love again. I truly love you, and were you mine it would be for ever. But you are not, and I am not a man to live life alone. Too much of a coward. But a poor player who needs a woman that he might see reflected in her eyes his image of himself as he would be.' He stopped, and after a moment continued, 'And, Kate, what of you?'

What of her? She could not go to Luke, for she had closed the door by her own folly. But there was one refuge, one answer.

'I will go to Bocton, of course.'

251

* * *

Alfred looked up crossly when Maggie flung open the door of the parlour with a crash; his face changed, however, as Katharine rushed in. He leapt to his feet, the *Pink 'Un* falling disregarded, and Sophy, dropping the teacosy, followed suit.

'My dear,' he said incoherently. 'What a surprise. I really do not know *what*'s going on at Newmarket.'

'Never mind Newmarket, Father,' she said, laughing. 'I'm here to know what's going on at Bocton.'

'There's no racing here, my dear,' he said, perplexed.

She flung her arms round him and kissed him. Just the same, thank heavens, the hair was a little greyer now, a little thinner. 'And Aunt Sophy. Do you live here now?'

'Good gracious, no,' said Sophy mildly. 'That would never do.' She turned slightly pink. 'I visit every afternoon, though, since Meg left. Now, Katharine, my dear, why did you not warn us you would be coming for The Case?'

'The Case?' she repeated blankly. In all the turmoil of the last weeks she had almost forgotten about it, forgotten that time was passing, that the world moved on its way while she had stood still.

'It begins in two weeks. You did know, didn't you?'

'No,' said Katharine flatly. 'I did not. I've been away from home visiting Mother,' she tried to say nonchalantly. 'Luke's in Leadville,' she said quickly, before they could ask.

'Why –' Sophy stopped, seeing the signs of strain on Katharine's face. 'I'll tell Maggie to get your room ready,' she said quietly.

Back in her room, with the old apple tree outside, the faded roses on the wallpaper and the chipped bowl on the washstand, Katharine felt as if she were a little girl again, lying awake listening to the sounds of the night outside. As if she'd never been to Leadville, as if Luke had never been, merely a dream turned nightmare, and now she had awoken to realise the dream had vanished. She had telegraphed him from Paris to tell him her plans. Told him that she had decided not to join Daniel, but was returning to Bocton. And told him that she loved him. There was no message in reply. Had he sent a letter perhaps? He would have written, wouldn't he, as she had now done too? Surely he would reply?

Bocton's green woods and welcome meandering paths were a haven in her unhappiness. Katharine half feared the house might have disappeared in her absence, and that no one had had the courage to tell her, and hurried the more through the grounds to reassure herself. When she emerged from the woods, golden with their changing leaves, and saw beyond them the unkempt gardens and then the house, half covered now by ivy and wistaria each vying with the other for conquest, tears of relief rolled down her face, as she gathered her skirts and ran, stumbling through grass and gardens, along the straggly yew hedge walk, across the knot garden still ablaze with late Michaelmas daisies

252

and nasturtiums. Someone had been working here, she noticed. Aunt Sophy? Maggie? She blessed them, and ran on until she could touch the front of the house itself, as if to assure herself that it was real, holding her breath as she gently tried to open the huge old wooden door. It was locked, of course, with ownership still in dispute. Later she would find her own method of getting in, but for the moment it was enough just to sit and look at it, finding a measure of strength in its serenity.

She sat in the garden by the old sundial, her hand tracing out the legend, 'Tyme wanes awaye'. And how much time she had wasted, following a will o' the wisp, just like her mother, seeking escape not solution. But she was not Elizabeth, who indeed had found a kind of answer, but Katharine. Katharine who had hurt Daniel, hurt Luke. She had not trusted or loved Luke enough. And he? He had made mistakes too, and the greatest of these was that he had changed, possessed by the lure of silver. But was that through her fault or because he had truly inherited the curse of the Stowertons?

What use to go on pondering, when always like an irrevocably tolling bell she heard his voice: 'It's too late.' There was always the future, wasn't there? Always hope? She looked at the old house, still standing, while not very long ago that had seemed impossible. It was still there – and so was Luke, if only she could reach out to him.

'Mr Stowerton, of course,' Mr Pinpole looked somewhat apprehensively at Alfred, 'will be our chief witness, the parcener to speak for the other four interested parties, since none of the others will be present.'

'I shall be delighted,' said Alfred happily, envisaging a courtroom entranced by his talks of trial by battle, of Stowertons long ago. 'I shall enjoy it.'

'That's rather what I'm afraid of,' said Mr Pinpole simply. 'You must confine yourself to facts, Mr Stowerton, and to answering Counsel's questions, or you will merely assist the other side.'

'Of course, of course,' Alfred waved this advice aside loftily, 'but a little colour always helps, does it not?'

'No, Mr Stowerton, colour is not required. Facts are,' Pinpole said with some asperity.

'I am surprised that Uncle Robert has continued with The Case at all,' observed Katharine, 'now that he has lost the chance to sell to the railway company, especially since it's the London, Chatham and Dover Railway that has won the right to build and not his own South Eastern.'

'I am afraid,' said Mr Pinpole in a burst of confidence, 'that the issue is even more contentious, since the railway is running into some difficulty over land purchase and indeed in raising money. I strongly suspect that Sir Robert only finally admitted the point about the wills in order to speed the hearing up. Speed it up, indeed!' He looked shocked, as though such a desire were entirely alien to the purpose of the law – as indeed it seemed to be, thought Katharine. 'And now

Mr Philip has married, there is a certain pressure for The Case to be settled, so that he may move into Bocton.'

'*What?*' Outrage so strong took hold of her that she almost bounced out of her chair. '*Never!*' she said sharply.

'I felt you would disapprove,' sighed Mr Pinpole. 'He married last year, a most – interesting young lady, if a little – um – unusual. They have a baby son. Charham they consider too small to live in, but Bocton offers scope, they consider. If the house itself were to be rebuilt of course.'

'Rebuilt? You mean that if they retained Bocton, Philip would knock the house down and build some monstrosity in its place?' she asked, horror-stricken.

'I believe that is his plan, yes.'

'He will not,' said Katharine slowly. 'I'll tell Luke . . .' Her voice tailed off. Tell him what? Tell him how, when he had not communicated once with her directly?

'Obadiah, have you heard anything about my cousin Philip's appalling plan?' Katharine followed after him agitatedly as he lumbered around the house, gloomily pointing out one defect after another.

'Yes, miss, I 'eard he were round 'ere, *and* 'er,' he added disapprovingly. Clearly Mrs Philip had not impressed. 'Estimating 'ow much it would cost to knock down, 'im an' Gouch that was, and rebuild a nice modern house with turrets an' pointed gables an' crenellations.' He snorted, quite forgetting that a year or two ago he had been an advocate of nice, solid, decent, modern buildings.

'He won't. We'll win The Case,' Katharine told him confidently.

'Mebbe. If de house do not fall down first,' muttered Obadiah, kicking at the decayed post of the old servants' staircase at the end of the East Wing.

'One more winter,' said Katharine firmly, 'and then it will be ours. We can do what we like to repair it.'

'Yes, miss. If you got de money, dat is.'

'Yes, I have.' She stopped. Had she? What was Luke doing about The Case? She didn't even know that much. The bank had informed her that money had been sent from America credited in her name, but no explanations, no letter, had come from him. Nothing.

Still hoping against hope that Luke might appear for The Case, since much to her relief the solicitors had informed her that their accounts were being settled and no instructions had been received as regards withdrawing the action, Katharine arrived in the corridor outside the Queen's Bench courtroom at the Royal Courts of Justice with her father and Sophy.

There were already three small groups gathered: Mr Pinpole, several clerks and the barrister Smithers-Drysdale, whom Katharine had not met but to whom Alfred spoke cheerily, like an old friend. The second group comprised the public, anxious to be present on the first day of what might prove another *Jarndyce and Jarndyce*. The third group consisted of Uncle Robert who bowed slightly on seeing her, tight-faced; an even plumper Philip; and David, whom she hardly recognised, so serious and grey did he look. Aunt Millicent was there, talking to a young woman who must be Philip's wife, a beanpole of a girl, angular, with hair brushed forward over her face giving her an air of great intensity, and clad in the most extraordinary garment Katharine had ever seen, with enormous drooping sleeves, no bustle or stiffening, and, most interesting of all – no corsets. She stared at Katharine through an eye glass then, satisfied, turned back to Millicent.

David alone came across and kissed Katharine's hand, murmuring words of encouragement. 'From all younger sons everywhere,' he said, without a smile.

Alfred had been persuaded into purchasing a new morning suit and was wriggling in the unaccustomed tightness of the outfit, and murmuring to himself the lines he had rehearsed in answer to Pinpole's careful questions. Why couldn't he come right out and tell the judge that the Stowertons had been a bunch of scoundrels since William the Conquerer, but that Robert was by far the worst? Still, one look at him and any decent judge would realise that.

'Mrs Stowerton, may I present Mr Smithers-Drysdale. Mrs Luke Stowerton.' Mr Pinpole was having difficulty in containing his self-importance and excitement. He was about to go down in the legal history books.

'An honour to meet you, Mrs Luke,' the voice boomed out, deep and gravelly. 'Such a pity your husband could not be here. So very interested in The Case. Pertinent comments, yes, most pertinent. A keen brain.'

'Yes, indeed. A great pity,' Katharine managed to reply. 'He is needed at the mines,' she explained inadequately. Such a strange-sounding reason here, so far away, so very far away from Leadville.

The court was impressive in its quiet ordinariness, until the judge entered, a vivid splash of colour. Even Alfred looked subdued. Katharine could see Mr Dean sitting further along the row, next to Aunt Sophy. They all looked like characters in a play, like Gilbert and Sullivan's *Trial by Jury*. She remembered Daniel and *Pinafore*, wondering where he was and whether he thought of her. Her love for him seemed a midsummer madness from which she had recovered, left only with a tenderness for a love that had passed.

To listen to the impassioned florid speech of Mr Smithers-Drysdale opening for the plaintiffs, a casual listener might have thought his clients on trial for their lives. There were almost tears in his eyes as he recalled the numbers of centuries in which the lands of Bocton, Charham and indeed Stowerton had been treated as subject to gavelkind, according to the Custom of Kent; he waxed indignant as he pointed out that according to the Custom it was for the defendant to prove the lands were not subject to gavelkind rather than he be called upon to prove they were. Records from the old Courts of Chancery would be produced, he promised, of the ancient Rolls of

Assizes, of Mortdancestor, of the Book of Aid; Lambarde would be quoted, Robinson, Somner, other authorities. '*Totus comitatus*,' he thundered, 'in *gavelekynde mutari*.' Then he seemed to have noticed the jury's fidgeting for he hastily switched to English. 'Who shall deny this right to a freeborn man of Kent?' The jury's faces brightened again.

Alfred listened approvingly. This was all right and proper, and it was only when Smithers-Drysdale came to the treason of William de Stoorton that he began to fidget. 'Treason, indeed! I'll give him treason,' he muttered. 'A Stowerton couldn't commit treason. Every other crime, yes, but not that.'

'The opinion of Justice Sir Anthonie Browne,' Smithers-Drysdale emphasised, 'was that having escheated to the Crown, the lands were thereafter granted to a common person, and should therefore revert to their former nature of gavelkynde and be partible among his male heirs.'

'Common, indeed!' snarled Alfred, having clearly taken against Smithers-Drysdale now. 'He was a Stowerton. I'll give him common!'

'Oh, Father, do be careful,' hissed Katharine in his ear. 'You're echoing Robert's case, not ours.'

'Eh?' He stared at her blankly, as a door to the courtroom opened and a clerk tiptoed in to summon Mr Pinpole. He crept out and was gone some considerable time. The clerk then reappeared, and summoned Alfred. Curiously Katharine followed, leaving Counsel still in full flood somewhere around the time of the Civil War.

In the corridor she found Father being vigorously hugged by a familiar figure. Uncle Jeremiah! Luke – her immediate wild hope – was he here? Only then did she belatedly assimilate the shock of seeing Jeremiah so unexpectedly. Beside him stood an old man about whom there was something faintly familiar, but she could not place him until the blue eyes were turned on her. He gave her a slightly crazed, far-off smile, and then she knew. It was Uncle Jacob: with his beard neatly trimmed, and conventionally clad save for a red checked shirt under his obviously new and uncomfortable morning coat and trousers. The appearance of Jeremiah and Jacob was clearly having dramatic and unexpected repercussions, and apart from Jacob, whom Katharine went to welcome with a glad cry, no one noticed her presence.

Sweeping aside all Pinpole's protestations, Jeremiah announced he was taking over the role of chief witness, to Alfred's joint relief and indignation. Then he pointed offhandedly at Jacob. 'Took him out of that shack of his,' he informed them, 'told him it was time he stopped acting like a damn' fool and joined the family again. Gave him the choice of going back after this is over and living with Augusta, or staying here. He reckoned he'd stay here when I told him what she's like.' Then he noticed Katharine and grinned.

'I am so glad you've come,' she said gently to Jacob. 'And why,' she enquired of Jeremiah, trying to keep her voice steady, to forget that this was Luke's father, 'were you so enthusiastic for Jacob's presence here at the hearing?'

'Old Jacob's got a piece of paper, haven't you? What you might call a surprise. Come on now, I told you you'd have to part with it.'

Grinning vacantly, Jacob produced a roll of parchment from inside his red shirt and handed it to Pinpole. The solicitor looked at it blankly and somewhat gingerly. Early-sixteenth-century script was beyond his expertise.

'Very interesting document this is, Pinpole, so I've found out,' said Jeremiah smugly. 'Concerns the conveyance of land, the old manor of Northwell, from William Stoorton to one Richard Plantagenet *before* the date he was arrested for treason, and without as was then usual, I gather, making stipulations for the land to revert to the Stoorton heirs after Plantagenet's death. Now when William was arrested, his wife went to Northwell for refuge, but when the king's men came along to assess the lands, they took the lot. Naturally, Richard Plantagenet was not going to make his presence publicly known by announcing Northwell was his. They'd have taken his head as well as Northwell, since there was a case for his being the rightful King of England. They didn't want any more Perkin Warbecks, especially one who might really be Richard's son.'

'And what do I do with this?' asked Mr Pinpole faintly, mopping his forehead, seeing his inclusion in the legal history books being more difficult to attain than he had thought.

'Use it,' said Jeremiah shortly. 'Northwell is now Stowerton House and park. It's gavelkind land and seized unlawfully by the Crown. It belongs to the heirs of Richard Plantagenet and, if they can't be traced, to the Crown itself, who ultimately owns all land in its realm.'

Katharine slowly digested the implications. 'You mean that Sir Robert doesn't own Stowerton but nor do we – if we produce this paper.'

There was a sudden disturbance. Mr Pinpole had fainted.

'Jeremiah, how very pleasant to see you again.'

Robert came out of court at the luncheon recess. He had been forewarned of his brother's arrival; Jeremiah had slipped into the seat next to Katharine's after Mr Pinpole had been restored to consciousness. Some sixth sense had made Robert turn his head from the front benches. One long stare, and he turned back. Then, as Pinpole urgently conferred with Smithers-Drysdale, to request an adjournment until the morrow in the light of unexpected new evidence, he moved out into the corridor to greet his brother.

Robert said nothing else and the brothers stood staring in silence for a few seconds, each weighing the other up.

'You have done well, I hear,' Robert said drily at last.

'No good at business, eh? That's what you told Father,' Jeremiah jerked out. 'Look at me. Second richest man in Leadville now – after my son.'

My son. After Luke, her husband. Katharine's heart leapt at hearing his name. But it sounded so strange, so far away, so unreal.

257

Millicent bustled out from the courtroom, and, when he saw her, an odd expression crossed Robert's face, Katharine noticed.

'By thunder, you've put on weight,' said Jeremiah, startled, and Millicent's face started to crumple. 'Suits you,' he added hastily. 'Fine-looking woman.'

Robert's face blanched in anger. Yet why? wondered Katharine. The remark was tactless of Jeremiah, but hardly warranted anger. Yet she would not like to have been the recipient of the look Robert gave Jeremiah, and uneasiness returned at the thought of these two, each a Titan in his way, battling out their long-sought revenge in the witness box.

What of Luke? Katharine fidgeted all through the long session with Mr Pinpole, waiting for Uncle Jeremiah to be free to join her for tea in the Hotel Cecil. It had taken some time to persuade Alfred to look after Jacob with Violet and Primrose, but now they were happily ensconced, gossiping away in another corner of the restaurant. At last Jeremiah arrived.

Pride prevented her from blurting out straight away the question on her lips. Instead she asked more about Jacob.

Jeremiah glanced smugly at the group in the corner. 'I told him he could have a nice life over here with Violet and Primrose. And there was gold in these islands . . . he'd forgotten about that. I told him you'd arrange something, so that he could go gold-hunting.'

'And that's why you came. To bring Jacob?' she asked drily.

He sighed. 'You understand me too well, niece. Daisy Petal reckoned I might as well come and get the old feud settled. She was tired of living with a ghost from the past, she said. She could fight Augusta but not Robert.'

She waited on tenterhooks for him to mention Luke, but he did not. Surely he had brought a letter or at least a message? But Jeremiah said nothing, and at last she could bear it no longer. 'How's Luke?' she asked in a voice that did not seem to be her own.

Jeremiah looked at her shrewdly. 'I did it,' he began unexpectedly. 'I ran off with Daisy Petal. And I can understand you doing it. Living with Augusta is too much for anyone, and Luke ain't exactly easy. But, remember, Luke's got a lot of her in him. He's just as obstinate. I told him it was his own damned fault. If he'd wanted a meek and pretty miss, he should have married one. Mind you, I expect you blame me, don't you?'

'Because you wanted him to come back to Leadville to run the mines? He didn't have to come, did he?' she pointed out bitterly. 'He could have refused and made the excuse of our marriage.'

'Oh, but he did have to come,' said Jeremiah grimly. 'Didn't he tell you? No, he wouldn't, the darn' fool. I'm no sentimentalist, Katharine. I wanted Daisy Petal and I wanted money. So I made a bargain with Luke – told him I'd cut off the money for The Case if he didn't come back and manage the mines for me.'

'No,' she said, her mouth dry. 'No, he didn't tell me.'

'He's an obstinate young fool. Still, I've made it up to him. I've given him the last shares in the Manhattan, all of it.'

'It's too late,' said Katharine dully. 'He's caught silver fever himself. And it's a fatal illness.'

Sick at heart, she threw herself into trying to forget Luke by absorbing herself in The Case itself, and it gathered in drama as days, then weeks, went by, each session dominated by black-haired Jeremiah as each point was made, culminating in a thunderous reading from the Book of Aid, the mediaeval document recording all lands held in Kent by military service. Bocton was not among them.

'I must say,' said Alfred, 'I don't much care for Robert, but I almost pity him with Jeremiah on the stand.' But in late November it was Robert's turn as the defence opened, his counsel having poignantly pleaded that shortly after Sir Nicholas's death a judge had ruled in favour of the lands being held of Knight's Service and thus subject to the Common Law of the land. To gainsay it after two hundred and fifty years was illogical, he pleaded. Moreover, although the King had inherited the lands in his Body Politic, not his Body Natural, the two were one, and therefore that the land should descend to the eldest son was obvious, just as if it had gone to the King's own heirs. Moreover, the Crown had a right to change the nature of tenure of gavelkind land, as established in the third year of the reign of King John. Moreover, Sir Nicholas was the grandson of William Stoorton, executed for treason. Could the Crown be seen to be condoning treason by granting it back to the family as if nothing had happened? Moreover . . . Moreover . . .

The Case ground on. Katharine was lost in the reams of mediaeval Latin, as lost as the jurors who, even when a translation was supplied to them, looked remarkably uninterested. Gavelkind, it was clear, was proving not nearly the excitement they had expected from all the rumours and rumpus about the case beforehand.

Even the newspaper reporters had lost interest now; one newsman only remained, and somewhat apathetically at that. As Robert's case wound on, however, and Pinpole began to look increasingly anxious, the reporter was to find his reward for perseverance.

'Most irregular, most irregular,' Pinpole moaned. 'Sir Robert is calling you as a witness next, Mr Stowerton.'

'*Me?*' Alfred looked delighted.

'Yes, but remember it is for the *other side*, Mr Alfred. Pray *do* remember that.'

'Of course, of course,' said Alfred happily, eyes agleam at the thought of a moment of glory after all.

'What do they want Father for?' asked Katharine anxiously.

'I have no idea,' replied Pinpole, 'but I fear it very much. Oh dear me, just when everything was going so well. Forgive me, Mrs Stowerton,' he added hastily, remembering Alfred was her father. He was right to be concerned, however.

'You are well versed in the history of your ancestors, are you not, Mr Stowerton?' Robert's counsel enquired.

259

'I am renowned for it,' replied Alfred modestly, thumbs in the pockets of his purple waistcoat.

'Do you recall an episode in the life of Sir Nicholas Stowerton in the year of 1579?'

'Certainly,' said Alfred. 'Just a story of course,' he added hastily, somewhat perturbed.

Katharine racked her brains, but could think of no such story. She listened with increasing anxiety. If it existed, why did she not know it?

'Would you care to tell us about it?'

'No,' said Alfred. Then quickly, in case this should be misinterpreted, he explained with dignity, 'It is not suitable when ladies are present.' How dare Robert question him about that old legend that only came out with the port?

So that was why she'd never heard of it! Katharine was aghast at what he might say, as indeed was Mr Pinpole, who was sitting bolt upright in his seat in trepidation.

'You are on oath, Mr Stowerton, I would remind you. You cannot refuse. However, I will make it simpler for you. I will relate it and you will tell me if it is correct.'

Alfred tightened his lips mutinously.

'In that year, so the story goes,' defending Counsel began, 'Sir Nicholas Stowerton failed to present his red rose at court on Midsummer Day, as was due in Knight's Service to Her Majesty the Queen. So incensed was Queen Elizabeth that she swept down to Kent to demand the reason why. She discovered Nicholas Stowerton in the most intimate circumstances, clasped in the arms of the lady he was shortly to marry. So jealous was Her Majesty that she immediately declared the lands forfeit to the Crown, barred Sir Nicholas from his house, and declared she would herself take possession that very day. She and her retinue entered, Her Majesty retired to the state apartments, her guards keeping the doors.

'Nervous though he was of meeting the same fate as his grandfather –'

'Just a moment,' Alfred interrupted, irritated, seeing his moment of glory vanishing. 'You're not telling it properly. *I'll* tell you,' he pronounced in lordly fashion. 'Her Majesty retired to bed, but at midnight sat bolt upright, awoken by a noise. Sweeping back the bed curtains she saw old Nick himself, bearing a red rose in fealty. He had smuggled himself in through the cellars and made use of a secret staircase.

'For a moment the Queen hesitated, furious at being caught at a disadvantage and somewhat concerned for her life. Her hand was on the bell rope. But Sir Nicholas rushed forward, rose outstretched in his hand, so that she might see that in its red petals was concealed a rich ruby . . .

'My rose in homage not to my gracious Queen but to her incomparable beauty,' declared Nick Stowerton.

'And the ruby, you rascal?' Elizabeth rasped out, gimlet eyes on him.

260

'So far above rubies do I prize the love of my queen that I risk my neck in bearing it to you.'

For a moment she wavered. She had but to call the guards and the Tower would boast another head. Yet Nick? Her handsome Nick? Her hand tightened on the bellrope, but she could not pull it. Burleigh would call her fool, but he had no liking of blue eyes and an impudent wit. 'Tell me Nick, before you die, why did you not inform me of that staircase?'

'That if my queen were in danger, I might save her,' he answered beguilingly. 'That if my queen had need of counsel, I might talk with her.' Then, coming towards her, blue eyes twinkling, 'That if my queen looked on her knight with favour, I might –'

'That's enough, Nick,' she stopped him. 'That if your queen had displeased you and you wished to murder her none might know, eh?' she probed.

'Had I wished that,' said Nick Stowerton slowly, 'I would have come armed. But I come bearing only this.' And tossed the rose on to the royal bed . . .

'Queen Bess threw back her head and laughed,' Alfred proclaimed. 'Forgave him, handed him back Bocton, and increased his Knight's Service to two roses a year.' He looked round happily at his captivated audience as he came to a triumphant conclusion.

Katharine groaned. 'Oh, Father, how could you?' she cried to herself. 'You've thrown the case away – oh, *Father!*'

'Thank you, Mr Stowerton,' said defending Counsel gratefully. 'That would establish, would it not, that Bocton was *twice* regranted by the Crown by Knight's Service?'

'Yes,' agreed Alfred happily, as Mr Pinpole completely abandoned hope of legal history books.

Robert's counsel, however, aglow at this unexpected ally, incautiously asked a further question. 'And that concluded the matter?' he added unnecessarily.

'Oh, no. You're wrong,' said Alfred, ever-anxious to be helpful. 'She granted the lands back, the story goes, not to . . .'

'That's enough, Mr Stowerton,' Counsel almost shouted, seeing possible quicksand ahead.

'My lord, he had asked the question, let the witness answer,' pleaded Smithers-Drysdale, clutching at straws. The matter could hardly be made worse now.

The judge frowned at this topsy-turviness, but perhaps because he himself was eager to enter judicial immortality, allowed the point.

'The Queen had a sense of humour, you see, and knew the Stowerton story, so she granted the lands, the story goes,' said Alfred, 'not to Nicholas, according to the Custom of Kent, but in trust for all the heirs of his body, the first of which, the Queen said to him that night –' He stopped, remembering why this was an after-dinner story.

'Speak up, Mr Stowerton.' The judge was getting interested.

'– was no doubt a-swelling in that young madam's womb.'

'Oh, Father!' Katharine flung her arms round him as he returned

261

to his seat, amid the gales of shocked laughter rocking the court at the defence's expense. 'You've won The Case for us.'

'Have I, my dear? How? I thought I was speaking for Robert,' he said, bewildered. 'Mr Pinpole had told me to assist him.'

The offices of Messrs Pinpole, Foggett and Dodson were given over entirely to a mood of rare jollity as Alfred insisted on celebrating the event. Mr Pinpole had ventured into a bright red cravat in honour of the occasion. 'I did not feel I should invite Sir Robert to be present, in the circumstances, though of course he is one of the beneficiaries.' He glared at the champagne as it took effect, as if to blame it for the singularly light-hearted manner it induced in its partakers. Jeremiah promptly recounted with glee his encounter with Robert after The Case.

'You have not won yet, Jeremiah,' Robert had told him coolly. 'I shall appeal.'

'I think not, Robert,' he had replied, almost crowing in triumph. 'Remember Uncle Jacob?' He brought forward the old man who beamed at Robert, shaking then pumping his hand, unable quite to take in who was who. 'He brought a most interesting paper with him, didn't you, Jacob? Let me tell you what it says.'

Jeremiah made no outright threats, merely, as Robert's face grew white and he spoke of forgeries, commented, 'Of course, of course, it *may* be a forgery. We could get the Wills Division to take a look at it. While your appeal is going on, maybe?' Robert had taken the point speedily.

'Bravo,' said Pinpole, clapping, hearing of this manoeuvre only now.

'Mr Pinpole,' said Mr Foggett, shocked, 'does this not smack of,' he lowered his voice, 'blackmail?'

'Quite,' said Mr Pinpole firmly. 'And very effective too.'

Mr Foggett subsided. Perhaps even he had had enough of gavelkind for a while. 'May I,' he said thoughtfully, 'propose a toast? That the Stowertons may never utter the word gavelkind again!'

'Mr Foggett,' Mr Pinpole pointed out, after another gulp of champagne, 'I should point out, The Case is hardly finished yet.'

'Not over?' cried Katharine. 'But we have won. Thanks to Father.' And Luke, she would have added, but could not utter his name.

'My dear Mrs Stowerton, *five* co-parceners have won The Case. That means that the properties of Bocton and Charham and the lesser possessions have to be divided into six, including Sir Robert's share, plus the future of Stowerton determined in the light of this document.'

'But Luke and I paid for The Case,' said Jeremiah indignantly. 'Don't that mean anything?'

'I am afraid the law is the law. I'm sure everyone will be very generous and accommodating,' said Mr Pinpole soothingly, 'in view of your financial backing.'

A shout of laughter from Jeremiah as he took in what would have to happen. 'You mean all the family will have to come together again? That's what I've been waiting for! Armageddon, by heck. Armageddon at last.'

'We could settle the matter by correspondence, perhaps,' said Pinpole doubtfully.

'No,' said Sophy sharply, before Katharine could speak. 'No. Everyone must come.' She looked round. 'If Jeremiah and Robert are to face each other, then all – Joseph, Albert and Mabel – must be here. Especially Mabel,' she added, almost to herself.

'And Luke,' said Jeremiah bluntly.

Katharine's heart turned over. Luke? Another chance? Another hope? She had weathered the disappointment this time, but how much worse would it be in six months, for that's how long it would take to gather everyone. How could she bear it? Yet how could she bear not to?

Chapter Fifteen

Anticlimax was not long in setting in. Katharine had six months to wait to know what Bocton's future might be – and to know whether Luke might come, tempted by curiosity over Bocton, if not by her. Yet she faced the unwelcome knowledge that there was no need for him to come, for Jeremiah had announced his intention of returning for the final confrontation with Robert. He wouldn't miss it for all the gold in Colorado, he said with relish. Her hope that Luke might come too was a forlorn one, yet slender as it was, it was something to cling to as the long months passed. Mr Pinpole despatched letters to Australia, France, Damascus (Mabel's latest address) and Leadville, and then settled down to the unexciting (to her, though he thrived on it) tasks of deeds to sign, and administration with the court over The Case – and, he added drily, the affairs of other clients.

January came and with it the snow. Once so happy here at the Dower House, she found the long dark days of winter passed slowly. Looking after Alfred and visiting Sophy were not enough to distract her, for somewhere, unreachable physically and emotionally, there was Luke. What was he doing? Had he found someone to replace her, a Daisy Petal? She cried into her pillow at night, deep muffled sobs that racked her body and left her tired and listless during the days. She could not even achieve anything at Bocton. Snow lay everywhere in deep drifts, making the trees and gardens, even the house itself, unreal, swathed in a cocoon of white. She tried not to worry about what harm the heavy fall might be wreaking on the already weakened roof, and of what would happen when it melted and yet more water poured into the West Wing. Cold whipped at her face, gentler than in Leadville but harder to endure here, lacking the icy bite of snow in Cloud City. Here snow nestled in drifts, on trees, and was already turning to slush where pathways had been trodden.

Katharine had seen little of Jacob; Violet and Primrose had greeted him with cries of delight and promptly proceeded to pamper him and generally fuss over him in their small cottage, all of which cosseting he treated with a sublime acceptance, as though he had been accustomed to such treatment all his life. In their disjointed way, they struck up a bond, and for this Katharine was grateful, for she herself would be poor company. How was she to fill in the lonely months of waiting? What point was there in simply staring at the old house when there was nothing she could do? She remembered her plans for a school, abandoning them without regret. Bocton had been intended as a home, and if it were possible that was what it should be again, however little hope there seemed of its being so. Luke was in Leadville, she in Kent, and he clearly wished it to remain that way. Suppose that Jeremiah arranged in June for Bocton to be Alfred's, or even his, and suppose she could restore it and live in it (and that, she thought wrily, only due to the silver she so much despised), what use in living alone? It would be a hollow victory. Bocton should be a shared home. Luke's words came back to her: 'There's nothing to keep me here, unless there's *someone*.' She was here, true enough, but he no longer wanted or loved her. She shivered with the cold. As soon as the snow melted, she must see what damage there was and start patching it up once again.

Then an idea came to her, so simple, so possible, she wondered at her stupidity in not thinking of it sooner. She snatched at it, plucked at it as a life saver. What should she do for these few months? Why, work on Bocton. Start restoring it . . . She had the money for what Luke sent her as an allowance was far, far in excess of their daily needs. Then she remembered, her excitement evaporating, that as yet Bocton was not hers; it belonged to five other parties. Yet even if Bocton were lost to her in the long run, she argued, the money was well spent. And with Bocton part-restored, not even Philip would pull it down later.

She was too proud to take money from Luke save for the barest essentials. Yet if she did not, to whom could she turn? And she could not continue to allow Mr Dean to support Father.

Alfred, however, had very firm views on the subject. 'Mr Dean insists on looking after me, Katharine. I refuse utterly to be supported by my own daughter. I have my pride to consider.'

'But he is no close relative, Father. It is not right.'

'I am told he has our interests at heart,' said Alfred. 'Moreover he enjoys my company.' He was most hurt.

'Very well,' Katharine capitulated. 'I shall ask him about it on his next visit, however,' she told him firmly.

'I suppose,' said Mr Pinpole somewhat reluctantly, 'there would be no barrier to your working on Bocton unconditionally in this waiting period, though of course you would be better advised to wait.' These young people. Rome was not built in a day, so why should Bocton be? 'However,' he added firmly, seeing signs of relief on her face, 'I feel that Sir Robert should be consulted as the co-heir on the spot.'

Robert? This might prove a stumbling block, bearing in mind Philip's rumoured interest in Bocton, let alone their other plans. Yet she still held the ace about the legal ownership of Stowerton. She remembered with amusement her conversation with Jeremiah just before he left to return to America. She had longed to ask him to plead her cause with Luke, to bear messages, but she did not. Instead she asked him the question which it had occurred to her had been left unanswered in Jeremiah's recounting of the contents of Jacob's letter.

'How did Richard Plantagenet pay for the lands he received from William Stoorton if he was only a humble brick-layer, or even a master brick-layer?'

It had not been Jeremiah who answered. It was Jacob who suddenly said, quite intelligibly and without his usual half-crazed smile: 'Paid with Richard III's jewels, o' course. What else did he have?'

'I must congratulate you,' Robert said after Katharine had seated herself at Stowerton House. His thin lips were compressed. 'You have great determination, Katharine. The result of The Case was, I confess, a surprise to me, and even yet I am considering an appeal.' His face was controlled, only his eyes speaking of his venom.

'To see Uncle Jacob was a surprise too, I imagine,' she said brightly.

Robert did not reply, but darted a look at Philip who sat quietly, yet an animosity registered on his face that had not shown on Robert's. At his side sat David, more subdued than of old, his face devoid of the youthful mirth that had characterised it and settled into serious lines. His spectacles made him look remote from the friend of her youth. If he still thought of Meg he had not mentioned her, though he was still unmarried.

'Indeed, yes,' said Robert. 'I imagine you had a hand in that, too, Katharine.'

'No,' she said honestly. 'It was Uncle Jeremiah.'

'Ah, yes, Jeremiah. And Luke too. I hear he has done well in his business.'

'You are right,' she said coolly. 'The Manhattan is the richest mine in Leadville, as rich as the Robert E. Lee.' What use to reel off these names? How could they appreciate what money meant in Leadville? How fortunes were made, fortunes lost, not anchored to roots that could endure like Bocton.

'You have done well for yourself,' said Philip with just the faintest suggestion of a sneer.

Blood rushed to her face at the obvious implication that she had chosen Luke in preference to Philip for monetary reasons.

'Especially as he does not seem to require much of your time,' Philip added.

'Shall we discuss Bocton?' she managed to say coolly, clenching her hands.

'By all means,' said Robert, satisfied now they had gained a point. 'I understand you wish to start restoring Bocton. We have discussed it,' he glanced at Philip, 'and feel it would be merely petty to forbid it. If it so happens in the end that Philip and I still own Bocton, we shall be the better for it.'

'And I,' put in David quickly. 'And I.'

There was a startled pause. Of course, Katharine realised, with the lands now established as subject to gavelkind, David had an equal right to inherit with Philip. That this was a new and unwelcome thought to Philip at least was clear from the appalled expression on his face.

David gave Katharine a twisted smile.

'And we shall, of course, do our best,' Robert went on smoothly, recovering. 'My solicitors feel we have a good chance. But by all means go ahead – without prejudice, of course. I should perhaps also mention that I propose to reopen Charham, with Pinpole's consent. Not for myself,' as Katharine opened her mouth to protest, 'but because our overseas visitors will require somewhere to stay in June and in the circumstances we feel that on this occasion Stowerton would not be the right place. Luke, of course, will stay with you.' Was there the faintest hint of interrogation in his voice? 'Albert, Mabel, and Jeremiah can have Charham,' he added dispassionately.

Luke at the Dower House? She ignored the wave of panic in her stomach. Suppose he would not stay there? And his mention of Jeremiah – was that why Uncle Robert had decided not to obstruct her? Because he was concerned more now with his feud with his brother?

'I heard Philip is planning to knock Bocton down, should he come into the property. Is that true?' she asked. A dead silence followed.

'Surely, Katharine, if Father and I do inherit Bocton, we can do as we wish – at last,' Philip said finally in a bored voice.

He had not denied it, but why, oh why, was Bocton still of interest? Of course! she thought instantly. Hadn't she read once that at the time the London, Chatham and Dover Railway was still running into difficulties over the building of the line, the South Eastern was now putting forward its scheme for a line from Lenham to Chilham? The LCDR was well underway with building now, but suppose somehow the SE had not dropped the idea of its line, but was still planning it? And suppose, just suppose, Bocton entered into these plans somehow? Yet none of this showed in her face. She too had learned to play games.

Albert read the letter from Messrs Pinpole, Foggett and Dodson thoughtfully and decided not to show it to Louise for a while. He would bide his time. Louise had been acting strangely recently; it must be her age. She was beginning to object to his visits to Paris to see Louis. It was almost as though she suspected he was encouraging Louis to play fast and loose on the town. If only she knew! Firstly, Louis needed no encouragement, and secondly it was sweet little Meg who needed watching, in his opinion. As a connoisseur of young married women, Albert knew precisely the point at which the delights of housekeeping and first love vanished into child-bearing and rearing, and could tell which of two paths they might then take – either they lost that bright sparkle and became devoted wives and mothers, pillars of society, or they did not, and the bright sparkle positively glittered. It needed no great powers of deduction for him to see that in Meg's case there were definite signs of glitter. Yet he could not convey this to Louise since where Meg was concerned, and particularly after she had produced two baby boys, his wife's normally sharp wits were definitely blunted. Sweet Meg could do no wrong in her eyes.

He straightened his cravat as he contemplated the June meeting. Would he go? Oh, most certainly. How could he miss playing, or viewing, the last act in the Stowerton farce? Besides, he might, with the right strategy, find himself the owner of Bocton.

Mabel Stowerton tossed Mr Pinpole's letter across the table to her wayward son, Agamemnon. A misnomer, she sometimes thought cynically. He was more of an Achilles' heel. He was eighteen now, and an unknown quantity, but she could deal with that. She had before.

'You're entitled to a sixth share,' she told him, 'on your father's behalf. Want to go, Gam?'

His dark eyes contemplated his mother for some time. 'No,' he told her. 'I'm sure, Mother, that you will do your best for me. Better than I could, for I don't know these people and you do. Besides, you play chess better than I.' He paused for a moment then added, laughing: 'I think Father would have wanted you to go, don't you?'

'Do you know, Gam, I think you're right?' she replied, pleased. 'I'll go.'

Luke Stowerton read Pinpole's letter quickly, impatiently. He did not want to be reminded of Bocton. He had done with it. Bocton meant Katharine. It had done so in 1880, and so it did now. How could he go, despite his sudden craving to be there, to see her? Yet he knew the pain, the opening up of the wound, would be too great, as it had been when her telegraphic message and letter arrived. He could not reply, and she had not written again. All communication was through Mr Pinpole nowadays.

The news that she hadn't run off with Pearson after all had been the final twist of the knife in the wound. Mingled relief with added bitterness. What did it matter? She had said she loved him. Of course she would say that now. She'd found out that Daniel was a worthless travelling player and so had gone back to Bocton, he reasoned, since she gave no reason for her decision. And now the gavelkind case had been won, despite the complications Pinpole mentioned, whatever they might be. Father had talked endlessly about The Case on his return and Luke had listened, but at the first mention of Katharine he had stopped his father firmly. He did not want to hear. So Jeremiah bided his time.

Deep lines were forming on Luke's face. He welcomed bitterness as a friend that he might not feel pain, might not have to examine his own share of blame, for that was a path he would not walk. Bitterness formed a scab that made it possible to ignore the wound that still lay beneath. He would write and decline the invitation to be present in June. That settled, he thankfully picked up the Manhattan yield figures. They made good reading. Last month had produced the extraordinary return of $125,000 during ten days alone, and overall the last three months had returned $522,000. He read them again, and then again. These at least did not deceive.

'Hell and Tommy!' Joseph stared at the official letter from Mr Pinpole, letting out a roar that had staff and Emily running. To hear him shout was unusual, to hear him swear positively alarming. Impatiently Joseph sent the staff away again. They returned, curiosity unrewarded, to their duties in the huge hotel now catering for Manly's growing number of visitors.

Joseph had grown plumper in three years. 'The sweet fruits of success,' said Emily kindly.

Success? But she was right, he supposed. It had gone well, thanks to her. The Stowerton Grand Hotel, right near the Corso, faced the blue Pacific. He'd been right about the visitors coming. More and more flocked off the ferries from Sydney, and to stay rather than just for the day as previously. And rather than stay in a hotel overlooking the harbour, they took the carriages provided free of charge by Joseph to bring them with their luggage to the Stowerton Grand.

'Poor old Governor Phillips wouldn't recognise the place,' said Emily, referring to the early governor who had named the cove Manly. She looked out along the elegant paved Corso, linking one side of the peninsula to the other, thronged now with elegantly dressed visitors, many of them staying in the Stowerton Grand Hotel. Their hotel.

'They've won The Case, Emily. The gavelkind case,' Joseph chortled now, waving the letter. 'What fun, eh? Poor old Robert,' he said with glee.

'Is he going to appeal?' asked Emily, with hazy recollections of the law.

'Apparently not. They want me to go for the cannibal ceremony in June to decide who gets what,' he replied with relish.

'But surely that young man who paid for it, Luke, would decide that? After all, you only put your name to it.'

'The law says differently,' said Joseph, suddenly obstinate. 'We're all equal and have an equal claim.'

'But the rights of the matter, Joseph –'

'Amongst the Stowertons, Emily,' said her husband grimly, 'there's no such thing as the rights of a matter. But I agree with you,' he said, a little reluctantly. 'Perhaps,' he looked at her anxiously, 'I had better be there?'

'Yes, Joseph,' she said bravely, facing the prospect of a further six months alone, 'perhaps you had.'

Obadiah Trant plodded up to Katharine as she shivered in Bocton's porch, sheltering from the cold winds of March. He had at last agreed that they might start on their work, and an initial survey might be taken.

'It don't look too happy, do it?' he summed up critically as they walked around the outside of the building. She was forced to agree. Brick and stonework crumbling, chimneys half falling down where pointing had worn away, tiles and battens vanished, exposing roof beams and rafters in places.

'Still, I reckon 'twouldn't take much to make it *look* decent again,' said Obadiah bravely. 'If I get Jethro . . .'

'Jethro, Obadiah?'

'Getting too old to do it all meself, Miss Katharine. 'Sides, I don't 'ave the 'elp I once did.'

She was puzzled, until she realised he meant her, and laughed. 'I can still wield a hammer, Obadiah.'

'But yew are a respectable married lady now, miss,' he said shocked.

Respectable? How Leadville would laugh at that.

'Nevertheless, Obadiah,' she told him gravely, 'I assure you I intend to help you. Bocton would never forgive me if I didn't.'

Her years of absence had not improved the house. The West Wing was almost entirely given over to rats, mice, squirrels, and more of the roof had given way. The ballroom where once she and Luke had found the line of the old kitchens was now a mass of fallen timber, laths and plaster.

'There be a lot of work 'ere,' pronounced Obadiah, understating the case so much that Katharine laughed. 'You sure you wants to be a-starting till you knows it won't be pulled down?'

'Bocton will stand for ever,' she said confidently.

'And there's summat else too. Which house are you be going to restore? De old 'allouse or Queen Bess's house?'

She hadn't thought of that. What should she do about the old mediaeval house still mostly hidden inside the Tudor mansion? Should they begin at the study where the beams had first been found, or . . . 'The Queen's Bedroom,' she said simply. 'Of course. What we'll do, Obadiah,' she went on excitedly, 'is restore the upper floor of the East Wing, do the roof first obviously, and the attic rooms, and the upper floor – what used to be the State rooms – that is the Queen's Bedroom and Receiving Room, and the master bedroom at the end of the wing. *And* we'll install a bathroom. Then we will have one floor ready to show in June. And this is the easiest and best place to start.'

Obadiah sucked in his breath. 'A bathroom, Miss Katharine? You allus did want to run before you could walk. Where's the water a-coming from? Ain't none that I know of that side of the house.'

Installing water would be costly indeed. 'We'll have to pump it from the wells, a pump-house maybe.'

Her face fell, and seeing that Obadiah said comfortingly, 'Now how about this? I'll put your bathroom in, and I'll lay de pipes inside, just so's all nice and ready. Now that won't be too expensive, Miss Katharine, and when all's settled like, then we think about pump-houses and the like.'

'Yes!' she said, her face clearing, trying not to think of what might happen in June. 'Oh, Obadiah, you're a genius.'

His wrinkled face flushed.

'The old dressing room can be a bathroom, and everything else can wait till June, except to tidy up the Great Hall.'

'And the study, miss? Do we cover dem beams up again? Mr Mayfield, 'e was asking me, miss.'

'Who? Oh, Roderick Mayfield.' She had forgotten all about him. And yet at one time he had been so important in her life.

'Put the panelling back, Obadiah. Bury the old house for the moment.' At the back of her mind was the thought that somehow it might prove a valuable card in her hand.

Elizabeth sighed as dear little Jean-Albert was sick on her velvet dress. She could have another one made, but nevertheless it was distressing.

'Klaus!' He looked up placidly from his book. 'I have been considering,' she informed him. 'I think I am too old to have another baby. Dear Meg's are quite sufficient. What is your view?'

'My view,' said Klaus, mightily relieved that this particular saga was over, and tactfully refraining from pointing out that nature would undoubtedly agree with her, 'is that I am selfish enough to be glad that I shall have you all to myself for ever.'

Elizabeth smiled happily. 'That's all right then.'

'And to tell you the truth, your two daughters, delightful though they are, seem to cause enough problems without adding more.'

'Yes, they do.' Elizabeth's brows knitted in thought. 'I'm concerned about Katharine. She wrote that Luke had not attended that wretched case, but that he might come in June for the final settlement. I wonder if he will?' She plucked at her shawl absent-mindedly. 'Do you know, Klaus, I think I might pay a visit to England just about that time. Would that not be maternal of me?'

'Most,' he said agreeably. 'Do you wish me to accompany you?'

'No,' she replied firmly. 'I like to alarm Alfred now and then. Afterwards I can relieve him by telling him I don't need a divorce. You don't mind, do you?'

'Dearest,' he answered, 'not at all.' Really, everything suddenly seemed most agreeable. That uncomfortable feeling that in ten or fifteen years' time he might be too old to accommodate Elizabeth's unpredictable passions was relieved. He embraced her. 'Always, my darling, always yours.'

'Did I hear you say you were going to England in June, Mama?' Meg swept through the door, her customary petulance suddenly giving way to interest.

'Yes, Meg dear, and your baby has just been sick over my dress.'

'He seems to like velvet,' she said vaguely, not bothering to remove him. 'I thought I might come with you. It's a long time since I saw Papa.'

Elizabeth eyed her suspiciously. Unselfish filial devotion in Meg was unusual. 'Would Louis accompany you?' she enquired.

'I shouldn't think so,' replied Meg brightly. 'The racing is good here in June, isn't it, Klaus?'

Obadiah's voice roared in song towards Katharine through the roof beams: 'Hearts of oak are our beams, hearts of oak are our pegs,' as she perched precariously on a tiebeam. He and Jethro, the latter a younger and less loquacious version of his father, had scrambled through above the ceilings of the attic rooms to effect repairs to the far end of the roof in the East Wing, but she had been forbidden to join them. Now he was busy at the front end, above the old study, where the mediaeval roof was all part of the one Great Hall. If she had needed further proof of the existence of the mediaeval house, it was here at first sight of the massive beams of the old house, one unbroken whole running the entire length of Bocton's façade. That Obadiah approved of his forefathers' workmanship was obvious.

'Burst dey 'ave,' gloomily inspecting a mediaeval joint, 'little lovelies dey are. Bolt and strap, Jethro. Bolt and strap wanted here . . . Dry rot.' Tones of disgust. 'We'll 'ave to 'ave this little beauty out . . .' Sounds of a saw. 'Gentle now. Don't 'urt de sound part. We'll splice de liddle ends together.'

At first Katharine had only been allowed to hand things to Obadiah and, mortifyingly, to Jethro. Now she had been promoted to sawing new rafters, even the trenail oak pegs cut from heart of oak for joints, which was precision work. But she was still forbidden to clamber along the beams.

Carefully Obadiah repaired the end of a tie beam by scarfing on a flitchplate; a cracked collar beam had a sound beam inserted along its length underneath for strength; clamps or straps appeared on other burst joints. Now Obadiah's face loomed up as he crawled towards her. 'It's only scantling,' he said consolingly, as she exclaimed at the mess not only on the floor beneath her, but whole rafters and beams that had fallen in from above when the roof had suffered. 'Not structural. Don't you worry, Miss Katharine. And careful now with those wooden pegs,' he roared in sudden ire, seeing her still clasping them in her hand as she disobeyed and clambered along. 'Dey be precious – begging your pardon, miss,' he added.

Where joints had cracked and rotted, he carefully cut new timbers, fitting new pegs in to their opposite notches. 'Dere dey go,' he remarked happily. 'De gentleman and ole lady fitted together as tight as – begging your pardon again, miss. Now I'll be awaiting another piece, just dis size, if you please, Miss Katharine.'

Obediently she struggled down from her lofty position and went down the staircase to the Great Hall temporarily appointed a workshop. There, looking distinctly askance at the wood shavings on the floor, and the trestles and saws, was the Blessed Damozel, as Katharine had nicknamed her – Amaryllis Stowerton. Katharine had discovered since their earlier meeting that her odd mode of dress heralded her as an Aesthete, harking back to uncluttered, unbustled, uncorseted mediaeval dress. Katharine viewed the matter of dress with great sympathy – after all, who was she to take issue, clad in bloomers or breeches? – but the expression of superiority irritated her. Pre-Raphaelite in dress she might be, as Rossetti-ish as the Blessed Damozel herself, but womanly submission seemed far removed from Amaryllis's thinking.

'Ah.' She eyed Katharine as she heard her approach, gazing at the bloomers in disdain. 'Philip told me to look round the old place again. I have to tell you, Mrs Luke,' she said stiffly, 'I am not impressed.

272

Moreover,' she added, 'I see you wear bifurcated garments. You are a member of the Rational Dress League?'

'And why are you not impressed with Bocton?' enquired Katharine sweetly, clenching her fists to remind her that control might be advisable. 'And, *moreover*, I am not a member of the League. I merely believe in practical dress, as you seem to yourself,' gazing at the shapeless dull red garment adorning Philip's wife.

'Damp. Decay. Rot. I couldn't live here,' Amaryllis announced, ignoring the comment on her costume.

'Then is it not fortunate that there is little chance of your doing so?' said Katharine.

Amaryllis stared at her for a moment, saying nothing. Then, obviously deciding Katharine must be humoured, told her placatingly: 'It will make quite a nice residence when the new house is built.'

'When,' said Katharine with deadly calm, 'is not the word I should have picked.'

Amaryllis regarded her blankly. 'You must come and visit us here,' she said briskly, 'when it's finished. Philip said you were fond of the place. You and your husband, the new Silver King.'

'The what?' Katharine stiffened, her mind abruptly taken off her murderous thoughts towards this woman.

'The Silver King. That's what he is called now, after a play that is on in London. It's about an Englishman who mistakenly thinks he has committed murder and flees to America where he gains an enormous fortune in silver, but is unable to return home. Years later he comes to England to find his wife and children in poverty. I read in a magazine that Luke Stowerton is now called the Silver King.' She paused, considering. 'Not, of course, Mrs Stowerton, that you are in poverty, despite this strange attire.' Another disapproving look at the trousers. 'And you have no children, have you, so it is not a close resemblance.'

'If you keep very still,' said Katharine sweetly, 'you will not alarm him.'

'Who?'

'The rat sitting on the floor behind you.'

But much to her surprise, Philip's wife did not scream and flee in horror. She turned round. 'I don't see him,' she announced. 'I would like to have done. All creatures of this earth were made for us to cherish, and not to eat.'

'I was not proposing to turn him into forcemeat,' Katharine muttered, defeated, returning to her work-post in low spirits. No wonder Mr Pinpole had said Amaryllis was determined. She was blinkered to all save her own path, yet Katharine found it hard to dislike her. There seemed none of Philip's maliciousness in her, and in other circumstances, in other times, her simplicity of purpose might have appealed. But where Bocton was at stake, this was not possible for the wife of the Silver King. Her heart tore wide open again. If Amaryllis was right, then Luke was further away than ever.

*   *   *

Charham was a small Queen Anne house set in formal gardens that lacked the wild spaciousness of Bocton. Being nearer to Stowerton House, Robert had seen to its upkeep after a fashion, and as it had only been empty since Jeremiah had left, not nearly as long as Bocton, it proved comparatively easy to reopen and reorder the house. Violet and Primrose had thrown themselves into the work with zest, while Jacob, who had lived there for some years, merely sat and gazed at his old home with a kind of vacant curiosity. Only when he saw the gilt of the picture frames in the main rooms did the blank look leave his eyes, as he ran his hands lovingly over the precious colour of gold.

Luke paused by his office window to glance outside, into the street seething and noisy as usual, but even so he did not take the scene in, for he was wrestling with the figures that the clerk had just presented to him. If the mine could keep this up for another year, he was reasoning . . .

'Good morning, Luke.' The door had opened quietly and a fashionably dressed young woman entered.

'Daisy Petal.' He went to her, greeting her warmly with real pleasure. He took her hands and kissed them. 'What are you doing here?'

'I've come down with Jeremiah. He has some business with his wife,' she grimaced. 'Former wife, I should say.' The divorce had gone through acrimoniously last year. 'I came to tell you we're to be married next week in Denver. You'll be there, won't you, Luke?'

'Yes,' he said, 'certainly.'

'I'm glad, for I doubt if his daughters will be. And besides, if you're there, everyone will perhaps stop thinking I'm after Jeremiah for his money,' she said cheerfuly. 'Or perhaps not, since you've got more money than you know what to do with.' She laughed. 'The Silver King.'

'What?'

'The Silver King. The newspapers have awarded Tabor's old title to you. It's a play we have just seen in Denver, Luke. I brought you an article about it – and about you.' She threw the newspaper on the desk, and proceeded to tell him the plot, but he did not take it in. He could see the headline, 'Silver King Luke', and his eyes remained on it, fascinated, repulsed. 'Jeremiah's quite jealous of you,' she said cheerfully. Then less cheerfully, '*You* don't think I'm marrying him for his money, do you, Luke?'

'No,' he said abruptly, coming to rather belatedly. 'No, of course not.'

'Good,' she said, and went quietly out, her task fulfilled. He did not see her go.

Almost against his will he took up the newspaper; there it was in black and white, his successful life story, and congratulations on having risen from young reporter to the Silver King himself. 'Bravo, Luke Stowerton.' Slowly he laid down the paper. A sense of revulsion so strong swept over him that he felt almost physically sick. They congratulated him for *this*? Where now was the young reporter with his hopes and dreams? *That* was Luke Stowerton, not this silver monument. Had he lost his way so far?

When Jeremiah arrived some hours later, Luke's plans were already made and unalterable.

Obadiah was tackling the biggest task first, the Queen's Chamber and the bathroom, for the bedroom beyond was in good structural repair and needed only redecoration. But the Queen's Chamber was undoubtedly in disorder.

'Oh, well,' said Katharine, as she and Obadiah regarded the task ahead, 'perhaps we'll find Sir Nicholas's secret door.' A grunt from Obadiah signified that he didn't hold with such whimsies.

Determined not to dwell on the past, she steadfastly refused to think about what had happened here less than three years ago. The hole was repaired now, joists and floorboards replaced; all that remained was for the lath and plaster ceiling to be repaired – a time-consuming task with its delicate ornamentation of rosettes with ER monogrammed on them. Then it would seem as if Gabriel Arch had never existed. As it did now. She felt tears sting at the back of her eyes and resolutely went to work cutting laths, hoping to vent her energy in sawing.

'Rot ahoy,' yelled Obadiah from above.

'Wet or dry?' she shouted back.

'Wet.'

She ran back upstairs to find him apparently paying homage to the fireplace, an original Elizabethan one, not a later addition. ''Tis rotten where de water's come down where de chimneys enter de roof,' he told her. 'Nothing serious. Jes' a little scarfjoint or two on de timbers up dere.' He tapped the bulging plaster round the fireplace as if to reassure it.

Just this, just that. It seemed to go on for ever. In the end, Obadiah pronounced himself satisfied and she was left to the unrewarding task of stripping the hideous heavy wallpaper, repairing the plaster beneath, and painting it the palest lemon tint.

Obadiah meanwhile could be heard exclaiming and tutting in the Queen's Receiving Room over the study. 'Sag' was a word she grew accustomed to. Jethro, as ever uncomplaining, was sent scurrying for flitch plates, straps. 'Joists have gone again.' Obadiah looked sadly at the huge tribes laid horizontally, and, muttering, set about repairs. 'We'll be needing a bridle scarf 'ere,' he told Jethro as Katharine came through to report she had finished.

'Another gentleman and lady joint?' she enquired mischievously.

Obadiah looked at her in reproachful silence, and she crept away in deep humiliation.

'I regret to say, Mrs Stowerton, that we have heard from Mr Luke that he will not be attending the June meeting.' Mr Pinpole averted his eyes while imparting the news, as if out of respect for his client's wife's feelings.

So it was all for nothing. Katharine realised that in her heart of hearts she had been doing the work on Bocton for Luke, and now he was not coming. She tried to tell herself the work was worth doing for its own sake, but for the moment without success. All she could think of was that Gabriel Arch would never see the Queen's Chamber restored to its full glory.

She walked slowly through the rooms when she went to Bocton later. They were pristine in their freshness, and needed only furnishing. Suddenly ashamed of herself for thinking Bocton not worth her effort, she vowed that she would go ahead; the rest of the Stowertons should see the glory of their ancestors even if Luke did not. And to begin with . . . she swept the dilapidated curtains from the four-poster with sudden determination. Aunt Sophy would receive a visit.

In the last few weeks she threw herself into the tasks of equipping the bathroom with lavatory stand, valve closet and bath. No matter there was yet no water! She cleaned the huge Bethersden marble columns of the ornate fireplace, a curious design of two columns flanking each side with painted panels in between, complemented above by smaller columns enclosing a pargeted plaster mount with the Stowerton arms and motto. It gleamed as she finished and she was proud of her efforts.

Then she dusted off pictures that had too long hung face to the wall: a Gainsborough, a Reynolds, a small Constable, and many works by lesser artists. Even a bad oil painting said to be of Queen Bess herself, red-haired, gimlet-eyed, sharp-featured, but wearing a ruby on one hand laid lightly across her breast. Suppose – she laughed – oh, just suppose the old story Father had retold was true? But how could it be? She and Obadiah had found no secret door.

Nevertheless she decided she would bring a painting of Nicholas Stowerton here, just for a little while, that he might hang by his Queen. But as she hung it the next day, the pale lemon of the wall caught and intensified the gold of his hair and she turned the portrait face to the wall lest she see Luke's reproachful gaze in the blue eyes of Nicholas Stowerton.

'Why do we always have these family meetings on Derby day?' moaned Alfred.

Despite herself, Katharine managed to laugh. 'I don't think it's done purposely, Father. It's just coincidence. Anyway, they are only beginning to arrive then. You can still attend to your bets.'

'Indeed,' he answered. 'I intend to. I fancy Beau Brummell.'

'No,' said Katharine, 'look at your cravat!'

'Very well then,' Alfred straightened the offending article, 'St Blaise.'

Still laughing, Katharine put on her trousers for her last visit to Bocton before the family began to arrive. Save for the flowers all was now done, and she would pick them on the way. Already Violet and Primrose were at fever pitch, rushing in circles round an unmoved Jacob. She walked through the gardens, showing signs of her care now. She had been touched at Maggie's dogged efforts to tend them in her absence, and had thanked her warmly. But now the gardens were hers once more. Lovingly, she picked some gilliflowers, their perfumed scent trapped headily by the red-brick walls, plucked some of the early roses beginning to colour the walls of the knot garden, the scents of the mauve and pink blooms filling the air, and then, almost as an afterthought or gesture to the past, Sweet Williams . . .

She entered the house, already smelling sweet from the beeswax polish she had used in the hall, but before she could arrange the flowers, she heard someone in the study. Obadiah? What was he doing here now? Hurrying, because she wanted to see him about the next stage of restoration, she ran towards the study, and cannoned into someone coming out. The impact knocked the flowers from her hand, gilliflowers, roses and Sweet Williams lying disregarded at her feet.

It was Luke.

What the hell was Katharine doing here? He had counted on her being at Charham to greet everybody. He was not ready to meet her yet. He wanted to go to Bocton first, take time to assimilate the place again. He would have to meet her some time, but why now, before he was prepared? Especially in Bocton, where of all places he might not be able to master his emotion.

Luke had not reckoned on the place still having such a pull. Its mellow grace aroused such a tide of memories in him that he could not stay in the gardens and had walked inside once more. Impulsively he followed his route of the first time. There was the window she had crawled through, mended now. This was the staircase he had climbed.

He walked up, slowly now, and there before his amazed eyes saw not the decrepit rooms he remembered, but a splendour of tapestries, paintings and bright colour as if he had walked back three hundred years into history. A carved wooden chair and oak table stood mid-centre in the Queen's Receiving Room; simple oak chests by the windows, through whose coloured leaded lights the sun streamed fitfully.

He walked quickly to the connecting door and opened it. The Queen's Chamber was before him. But not the one he remembered. There was no sign now of Mr Gabriel Arch's hole. No sign of the mess of fallen plaster and decayed wood. Instead the four-poster bed dominated the room, its ornate carved wood gleaming with polish, hung with new embroidered curtains and laid with glowing crimson coverings.

On the plain freshly plastered and tinted walls hung two portraits, one of Queen Bess, surely, and the other . . . ? Curious, he strode over to it, and turned it round. Why, Nick Stowerton!

Luke stood face to face with his own likeness for a moment, moved almost to tears, then hurried on. A bathroom. He stood stock still and looked around, bewildered, wondering whether it were a trick of the light or of his tired brain. There was even a valve closet. Experimentally he pulled the chain. No water yet. He smiled. There was hard work indeed here, and he knew who was responsible. Not Pinpole's doing, or Robert's. Only Katharine's.

He went through to the master bedroom and stood looking out over the gardens at the rear of the house, at the lake and then the fields stretching into the hazy blue distance. This was the house that Nicholas Stowerton knew and loved, brought to life again by someone who loved it as he did. Unable to bear it, knowing he must leave, and leave quickly, he ran down the servants' staircase to the ground floor and back along the wing, picking his way through the dust and debris to the study. He ran through the door to reach the air – and cannoned into Katharine coming in.

Her face was drawn, healthy with outdoor life, but with a sadness about it that was new. Sadness for Pearson perhaps? he thought involuntarily. He caught hold of her to prevent her stumbling, such was the force with which they had collided, and an almost physical shock ran through him at touching her again. He dropped his hands quickly, staring down at the scattered flowers. Sweet Williams . . . Where was yesterday? *Where?* Yet his face registered nothing of this, and the tremble in his voice was lost to her.

'Katharine, I intended to visit you at the Dower House.'

'You said you weren't coming,' she blurted out, on the verge of tears, longing to throw herself into his arms but holding back for pride as his blue eyes stared impassively at her.

'I'm sorry if it has annoyed you,' he said coolly.

'I'm not annoyed,' she cried vehemently. 'I *wanted* to see you.' How could she convince him? How to pass the guards and reach his heart?

'There is much to discuss – financially,' he added, in case there were doubt in her mind. 'And the future, of course.'

'Of course,' she said, through white lips, bending down to gather up the flowers. 'You will stay at the Dower House?' she managed to say.

'No,' he said, almost curtly. 'I understand the solicitors have reopened Charham. I shall stay there with my father. That's where I was born, after all.'

She looked at him, aghast. 'You cannot,' she burst out, 'you cannot do this to me! Whatever your feelings for me, just consider.'

He thought of the talk, the gossip, and unwillingly saw what she meant. This was between himself and Katharine, not the whole family. 'You are right,' he said. 'At least for the sake of Bocton and the success of the meeting, we must appear to present a united front.' He had not intended cruelty, but she blenched, wanted to cry out: *That's* not what I meant. Instead she said proudly: 'There is a spare room at the Dower House, you know.'

'Very well,' he said woodenly. So she was making it clear that she did not want him as a husband? 'And I shall leave immediately after the meeting.'

'For Leadville?' she asked flatly.

'No.' Katharine looked at him, startled by his reply. 'For Bucharest.' Then, as she looked totally bewildered, he smiled faintly. 'I have sold the Manhattan. I am sure you will approve. I have left Leadville.'

'Oh, Luke!' She threw her arms round his neck, full of hope at last, happiness and relief spreading through her. He stood very still and did not respond. 'If only we could win Bocton – you see I have begun to restore it,' she said nervously, feeling his lack of response. 'We could live here, get to know each other again, get to love each other again.'

He gently removed her arms, trying to still his trembling hands, quiet his beating heart.

'No, Katharine, you do not understand. I do not plan to live in England. I plan to do what I had always intended before I met you: to travel the world and write. I shall see you have enough money to restore Bocton if we can persuade the other five parties to let you have it, and so far as the world knows we are still husband and wife. I shall be away most of the time, that is all. I will pay occasional short visits so that it will not appear too strange. It will not be easy, but it is a method of life.'

She seemed frozen into immobility. He had not consulted her or discussed it. 'You sound like Mr Pinpole,' she said at last, the ache in her heart almost choking her. 'But I can't say to Mr Pinpole what I say to you – that I love you, Luke.'

'It's too late,' he said quickly, flatly. 'Too late. There has to be more than love.' He had rehearsed these words and they came out now meaninglessly. 'And now I must go, if you'll excuse me?' He walked away on trembling legs, certain she must see the effort it cost him. Once outside he saw the bright air, the hope of a new life that would hold no pain. Soon he would escape, once the meetings of these long weeks ended.

Left alone, Katharine stood incapable of movement, her hopes and dreams as crushed as the solitary Sweet William that had lain beneath his foot.

Only Elizabeth, who had to Alfred's disgust and Albert's nervousness arrived unannounced with Meg, guessed that something was wrong.

'I know Luke's staying in the Dower House, darling, but somehow – I don't think,' she smiled brightly, 'things are quite *right*, are they?' She appeared in the garden one day as Katharine was vigorously attacking spring weeds.

'He doesn't want me, Mother.'

'Nonsense,' said Elizabeth briskly, more confidently than she felt. Luke had been deeply hurt. However, much of it was his own fault from what she could gather, so there was scope there. Yet men could change. They were odd creatures when you understood them as she did. She remembered Miguel: how he had simply stormed off just because she had had that meaningless flirtation with that stunner of a prince. He had never come back. She had waited two whole months.

'No, Luke has told me so. He has sold the mine and is going to travel the world.'

'They used to join the Foreign Legion in my day,' observed Elizabeth nostalgically.

'Oh, Mother, be serious,' said Katharine wearily.

279

'I am,' she said indignantly. 'A young French officer I knew did just that.' She paused. 'But you know Luke best. I don't see that I can help.'

'You used to say that all men are basically the same,' said Katharine desperately.

'That is true,' admitted Elizabeth, 'but they have differences too, and Luke is not a type I have had experience of. There was the Honourable Gerald, of course – he had a stiff upper lip too.'

'So what did you do in these circumstances?'

'Oh, darling.' Elizabeth looked helpless. 'It was the reason I left him. That lip was far too bristly for me. Then there was the Duke of Firth, of course – I did have a big disagreement with him.'

'And how did you resolve it?' Katharine asked eagerly.

'I went to his room in the castle in a long pure white satin mantle,' her mother sighed, 'and a rose in my hair.'

'How did that help?'

'I wore nothing underneath,' said Elizabeth simply. 'It was rather draughty going up all those castle steps, but worth it. Oh, yes, well worth it.' She smiled dreamily. 'I remember he particularly admired my eyes.' Those same dark eyes twinkled now.

'Oh, Mother, be serious. Can you really see me doing that to Luke?' said Katharine impatiently. 'He'd shut the door in my face in his present mood.'

But Elizabeth was not listening.

'And then there was Medjuel. I made love under the stars with him – unless it was too cold. I had not seen him for many months when he was wandering with the Bedouin, and so I arranged to arrive in his tent in a cake – or was it a carpet?'

'I think that was Cleopatra,' said Katharine drily.

'Oh no, darling, definitely Medjuel,' said Elizabeth happily. 'I remember it was so uncomfortable crawling out of it. It quite spoilt the effect. You must remember, Katharine,' she said seriously, 'that seductive though it is to recline nude on a bed or sofa, it is far from elegant to crawl on all fours out of a roll of carpet.'

'Oh, Mother,' said Katharine, torn between tears and laughter. 'I don't think this is going to help.'

'You'll find a way, Katharine, if you love him enough. The heart always does,' sighed Elizabeth happily, going in search of Alfred.

'You'll find a way . . . .' But where? How? Katharine ran to find comfort in Bocton, unable to bear the Dower House any more. Luke was pleasant, polite and considerate to her, chatting to Alfred as if nothing had happened. It was unbearable. She heard his door shut quietly at night, shutting her from his life, leaving her body aching, restlessly hoping he would come to her. But he did not.

Bocton was where it had all begun. In the Queen's Chamber. And here it had finished, when last week Luke had told her his plans for the future – which did not include her. But Bocton had been threatened, and she had refused to accept it. Now it was coming to life again.

Somewhere, somehow, there must be a way to win Luke back to her, too. She wandered round the Great Hall and into the study.

And there an idea came to her – just the germ of an idea, not much, but enough to cling to.

If she could not, then Bocton itself would woo him back.

Chapter Sixteen

Mr Pinpole's chest seemed to have expanded by several inches as he bustled importantly into Charham. Five double victorias awaited the Stowerton family outside. Gathered in Charham's morning room were Violet, Primrose and Jacob, Elizabeth and Meg, Robert, Philip, Amaryllis and David, Joseph, Albert, Mabel, Sophy, Mr Dean, Alfred, Jeremiah and Luke – at first somewhat stiltedly conversing, then somewhat more animatedly, as the room showed definite signs of overcrowding.

'It's like the day of the treasure trove, isn't it?' announced Mabel happily. 'I remember George telling me all about it.' There was a sudden hush as animation was replaced by apprehension, and the holiday feeling vanished into unease. But as Mr Pinpole gathered his charges together, and they meekly followed him down the steps to the waiting carriages, optimism reasserted itself – in all save Luke.

Where was Katharine? He tried to dismiss her from his mind, but thoughts of her refused to budge. Why was she not here, today of all days? He told himself that she was probably at Bocton making final preparations for the tour of inspection, yet this explanation did not entirely satisfy him. He had naturally expected to escort her to Charham, and had told her so at breakfast-time, but she had refused, murmuring that she would join him later. To question her further would have meant displaying a curiosity, the existence of which he refused to acknowledge.

Charham had been as uneasy a place in which to stay during the past few days as the Dower House. Only Jacob and Elizabeth seemed oblivious of the strain. Alfred had objected vociferously to Elizabeth's presence at all, claiming she had no right to be there, or even if she had it was not going to be exercised under the same roof as Albert. She had merely retorted that in that case she would move to the Dower House as she surely had every right to do, as his wife? At her mention of the dreaded word, Alfred had promptly capitulated, on condition that she came nowhere near the Dower House again. She had smiled sweetly and somewhat abstractedly.

In a victoria awaiting Mr Pinpole's return sat a sober-looking valuer from Young and Gardner's of Canterbury, present in order that the relative values of the properties might be assessed, and the delicate matter of division thereby given a sound financial basis.

The tour of Charham had already taken place, unobtrusively. There was, however, no doubt about who intended to live there, regardless of right. Violet and Primrose had proudly welcomed their guests on arrival and today upstaged Mr Pinpole as hosts, much to his annoyance.

'This place will suit you nicely, won't it?' Mabel had barked in approval while they were awaiting Mr Pinpole's arrival, as Primrose revealed plans for redecorating the morning room in Chinese-style. Mabel had thus put into words what the other Stowertons present had refrained out of tactfulness from querying.

'Oh, yes,' said Violet enthusiastically, 'I like it. Don't we, Primrose?'

'Indubitably we shall be staying on,' she confirmed gravely. 'And dear Jacob too,' she added. He grinned toothlessly, momentarily distracted from the toy soldiers gathering dust in a corner cupboard.

'It used to be Jacob's home for a while, so George said,' Mabel pointed out.

'I don't recall these ladies as co-parceners in this case,' observed Albert pleasantly. 'Perhaps I have been misinformed.'

'You'd turn 'em out, would you, Albert?' Mabel snorted.

'It isn't up to Albert,' Sophy said sharply. 'It will be settled by the solicitors, with our consent, at the meeting.' A meeting she dreaded.

'You may sit next to me, David,' Meg commanded, seating herself in the victoria. 'It is such a *very* long time since I had a chance to talk to you.' She smoothed the folds of her dress, well aware that the latest slim Paris fashions suited her well, and that motherhood had only enhanced her charms. True, walking was a little difficult with one's skirts restricted by strings holding back their fullness, but then she had no intention of walking far at all, and the outline of one's limbs showed to great advantage while sitting.

David flushed. 'I'd be delighted, Cousin Meg,' he said woodenly, though the strain on his face did not suggest delight.

Elizabeth, thwarted from keeping as close an eye on her daughter as she would have wished, consoled herself by sitting herself between her husband and Luke. 'There now,' she informed Alfred serenely, 'isn't this nice?' He did not agree. Such close proximity to Elizabeth was something he preferred to avoid.

There were other Stowerton properties, widely distributed, besides Bocton and Charham Manors. Chief of them were Charham Home Farm, Stoor Mill, Charham Forge, Chelsdon Farm (all that remained of a minor mediaeval manor attached to Bocton), several groups of cottages, and the Stowerton Arms in Bocton Bugley.

Tramping round muddy farms was not part of Elizabeth's plan for her day. Instead she had earmarked dear Luke for a motherly talk. He, however, well aware of her intentions, excused himself on the grounds that it was essential for him to view all the properties to form his own opinion of their value.

'But isn't Jeremiah the beneficiary?' she asked innocently.

'I do have a certain interest,' Luke said pleasantly, and recognising her match when she saw it, Elizabeth gave up.

Chelsdon Farm was almost entirely given over to hop-growing, although there were also a few orchards of cherries. The tenant farmer watched suspiciously as the valuer walked round the dilapidated farmhouse, and a group of ladies and gentlemen, apparently dressed for a day at the races, proceeded to invade his domain.

Luke walked by himself, appreciating the old flint oasthouses with their white-painted cowls and finials, and the hop gardens full of the young plants now beginning to spiral up the strings. Behind him, Jeremiah tramped happily round recalling his youth and their hop-picking days with Sophy. 'Daisy Petal would have liked this, Luke,' he shouted somewhat regretfully. Luke turned and grinned. Daisy Petal would look almost as out of place here as did Elizabeth, exotic flowers growing in a wild meadow. 'This takes me back,' Jeremiah sighed. 'Remember when we raced to see who could fill a basket of hops quickest? Slowest got tipped in. That was Joseph.'

'Yes, but you cheated,' he said without rancour, having overheard.

'I did not,' said Jeremiah, astounded.

'Yes, you did,' Joseph repeated. 'George saw you.'

'He couldn't have done,' said Jeremiah flatly. 'Because I didn't.'

Would he have cheated then? Had he needed to cheat? Surely not. What could he remember clearly enough of the hopes and fears of that thirteen-year-old boy that he could be so sure now? Yet he *was* quite sure. He felt the old bitterness begin to rise again, unbidden. But for what cause? He eyed Joseph caustically, on the defensive. 'George always said you'd have to be watched, Joseph.'

Joseph stared at him, bewildered, unable to cope with this accusation that stemmed from so long ago. He longed for Australia, so far away, so clear, so straightforward, so welcoming. There lay his future, the millstones of forefathers fallen from his neck, dissolved by distance. How he longed for it, even though he knew he could not leave Kent without knowing what would happen. But why? Why?

'You cheated,' he said again slowly, for he remembered it so.

'You're making it up,' said Jeremiah vehemently. 'Just like you did on the treasure trove day.'

'I did not.' Three clipped words. 'You took my part over the treasure trove, anyway. So you knew I was right then.'

'No,' said Jeremiah simply, considering. 'I just wanted an excuse to hit Robert. Just like you did, only you were too small to do it physically. You had to do it your way, challenge him for the cup. Fight him as you could. That's what we all did.'

'And we're still doing it,' said Joseph. 'Aren't we? Fighting him for Bocton. All of us.'

'Do you want Bocton?' asked Jeremiah curiously.

Joseph wanted Australia, yet he wanted Bocton too, for it was a symbol. Only then could he be truly free.

Luke had ceased to think for the moment about who and what. He was looking in horror at the poverty in which the tenants of the labourers' cottages lived. He tried to compare it with Leadville, but gave up. Impossible here to imagine the noise and bustle of Leadville, where none was poor save those who let a fortune slip through their

284

fingers. Here there was precious little to slip through anyone's hands. When he owned Bocton, he would try to improve the lot of the tenants. Give them bathrooms, improve their plumbing. Surely the risk of cholera and typhoid must be great in these primitive conditions? Nothing had been done to these cottages for years. Not worth it, Robert would say, seeing the amount of rent they paid. When he owned Bocton, Luke vowed fiercely, he would . . . Then it struck him. He would not be here. He remained talking to a tenant for a few moments, until Robert walked up to him.

'Why is not Katharine with us today?' he said, not bothering to apologise for breaking into the conversation. Tenants were like servants to Robert.

'I imagine she is at Bocton,' said Luke evenly. 'She is naturally eager to present it at its best.' Though why should she, he suddenly wondered, if she wished to keep Bocton for herself? Pride? Integrity? No. He could not now relate such words to her. Katharine had left him for another man and then come running when he did not want her after all. Bitterness made his voice sharp to Robert.

'You still have plans for Bocton?'

'I have as much right as anyone else. More, in fact, since I am the eldest.'

'You still wish to have it so that my father does not, is that it?' Luke pressed on, ill considered in his anger.

Robert raised his eyebrows. 'I can see that you will attend the meeting as objectively as could be expected of Jeremiah's son.'

Luke swallowed, annoyed at himself for having been betrayed into a miscalculation. 'My apologies, Uncle Robert. You must forgive me. It seems,' he gave a twisted smile and a bow of apology, 'the Stowerton disease is affecting me.'

Robert glanced at him, saying almost humanly, 'I have often wondered how the disease occurs, Luke. Whether it is hereditary or –' He hesitated.

'Or?' Luke prompted, curious.

'Engendered,' said Robert slowly. 'I suppose the meeting will tell. I warn you, nephew, I do not intend to be generous. I have decided not to appeal, but I go no further than that.'

'I intend to settle any differences between the six of you with money if it cannot be resolved by bricks and stone.'

'Money does not answer every need,' said Robert sanctimoniously. Luke looked at him curiously. Was this merely a platitude, or did Robert too have an emotional stake in the settling of old scores – other than his feud with Jeremiah?

At last the carriages arrived at Bocton. Luke looked at the building and tried to be objective. But he thought of Katharine who must be inside, and felt so fiercely protective he had to resist the urge to see these people as intruders. Intolerable to think that others might lay claim to Bocton. Yet he was aware that he must move carefully. He sensed that the Stowerton cauldron was once again awaiting an opportunity to boil over, and whatever happened he did not want Bocton to be the catalyst.

He strode forward, half expecting that Katharine would be there in the entrance to meet them. For a moment, as he saw the hall empty, he felt an emotion that he told himself was relief. It was only then that he looked again at the great entrance hall itself. In place of neglect and decay were the smell of beeswax polish and bowls of flowers that brightened the old oak table and chests, complementing the sunlight that filtered in through the leaded windows. The staircase gleamed with polish almost as though it awaited the foot of Her Majesty Queen Elizabeth herself. Luke pulled himself back into the present, reminding himself ruefully that the future of Bocton was still undecided – it depended on those gathered here today. He caught his father's eye as he ran his hand over the carved lion proudly adorning the newel post on the staircase, and knew Jeremiah was thinking exactly the same as he – though for a different reason.

Luke watched almost jealously as the Stowertons wandered round the hall, touching, peering, reacquainting themselves with an old friend, for this was a different Bocton to the one they had seen three years ago. Jacob ambled over to the fireplace, running his hand over the ornate wooden columns that flanked it, then the coat of arms carved into the entablature between them, over the fireplace. He peered up the huge chimney, making a face at the fire dog; then he burrowed under the table in the hall, emerging the other side satisfied. He had found his initials, carved illicitly long since into the oak.

Unable to watch, so possessive did he feel, Luke hurried over to the door of the study. He turned the knob without success and pushed harder, assuming it stuck. But in vain. The door was either locked, bolted or wedged from inside. Slightly puzzled, he followed Mr Pinpole's flock to the first floor, since Pinpole had elected to display the restored rooms first. Luke brought up the rear, unwilling to talk even with Father about what was to come. He did not understand why this should be, save that Katharine was concerned in it somehow.

Even Robert looked impressed at the State Rooms, and general interest tangibly quickened as Bocton's potential was made so evident. The only person who showed little sign of being impressed was Amaryllis, who looked down at the polished wooden floors with their simple rugs and observed with disdain: 'Cold. But something might be done to improve these rooms, I suppose.'

Luke stared at her, wondering if he had heard correctly, if she had eyes to see. It was perfect now, as though Queen Elizabeth herself had left but yesterday, as though the ghost of Nicholas Stowerton still haunted these sun-filled rooms. To sleep here would be to dream of kings – or Katharine. He was brought up against the sharp edge of memory. Meg was pulling idly at the covers, and it was all Luke could do not to drag her away from the bed.

'Your work?' he forced himself to ask Sophy, indicating the curtains on the bed.

She nodded. 'I did them for Katharine,' she told him quietly. 'Where is she, Luke?'

'I don't know,' he said in irritation, as though Sophy accused him of spiriting her niece away. Seeing her look at him as if with reproach, he added angrily, 'I expected her to be here.'

Even Amaryllis was impressed by the bathroom, until she discovered there was no water. Her face then resumed its normal look of disdain. 'I don't want all the effort of trying to lay pipes in an old house, Philip,' she complained. 'I'll have to pull it down and start again.'

Even he looked somewhat uneasy as Stowerton heads turned first to her and then to him in surprise. Luke was hard put to it not to retort that with her devotion to mediaeval dress, the house should suit very well as it was. He thought better of it, and walked quickly away. Mabel was unusually quiet as they finished their tour of the restored rooms and descended the small staircase at the end of the wing. She could see Gam doing very nicely here if he chose to come in a few years' time. Yes, she would do what she could . . .

From the atmosphere it was clear that spirits were fast falling as the party worked its way back along the ground-floor rooms, which showed the true extent of Bocton's decay. Only Luke and Jeremiah remained gripped by the house's spell: Jeremiah because of his fanatical determination, Luke because he found himself already making plans. This the drawing room – and billiard room – and the study. What they could do once they had pulled down the old plaster, uncovered the beams and posts from their centuries of hiding! Some would be rotten, of course . . . Luke's imagination began to work as he envisaged the Great Hall with its ceiling removed, so that it too was as it once had been, the fine roof exposed, not hidden.

'Strange,' observed Mr Pinpole at the door of the study. 'I cannot open the door. How odd.'

'Let me try.' Luke put his shoulder to the door, but it did not budge. 'It won't move,' he said abruptly. 'We'll have to go back the way we came.' He eyed the door, fighting suspicion, trying to drag his mind to the question of the West Wing where what remained of the party's early enthusiasm drained fast as its devastation became fully apparent. Amaryllis gave it one glance and retired to the hall again, her decision at least made. The men advanced further in, picking their way through the rubble of fallen plaster and rafters, avoiding looking at each other. Even Mabel, struggling after them, began to have second thoughts as to whether Gam would thank her for landing him with this. But the land, she thought – that at least was worth something.

Luke came to a decision, having wrestled with his suspicions. Abandoning Mr Pinpole's strenuous efforts to put the West Wing in a flattering light, he strode back across the entrance hall, the rest of the party wandering desultorily after him. He pushed savagely at the study door again. This door wasn't locked, he was sure, but there was something behind it, for it budged a little. With growing anger, he realised for certain that someone was in there, and the likelihood was that it was Katharine. What she was doing he had not the slightest idea, but he was going to find out.

'Katharine,' he yelled, 'open this door. The family needs to inspect the room.'

A second's pause. Then: 'Just a moment,' her voice called out gaily from within. There were sounds of furniture being scraped back across the floor, while Luke, annoyed to be made to look foolish, prayed that she would not be revealed in bloomers, wielding hammer and saw. But as the door was thrown open, it was clear to Luke and to everyone that Katharine was not in bloomers but in a becoming summer dress of delicate cream silk – an image rather spoiled by huge ungainly working gloves. Moreover she was not alone. With her was a man Luke recognised faintly, then with growing certainty. It was Roderick Mayfield and, even more irritatingly, both of them seemed far more interested in removing rotten laths from the wall than in greeting him, much less the Stowerton party.

'What do you think you're doing?' he enquired with dangerous calm, oblivious of the rest of the party in his anger.

Katharine looked up, startled. 'Oh, I'm so sorry, Luke. I *am* being rude. It's just that Roderick and I are at a particularly absorbing stage of our work. You can see here the grooves into which the oak staves were fitted, before the hazel wattle was woven round them. Of course, much has rotted, but you can make out a main post here and –'

'Perhaps, instead of lecturing us on mediaeval history, Katharine, it might be more polite to introduce Mr Mayfield to the family.' He swallowed, furious with himself for the sarcasm yet unable to prevent it. They might otherwise wonder who he is and why you lock yourself alone in a room with him, he was tempted to add. Had she no thought for her reputation – or his? And just why had she locked the doors? Or was Mayfield . . .?

'Oh, yes, how rude of me,' Katharine agreed immediately and disarmingly. 'May I present the Honourable Mr Roderick Mayfield, a prominent member of the Kent Archaeological Society? He has many demands on his time and could spare me only this morning.' Luke noticed the slight start of surprise Roderick Mayfield gave, and his eyes narrowed. 'So I'm sure you'll forgive me for wanting to take advantage of every moment he could spare to give his advice,' she finished appealingly.

Alfred frowned. There was something very strange here. After all, Katharine was a married woman even if it seemed to be an odd sort of marriage. Still, he thought with relief, if Luke didn't object, it was no business of his to do so.

'I understand you are joint inheritors of this property. I must congratulate you all,' said Mayfield, his dry voice sounding almost animated for once. 'Mrs Stowerton has no doubt told you the good news.'

Luke stiffened, and the rest of the group looked interested.

'We are quite sure now that the old fifteenth-century house of Thomas Stoorton still lies within the walls of Bocton. Nicholas

Stowerton simply incorporated the old house within the new.' Only Robert's face showed any signs of comprehension. 'Our plan therefore is to tear down this rotten panelling, exposing the old timber frame – taking off the old wattle and daub too, of course. And removing this plaster ceiling, since I suspect there is a remarkably fine dragon beam plastered in, and Kath— Mrs Stowerton and I feel a most attractive room can be made here.'

Luke held himself in check, a pulse beating furiously in his temple, but whatever he intended to say was forestalled by Robert. 'Might I point out that the owner of Bocton should decide such matters, not yourself and my niece, sir? Though we are grateful for your guidance, of course,' he added as an afterthought.

'Naturally Mrs Stowerton has explained the position to me,' Mayfield said stiffly. 'Whoever inherits would need expert advice and I have offered my services accordingly.'

As Mayfield found himself the centre of a barrage of questions, the first shot by Mr Pinpole who had a feeling he was being outwitted but was not sure how, Luke grabbed at Katharine's arm, none too gently, and took her aside. 'Do you not feel,' he asked her grimly, 'I might have been consulted since I have some slight say in the matter, considering payment is made by me?'

'I'm sure Mr Mayfield would be delighted to discuss it with you in more detail,' said Katharine readily, a degree of puzzlement entering her expression.

'Whether he is delighted or not, I intend to have a few words with *him*,' Luke replied shortly.

'Splendid,' said Katharine cordially. 'You will have every opportunity, Luke. Mr Mayfield is coming for dinner this evening.'

In the victoria again, Mr Pinpole mopped his brow. It had all gone reasonably well in the circumstances, had it not? Apart from Mrs Stowerton's strange behaviour. 'I thought everyone was remarkably co-operative and good-humoured. I don't foresee any difficulty there at all.'

The valuer cast a puzzled look at him, not knowing the particular trouble Pinpole had foreseen. 'I'll have the figures in about a week,' he assured the solicitor.

'Splendid,' said Mr Pinpole fervently. 'We will hold the meeting on, let us say, June the sixth. I am sure everyone can keep themselves amused for a week here, now they are getting on so well together. It is quite heart-warming to be present at these family reunions.' Relief for once overrode his customary caution.

Luke dressed carefully, cursing as he tried to adjust his white tie with hands still shaking from belated rage, the reason for which he could not entirely analyse. He was both relieved and annoyed to find that there were to be guests other than Mayfield.

Unasked, Elizabeth and Meg had announced they would be present, and Sophy and Alexander Dean too, who *had* been invited. Luke was particularly glad of the latter. With his and Alfred's presence, he could avoid talking to Mayfield, at least under Katharine's scrutiny, before he was ready. Perhaps over port he would be able to enquire just how this cosy arrangement had come about, and how often Mayfield had visited, and if he intended to . . .?

Luke stopped this train of thought on the brink, seeing the pitfall into which he was tumbling. He almost laughed aloud. So Katharine hoped to make him jealous of another man? She might have chosen better than Mayfield, he thought, feeling superior to her naivety, pleased that he had realised her intention and that it was one so easily foiled. At least Pearson had shown every sign of taking a normal interest in women, unlike Mayfield. Poor Katharine, he almost felt sorry for her. Well, she'd be disappointed. He had no intention of accusing Mayfield at dinner of taking a personal interest in Katharine, and giving her the satisfaction of his behaving as a jealous husband. He would treat Mayfield objectively, as the historian he was.

The evening did not begin well, however. All his questions to Roderick Mayfield about the house were politely answered, but briefly, as though to an interested dinner guest rather than the person who would have to fund his suggestions.

'And what do you advise about the Great Hall?' Luke said in desperation, getting nowhere on details fo final decoration of the study.

'I have not yet discussed that with Katharine. We are waiting for an inspection of the roof with Mr Trant, and then we will decide.'

'I presume you will also be consulting me?' Luke asked ironically.

'Naturally, naturally, though I think you will find everything will be under control, Mr Stowerton. You need have no fear as to the result of our labours.'

'No doubt, but –'

'Mrs Stowerton is a most capable lady,' Roderick assured her husband. Katharine looked modest. 'You could not have entrusted the work to safer hands. Great damage can be done when insensitive tools are at work. I recall a church near Rye . . .' The conversation was implacably manoeuvred away from Bocton, aided by Elizabeth who had singled out Mr Dean for her attention.

'Do excuse me,' she smiled her sweetest smile, 'but just who *are* you?'

'I introduced you, Elizabeth. Alexander Dean,' put in Sophy quickly.

'Nonsense,' said Elizabeth briskly. 'Your name is not Dean.'

A startled silence fell. 'You are misinformed. My name *is* Dean, Mrs Stowerton,' he said at last.

'No, you're Alexander Bishop,' she informed him. 'Dean, indeed!'

All faces turned to Alexander, who looked round the table with brick-red face. 'I plead guilty,' he said slowly. 'Yet it is but a short step from a Dean to a Bishop.'

'Would someone please enlighten me?' asked Alfred plaintively. 'Bishop or Dean, what does it matter? He has the interests of our family at heart,' he repeated virtuously. Particularly of Alfred, he might have continued, if given to self-examination.

'It matters a great deal,' said Elizabeth brightly. 'Mr Bishop is a leading London publisher. I find it strange that he should bother to conceal his name merely for the purpose of supporting your betting activities, Alfred.'

Dean said nothing, torn between confusion and anger.

'How did you get to know him, Alfred?' Elizabeth asked curiously. 'I had not thought the literary world your province. You *are* a dark horse.'

'Me?' glared Alfred. 'I didn't. He's a relation of yours, he said. I remember it distinctly. Came down here after you disappeared with that blasted fellow and told us he was some kind of second cousin of yours.'

'I wish he had been,' commented Elizabeth, sizing him up. 'Unfortunately he is not. I have no cousins, second or otherwise.'

'Someone must know you, Dean – er, Bishop,' Alfred pointed out reasonably. 'Dammit, you've been supporting me and my family long enough. You didn't just wander in off the street, did you?'

'Indeed not.' Alexander was recovering now. 'And, incidentally, Dean is my real name in a way. It is one of my Christian names given at birth, after my mother's family. As to why I came here, I met –' a quick glance '– Miss Sophy in London at one of her charitable events, and she told me of your plight. And I might add, Mr Stowerton, that I have felt it an honour to support you,' he ended up quickly and warmly.

'Very right and proper,' approved Alfred.

'But, Mr Dean,' Katharine began impulsively, very puzzled. Complete strangers, however charitable, did not rush to support impecunious families. There must be some other reason. Then she reflected on what this might be.

Luke, who had come to the same rapid conclusion, turned to the one infallible source of alternative conversation. 'Perhaps you could tell us who's running at Ascot this year, Mr Stowerton?' Sophy breathed a silent thank-you.

'I cannot think what you see in Mr Mayfield, Katharine,' said Meg carelessly, as the ladies took coffee waiting for the ritual of port to finish and the gentlemen to rejoin them. Elizabeth was plying Sophy with questions about Alexander Dean, all of which she seemed to be calmly stone-walling. Katharine tried to pay attention to her sister, worried as to what might be happening in the dining room, though powerless to prevent it, whatever it might be.

'I see a lot of information about mediaeval houses in Mr Mayfield, Meg,' she replied calmly. 'May I help you to cream?'

'Yes. I must say, Katharine, you are more of a sly old puss-in-boots than I'd thought.' In Meg's eyes this was some kind of recommendation.

Elizabeth, however, eyed her daughter with new respect. She didn't know exactly what Katharine was after, but there was a definite change in her that that dried-up stick Mayfield was unlikely to have occasioned. Perhaps Katharine took after her more than she had realised. First Daniel, then Roderick . . . yes, Katharine was a girl of spirit. All the same, Elizabeth was worried.

At the end of the evening Alexander Dean escorted Elizabeth, Sophy and Meg home in his carriage. Luke came to the door just in time to see his wife's hand being kissed by Roderick Mayfield, who was about to mount into his brougham.

'Thank you very much, Roderick,' he heard her say. Thanking him? For what? He quelled such thoughts instantly. No playing into her hands. How easy it was to outwit her.

'Until Thursday, then, Katharine.'

The day after tomorrow? Was the fellow taking up residence?

'And just what is happening the day after tomorrow?' He strolled up the path to meet Katharine, deliberately casually, as she turned to come back to the house.

'That's when we shall inspect the timbers of the Great Hall and decide what we shall do with it.'

'*We*? I take it *I* am included?'

'Oh, no, we won't need to worry you, Luke. We can tell you about it afterwards. I think you and your father have enough to do in ensuring Bocton is kept safe from Uncle Robert. And, after all, you are not planning to live in Bocton, so the finer details can be of no consequence. You can rest assured Obadiah will not cheat you in the way of bills.'

'That doesn't mean I'm not interested,' he managed to say coolly.

'I don't understand why,' she said, perplexed. 'Have I annoyed you by spending your generous allowance to me on Bocton?' She looked so appealing, so young, so beautiful, he could not believe even now that the intervening years had changed her so little. He had merely to put out a hand to touch her breast, where the creamy skin emerged from the deep red lace of the low bosom of her dress. In former days he would have done so, taken her into his arms and then to bed . . . No longer, no more.

'I'm not angry, Katharine, merely annoyed that you purposely made me look foolish this afternoon.' He tried to reply with controlled voice, but failed to keep it from rising.

'Foolish? I don't understand.' She looked alarmed, almost close to tears.

'You were in a locked room with another man,' he shouted, goaded beyond endurance.

'But it was Roderick!' she said, astounded. 'Oh, Luke, you surely cannot be jealous? After all, you did say yourself that he is not a man who likes women in that way.' Her eyes gazed innocently at him, and he cursed himself for having fallen into her trap. But he would escape, he was not so easily overcome.

'My dear Katharine, you can spend all the time in the world with Roderick Mayfield, or any other man for all I care. Just don't do it in a locked room when other people are present in the house. I dislike being made to look foolish.'

'Oh, Luke.' She began to laugh. 'And you the man who waded

fully dressed into a lake carrying an open umbrella,' she said softly.

The night air was sweet around them, filled with the scent of roses. He could find nothing to say as she ran back to the house, the sound of her laughter floating back to him, left alone and silent on the brick path.

Mr Pinpole walked into Charham on this occasion with a definite sense of foreboding, despite his earlier optimism. He wished he had stuck to his guns and held the meeting in his offices, but Messrs Foggett and Dodson had decided that these could not comfortably hold all the people who either had a claim to be present or an interest in being so. Of the alternatives, Charham seemed the obvious place.

On this occasion, however, the gathering had arranged itself into groups of allies. Katharine was next to Luke, acutely conscious of his physical presence. She had only to reach out a few inches to touch his arm. The temptation was almost overwhelming, but she resisted. With them was Jeremiah. Alfred longed to join them but was firmly sandwiched between Meg and Elizabeth, who had also attached herself to Alexander Dean. Sophy sat apart with Katharine and Luke. Robert was with his solicitor, Philip, David, Millicent and Amaryllis. Violet, Primrose and Jacob formed another group, leaving Mabel oddly linked with Albert. The latter had done his best to keep away from Elizabeth and was somewhat piqued to find she did not appear to mind, Alexander Dean apparently proving a greater attraction.

'The six co-parceners or their representatives being present,' Mr Pinpole began nervously, 'I will proceed to list the properties at issue and their respective values. You are of course at liberty to challenge the latter. Bocton Manor £10,000, Charham £2,000, Charham Home Farm £900, Bugley Mill £400, Chelsdon Farm £800, Stowerton Arms £500, cottages and forge together £1,000. Rents have of course been taken into account in reaching these valuations.'

Pinpole looked round and was comforted to find that apart from a little shifting in their seat, no one seemed to have a violent reaction to this. 'Splendid,' he said, relieved. 'Now,' he beamed, 'I put this suggestion forward for discussion: as the expenses of the recent High Court case have been paid for by Mr Jeremiah Stowerton, and his son Mr Luke Stowerton, it would seem fair to me that he should have first choice of residence and indeed the major share of these properties with financial adjustment if deemed necessary, and he has indicated he is prepared to do so.'

'I paid rather heavier expenses,' pointed out Robert coolly. 'Since judgment was erroneously given against me, I also bear the majority of those of the plaintiff apparently. This invalidates your point, and as eldest I consider I have first choice.'

'But you opposed the issue, Sir Robert,' Pinpole cried, appalled.

'That appears to me immaterial for this point. Since you are prepared to take Jeremiah's expenses into account, you must also take mine,' said Robert, speaking quickly to his solicitor who caught Pinpole's eyes.

293

Almost indiscernible gestures were made that discussion would take place later between two gentlemen of the same profession.

'Isn't the law that we all share equally?' enquired Albert, after a whispered conference with Mabel. 'Correct me if I am wrong. And moreover, as far as choice goes, I believe the law of gavelkind grants protection by the family home to the youngest, not the eldest.'

Pinpole gulped. 'It seems to me that in this case exception should be made,' he announced quickly, 'especially as some of you live abroad and have your own hearths there to protect you,' he added meaningfully.

'Might want to return to our roots,' pointed out Mabel.

'That is true. I propose therefore that the smaller properties be allotted to those who live abroad.' Seeing instant signs of dissent, Pinpole hastily added, 'This is merely a proposal for your consideration. Of the major two properties I propose that Sir Robert should take Charham, Mr Alfred the lesser properties of the Bocton estate to provide him with an income together with the Dower House and Lodge, and Mr Jeremiah, Bocton.'

There was an instant outburst of discussion, dissent and disapproval, but over it all rang the voices of Violet and Primrose in unison. 'Oh, no, that won't do. We are having Charham.'

'For yourselves? But I regret –' Mr Pinpole attempted to come to terms with a nightmare he had convinced himself was banished.

'For us and *Jacob*,' they amended happily.

'Unfortunately, ladies, you were not parties to The Case,' he said somewhat snappily.

'That is true,' observed Primrose. 'However, we do not consider Robert should have it. Now that this case is won, thus proving that the land is subject to gavelkind, we could most certainly open up the previous case again, with dear Jacob's help, and *win*. So we would get it all,' she added, to make it quite clear.

'Dear ladies, we have been into this before,' Mr Pinpole said desperately, perceiving a yawning chasm. 'You do not possess enough money to bring the case.'

'We possess Jacob,' said Violet brightly, patting the old man's knee affectionately. 'So both Nathaniel's brothers are represented. And we have Jacob's interesting deed of sale regarding Stowerton.'

Robert stiffened.

'*I'll* pay for their case,' shouted Jeremiah happily, 'provided you let me have Bocton at the end of it,' he added to the twins.

'Certainly, Jeremiah. It is Charham we want. Shall we draw up the agreement now?'

Mr Pinpole was a drowning man, but salvation came from an unlikely quarter.

'I think you are all ahead of yourselves,' said Robert smoothly. 'I have no intention of being fobbed off with Charham. I want Bocton.'

Mabel barked with laughter. 'Anything Jeremiah wants, eh, Robert?'

'You won't get it,' said Jeremiah, folding his arms truculently.

'My dear brother, I can appeal. I do not believe, after all this time, that that ridiculous document Jacob possesses is valid. What proof of sale is there? It is merely a deed of transfer of property, and invalid without proof of payment. The jewels, indeed! They are a mere fabrication, like the whole story of Richard Plantagenet. The risk to Stowerton Park is infinitesimal, and no Crown barrister would take on such a ridiculous case merely to prove it Crown property, or indeed take on the ladies' case for the entire Stowerton estate.'

'Think not?' barked Jeremiah.

'It would be fun,' said Mabel brightly. 'Like the day of the treasure trove again.'

'I hate you, Robert! I hate you.'

Robert sneered. He was the eldest, the cleverest, he was unbeatable. Brain would always win over Jeremiah's undisciplined flailing arms. How could the fool think he'd ever beat him, Robert? The silver cup was Robert's by right. Now Jeremiah was claiming Joseph had found it first. Nonsense!

'You'll pay for this,' said Jeremiah, hands clenched by his side.

'It's mine,' said Robert, laughing at him.

'Don't hit him!' shrieked George.

Jeremiah cast one glance at him, and ignored him. The punch landed on Robert's chin, but Robert was tougher than he looked; he staggered but did not fall until Jeremiah threw his whole weight against him. Then they were pummelling each other, fighting, rolling over and over in the muddy grass. When at last, bleeding and dirty, they were separated, Robert aimed one last blow at his brother, vicious and below the belt, as Jeremiah was being pulled from him. Only Sophy saw what happened.

'I'll never forgive you that, Robert, as long as I live,' said Jeremiah when he had recovered, to find Robert standing over him, leering, with triumph. 'I'll get my revenge . . .'

'You always did lose, Jeremiah,' said Robert unemotionally. 'For all your riches, you'll never win what you really want. Not against me. Look at you. Neither of you –' he glanced superciliously at Luke '– can keep a woman.'

'Why, you cockless creeper!' Jeremiah flung his chair back so hard it crashed to the floor, as in two strides he was across the room, towering over Robert, pulling him to his feet by his collar, glaring straight into his face as Philip ineffectually tried to pull him away. He drew back his arm, but Luke grabbed it.

'Not this way, Father,' he cried, choking with anger himself, but able to see Robert's intention. He pushed Philip away with one hand planted full in his face. Jeremiah pulled free, pinioning Robert's arms behind his back with one large hand, gripping him by his collar and glaring into his enemy's eyes, shaking him to and fro. 'You talk of not being able to keep a woman. *You* of all people. When your own wife . . .' He began to laugh wildly, throwing back his head. Robert for once had miscalculated.

At Robert's side Millicent was sobbing loudly, head in her hands, praying to avoid the shame of what might come. 'Don't, Jerry, don't!'

At the sound of her voice, the affectionate nickname, Robert redoubled his efforts at freedom, still held in Jeremiah's vice-like grip, kicking his captor viciously between the legs to free himself.

'Stop, it's all happening again!' Sophy cried out in horror. Too late, as Jeremiah released his hold, staggering back. He collapsed to the floor, groaning.

Violet and Meg began to scream, Elizabeth threw her arms round Albert who was laughing like a maniac, Mabel stood completely still. Only Luke and Katharine rushed to Jeremiah's aid as he coughed and spluttered on the floor. Millicent was still crying, clutching at Robert who ignored her as he watched Jeremiah's pain impassively.

Jeremiah brushed Katharine and Luke aside, and clambered to his feet unaided. His black eyes darted to Millicent. 'You picked the wrong one,' he said hoarsely. 'I told you so.' Contemptuously he jerked his head in Robert's direction. '*He* hasn't got any balls to kick!'

Alfred sat rigid at this appalling language before ladies. Mr Pinpole was frozen to his chair, but he was not a solicitor for nothing. 'I shall adjourn this meeting for one week,' he announced with what dignity he could muster. 'I shall then expect you to put before me a reasonable scheme for the division of the property, agreed by you all. If you fail, you accept mine. If this does not prove acceptable, then you are at liberty to offer the matter back to the Courts for adjudication. I regret that in that event I should be unable to take the case.'

He rose somewhat unsteadily to his feet and marched outside to his carriage, ordering the driver to return immediately to Canterbury. Once through the Charham gates, he had a moment's pause for thought. He ordered the driver to stop at the first public house he came across – the first, as a Chapel man, that Mr Pinpole had ever visited in his life. There he indulged in a large whisky. He did not even notice that the public house was called The Stowerton Arms.

Chapter Seventeen

Luke left the Dower House with relief the following morning, glad to be away from the frustration of living so close to, and yet so far from, Katharine. Even Alfred provided a welcome respite from having to see her irritatingly cheerful self, and from that part of him which instinctively longed to touch her every time she passed close – until his other self checked the involuntary movement. He should be glad that she was happy, relieved that she was so absorbed in restoring Bocton, so why was he not?

It was natural, he told himself angrily, that here, where only three years ago he had dreamed such dreams, seen his future based, he should be restless now that the door had been closed against him. The red peg-tiled roofs of the houses that nestled in the curves and folds of the hills, intermingled with grey stone churches and white-painted cowls of the oasthouses, spelled a scene of peace and tranquillity from which he was barred. His room at the Dower House still contained many of Meg's childish possessions, evoking his own memories of childhood more strongly than Charham where he had been born. There the room that had once been his nursery contained nothing that spoke to him so clearly as the Dower House, for his had been a hard childhood, only enlivened by his cousins and friends. From there he had been snatched away to America, to an increasingly grim existence where his only refuge had been the lightheartedness which he placed between his parents and himself. 'You're never serious,' he heard Katharine accuse him once again. Had that been three years ago? Never serious . . .

Luke stood by the lakeside and looked down into the water at his reflection. Even the ripples on its surface could not disguise the hardness of his face now. Perhaps if he'd grown up in Kent, it might have been different. Yet would he have missed the vigorous optimism and strength that America had given him? During his youth it had been a land racked by civil war; it didn't touch them directly in New England, but all the same he knew as he grew up that this was a country on the march, which had imbued him with its strength just as much as Bocton had in its different way. He told himself that what he had taken to be the strength and integrity of England was really an age-old cunning; the land deceived, as did Katharine. He thought of Sir Nicholas's motto above the chimney in the Queen's Chamber: *Fides non Fraus*. Loyalty not deceit. Yet how shallow that had proved for the Stowertons, and Queen Elizabeth herself was hardly known for blunt straightforwardness.

Katharine – no, he would not think of her. Was it not enough that

297

he had to sleep in the room next to hers, convince himself that his own wakefulness and uneasy sleep were due to light evenings and early dawns, and not desire? It could not be desire, for he had desired a Katharine who did not exist. A Katharine who could never betray.

Luke walked up through what had been formal gardens towards the rear of the house, then round the East Wing to the front entrance. Here was Bocton, where it had all begun. But what was the beginning? Himself and Katharine? Or were they caught in a much older story, that began three hundred years ago with Nicholas Stowerton? Or even earlier, with William Stoorton and Richard Plantagenet? He hurried past the house into the overgrown yew walk, where the lichen-covered statue of Cupid and Psyche at the far end seemed to mock him, the arrow pointing directly towards him. It was fortunate, he thought ironically, that now he had a stone for a heart. Nothing could touch him any more.

The sound of laughter from the gardens in front of the house attracted his attention. Katharine's. Restraining the impulse to run towards the sound, to see what could make her laugh so, he continued down the walk, ignoring it. Yet at the end his steps hesitated and he could not resist the temptation to glance back. There in the knot garden he could just glimpse Katharine, Roderick Mayfield and, to his sudden relief, Obadiah Trant – yet why he should be grateful for the latter's presence he hardly knew as he was quite certain of Mayfield's sexual proclivities. Katharine appeared to be showing them plans or drawings of some sort. The sunlight was gleaming on her chestnut hair; she wore it looser now, no longer tied back in a chignon. Today she was wearing her bloomers or breeches he deduced, from what he could see of her severe neckline. No frills and muslin dress today. He could see her profile etched against the light as she leaned forward over the plans, sharp and classically clear.

His imagination brought to him the softness of her cheek, the gentle swell of her breast. Impatiently he checked himself. What matter? That was past. Katharine was discussing plans for Bocton, no more, and was unaware of his presence. So he would stroll up, merely displaying interest in Bocton. After all, he told himself, he had the right. But he would go slowly, lest she glance up and thought he was hurrying to her.

To Katharine it seemed her tension was so acute he must observe it. For he was there, she knew it as clearly as if he had shouted his presence. She struggled to retain her composure, for she would need it.

'You mean we could leave the whole hall open to the roof again, Roderick?'

'It would look splendid, I feel.'

'But might the staircase look somewhat strange if we take the ceiling down above it?' She hardly heard his answer, so aware was she of Luke's measured approach. He was nearly here, he must be.

'Good morning.'

Katharine looked up brightly, as if startled. 'Oh, Luke, I'm so sorry.

298

I didn't hear you coming. We are just discussing the restoration of the Great Hall. It will be quite extensive.'

'Indeed,' he said drily. 'And might –'

'Merely plans, I assure you, Mr Stowerton,' said Mayfield hastily, correctly interpreting the look on Luke's face. 'It would be too expensive and far-reaching a project to begin before ownership is finally settled.'

'It is good of you to consider my finances,' he observed.

Katharine gave him a bright smile. 'Besides that, we couldn't bear to begin the work and then find that Bocton went to Uncle Robert after all.'

Unreasonably deflated, Luke hovered undecidedly as her eyes strayed to the drawings again. 'What are these plans?' he asked abruptly.

Katharine glanced at Mayfield and Trant, smiling in a way he irrationally defined as conspiratorial, and gathered up her papers hastily. 'Oh, we won't bother you with the boring side, will we, Roderick? Not till it's all settled. It would spoil the surprise.'

'I don't want a –'

'They are merely suggestions of mine,' said Mayfield uneasily.

'What are?' said Luke, diplomacy beginning to desert him.

Obadiah Trant coughed. 'Miss Katharine, she's got ideas enough for ten 'ouses, her and Mr Mayfield here.'

'That I am aware of, Mr Trant,' snapped Luke, 'since *Miss* Katharine is my wife,' he added unfairly, aware that he was descending to pettishness but ceasing to care. Katharine had an infuriatingly superior look on her face that he longed to shake out of her, kiss out of her . . . He controlled himself quickly. 'No doubt when you have decided on your course of action, I will be informed – with an estimate, Mr Trant,' he said unemotionally.

'Of course, Luke,' said Katharine warmly. 'Now if you'll excuse us? Roderick is pressed for time and we must begin.'

Begin? Begin what, he wanted to know, but since he was obviously not to be included in the party, and pride forbade his accompanying them unasked, he bade them good day and walked away as though he had somewhere else to go. If only he had! The whole world was his, but suddenly the idea of Greece or Italy or wandering the deserts, which had seemed such an escape while sitting in his Leadville office, failed to exercise the same magic.

Was he jealous? What man in his senses could be jealous of a sixty-year-old builder and a dried-up bachelor who preferred young men to women?

And who, he reminded himself, would be jealous of a woman who had proved so disloyal? He sought out his old bitterness as a refuge, but for once it failed to comfort.

'This takes me back,' said Jeremiah, happily tramping round the old watermill. 'I used to play here as a boy. Mother never knew, of course.' Mabel plodded after him, feet in sturdy boots, a thick tweed skirt flapping round her legs. Yes, it had been a good idea to come out and look round the place, get the feel of the real England again.

'There were a couple here, the Palmers – I used to play with their son.' His black eyes brooded on the past. 'Such larks. Then Robert found out that I was friends with the miller's son, and that put paid to that. Father put his foot down.' He shook his head ruefully. 'That's why I like America. None of that there. Nor where you are, I suppose, Mabel? Only here in England. I brought Luke up to believe we're all equal before the Lord.'

He ignored the fact that his wife took a different view from the Lord and his daughters had suffered accordingly. But Luke – he was a fine boy. Jeremiah could see that now, thanks to Daisy Petal. The last thirty years seemed a black cloud out of which he had been propelled by her presence, and, being Jeremiah, he gave no thought to those he had left within it.

'That's when you began this feud with Robert, was it?' asked Mabel.

Jeremiah shrugged. 'That and other things.' One row after another, culminating in Millicent. She had had the same wild streak as he did. They'd shared the same passions, the same exuberance, the same lust – even now, he was stirred when he remembered her as she was. Looking back, they were lucky that she hadn't conceived. They never gave it a thought. He hadn't even known Robert was interested in her – well, not *seriously*. Yet suddenly she announced she was marrying his brother. Looking at her now, it was hard to imagine the lusty girl he'd known. Over thirty wasted years of marriage to Augusta, and well over thirty years of bitterness towards Robert. And they had soured him. Why should he waste more? Daisy Petal was right. This affair must put an end to it.

'He'll never let you have it,' said Mabel smugly.

'Bocton?' Jeremiah said sharply.

'Yes. That's why he wants it. And he'll stand a good chance too, being the eldest. You mark my words, he'll get it.'

'Never,' said Jeremiah, enraged. 'Never. I'd sooner Alfred got it.'

'That's tantamount to letting Luke have it, since Katharine and Luke are married. And don't forget, Katharine started all this off. Think Robert will forget that? Never.' She walked briskly back towards the carriage as Jeremiah scowled.

'It is most kind of you to escort me to Canterbury, David.' Meg laid her white-gloved hand lightly on his.

He had not realised before that Meg was so interested in Kentish history, and was far from loth to have such a companion to show round the cathedral. Conversation was somewhat stilted to begin with, but as he relaxed, getting used to her presence at his side, she waxed more voluble. 'It is so very, *very* nice to be with you again, David,' she told him softly.

He looked at her sharply. 'I never noticed much inclination before

300

you were married,' he said drily. He had no intention of raking up the unhappiness of the past.

'Marriage and motherhood teach one a lot,' said Meg soberly. 'They have made me realise the important things of life, like companionship and having things in common. And, oh, David, if you only knew how unhappy I've been!' She turned away quickly and buried her head on his shoulder.

He cast an anguished look at the rigid back of the driver. 'He's cruel to you?' he asked fiercely.

'No, not cruel. Indifferent.'

'The blackguard,' said David vehemently, suddenly wondering how anyone could be indifferent to Meg.

'You see, he – he – seduced me before we were married,' she hissed tremulously in his ear.

David started violently, shocked beyond measure, even though somewhere at the back of his mind was the regret that had he known Meg was so susceptible, he might well have done the same. 'He's French, of course,' he declared, as if this explained everything, '*and* he's Albert's son.'

'I should have known better, but I was so young.'

He pushed behind him the treacherous thought that she had not been so *very* young, and squeezed her hand instead.

'Oh, David, I need friends.'

'You can always count on me,' he declared. 'Dearest Meg.' He kissed the little hand fervently, wondering whether during the course of the day an opportunity might arise to change the target of his lips and touch hers.

Meg managed to look modest. 'What do you think will happen to Bocton in this silly old case?' she enquired, apparently eager to divert David's enthusiasm.

He shrugged. 'I think Father will get it. Can you see any way he would allow Uncle Jeremiah, or any of his brothers for that matter, to have it? And he is the eldest after all. There is evidence from the past to suggest that the eldest has first choice in such cases.'

'But of course,' said Meg thoughtfully, 'it is a little less likely since he did after all lose the gavelkind case.'

'Do you want Bocton?' asked David abruptly. 'Or Uncle Albert? Uncle Alfred perhaps?'

'Me?' asked Meg quickly. 'It would be nice to live back here, of course, very nice. But I cannot see how Louis would fare in England. He is so very fond of Paris.' (And any fashionable city with lots of attractive young women in it, she thought sourly.) 'However, it would be nice for me to have a little place to stay when I come over.'

David's heart took a gigantic bound, leaping over his vow of caution. 'When you come over?' he echoed slowly.

'Yes,' said Meg, smiling at him. 'I've decided I'm too much in France. I miss my family.'

Philip too was thinking of Bocton, sandwiched between his father's desire for it and his wife's, for vastly different reasons. He too wanted

301

Bocton – for it would prevent Katharine's having it. True, his rancour had been somewhat mollified by discovering that her marriage could hardly be progressing well, despite Luke's money. Poor Katharine. She must be rueing the day she had rejected him, Philip. And would do even more once he owned Bocton! Aunt Mabel had been quite right to point out that Jeremiah would fight to the death for Bocton, and yet Robert would never let him have it. Neither would allow the other to possess it.

So, Philip went on to think, if it were allotted to one of the overseas family members, then a private sale at advantageous terms could easily take place thereafter. And who better than he to buy it? No one, not even Father, could manage the Bocton estate as well as he could: sell part of it at a good price, knock down that ruin in order to build – and have the great pleasure of seeing Katharine and Luke discomfited. How subtly clever Father had been to allow them to continue the restoration; their anguish would be all the more bitter when they lost it. And lose it they would. He and Father would see to that.

'Keep your eyes open, Luke,' Jeremiah warned him. 'Something's going on. I don't know what it is, but it's dirty work. You can count on that where the Stowertons are concerned. Sophy's all right,' he amended. 'But watch the rest. They haven't changed.'

Luke tried to watch, but could not take it seriously. More and more he found himself obsessed by Bocton. He was going to find out what was happening there, and be damned if he would be thrown out by his own wife. Only yesterday she'd demanded more money as cool as anything, and then refused his offer of practical help. He was going to find out what was going on.

Fired with determination, he walked over to the old manor house. At first he thought the place deserted. Then he entered the study . . . and stood still in amazement. The room looked much larger. It *was* much larger. Silvered oak beams stood exposed, polished with beeswax, its smell mingling with chemicals in the air. Something for the woodworm and rot perhaps? The front wall was stripped back to the Tudor brickwork; before it, with a gap of about twelve inches, a row of oak posts stood exposed, with curved braces from post to wall plate at either end of the old timber frame; the brickwork walls had been plastered and painted, a bookshelf placed, obviously experimentally, in the gap between posts and wall. Furniture had been polished and treated, judging by the smell, rugs and pictures adorned the room. The other outside wall remained much as it had been, but above the front corner of the house the ceiling had been partly removed and an ornamented dragon beam which supported the jetty overhang had been exposed, as well as some floorboards.

Luke wandered over to the outside east wall, where a start had been made on stripping the plaster, and began idly to tear away some of the rotten panelling himself. Curiosity then excitement at the unknown rose in him. Then he heard a peal of laughter – Katharine's – coming from high up in the Great Hall. He strode outside, angry to think she had been there all the time and had not bothered to greet him though she must have heard him arrive. He bounded up the stairs to find ladders placed through a hole made in the Tudor ceiling into the roof void. Inside, an oil lamp glowed dimly. She was perched just inside the roof, her face turned not to him but towards the interior, calling to Mayfield or someone else beyond. White with fear for her, he stood mute lest the sound of his voice disturb her balance. He would go up, order her down. No, he couldn't do that. He must endure it, go up carefully.

'Far collar rotted.' Obadiah's faint muffled voice could be heard.

'Far collar brace rotted.' Mayfield's voice. Katharine's job was obviously to write it all down, as streams of measurements began to follow.

'Dis tie beam, 'e got de bad shakes,' Obadiah pronounced.

A muffled shout, a snap, a crash.

'Are you all right, Roderick?' Katharine shouted in fear.

'De rotted purlin. Mr Roderick all right.'

Luke's head slowly appeared in the roof void at her side. 'Katharine,' he asked quietly, 'please come down. You are not safe there.'

'Oh, I am,' she said gaily, dismissively. 'Luke, as you are here, would you mind preparing the refreshments for us? I think Roderick needs a short rest. You will find them packed in my basket downstairs. We will be down shortly.'

Rage fought pride. Pride won, as Luke descended the ladder again, getting out the refreshments as ordered. Biscuits, ginger beer, ale – and three glasses. He would walk away, leave them to it, yet something held him back.

'Thank you.' Katharine smiled at him vaguely – as she would one of the helps, Luke thought bitterly – arriving with Mayfield, who was limping slightly, and Obadiah.

'Thank you, Katharine. This is most welcome.' Mayfield bit absently into a Maid of Honour cake. 'Now, have you considered the plan we spoke of the other day, Trant?' he asked, ignoring Luke, who stood unrefreshed. Be damned if he'd take anything! He handed the plate to Obadiah.

'Thank 'ee, Mr Luke,' said Obadiah, gratified. 'Now dat's a nice idea, Mr Mayfield,' he went on approvingly, 'but all sorts of things do happen when you do remove ceilings . . .'

'Remove ceilings? *Which* ceilings?' asked Luke sharply, forgetting his resolve to remain aloof.

'I'll explain later, Luke,' said Katharine. 'Do excuse us now, though. This is our last meeting before the ownership is decided, and if – *when* – we get Bocton, I'd like to be able to start right away, with our plans decided.'

'Katharine, perhaps as Mr Stowerton will be paying, we had –'

'Of course, if you think so, Roderick,' she replied instantly, turning to Luke. 'Our plan is to remove this Tudor ceiling, save at the two ends so that the chimney stack is left undisturbed. Then we will start in the West Wing, where the original buttery and store room would have been, to see whether, as Roderick thinks, there may have been a gallery there – in Elizabethan times at least, when Nicholas converted the house.'

'Overlooking the hall, for minstrels to use?' Despite himself, Luke was displaying his interest now.

'No doubt we can discuss this when the ownership is decided,' said Mayfield tactfully.

'Oh, yes, Luke. We'll tell you all about it in detail. If you're here, of course.'

He glared at her furiously. How could she refer in front of others to their plans for a separate life? 'Why shouldn't I be here?' he enquired blandly.

'I imagined you might return to Leadville to clear things up there first,' she explained innocently.

'No,' he answered shortly. 'I want to be here when it's discussed,' aware he was beginning to sound like a petulant child.

'Thank you for the refreshment, Katharine.' Mayfield set down his glass. 'Now if we might begin again.'

'Do you require help?' Luke asked stiffly, as they returned to their work.

Katharine leaned over the curved stair rail. 'Oh, no, thank you, Luke. It's very good of you, but it would take too long to explain about the beams and just what we are looking for.'

He had been politely but firmly dismissed, with no option but to leave. Luke walked out of Bocton with conflicting emotions, chiefly anger against Katharine, or was it the world? What she said made sense – they knew what they were doing, and he would only be a hindrance. Yet he could learn, couldn't he? He had done all right when he and Katharine had explored the West Wing three years ago. Why should he not now?

Because he wouldn't be here later, he realised bleakly. He would not be here to find what secrets the old house might hide, or see it come to life, little by little, to reveal the heritage of Nicholas Stowerton.

Hardly knowing what he was doing or where he was going, Luke began to walk around the outside of the house. He glanced up at the old chimney. 'Grow rich in that which never taketh rust . . .' All very well for Sidney to write that in Penshurst, so full of worldly treasures, or was the poetry he left his legacy to the world? Sidney was happily married, too, like Nicholas Stowerton himself.

Jealous? Yes, he was. Not of Mayfield, however, he told himself quickly, but of Bocton. He wanted it as he had never wanted anything before – except Katharine. And that was over now, and had taken Bocton with it. Or had it? Suddenly he thought back to the hopelessness of the situation three years ago. He had turned matters to his own advantage then. Could he not do so again? Not to win Katharine, for that was finished. She was making it clear that they had separate lives; her way lay through Bocton, his elsewhere. That was what he had informed her was the position, and she was accepting it. So why did he have this odd feeling that she was controlling events? Luke was not accustomed to letting people get the better of him. Only Pearson had taken him by surprise, and never, never would he forget it. Leadville had blinded him – but Bocton, yes. With Bocton on his side, he might win yet. What the prize might be, he did not ask himself, for the quest itself blinded him.

'I will not,' declared Alfred firmly, 'sit in the same room as that man.'

'If you don't,' replied Sophy, equally firmly, 'you will not have a chance of owning Bocton.'

'Do I want to?' asked Alfred plaintively.

'You need to *appear* to want it,' Sophy told him.

'Very well,' he agreed. It seemed simpler. 'I'll come. But I want to be at least eight feet away from that fellow, so that I can count to six before I hit him.'

He stomped over to the Lodge that afternoon, relieved to see that tea in the garden was on the agenda. Good. He might feel less like thumping the fellow in the open air. He looked round somewhat nervously in case Elizabeth was lurking. He didn't entirely trust Sophy, despite her assurance that Elizabeth was safely out of the way. Sophy was getting to be too much of a manager.

Joseph balanced a delicate bone china cup awkwardly on his knee. Thank goodness Emily did not go in for this ritual. Tiny cakes and dainty sandwiches – he supposed vaguely that Sophy was glad to find something to do all day.

Albert looked perfectly at ease, one elegantly trousered leg over the other, surveying his brothers and sister sardonically. 'Could this gathering, dearest Sophy, have anything to do with the ownership of Bocton?' he enquired amicably.

'I felt we ought to discuss your intentions,' she said flatly. 'Since Robert and Jeremiah are at daggers drawn, they are most unlikely to agree to either of them getting it. Not without a court action.'

'So you want to know where the rest of us stand, eh?' barked Mabel, setting down her cup. 'What use would Bocton be to me, Sophy? I'm away all the time. Easy answer, there. How about you, Joseph? You're in the same boat. No way you want it, eh? Not only Bocton, you more or less thumbed your nose at the whole lot of us the day of the treasure trove, didn't you?'

He muttered something, looking into his cup as though it might provide the answer.

'Anyway, you wouldn't get it,' said Mabel. 'Not living in Australia. Not unless you let it to Alfred here. Or Luke and Katharine.'

Sophy looked up sharply.

'It would upset Robert if I said I wanted it,' said Joseph belligerently.

Mabel agreed, nodding her head vigorously. 'No one else would agree, though, not unless we come to an understanding.'

'Albert?' asked Sophy quietly.

305

'It's quite a nice little dump,' he said. 'Why not? I do have a sort of claim after all, being the youngest. As I pointed out before, the Custom of Kent awards the family home to the youngest.'

Alfred snorted. 'That's for boys under fifteen, not for roués of forty-five.'

'Nevertheless, I have no roof to call my own,' Albert said plaintively, 'and I am not yet forty-five. I could make quite a telling case to Mr Pinpole.'

'You're trying to provoke me – us,' amended Alfred testily.

'Not in the least. Moreover, Alfred, I have a son married to your daughter. They have sons, and Bocton would make a fine family residence for them. I do feel they should appreciate the English side of their heritage.'

Alfred's eyes bulged, and Sophy interrupted quickly. 'I think Jeremiah should have it,' she said stoutly. 'He paid for The Case. It is only fair.'

'When were the Stowertons ever fair?' enquired Mabel with a cackle. 'Never, from what George told me. He was always the fair one, the peace-maker. He was glad to escape.'

'He left last,' said Sophy shortly.

'He enjoyed England – without his brothers,' said Mabel wrily.

Sophy was remembering George, her elder brother. Always comforting, always encouraging. 'Don't be afraid, you can do it,' he would say. Though somehow she never could, and would return in tears. So well meaning, so kind . . . She pulled her thoughts back to the present.

'If Jeremiah and Robert cancel each other out,' said Mabel practically, 'we may have to look for someone else acceptable to us all.'

'And who would that be?' asked Sophy quietly.

'Me,' announced Alfred happily, to an embarrassed silence.

'I feel,' said Mabel slowly, breaking the silence, 'that it might be wise if as well as stating our own preference for which property we should own, we also state one other person for Bocton in case we do not get our own preferences. I'll put this to Jeremiah and Robert, too, if you like.'

'Suits me,' declared Alfred, relieved that some kind of sensible suggestion had been made, and he could get back to the safety of the Dower House and away from that blasted fellow.

Amid the general approval, only one person dissented. And she did not have a vote.

Meg twirled her pink parasol lightly, and smiled at David in pure pleasure. Although the day was warm, the Charham folly by the lake, used as a summer house, was much more attractive than being outside, for today was the day Meg had decided she would allow herself to be seduced.

She sank on to the chaise longue while David hovered anxiously, not quite sure of his role.

He was left in little doubt when Meg's limbs moved sensuously under the muslin dress, then swung off the chaise, exposing quite a lot of white-stockinged limb. She made it clear he was to sit by her, close to her: 'Because you are my very best friend, David,' she whispered. 'My *very* best.'

That would teach Louis, she told herself afterwards with satisfaction. True, he would never know, but *she* would have the benefit of knowing. And David was very sweet. In a way. Full of sleek contentment, Meg ran up the stairs at Charham to change for dinner. And sighed. Another of those dreary family repasts with Mother ogling Father-in-Law to annoy him, Violet and Primrose forever rattling on about China, and that awful old man dribbling his soup. She sniffed as she reached the first floor. A distinct smell of Paris perfume. Mother's. She must be ahead of her, on the next flight of stairs. No, she wasn't. She sniffed again. The smell was from *this* corridor. Intrigued, she walked a little way down, and heard a most interesting conversation through a half-open bedroom doorway. Father-in-Law's bedroom.

'*No*, Elizabeth.' Sharply.

'Albert, you never used to be quite so shy.'

'I'm older.' Goaded.

'I'm sure you could still make love, if I help you, darling. I know how.'

The sound of Albert's voice choking with rage. 'Of course I *can* still make love, Elizabeth, if I want to. But I've got a wife . . .'

'You seemed to have forgotten her when I saw you at Longchamp with that attractive young lady, darling. Oh, Albert, have I changed that much? Remember the Trevi fountain?'

Meg listened, entranced. From the silence she concluded that Elizabeth had overcome her victim's scruples, until there was an agonised shout: 'Go away. Get off me, woman!'

Then the sound of her mother's tearful voice. 'Oh, *Albert*! It's because I'm old, I'm ugly . . .'

'No.' Chivalry had not quite deserted him. 'It's because the door isn't shut.' He was clutching wildly at straws.

'Is *that* all?' said Elizabeth, relieved. 'At first I thought you didn't want me. Just a moment.'

There was the sound of something that might have been the cry 'Don't', and then the door was firmly shut. And Meg could hear quite distinctly the sound of a key being turned.

'Where are you going, Father?' asked Katharine, puzzled, seeing Alfred sitting patiently in the trap outside the Dower House.

'Eastwell,' he said complacently. 'Luke's arranged it. He wants to investigate the old legend of Richard Plantagenet.'

'Why?' The word burst from her before she could reflect. Why did Luke want to know about the old legends? she thought mutinously, regardless of the fact that this was a sign of exactly what she had been aiming for. He strode past her at that moment, with a courteous 'Good morning', leaving her extremely disgruntled.

307

'Why don't you come,' asked her father idly, 'if you're interested?'

Luke said nothing, apparently engrossed in a guide to Kent. She would not, *could* not go, Katharine decided, unless he asked her. But he did not. She hesitated while he laid aside the book and gathered the reins in his hand. Perhaps . . . She stopped, pride keeping her from submission. Then: 'I do wish to visit Charham. Perhaps you could call there on the way back?' she compromised.

'Certainly, if you wish,' said Luke agreeably enough, yet a distinct note of boredom in his voice.

She bit her lip as he jumped down, and with what grace she could muster, accepted his hand up into the trap. Even this slight contact set her heart racing, and she had to force herself to maintain her pleasant smile of polite interest. 'Why are you going?' she enquired offhandedly.

'I thought your father would be pleased to rootle out evidence about his old family legend. Also, I'm interested myself,' Luke added, 'in case we get Bocton.'

She digested both the disagreeable sound of 'in case' as though he admitted doubt, and also the fact that Luke was confessing to interest.

'You think that the ghost of Richard Plantagenet will pop up and point you the way to his jewels?' she asked, endeavouring to maintain a lighthearted attitude.

'Never speak slightingly of ghosts, Katharine,' said her father reprovingly. 'It's almost Midsummer Eve.'

'What of it?' she asked.

'That's the time that the ghost of Nicholas Stowerton rises from his grave to present his ruby to the Queen in her bedroom.'

'I don't believe it,' she said indignantly. 'You never told me that before.'

'I couldn't,' said Alfred, hurt at his veracity being questioned. 'Not without your knowing the full story – and that, as I said before, is not in my view a story for ladies. In fact, the ghost appeared to Jacob when he lived in Bocton as a boy. No one's slept there since.'

'Perhaps the ghosts of Plantagenet and Stowerton have been battling it out together,' said Luke lightly.

Katharine sat tensely as the trap jolted through the lanes, thinking of their trips to Georgetown and the night that had followed one of them, when it had seemed that nothing could ever spoil their happiness again. How wrong she had been. Luke no longer cared for her, for surely otherwise they could have mended their differences by now?

The tiny village of Eastwell was almost entirely enclosed in the huge estate of Eastwell Park, the home of the Duke of Edinburgh. 'The best venison in Kent comes from here,' Alfred informed them, as they passed huge herds of deer grazing on the green turf, after Luke had spoken to the lodgekeeper.

'How do you know, Father?' Katharine asked suspiciously.

'My dear,' he informed her, 'I was invited to luncheon by the Duke.' He looked modest. 'My fame as a raconteur has spread rapidly, thanks to Robert's Counsel's wisdom in calling me as a witness.'

The church where Luke had arranged to meet the Rector was on the south side of the park. Determined to betray no interest, Katharine stood to the rear of the group as they toured the old flint building, admiring the monuments to the owners of Eastwell, including Sir Thomas Moyle, Richard Plantagenet's benefactor.

'This is the only one,' the Rector pointed to an unmarked tomb in the chancel, 'that could possibly be Plantagenet's, but there's no evidence as to whether he was buried in the church itself or in the churchyard, so I am afraid it will remain a mystery.'

'But there's no doubt he was buried here?' asked Luke.

'Oh, yes.' The Rector showed them the old church register, and Katharine could no longer disguise her interest, coming quickly to join them. *Rychard Plantagenet was buryed the 22d daye of December, anno ut supra*. The year was 1550. 'This tick,' the Rector pointed to a curious symbol, 'before the name indicates the deceased as of noble birth. So there you are, Mr Stowerton,' he said brightly to Alfred, whose fame had spread since the case, 'evidence for your legend.'

It was, however, the only tangible evidence. The small hut that Richard had asked permission of Sir Thomas Moyle to build for himself had been pulled down when the field he chose became part of the new Eastwell Park long after Moyle's death. All that remained was a story that the nearby spring was called Plantagenet's Well.

'That's all there is?' snorted Alfred forthrightly, looking at it in some contempt.

'This and the correspondence in your own library.'

Alfred looked puzzled.

'Your own bound volumes of the *Gentleman's Magazine*, Alfred,' Luke told him gently. 'Have you never read the correspondence there?'

'Only about horses,' Alfred told him, somewhat shamefaced.

'I guess the horses in these issues are long since dead, for the correspondence took place way back last century, when someone wrote with information given by one of the later occupants of Eastwell about a family tradition. Apparently, after Sir Thomas Moyle bought Eastwell in 1543 or four, he saw his chief bricklayer reading a book in Latin, and on being questioned, the old man told him that until he was about sixteen he had been boarded with a schoolmaster who taught the classics; he knew no relatives, but a gentleman came to pay his expenses once a quarter. On one occasion he was taken to see a splendid mansion where he was given money by a man wearing a star and garter. Then, in August 1485, he was taken by horse on a long journey to Leicestershire, to Bosworth Field, where he was escorted to Richard III's tent. The King informed him that he was his illegitimate son, and that if he were to win the battle on the morrow, he would formally acknowledge him as his son and heir to the throne. By this time, I guess you'll remember, Richard's only legitimate heir had died.'

Luke broke off, for Alfred's interest had waned with no mention of

Stowertons, and he had no intention of satisfying Katharine's curiosity without prompting.

'What happened?' she demanded, pride unable to restrain curiosity.

'"If I lose the battle I lose my life too," the King told him,' Luke continued, somewhat unwillingly, before he too became absorbed in the story, '"but I hope to survive both. Do you stand in such a place (and he showed him where) and you may see the battle out of danger . . . If I should be so unfortunate as to lose the battle, then shift as well as you can and take care to let nobody know that I am your father for no mercy will be shewed to anyone so nearly related to me." Then the King gave him a purse of gold and dismissed him. That's about the lot, I reckon,' Luke finished more off-handedly than he had begun, as if suddenly recollecting to whom he was speaking so animatedly.

'Suppose it wasn't gold but jewels,' Katharine began eagerly, then remembered she was trying not to display undue curiosity.

'Well, he did lose,' Luke went on, unable to resist a grin of triumph, 'and so our Richard made off to London, sold his rich clothes and horse, and promptly apprenticed himself to a bricklayer. Then he apparently disappeared from historical record until Sir Thomas Moyle discovered him, years later. By then he must already have been in his mid- to late-seventies, since he died at the age of eighty-one only a few years after he built his little house – having turned down the offer of accommodation at Eastwell. So,' he ended thoughtfully, deliberately looking away from Katharine to where Alfred was by now strolling round the field, 'what was he doing in the meantime?'

'Trying to procure a house for his old age, with his one source of wealth,' said Katharine eagerly. 'It fits. Oh, Luke, it fits –' She broke off with a scream as her excited movements caused her to catch her foot in the back of her skirt, sending her slipping down the bank of a small stream.

'Careful.' Luke's arm shot out as she started to fall, and the grip of his hand on her wrist hurt but saved her. She scrambled back up the bank with his help and he put both arms round her to steady her, quickly releasing her again.

'You nearly lost me then,' she said inanely. Lost? How stupid. He did not want her.

Luke stared at her across the inches that divided them. How long ago they had stood thus on the threshold of love . . . and how near again it suddenly seemed, how possible once more. He had but to make a move and she would be in his arms, never to leave again. 'Katharine,' he began hoarsely, but he would not, could not, continue.

'Yes?' she said jerkily, knowing that he had only to say one more word and she would throw herself into his arms. But no word came.

Chapter Eighteen

On this occasion, Mr Pinpole intended to take no chances. The Stowertons would meet at the offices of Messrs Foggett, Dodson and Pinpole, in as intimidating an atmosphere as he could contrive. This time there would be no intimate circle of chairs; there would be rows, facing one end of the room, and facing them would be Mr Pinpole, Mr Foggett and Mr Dodson.

Katharine too had made careful preparations, dressing with care, as she had done on that very first meeting with her relatives. It seemed so long ago now, yet it was only three years. And, as then, so much depended on this one day. The future of Bocton would be decided for good today, for even the Stowertons would surely not let the matter go to court. Not only Bocton's but her own future was at stake. She had heard Luke go downstairs a few minutes ago, and her fingers trembled slightly as she adjusted her new fashionably high gable hat, befeathered and ribboned. She made a face at herself in the mirror for such concession to fashion, yet it set off the plain dark silk dress tightly drawn back with its fullness behind, over the ridiculously uncomfortable bustle that was once again *de rigueur*. Only for such an important meeting would she have bowed to the dictates of fashion.

Taking a deep breath, she opened her door and walked down the stairs to meet Luke and her father. Breakfast had been a silent meal. Now Alfred glanced up happily at her approach. 'Ah, Katharine, I was just saying to Luke that if we get this meeting over quickly, I might visit the cricket match in Canterbury.'

She said nothing, amazed at her father's ability to skim over the dramas of life. Could he not see that whatever the outcome of this meeting, it was hardly likely there would be time for sporting events?

Luke murmured something polite, his eyes on the new hat. Was that admiration in his glance or should she feel guilty for buying it? He had reproached her often enough for not spending money on clothes. His glance seemed friendly enough, however. Perhaps he too appreciated that today they had a common aim.

As if sensing the emotions that her face did not display, Luke kept her hand in his slightly longer than was necessary after handing her up into the carriage, but as she turned to him in gratitude when he sat next to her, he dropped it, as if annoyed at having been betrayed into a sign of any interest other than a business one.

As the carriage drove through the streets of Canterbury, Katharine

envied the people hurrying about their daily lives. Not for them this
overwhelming dread of what the day might bring.

They were the last to arrive. Not that there were so many at this
meeting as on earlier occasions for Mr Pinpole, perhaps excited by his
new assumption of power, had excluded all those not directly involved.
Only for Luke had he made an exception, since he had paid for The
Case, and for Katharine and Sophy. Violet, Primrose, Meg, Philip,
David, Jacob and Elizabeth, to the dismay of some of them, had not
been asked to attend.

Violet and Primrose had been the most vociferous in their com-
plaints.

'I am afraid,' said Mr Pinpole to his partners, with some perplexity
that anyone could find such difficulty, 'they do not understand the law.
The fact is that an action dropped some fifty years ago has no bearing
on the results of the present one. I have told them their interests will
be taken into consideration, but it did not seem to satisfy them.'

There was a strained silence in the room as the Dower House party
entered and took their places. Luke, quickly glancing round, observed
Mr Pinpole's plan, and positioned himself at the rear next to Alfred and
Jeremiah, having seated Katharine next to Sophy in front of them. She
held up her chin proudly, refusing to display any sign that this was
other than completely to be expected.

'I trust,' Mr Pinpole asked severely, after his opening preliminaries,
'that you have reached a consensus?'

'I regret not,' said Robert, after a moment's pause, as if to see
whether Jeremiah would make a bid for party spokesmanship.

'In that event,' said Mr Pinpole, with some relief, 'I must ask you
to abide by my decision.'

'That won't be necessary,' said Robert. 'My brothers and their
representatives have reached a decision of sorts, in which I concur.
Since Bocton appears to be the property most at issue, we propose
to hand you our individual choices as to whom should possess it. We
shall also provide you with our individual *second* choices.'

Mr Pinpole looked wildly towards his partners for guidance. There
seemed no theoretical objection to this, but where the Stowertons
were concerned, there were likely to be hidden pitfalls. Messrs
Foggett and Dodson provided no guidance, and thus Mr Pinpole
was obliged to receive the papers handed to him by the six heirs,
one by one.

Katharine watched as Alfred handed over his. She had not seen
him write it, but all had been settled, she tried to tell herself with
conviction. He would nominate Jeremiah, with himself as second
choice. Why then was she uneasy – an emotion that she sensed Luke
shared. The whole week had been strange, now she came to think
of it. Concentrating so hard on her unhappiness over Luke, and on
Bocton itself, perhaps she should have paid more attention to what
was going on between Father and his brothers. She had seen little of
Alfred or of Jeremiah. There had been constant meetings, to which
she was not invited. What now seemed most worrying was that Sophy

had been mostly excluded from them too. It was natural, Father had told her, that only the beneficiaries should be present. That was true, but . . .

Katharine's forebodings increased as she saw Mr Pinpole's face whiten as he anxiously conferred with his colleagues. Finally he spoke: 'We appear,' he announced drily to the ceiling, unable to look these terrible clients in the eye, 'to have six different solutions offered. In each case it would seem that you would like Bocton for yourself.'

Katharine's heart sank. She had been right to fear today.

'However,' Pinpole continued, seeing a chink of light at the end of the tunnel, albeit not a chink he would have chosen, 'your second choice does offer unanimity.' He looked around with an expression of bright optimism that his instinct was telling him was misplaced. 'It seems that Mrs Mabel Stowerton, on behalf of her late husband, is the second choice of you all.'

Mabel! 'Of you *all!*' Mr Pinpole had said.

Katharine let out one cry. She was aware of Luke gripping the back of her chair from behind, not in comfort, but in warning. But of what? Of what? *Mabel* to own Bocton? How could it be? Why should Father have nominated her? Why Jeremiah? This was what came of loving Bocton too much and ignoring the Stowertons. Had not Jeremiah always said they were not to be trusted? But Father – how could he do it? And *why* cut out Jeremiah, who was the obvious choice for him? Her head spun with confusion and horror.

'No!' One explosive syllable broke the tense silence after Katharine's cry, not from her lips or Luke's but from Sophy's. She stood up, trembling, hands gripping Robert's chair in front of her. 'Are you all mad?' she hurled angrily at her brothers.

'Sophy!' barked Mabel, the picture of innocent outrage.

'Miss Stowerton!' Mr Pinpole said in unison, glad of his authoritarian position. This was what came of his liberal attitude in allowing her presence. He was horrified that Miss Sophy of all people should be the one to stir conflict. 'Do you have some legal reason for objecting to this decision? If not, I must ask you to take your seat again and remain silent.'

She stood where she was. 'Legal?' she said. 'Legal is not the point. I know just cause and impediment.'

'It –' Pinpole began indignantly, but all eyes save Mabel's were on Sophy, not him.

Mabel folded her arms and sat bolt upright, a gleam in her eye. 'Get her out of here,' she told the solicitors unemotionally. 'She has no standing in these negotiations. I demand she be removed.'

'No,' said Katharine.

Mabel did not even glance at her.

'And her,' she said. 'That niece of mine too.'

'I will not go,' said Sophy steadily, 'and nor will Katharine.'

'I regret Mrs Stowerton has a point,' Pinpole began. 'Perhaps Miss Sophy, you would –'

313

Jeremiah stood up. 'She's our sister,' he said gruffly. 'Let her speak. Do you agree?' He looked at Robert first, then the others.

'Certainly,' said Robert. 'I see no reason why not.'

A faint look of surprise flashed across Jeremiah's face.

Sophy seemed hardly to have heard, so lost was she in the past. Then she looked directly at her five brothers, with whom she had played and shouted joyfully in Bocton's gardens forty-two years ago, the day of the last treasure trove. But on that day there had been not five, but six of them. 'What,' she asked these five middle-aged men, 'do you remember of your brother George?'

A puzzled silence was broken first by Jeremiah.

'He was the peace-maker,' he said almost angrily, surprised she could ask. 'Good old George.'

'He was the best of you all,' said Robert quietly, venomously. 'He was the only one of you who bothered to talk to me as though I were his *brother*.'

'He mended that boat of mine you broke,' Alfred said to Joseph without rancour. 'He was kind.'

'He looked after me,' said Joseph gruffly. 'I miss him.' His eyes filled with tears for a long-lost youth.

Only Albert said nothing, bright eyes darting from one to the other.

'You must remember, Sophy,' said Jeremiah fiercely to her, angry that his idol was being questioned. 'You think the Stowertons are good at quarrelling now. Without George, we'd have torn each other to pieces years ago.'

'No,' said Sophy wearily. 'That's not so. I used to think so too, until Mabel came here. Then I began to wonder. We all saw George as the peace-maker, the one in the middle between the older brothers and the younger, the amiable one, anxious to help, soothe, unite. Has it ever occurred to you that he was nothing of the sort? That *he* was the trouble-maker; that he found it fun to set brother against brother, to manipulate, and manoeuvre. *And now she's doing the same!*' pointing at her sister-in-law.

'Sophy!' barked Mabel, dabbing at her eyes with a large checked man's handkerchief. 'Say what you like about me, but I won't hear George vilified now he's dead, and not here to defend himself. Are you going to listen to this jealous rubbish?' She turned to her brothers-in-law, who, recovering from their initial shock, were uneasily considering this disloyalty to the memory of George.

'Quiet, Mabel.' Robert was listening intently. 'I intend to hear more.'

'You,' hissed Mabel reproachfully. 'You whom he befriended most.' Robert flushed.

'It was the day of the treasure trove.' Sophy's voice cut across, determined to win them to her. 'Joseph, tell us what you remember.'

He looked embarrassed, bewildered. 'You can't say bad things about *George*! He looked after me.'

'Just remember, Joseph.'

314

He looked obstinate, then seeing he had no option, that curiosity was replacing puzzlement on his brothers' faces, began slowly: 'I was going to find the cup that year, and I *did*. I went through the shrubbery and there it was in the old beehive, like a sort of grail.' He was back in his childhood, the silver gleaming, just waiting for him to stretch out his hand and pluck it from its hiding place. 'And then Robert came up behind me –'

'I did not.' Three clipped words.

Joseph continued as if Robert had not spoken, '– and told me to leave it there. That it was mine this year, that he would guard it for me, while I went to find the other toys. And I trusted him, so I did.'

'Why do you say you trusted him, if you thought it was Robert?' asked Sophy. 'You had never trusted Robert, had you? None of you did. He had never tried to win trust.'

'That's right,' said Joseph, puzzled, shaken for a moment. 'That is odd.' Then: 'But when I came back, Robert had the cup and refused to tell people it was mine, so it must have been him.' He glanced across at his brother venomously.

'And how do you claim you found the cup, Robert?'

'I worked out where it was and found it in the beehive,' he said in his dry voice. 'There was no sign of Joseph and I never spoke to him.'

'And how did you work out where it was?'

He shrugged. 'I was sixteen, and it was a game for children so it was easy. I just guessed. No . . .' The hot summer's day; boys' voices echoing in the distance, misted by time. 'No,' he said, considering, startled at what memory retrieved from the chasm of years, 'it was something someone said gave me the clue. I can't remember . . .' He looked at Joseph directly, yet seeing not the middle-aged man he now was, but a boy with desperate longing in his eyes. A longing that he had assumed at the time to be so acute he would lie. 'Help me. Think back, Joseph,' Robert added urgently. 'Think back.'

Joseph stared steadily at his hated brother. That hatred of Robert had obliterated everything from that day, except his need for revenge. His hand was stretching out, almost touching the cup, when the voice spoke. Robert's . . . He could not get past the hatred. It rose before him like a sickening, enveloping fog. If only Emily were here . . . Slowly the blanket became less suffocating, the mists rising from that summer's day and leaving a blue sky of certainty. 'It wasn't you,' he told Robert in wonder. 'Alfred?' he continued, almost hopefully. 'Was it you?'

He shook his head, bewildered. 'I was with Jeremiah.'

'I was with Sophy,' said Albert, alert now, all languor gone.

'George?' asked Joseph of his brothers.

They looked at him, unable to agree, unable to deny, unable to comprehend.

'George tried to stop Robert and me fighting,' said Jeremiah flatly.

'Did he?' asked Sophy quietly. 'Think about it.'

'Don't hit him,' shrieked George.

Jeremiah hadn't been going to, but suddenly Robert's smug complacent face, exuding undisguised triumph, was too much. He'd

315

launched himself at his brother, George dancing round. 'Don't, don't, *don't*! You can't hate him that much, Jerry.'

But he did, he did – didn't he?

'I can't believe it.' But there was no conviction in Jeremiah's voice any longer.

'I can,' said Robert suddenly. He had been turning it over in his mind, looking at this new angle, this new possibility, almost as dispassionately as if it were a business venture. Could George have been the barrier between his brothers and himself, the reason that the differences provided by age had been accentuated into an unbridgeable gulf? 'He was in the middle. It was his way of getting power, was it not?'

'Yes,' Sophy answered quietly. 'He liked power. I saw a different George from you, but it took me a long time to appreciate what I was seeing. Even when Albert ran off with Elizabeth.'

An electric silence fell.

'Sophy?' demanded Alfred in wondering tones. 'Are you trying to make excuses for that scoundrel?' He jerked his head towards Albert who looked completely flabbergasted at this unexpected light thrown on his own iniquities.

'No,' she said, smiling faintly. 'For we all bear the responsibility for our own actions. But a seed can be planted. In this case, I think it was Adam who took the apple, but the serpent had put the idea in his mind. Perhaps in Elizabeth's also.'

'Wait a minute!' Albert exclaimed thoughtfully. 'George certainly suggested I stayed at the Dower House, reminded me how attractive Elizabeth was, and told me how bored she was with . . .'

'You blasted – *fellow*!' Alfred was on his feet, remembering just in time the presence of ladies.

'I'm telling you what George told me,' said Albert a trifle smugly. 'It wasn't necessarily the truth, though I thought it was then. Is that what you mean by a serpent, Sophy?'

'Yes,' she said. 'He didn't always succeed, of course. It was a game. I think you and Elizabeth were his major and final triumph. You and George left shortly afterwards, didn't you, Mabel?'

She had sat so silently all this while, they had almost forgotten her. 'And what if all this nonsense is so?' she said smugly. 'How does that affect me and my rights?' she demanded of Pinpole.

'Quite a lot,' said Sophy forthrightly, answering for him. 'Because you play the same game, don't you, Mabel?' She looked at her brothers calmly. 'Mabel is always there, always stirring the pudding gently. Always suggesting, never asking. How do you think you all came to put her name as your second choice for Bocton? Think back.'

They looked at Mabel, uneasily remembering the quiet reasoned talks, the frank discussions, the unassailable arguments against one or other of their brothers.

'Why should Mabel want it for herself?' demanded Alfred, bewildered.

'That's easy to answer,' said Sophy briskly. 'Partly because she has

316

two children, but mainly to prevent any one of you getting it. Perhaps she sees it as George's vengeance for dying young and being cheated of further mischief-making.'

Mabel rose to her feet.

However could she have thought her face amiable? thought Katharine, dazed. It seemed now almost ugly in its viciousness. 'Do you believe the jealous ramblings of an old maid?' Mabel asked the five men briskly.

The way their faces turned away from her seemed answer enough, for she screamed out: 'And what of her? Little Miss Sophy, always the good girl, always so meek and mild, devoted to charitable works. Like hell!' She gave an ugly laugh. 'She's been Alexander Bishop's mistress for over twenty years.'

'Be quiet,' shouted Katharine, instantly and angrily. Ever since the revelation of his identity, she had realised the situation, and it had lain comfortably between her and her aunt, accepted and unspoken. Sophy kept silence as if she had expected this rejoinder and calculated for it.

'Though perhaps "mistress" is the wrong word,' sneered Mabel, 'since Sophy has enough money to have paid for The Case several times over. You did not know that, did you, Katharine? *Her* money's been supporting you all these years, not Bishop's.'

Katharine turned sharply to Sophy, caught by the unexpectedness of this attack, unable to grasp it, looking in bewilderment to her aunt for enlightenment.

'Tell them, Mabel, everything,' said Sophy almost politely. 'Let's have done with it.'

'And you want to know where the money's come from? Our modest Sophy is one of the queens of the circulating libraries, read avidly for the purple of her highly passionate romances. All based on experience with Mr Bishop, of course. *By the Moon's Burning Light, The Rose of Passion's Garden, The Desert and the Lady* are all written under the name of Lady Wittisham – our Sophy.'

Katharine rose to her feet and walked over to Mabel. 'Leave,' she said thickly, '*now.*' Time enough to grapple with the implications of this astounding information once the serpent had gone from their midst.

Mabel roared with laughter as she went to the door. 'George would have enjoyed this,' she said with satisfaction. 'I certainly did. You can write to me, Pinpole, and tell me what property you assign to me, or else send me the money. I imagine it won't be Bocton. In any case, I've had my money's worth already. Oh, and by the way,' she added, 'if you want to know what George was doing on the Gold Coast when he was killed, he was selling the natives arms – just as he did all over Europe, Asia and Africa. As you've all so suddenly appreciated, he did so enjoy stirring things up. Tarnishes the precious Stowerton image somewhat, doesn't it?'

She gave a last harsh cackle and the door closed behind her. Five brothers looked on their sister with new eyes.

'Can you forgive me, Katharine?' Sophy looked at her niece. 'If I'd

317

paid for The Case, I knew it was inevitable there would be more rows, more quarrels, and I couldn't bear it.'

'How can I criticise you,' Katharine replied warmly, 'when you supported my sister, myself – and Father – all these years?'

Sophy smiled faintly. 'And in such a way? All those romances that Meg so avidly used to read. If only she'd known!'

Katharine laughed and said softly: 'I'd rather have been brought up by love than horses.'

Alfred caught the last word, and his eyes strayed to the *Pink 'Un*, neatly folded, awaiting his attention on his lap.

'It seems I was wrong in hitting you the day of the treasure trove, Robert,' said Jeremiah gruffly.

'Yes,' he said matter-of-factly. He hesitated. 'And perhaps I did not fully appreciate how my younger brothers felt.'

'Ah, well,' said Jeremiah, sighing, 'it was all a long time ago.' He put out his hand and, after a split second's pause, Robert took it.

Mr Pinpole began to come to life again. He coughed gently. 'Might I ask,' he enquired a trifle plaintively, 'what is to be the future of Bocton?'

Impulsively Katharine turned to Luke in the carriage going home, Alfred having driven with Sophy in order, he announced, 'To hear more about the writing of romance.' Perhaps he too might take it up. The romance of the turf – now there was an idea.

'I feel,' Katharine announced, 'as if the man in the moon has descended to earth and waved a magic wand.'

'We've got more than green cheese,' Luke said, smiling, unable to hold back his elation.

We. He had said *we*. 'I think his name is Sophy. To think she was writing all that time, and we never guessed. No wonder she wanted to move from the Dower House. It can't have been easy to write romantic novels with Father thundering about.'

'Or to conduct a love affair.'

'Luke!' she laughed, half shocked, then she sobered. 'Poor Sophy. How sad that she can never marry him. Unless his wife dies, of course. He has not seen her for thirty years – they were only married a year, so Sophy says, before she refused to make love to him again. How could she . . . ?' Katharine broke off as she was aware of Luke's silence at her side. Isn't that what she had done? Refused to sleep with him at first, no matter for what reason?

'Luke,' she began hesitantly, 'now the Stowerton feud is no more, now we have Bocton, could we not –' his sudden stillness frightened her, but she swept on '– be lovers again. A new start, begun today of all days?'

The fields went by in a blur of unreality. Only this was real, this moment.

Fear filled him, a fear of events beyond his control. Bocton was theirs, could swamp him with its tentacles, lure him with its magic, so that blindly he would trust again.

'No,' he said, as though to ward off some destiny he was not yet prepared for. 'No, it is too late,' he repeated, snatching at the only words that had the power to stop him taking her into his arms and kissing his doubts away.

'Now,' Jeremiah declared grandly, 'I shall view my property,' flourishing the key to the old oak door. 'I shall enjoy one last look before I sell it to Luke. And I'm going to make it a condition of the sale that Daisy Petal and I can come here as often as we like.'

'Granted,' said Katharine, torn between the hurt that consumed her and exhilaration that Bocton was at last theirs.

The division of the property, to Mr Pinpole's amazement and delight, had taken a mere thirty minutes, now that harmony had come to the Stowertons for the first time since Nicholas's death. Jeremiah took Bocton; Alfred kept the Dower House and the Lodge, plus sufficient income to keep both running; Joseph took Charham, on the understanding Violet, Primrose and Jacob should live there till their deaths; Robert took Charham Home Farm and Mill, plus most of the Charham grounds; Albert took the Stowerton Arms and cottages. Working out monetary compensation to bring all to equal shares would keep Messrs Pinpole, Foggett and Dodson in employment for some time, and they eagerly anticipated the opportunity of control of this area with no interruptions from the Stowerton clan.

Jeremiah heaved a sigh. 'I almost feel sorry for Robert. He looked quite human when he signed Bocton away. Still, he didn't want it for its own sake, only to spite me,' he consoled himself. 'That's why I wanted it too – to spite him. Well, it's best in your hands, Luke.' He looked round the old hall, peeling, damp and uncared for, despite all Katharine's efforts. 'Pile of rotten old wood, isn't it?'

'How can you say that?' said Katharine indignantly. 'You wait until this hall is restored, when that ceiling is taken away and the roof opened up.'

'Draughty.'

'You can't compare this with Denver,' she said, not noticing his grin. 'Look at that fireplace.' She pointed to the old inglenook in the hall.

'And look at that.' Jeremiah jerked his thumb towards the storm-struck West Wing. 'Worth all the fighting, was it?'

'Every bit,' said Katharine stoutly, and they laughed, just as Luke came in to join them. Immediately Jeremiah noticed a change come over Katharine. She seemed to shrink inside herself, her voice sounding artificial. 'When Mr Mayfield and I have finished, you'll see most of the old mediaeval house itself, I promise. Excuse me, I need to open the windows upstairs.'

Jeremiah glanced curiously at Luke when she had gone. 'You're a fool, Luke, leaving her so much with him. You know what you're doing, boy?'

'I know just what I'm doing,' he retorted evenly, 'and there is nothing to fear from Mayfield, I assure you. He's a nancy.' Fear? Why had he used the word fear?

Jeremiah frowned. 'But you'll be living here, won't you?'

No. Katharine will be here alone,' said Luke stiffly. 'I'll come when I can, naturally.'

Jeremiah sighed. 'You take after your mother, you obstinate young devil. Cut off your ears as well as your nose to spite your face.'

Luke was silent. There was nothing to say. He was powerless to do anything about the situation, even had he wanted. It was as if his heart was dead. Trust was gone, and taken love with it, he told himself. Once across that river, it could not be recrossed. All he could do would be to search out new lands, new ways of life. He glanced up to see Katharine coming down the stairs to rejoin them.

'I'll show you the study, Father,' said Luke quickly. 'You can see what's being done there to the old house.'

'It's locked, I'm afraid, Uncle Jeremiah. Mr Mayfield thought it better,' said Katharine brightly, despite the effort.

'Did he indeed?' said Luke grimly. 'Might I remind you that Father is the owner now, Katharine.'

'*Roderick* says it is not safe while we are taking walls and ceilings down,' she replied lightly.

So she was still playing her childish game, was she? Even Father must be able to see how transparent the ruse was. Inside him the longing to see the room, to display its secrets, was battling with not wishing to play Katharine's game.

Jeremiah remained silent, summing up the situation and deciding his best course was to stay out of it.

'You'll see the room before you go – both of you,' she assured them anxiously. 'Only I do want you both to see it at its best.'

'I would like to be consulted as to –' Luke began, then stopped. He would *not* betray undue interest in Bocton. Anger began to rise in him. He was being deliberately kept away from the work for which he was paying, he reminded himself. Then he acknowledged to himself that it was not the money – it was Bocton itself from which he resented being excluded.

'Sister Meg, how pleasant to see you.' Luke waylaid her at Charham, whither he had gone for exactly that purpose.

She smiled artificially, nervous at having been caught after deliberately avoiding him. 'You're always so busy with Bocton and Katharine, Luke.' She could hardly have said anything more calculated to annoy him.

'I wanted to inform you, Sister Meg, before you hear through my lawyers, that I have withdrawn your allowance.'

'What?' The blood drained from her face. 'You can't do that,' she cried shrilly.

'Why not?' he asked unemotionally. 'I have already paid you more than was agreed at the time of your wedding.'

Her anger flared. 'It was to continue,' she said viciously.

'I think not. Do you,' he asked, 'have tangible reasons why I should continue to pay?'

Her eyes fell away from his.

'You are disappointed, naturally,' Luke went on unemotionally. 'Now, however, that Albert has come into his inheritance, I expect he will see to the needs of his son – and grandsons. Would you not consider that just?'

'Grandsons,' she echoed, clearly debating whether this still had bargaining power in it or not.

'Yes,' he said curtly. 'Would you dispute that Louis-Luc is Albert's grandson too?'

She turned on her heel and flounced away, seriously upset. She was astute enough to see that she had no bargaining power left in Luke. Albert, however, was a different matter.

'What's the matter, my beautiful Meg?' David leaned over her anxiously.

'Nothing,' she said disconsolately, pulling the sheets around her.

'Are you worried in case anyone knows I'm here?' he pressed her.

'No.' She laughed scornfully. 'Only Jacob's in and he wouldn't notice if I walked down the corridor stark naked with you.'

'I think he would,' said David seriously.

'Are you happy with this ridiculous settlement?' she asked suddenly.

He shrugged, slightly put out at talk of business after the love they had just shared. 'I'm a younger son – what can I expect? Philip will get Stowerton. I may get the farm, if I'm lucky. I might like that,' he said with more enthusiasm. 'The old tenant farmer's getting old and has no children. I might like being a farmer.'

'You'll be all smelly when I come to –' Meg ran a finger down his chest.

'To what?' he said huskily.

'To visit stuffy old Katharine,' Meg pouted. 'To think,' she burst out, 'how much she's got while I've got nothing. It's dreadful what Luke has done to us!'

'Luke?' asked David, bewildered.

She could hardly tell him about the allowance, or the reasons he had withdrawn it. 'He's given all the money to Father,' she pouted. 'He'll gamble it away and there'll be nothing left for me except to share the Dower House and the Lodge with Katharine as an inheritance, and I expect Sophy will go on living there for ever anyway. All that money wasted on Father.'

'But you have a husband to support you,' said David, completely bewildered at this unusual pillow talk.

She could hardly tell him that she wanted money of her own, and that Louis was as feeble a manager of money as she was herself, so she kissed David passionately. Even if he was going to be a farmer, at least he would provide some diversion in England. Still deep in this slightly consoling thought, she later accompanied him as they hurried down the stairs from her room. As they descended the last flight, she heard David exclaim and looked up to see her father-in-law, Albert, at the foot of the staircase, looking at her

321

with a most peculiar expression. How *very* provoking. She held her head high.

'Good afternoon, Father-in-law,' she trilled in her light, clear voice. 'David and I have just been discussing Kentish architecture in the library.'

'I hope you have had an instructive time,' said Albert evenly, filled with such rage he surprised even himself. 'Good afternoon, David.' It was a dismissal, not a greeting. He knew well enough that David was unlikely to have been the instigator of this affair.

'I hope, Uncle –' David began.

'I said, good afternoon.'

David went, torn between relief at this release and a feeling that he was hardly behaving in gentlemanly fashion. Meg was not so fortunate as David. As she turned from the door, Albert awaited her. 'A word with you, daughter.' He was shaking with rage, surprising even himself by the strength of his feelings.

'You whoring tart,' he addressed her sweetly.

She stiffened, prepared for battle. 'Are you going to tell Louis?'

'Be quite sure that I will.'

'And how about him amusing himself all over Paris?'

'That is his own affair. He is a man. You are not. I feel it important he should know he appears to be in danger of fathering a child who is not his own. If you conceive, either now or in the future, I shall tell Louis to make full enquiries.'

'How dare you?' she burst out, aggrieved. 'You complain about me and David. What about you and Mother?'

Albert stiffened virtuously, ready for this. 'What happened between your mother and myself was years ago, Meg, a true and lasting love. Hardly something to be compared with a squalid little tumble in a handy bedroom. Your mother is honest. She does not commit adultery behind her husband's back.'

'Like you,' sneered Meg. 'What about you and her the other evening?' This was a shot in the dark, for she was by no means sure of her facts. The look on Albert's face was confirmation enough, however, and a happy complacency succeeded Meg's worry.

'I was trying to get her to go away,' Albert said ungallantly, if truthfully. No need to confess that he had succumbed, and how enjoyable it had proved.

'Do you think Madame la Comtesse will believe that?'

Albert's face went white. 'You little blackmailer.'

Meg burst out laughing, taunting him, and in a fury he strode to her and gripped her by the arm, dragging her up against him in uncontrollable anger just as Alfred came through the door in search of his daughter: an arrangement that Meg had completely forgotten.

'What the hell are you doing?' Alfred roared, forgetting all about the new brotherly friendliness and the feud of the Stowertons being over as he saw that blasted fellow physically attacking his daughter. Meg promptly began to cry, and Alfred launched himself at Albert, dragging him away from her, and, with his far greater bulk, flinging him in an undignified heap on the floor.

Promptly Albert struggled to his feet, warding off Alfred's second attack, shouting: 'Don't, don't, I'll explain!' Then remembering he couldn't as Alfred aimed a second blow at him.

'Why, Alfred,' came a pleasant voice, as Elizabeth sailed into the room, attracted by the sound of altercation. 'Oh, *Alfred!*' seeing her husband and lover so engrossed. 'So you do care.' She launched herself happily into the fray, trying to free Albert, but only succeeding in giving Alfred time for another punch.

The three of them danced round in a frenzied triangle for a moment or two, while Meg took the opportunity to vanish from the scene.

'Get off, woman,' roared Alfred, trying to free himself from her embraces in order to get at Albert again.

'Alfred, don't hurt him. For my sake,' she pleaded dramatically.

'I'll hurt him all I like.'

'But I love you,' Elizabeth threw in on cue, somewhat exaggeratedly.

'Eh?' Both men turned to her, since it was by no means clear to whom this was addressed. Albert recovered the quicker of the two, aiming a punch at Alfred's ample paunch and sending him backwards into Elizabeth's arms.

'Come along, darling,' she crooned, leading her panting husband away.

'I wasn't fighting over you,' he yelled, irritated, as soon as he could speak.

'Of course not,' she soothed. 'I understand. Of course you wouldn't want to admit it. But now I know you love me still, I'm so pleased, darling. It makes all the difference. Now I know I can return to you if ever I am in need. When we are old . . .'

'No,' howled Alfred, seeing the abyss ahead into which fate was so unceremoniously tossing him.

Luke fumed, unable to believe it even now. He was locked out. First locked out of the study and now apparently out of Bocton itself. Katharine must be out of her mind. Was she closeted in there even now with Mayfield? There was no sign of his carriage, but it might be in the stables. He'd go and see. No, he wouldn't. He wasn't interested. Anyway, he wouldn't put it past Katharine to have locked herself in alone. She seemed determined to keep him out, goodness knows why. All this talk about surprises being prepared for him was simply to annoy him, for the more he protested, the more he betrayed interest and thus played into her hands. After all, he reasoned, he was going away. What interest could he possibly have save that of the best interests of the house? And for that he should leave matters to Katharine and the expert Mayfield.

He walked round to the side of the house, as if to expunge his resentment at even thinking of the fellow. He could climb in at a window, he supposed. No, he would not demean himself. He had tried to keep away from Bocton, but saw no reason that he should not at least see the place a little before he left. After all, he'd been through a great deal to attain it. Father and he had signed the contract of sale now, so it was legally his. *And he was damned well going to enjoy it.*

It irked him even more that Katharine had taken his father round several times, but not him. Father had even come back saying Mayfield had some good ideas. Did he indeed? Luke felt an outsider, but was not sure how to remedy it. After all, from Katharine's point of view she had some justice on her side. He had said he was leaving Bocton, and leaving her. She should make a life for herself. Very well. She was. But he hadn't intended her to laugh in his face. A certain sadness would become her, he thought savagely. Unless – fear gripped him – she was intending to move Pearson in? No, surely not. But he grappled with this unpleasant thought for some while, wondering whether her allowance could not be made dependent on her living alone. No, she would not flout convention so, he reasoned. But what if . . . his mind leapt . . . *Sophy* moved in. Both their lovers would be free to come and go as they pleased. Sweat broke out on his face.

'Good morning, Luke. I thought I heard you.' Katharine, bright, breezy, undisturbed by the dark thoughts in his mind, came hurrying round the corner. In her hand was a key. He would not comment on it, he had too much pride. He wanted to puncture that air of indifference, that bright enthusiasm for something that should have been shared, and because of her – him – both of them, was not.

'I'll have a spare key cut since you always seem to be here,' she told him brightly.

'Nonsense,' he told her curtly, thinking how well the green-gold colour of her dress suited her, and, yes, how happy she looked. He was amazed to find how much he minded. 'I've hardly been near the place.' Happy? How could she be? Unless – suppose he were right about Pearson?

Against his will he recalled how she'd looked in Georgetown. Just like that. Only then it had been for *him*, not Pearson, not Mayfield, not Bocton. But his memories of Georgetown must have been his imagination. He had wanted to believe she loved him and persuaded himself that she did.

'Had you tried to get in?' she was asking.

'No,' he said quickly, too quickly. 'Why? Is it locked?'

'Of course,' she said, surprised. 'We don't want anyone breaking in, do we? Your father gave me the keys, so naturally I keep them.'

He wanted to say he had a right to be consulted, he wanted to say he should hold the keys, that if he were of so little consequence he would cut off the money, he wanted to say how much he wanted to share Bocton with her, he wanted to say – No, it was the impulse of the moment and it would pass. Her eyes were so clear. Why had he never noticed before? He turned quickly to the side of the East Wing, staring up at the Queen's Chamber and the old chimney stack at its side.

'And thou, my mind, aspire to higher things,' he said out loud, though he did not realise he had spoken.

324

'What did you say?' she asked, disconcerted.

He jumped. 'It's the line before that quotation from Sidney up there.'

'"Aspire to higher things". Higher things,' he said abruptly, inanely, wishing she would not stare at him so, piercing him through like the rose's thorn. 'Do you think he was thinking of the chimney when he wrote it? And the smoke curling up. After all, he put his badge on it.' He patted the huge old stack in front of them, jutting out from the wall, huge at the base, tapering off high up.

'It is quite high,' she pointed out idly. 'Though, I don't know why it's there at all; there's no fireplace.'

'Yes, there is,' he said, surprised. 'It's the fireplace in the Queen's Chamber.'

'On the first floor, yes, but not down here. Most of the stack is so wide it was obviously meant to serve four fires – in the Queen's Chamber and below, and the Queen's Receiving Room and the study below. Though that seems excessive, since in the study and Receiving Room it would face the inglenook on the opposite wall.'

'So why is there this huge base?' he retorted. 'Of course!' He broke off as he saw her staring at him. It came to them at the same time. Katharine was quickest, waving the key in her hand.

'Give it to me, it's my house,' he roared, racing after her as she darted back to the porch entrance. His long legs were easily covering the distance between them; then he changed his mind and lithely climbed in at the hall window. But he rattled at the door of the study in vain. It was locked.

'It's mine,' she panted, racing up to him. 'I've been doing the restoration work on the study.'

'I paid for it.' He caught hold of her and seized her, turning her to him, holding her tight against him while he tore the key triumphantly from her hand, feeling her heart thudding against his as she wept and shouted in vain. He turned the key in the study door, blocking her from entering with his body, then locking the door against her again so that she beat and howled on the outside in vain. He rushed to the wall and began to pick at the plaster, cursing because he had no tools.

Engrossed, he failed to see Katharine clambering, skirts hitched up, through the window; she was inside and climbing down before he was aware of her presence: then as he saw her, he rushed to prevent her approaching the wall, picking her up bodily and dumping her none too gently in a chair.

'Got you, my lady,' he shouted in triumph, as he held her down by main force.

'Let me go,' she yelled. 'You *would* have to do it by force. You haven't the brains to do it any other way. Let me go!' Tears of rage streamed down her face.

'Do I tie you to this chair or do I have your word that you will stand by and watch quietly while I investigate?'

'We must *share* it,' she said.

'You haven't done much sharing this last month,' he answered with satisfaction.

'That was different. You know it,' she hurled at him, struggling up and being pushed down again.

'Right,' he said grimly, looking round quickly for something with which to tie her up.

'Don't,' she yelled, as he sat on her to keep her still while he tore a cover sheet into pieces. 'You're hurting me. I won't interfere.'

'Your word?'

'Yes.'

He watched her suspiciously for a moment, and she sat quietly and obediently. When she saw his eyes still on her, she sighed heavily and went to stand on the far side of the room, holding her hands submissively before her. He turned to the plaster again. 'I need a hammer or pick,' he said peremptorily, in the hope she'd not question it.

'Go and get one,' she said sweetly.

'Only if I have your word not to lock me out.'

'You don't,' she told him smugly.

'Then I'll tie you up or take you with me.'

'I'll get you the hammer,' she retorted mutinously, defeated. She fetched one from the tool dump, and he set to tearing at plaster, regardless of his bleeding hands. Unable to resist, she came over to help – or rather to see what was happening.

'I thought I told you to go away,' he said, panting, as a chestnut head of hair appeared next to his in the hole he had made.

'You need me,' she said shortly.

'Like hell,' he retorted.

'Make a bigger hole. Hurry up,' she ordered him.

'I'm working as quick as I can.'

'Roderick's quicker than you.'

'Saint Roderick isn't here,' he shouted at her.

'He should be. He knows what he's doing.'

There was an exclamation, then he pushed her head out of the hole, followed himself, stood up and seized her by the shoulders. '*Will* you be quiet about that blasted man?' he said through gritted teeth.

'Yes, Luke.'

Satisfied, if suspicious at this meek submission, he began to work again, with her help. 'There's nothing here after all,' he said, disgruntled. 'It's all been for nothing. They probably put a flue here in case it was needed, but never used it.'

'Are you sure?' She could have cried with disappointment.

'Look for yourself,' he said. 'There's more spiders than jewels.'

She needed no second bidding, but clambered bodily into the hole as he pulled out his head. And gave a cry.

'What?' he asked sharply.

'Oh, Luke. It *isn't* a flue. Come and look. No, you're too big. It will only take one at a time. We'll have to switch places.' As covered in cobwebs as Miss Havisham's wedding table, she climbed out and was

326

pushed to one side by Luke. Once in, she heard him draw his breath. Then saw him moving, exploring, in the dark.

'What's happening, what's happening?' She hopped up and down.

A muffled voice. 'I think we've found Nicholas Stowerton's staircase into the Queen's Chamber. I'm going up.'

'No,' wailed Katharine. 'I want to.'

'There might be loose bricks. It's dangerous. I'm going.'

'I don't care,' she said pleadingly. 'I'm smaller. Oh, Luke, let me.'

But there was only the sound of scrabbling and Luke's curses for answer.

Quickly, Katharine ran out of the study, heart thudding, up into the Queen's Chamber. Even as she entered she could hear scuffling by the side of the marble fireplace. Then the painted panel between two of the marble columns swung open and Luke stood blinking into the light of day, covered in dirt and cobwebs.

'Enter, handsome Sir Nicholas,' Katharine bade him graciously, reclining full-length on the bed.

Luke laughed aloud, unable to conceal his delight. He strode over to her and for a moment she thought from the look on his face that he would embrace her, but he merely took her hand and pulled her off the bed. 'Come and see,' he said simply, 'come and see. I think it's safe for you to go down with plenty of light now at both ends. It doesn't appear to have rotted, but be careful.'

She began to pick her way carefully, then shrieked.

'What is it?' Luke called anxiously.

'Spider,' she retorted meekly.

'I thought you'd met the ghost.'

'There's no room for a ghost. I wonder *you* got up here at all.'

He pulled her out at the bottom, but let go of her hand immediately.

'Shall we cover it up again?' she said eagerly. 'So no one knows but us?'

He looked at her enigmatically. 'If you wish,' he said. 'I'll get some boards and do it now. So that's how Sir Nick took the red rose and ruby up to her and recorded it outside on the chimney. "Grow rich in that which . . ."'

'No, that's not right,' she interrupted, frowning. 'That inscription was put on the chimney at the same time the house was built. He can't have meant an event which took place six years later. He must just have thought it a convenient place to put a –' She broke off as their eyes met.

'Katharine,' Luke said slowly, 'what exactly did Mayfield tell you about how this part of the mediaeval house was organised? Was it that it formed the private apartments of the owner and the upper room was where the master and his lady slept?'

'Yes. Where the Queen's Receiving Room now is.'

'Then if they slept there, did they not have some kind of privy?'

'Yes, you remember Roderick said there would have been a garderobe there. It jutted out over the ground beneath at the far side end of the building. But that would have been taken away when Nicholas –'

'Wouldn't it have been just about where this chimney is?'

'You mean that obstruction just as the little stairs turn towards the top into the Chamber? But that isn't tall enough for a garderobe.'

'But look, the study and the rest of the ground floor in this wing are different,' Luke said, sketching rapidly on a piece of paper, 'I guess by a foot or so. Yet on the first floor they're all level, so that the garderobe would have been partly between the new Queen's Receiving Room and what's now the study.'

Katharine peered over his shoulder at the sketch. 'You mean where the bread oven is in the Queen's fireplace was really part of the old garderobe?'

'Bread oven?' said Luke, astounded. 'Do you think Queen Bess spent her nights tossing lumps of dough around?'

Katharine went red. 'Roderick said –' she began weakly.

Luke began to laugh helplessly, shoulders shaking, while she stood fuming at her own stupidity.

'Luke, come back!' But she was too late. He was tearing up the main staircase almost before she realised what was in his mind. Without thinking, she followed him, weeping with frustration as she yelled at him to wait for her. By the time she was in the Queen's Chamber she was too late. The panel was shut and she had lost her chance of getting to the fireplace first up the old staircase.

'Open it!' she ordered. '*Open it!*'

'No,' came a muffled voice from within, jeering.

'Luke,' she wailed, 'You can't. Bocton's mine as well as yours.'

'*You* didn't care about that,' he yelled.

'Please!'

Nothing. Then slowly the panel swung open and she threw herself into the hole, crouching at his side, her hands by his exploring the obstruction.

'No flue here,' said Luke briefly. 'There's room to stand up. It's the old garderobe all right.'

'Mind you don't fall through the hole,' she said brightly, and felt him shake with laughter in the dark next to her.

'I reckon we're kind of standing on the old mediaeval floor,' he said thoughtfully. 'Now if when they constructed the Elizabethan floor which is partly over the garderobe as far as the level of the new outside wall, the point where the staircase meets it, that would give a nice secret hole of about one foot in depth and width, and three feet wide. Right in front of us, below our foot level.'

'How do we get in to it?' she cried.

'Get an axe,' he commanded.

'We can't, Luke. Roderick would be horrified if we destroyed part of the mediaeval house.'

'*Get an axe, woman!*'

'I'll get a small one,' she compromised feebly. 'Wait, *wait* for me.'

She hurried back with the small axe Obadiah used for chopping rotten wood.

'Stand back,' he ordered.

Bits of wood and plaster flew in all directions, making Katharine cough as the dust entered her throat, and she scrambled back into the Chamber. The same happened to Luke, for he soon squeezed up past her into the bedroom.

Choking and spluttering, she flung open the casement window. The June sunlight streamed in and they gratefully breathed in the fragrant air from the garden.

'Next time you restore a house,' Luke said, coughing, 'lay the water on first, will you?'

She giggled. 'There's some home-made lemonade downstairs,' she offered.

Luke seemed suddenly to realise to whom he was speaking so companionably, and immediately awkwardness descended. 'Thank you, I'm better now.' And he quickly returned to the hole he was making in the wooden boards by the side of the small staircase. At last the hole was big enough for him to get his arm inside.

'Let me do it, Luke. Please.'

'No,' he said, grunting at the effort.

'Why? Do you think Nicholas put a poisoned dagger in there?'

'Might have done,' Luke said reasonably. Then, 'There's something . . . something . . . if I can reach.'

He tore another piece of wood away. 'It's a box,' he said in triumph.

Then Katharine was beside him, squeezing and scrabbling as they prised their trophy out.

Something made him want to give her the honour of carrying the box into the light, and she looked at him gratefully. Some day she would thank him, now she was too excited.

Much of the wooden box was rotten. No need to wonder how they could break the lock. She held the box aloft, and they both eyed it.

'Look,' she whispered, 'at the faded paint on the lid. The Plantagenet badge. Yellow broom sprigs on a red ground.'

He moistened his lips nervously. 'It could be –' he said guardedly.

Katharine's eyes sparkled at this nonsense. 'It must be,' she said firmly. 'Can I open it?'

'No. Just in case. Clear the rugs away. We'll kick it open.'

'How melodramatic,' she said, but let him have his way.

With one sharp kick, the lock gave way, the clasp springing up from the splintered wood. She watched as he positioned the top of his boot to kick the box open. It seemed to take for ever. Then it moved, the leather toecap moving through the air, the lid flying up, and two heads bent over the contents of the long-concealed chest.

And then they saw what it contained.

Chapter Nineteen

'The birthday of my life is come,' quoted Katharine slowly, breaking the long silence after the first sharp intakes of breaths. Rubies, emeralds, diamonds, agates, amethysts, looking like dull-coloured glass after their long concealment, hidden for at least three hundred years. On top of its colourful bed rested a small gold crown ornamented with rubies and emeralds and a central diamond, winking as it caught a sudden beam of sunlight coming in through the casement.

Luke put out his hands and shut the box sharply.

'Why did you do that?' she asked, amazed, her voice still trembling slightly from the shock of their discovery.

'I thought they might vanish,' he said, slightly shamefacedly.

'They haven't,' Katharine pointed out. 'There are no leprechauns around here.' Gently she reopened the box, reverently lifting out the crown and placing it on the bed, then letting her hands run through the bed of jewels beneath.

'Take care,' said Luke sharply.

She looked at him and smiled. 'Poisoned daggers? No, there's nothing here but gems. Oh, yes there is.' Her fingers fastened on something else, a small roll of parchment, which she carefully withdrew and which was almost snatched from her hands by Luke.

'It's an inventory,' he said, brow wrinkled as he stared at the old script. 'Of the jewels, I think.' He could not keep the excitement from his voice.

'Why did I waste my time learning Latin,' he muttered impatiently, 'when I could have been learning mediaeval script?'

She peered over his shoulder. 'Item,' she read.

'Thank you, Katharine. That much I could manage.'

'A crown of something . . . Anne . . .' she continued, undeterred.

'Neville,' he finished. 'It must be. Richard's wife.' His voice ended almost in a shriek.

'Thank you, Luke. I did know,' she laughed, almost crying with the same excitement.

'Item,' he read on, the words coming out one by one. 'Ruby . . . something of . . . another Neville, Cedric – no, Cecily. That was Richard's mother, wasn't it?'

'The Rose of Raby, yes. And here's her necklace.' She held it up, light catching the dull red of the stones, suffusing them with warmth.

'Wear it,' he said abruptly. 'And the crown.'

'No,' she said quickly. 'No, I couldn't. Not yet.'

He did not press her but read on down the long list, making out words here and there. 'Most of them,' he said, 'seem to belong to – or have come from – a count. Listen: the diamond . . . as Pomfret . . . that must be this.' He picked up a diamond larger than the rest. 'That and other items have Burgundy or Charolais after them.'

'Same man,' she told him. 'The Count of Charolais became the Duke of Burgundy. So that's where Richard got his secret collection of jewels that nobody knew about.'

'Let's put them back,' said Luke abruptly.

'Back?' she repeated, stupefied.

'Perhaps legends shouldn't be too real,' he said uneasily.

'What you really mean, Luke, is: who do these belong to?'

'No doubt of that,' he said. 'Not us.'

'The crown would be treasure trove, and there'll have to be an inquest because it's of gold. But the jewels themselves aren't subject to treasure trove. They're ours.'

'Are they?'

She stared at him, not understanding. 'Of course, you own Bocton now. The papers are signed.' But even as she spoke she followed his reasoning. They could still think as one though they no longer slept as one.

'Have you thought,' he continued, 'what would happen if we burst into Stowerton House or Charham with the news that Richard III's jewels had been found?'

'You mean the quarrelling could start all over again,' she said wearily. 'I'd forgotten, Luke. Goods don't get divided between all the sons under the Custom of Kent. They pass by will only. And that means Robert. Or would they belong to the owner of Bocton?' She slumped down, looking at the jewels in front of her.

Luke shrugged. 'Or to any member of the family who wants to make a claim. Katharine, let's brick the box up again for a year or two, then when all the ripples of this case have died down, we'll re-find it and announce it . . . propose we give the money to found a hospital. Or a home for exhausted lawyers.' He grinned suddenly, years falling from his face.

Katharine laughed. 'Poor Mr Pinpole. To add treasure trove to his worries just at the moment would be too much. Very well, let's bury them again. Here,' she said spontaneously, closing the lid, 'you can do it. Nicholas Stowerton can hide them once again.'

She watched him close the lid firmly, and disappear through the panel into the dark hole beyond. It seemed to take a very long time. Then she heard his voice, disembodied, urgent. 'Katharine, can you light a candle and bring it here? Quickly.'

She obeyed quickly, wondering what could be the matter. She held out the candle inside the cavity, wrinkling her nose at the smell of the foul air coming out.

'What is it, Luke?'

I can't – get it back,' he panted, with sounds of shoving. 'There's something wedged. It's another box,' he shouted.

'More jewels?' she asked.

'How do I know?' he retorted, and she felt foolish for asking. 'Here, take the jewels again.' He handed her back the box and struggled with the unseen object, cursing. 'Ah!' Triumph in his voice.

'It's not jewels,' said Luke, gasping with the effort. 'Too light.' He climbed into the Queen's Chamber through the panel and they knelt over it.

'This,' said Katharine carefully, 'can only be an anticlimax. It's probably his laundry lists.'

'No Plantagenet badge,' he pointed out.

'Maybe it's Nicholas's laundry.'

'This time I will use a stick to open it,' Luke said thoughtfully.

Despite Katharine's cry of impatience, he ran downstairs and came back with a long piece of wood, with which he prised the lid undone. It came up easily enough, with no daggers and no false bottoms being revealed. It contained merely scrolls of parchment.

'I told you,' said Katharine resignedly. 'It's the laundry.'

'Do *you* keep laundry lists?' he asked pointedly.

Gingerly, Luke began to unroll one. 'It's no use,' he said after a few minutes. 'It's this mediaeval script. It's worse than the other because it's not a list. It's –'

'I know what this is,' said Katharine eagerly. 'It's the same as Jacob's document. It's the other half of the transfer of Northwell to Richard Plantagenet by William Stoorton. Look, see where it's torn at the bottom – I'm sure Jacob's half would fit into this.'

'But what is it doing here in Bocton?' asked Luke, frowning. 'Jacob would have his half from the family papers, but why should Richard's half be here?'

'With his jewels,' said Katharine, then stopped to think more carefully. 'You're right, Luke, that can't be the case. Richard wouldn't leave his part here. Let's look at the other documents.'

Half an hour later she gave up. 'It's no use – I can only make out the odd word.'

'Me too.'

She looked at him, eyes glinting. 'I know who *could* read them for us. Roderick Mayfield.'

'No.' Sharply.

'Why not?' she asked innocently.

'I don't want him knowing the affairs of our family.'

'I'll ask your father's opinion. Perhaps Robert's too.'

Dead silence. She wouldn't. Surely she wouldn't. But this new Katharine just might.

'Very well,' Luke said stiffly. 'But I shall be present.'

'Naturally, if you feel I need a chaperone,' she answered gravely.

'I –' he began, cornered, unable to say yes or no.

'Perhaps you're right,' she said, interrupting. 'I am a married woman after all.' A pause. 'I'll go with your father.'

Charham looked like a storage depository, as some Stowertons prepared to take their departure and others to move in permanently. Mabel had gone. Immediately the party had united, the remaining days flying by in an orgy of family reminiscences, and present enjoyment of close relationship.

Joseph, now anxious to be away, beamed at everyone, unable to say much but shaking everyone's hand vigorously – even Robert's. 'If you're ever in Australia,' he assured them all anxiously, 'Manly is the place to come. You'll love it . . .' Already his thoughts were far away, to where the blue Pacific lapped a golden beach; where the streets of Sydney enticed, and Emily waited.

Only Philip stood mute, with a hypocritical smile on his face. One day his time would come. Albert shook hands awkwardly with Alfred; cordiality was a little strained, but the willingness was there. It was a start. Albert averted his eyes from Elizabeth, who floated around beneficently, bidding farewell to everyone. Alfred had been alarmed to find she was not yet leaving, and had to be reassured that her ticket was truly booked and that she had every intention of being back in Paris in time to prepare for the winter. That the villa Klaus had taken was in Cannes was a fact she had not yet passed on to Albert.

'If ever you come to Cannes,' he assured Alfred fervently – then remembered the last time Alfred had visited the town. 'Paris,' he amended quickly, 'we'll go to Longchamp.'

Alfred glared at him balefully, but was able to recognise an olive branch when he saw one. Besides, to go to Longchamp again might be no bad thing, especially if the blasted fellow paid.

Katharine went into Sophy's small parlour. It was the first time she had seen her aunt since the meeting.

'Can you forgive me, Katharine?' Sophy began without preliminaries.

'There is nothing to forgive, Aunt Sophy. Only thanks on our side,' said Katharine ruefully. 'You have been working all these years, and we have benefited. Well, no more. I shall see you do not have to work again.'

Sophy smiled and drew her to a chair. 'You don't understand, Katharine. I enjoy it.'

She was taken aback, then wondered how she could have been so stupid. Had she not demanded for herself in Leadville the right to work? 'Forgive me,' she said sincerely. 'That was clumsy of me.'

'Katharine,' Sophy said hesitantly, 'I do not intend to change my way of life, you know. If you feel the family are embarrassed in any way, then I must move, make different arrangements for myself.'

'Sophy,' said Katharine earnestly, for the 'aunt' posed a barrier which no longer existed, 'you are so fortunate. If I could choose between being with the man I love without a ring, and having one but being parted,' her voice trembled, 'which do you think I would choose?'

Sophy simply rose and took her in her arms. After a few moments, she voiced the other question. 'Do you truly understand why,' she began in a low voice, 'I could not pay for The Case? I thought at first the feud might be ended if everyone came together – and then I realised that with Mabel there, there was no chance. I could not bear to watch it all happening again. I was wrong, and it has come right, but I could not know that.'

'Yes,' said Katharine, 'it has come right.' And it must stay that way.

Katharine impatiently crammed on her hat. She was late for meeting Luke at Bocton, after seeing Roderick that morning in Ashford. Yet before she could leave the Dower House, there was yet another interruption.

'Is Meg here?' David strode into the morning room, ignoring Maggie's vain attempts to announce him.

Katharine looked up, startled. 'Meg? No, David.' With sinking heart she realised what her parents had been hinting at; she had been too taken up with her own problems to take notice. 'She's already left,' she said gently. 'She returned with Uncle Albert.'

'But she loves me, she said she loved me!' said David vehemently, unable to take in the fact that Meg had left without saying goodbye.

'In her way, David,' Katharine said helplessly.

'She said she would come back,' he told her defiantly. 'On frequent visits. Her husband leaves her alone too much.'

'Don't waste your life waiting for her, David,' Katharine pleaded.

'Why not?' he asked, surprised. 'I never wanted anyone else. And, yes, I know,' he added, 'that she is selfish, self-centred, and that she was using me to feed her vanity. But she loves me, Katharine. She does, whether she realises it or not.'

'But what sort of life is it simply to wait for a few snatched moments, David?' she asked, horrified.

'It is better than nothing,' he replied simply.

'No,' said Katharine firmly. 'It is not. David, you used to have such plans for life, such hopes. Even if Meg does not share them with you, can you not still search them out?' But who was she to preach? she thought bitterly later, when, half persuaded, David had left.

Luke looked up irritably, as she hurried into Bocton.

'Where have you been, Katharine? I've been struggling with this cursed fireplace all day. If we're going to have this place presentable by Midsummer Eve for the family dinner you're all so enthusiastic about, we need to hurry.'

'Come into the study, Luke – I've something to show you.'

Somewhat unwillingly, he followed her into the study and she emptied her bag of papers on to the desk.

'I've been to meet Roderick, and he's explained what's in these. Look, here's his translation. And guess what –'

'You've what?' he demanded with a voice like thunder. 'How dare you, Katharine?'

'Why not?' she asked innocently.

'You told me you'd tell me when they were ready.' He was beside himself with rage.

'I didn't think you were that interested,' she began, but he caught her by the wrist and pulled her to him.

'You know very well what we agreed. How could you do it, after I shared discovering the jewels with you?'

'You couldn't very well help it,' she pointed out calmly. 'I was here.'

'It's time you realised this is *my* house, and that if I choose I can turn you out tomorrow, and consign you to a two-up, two-down cottage in the grounds.'

'How?' she enquired sweetly. 'You won't be here.'

'I'll sell Bocton,' he said bluntly.

'That's just a threat,' she replied, trembling all the same. 'You love it too much.'

Silence.

'Katharine,' he said dangerously after a moment, 'what did he say?' He took up the parchments.

'Careful,' she said in alarm, 'they might crumble if handled too much, Roderick says.'

'Then where are his transcriptions?' Luke enquired in a clipped voice.

'Here,' she said meekly. 'And *this* is the one that will interest you most.'

He took the paper covered in Mayfield's impeccable handwriting and read in silence:

x May AD M.D.LI.

I, Eleanor, wife to Richard Plantagenet formerly of the manor of Northwell and son to Richard of York, by the grace of God former King of England and unlawfully killed on Bosworth Field, was formerly wife to William Stoorton of the manor of Bocton, and do hereby solemnly swear, as I shall someday soon stand before my God, that my son Philip, father to Nicholas known as Stowerton, though begotten of the aforesaid Richard in avowtery [adultery – RM] was yet born in lawful wedlock. Wherefore I charge my grandson Nicholas that when the time shall come he rise up and rid the land of these upstart Tudors.

Luke looked up at her without animosity now. 'But that means . . .'

'Yes,' she said simply. 'Nicholas Stowerton wasn't a Stowerton at all. He was a Plantagenet, and some might claim the rightful King of England.'

'Do you think Nicholas knew of this?' he asked in wonder, trying to grapple with the implications. 'Why would he bury the evidence?'

'He could hardly announce it to Queen Elizabeth,' Katharine pointed out. 'William Stoorton had already lost his head for treason. Whether Nicholas was his grandson or not, he might provide another rallying point for dissenters to Tudor rule, just as Perkin Warbeck had earlier. I think she'd have had him in the Tower as soon as the dreaded word Plantagenet was mentioned.'

'Wait a minute,' said Luke, sitting down with his head in his hands. He sat for a moment or two, thinking rapidly. Then he started to laugh. 'Katharine, have you thought out what this does to the legal position on Bocton?'

'Bocton?' she cried in alarm. 'What do you mean?'

'If a case is made for Nicholas being the rightful King of England, then he would hold Bocton as the Crown – and it would be passed on to his eldest son. And *his* eldest son, and so on.'

'Luke,' she clutched him in alarm, 'you mean that Robert could *truly* own Bocton?'

'There might be a case,' he said, grinning. 'On the other hand, let's accept Elizabeth as the lawful monarch by then. Robert's case that as Nicholas was grandson to William Stoorton the lands could not revert to gavelkind tenure, is demolished. He *wasn't* a Stowerton, so the lands *would* become subject to gavelkind again, if you accept Sir Anthonie Browne's judgment.'

'Poor Nicholas,' exclaimed Katharine, after she had absorbed this. 'How ridiculous. He could only show the lands were subject to Knight's Service, and not gavelkind as the Queen had decreed if Father's legend is true, by accusing himself of treason. No wonder he buried the jewels again and didn't leave a will.' She started to laugh.

'I think,' said Luke, 'perhaps we'll put these papers away again *now*. I don't think Pinpole deserves to face this one just yet.'

As they walked up the staircase to the Queen's Chamber, their sudden rapport deserted them. Silently they entered the room which held so many memories. He took the papers from her and replaced them in their box, then he opened the panel and placed the box back in its hiding place. 'What about repairing the wall to the staircase?' he asked stiffly. 'In case anyone should come across it, like we did?'

'I'll do that – after you've gone,' she said with difficulty.

'Katharine . . .' He found to his surprise he was holding her arm.

'You still intend to go?' she asked, her pride giving way.

'I'll stay for the feast,' he said gruffly. 'Then I shall leave.'

'You are sure, Luke?' Her lips were very close to his. He dropped her arm quickly. He had been betrayed in their common love of Bocton into an emotion for something that did not exist, for it had been broken, and once broken could not be mended. Yet as he looked round at the Queen's Chamber, at the vast four-poster bed, he thought how easy to carry her there now, to love her as though the rift had never been. The chasm crossed in seconds, with no words, no blame, no regrets, only love shared.

His arm moved infinitesimally towards her, then he stopped. Suppose it were to happen again? Once betrayed, that line that held them together had snapped forever. If mended, the link would be weak, not true gold.

'Yes,' he said at last. 'I shall go.' Not realising how long it had taken him to speak.

'Luke, we could try –' she cried, sensing his hesitation.

'No,' he said dully, and a chill filled the room. 'It is too late.' And with an effort he looked her straight in the face and there were only coldness and bitterness in his blue eyes. 'There is nothing left,' he said unemotionally. 'There was no love when we married (Let her deny it, he was thinking) and none grew. Perhaps it was my fault, perhaps yours. We both tried, we both failed.' He could not bear to look further at her, and ran quickly down the staircase and outside that the cool air might take the sting from his eyes.

Katharine half staggered, half fell on to the bed. She had tried, but failed. Her great plan that she had been so sure would succeed, to make his love of Bocton the spur to send him back to her, had not succeeded – and for the one reason that she had not taken into account: that she had refused to see, though it stared her in the face. Luke did not love her and never had. Her plan had succeeded only in proving that it was Bocton that had drawn them together in the first place, and not love. Not on his side, at any rate. For her, the two were so intermingled that she could not now separate one from the other. What point was there in Bocton if there was no Luke? Or, worse, a Luke who returned only from time to time as a polite visitor, while she grew older and older, childless and loveless, imprisoned in the house that she would have desired full of love.

Despair engulfed her, too deep even for tears. There was nothing more she could do. The Queen's Chamber, so richly restored and glowing around her, was all for nothing. Her whole life had been directed to this one moment of triumph, when Bocton should live again in the glory it had known, but now she wanted it no longer – not without Luke. The portraits of Nicholas Stowerton and his Queen on the walls seemed to gloat over her, as though they had achieved a serenity that she could not. They had found a way that was blocked to her.

Another few days and Luke would have gone for ever in spirit, if not physically. He would return only as a stranger. But now she had played her last card, for if Bocton could not win him back, how could she?

The bright disinterest of Nicholas Stowerton's likeness mocked her. Mocked? No, perhaps it was challenge. Perhaps an expectation that where he had not admitted defeat, neither should she. But, unlike his, her red rose had been offered and rejected. Yet those blue eyes refused to leave her, still held her in their grip as though Nick Stowerton and Bocton both could give her strength.

Bocton alive again, Bocton resounding to the sound of laughter, of crackling meat cooking on the spits, of madrigals sung from the galleries, of wine being poured into flagons. Ah, yes, it were a brave way to go, with head held high.

Katharine flung back her head, and addressed Sir Nicholas Stowerton: 'Very well, my Nick,' she said softly, excitedly. 'I promise you we'll have one other gaudy night.'

*　　*　　*

The ghost of Nicholas Stowerton peered anxiously through the window of his Great Hall. His work was nearly done now, his secrets unveiled, and he need remain with his beloved Bocton no more. He gazed enviously as he saw the huge oak table decorated with flowers, the finest glass and china, roses wound around his oaken staircase. Red roses. And that was only right for this was Midsummer Eve, when he should do homage to his Queen at court. Or did she come to Bocton here? He rubbed his tired eyes. He was confused, he had needed sleep so long . . . for tomorrow was the day he must attend the court. And this was Midsummer Eve, and the roses were in bloom. There in his fireplace a fire blazed, with meat cooking on the spit. But why there? Why not in the kitchens? There was something passing strange here. And guests, phantom shapes, he faintly recognised and went to welcome. But no sound came from his throat. No ordinary guests these, they were Stowertons. So all was well, wasn't it? And surely the Queen slept here tonight that he might do her homage?

The firelight warmed the pale flickering light of the candles placed in huge candelabras in the hall, making the gathering ghostly, unreal in their Elizabethan dress. Only Alfred had resolutely refused to put on this ridiculous attire and warmed his tails in front of the fire. Jeremiah, Alexander, Luke, Sophy and Elizabeth had entered into the spirit of the festivities. Jeremiah had taken advantage of his comparative slimness and was strikingly attired in a black and gold doublet and matching short cloak. Alexander, well used to Elizabethan dress, followed suit in red, with a dashing ruff that suited his classical features, and Luke somewhat reluctantly had donned ruff, deep blue doublet and pale blue trunkhose, cursing Elizabeth who had dubbed herself mistress of the robes and provided the apparel. Her own was a rich red farthingale dress with a deep-pointed stomacher, and in deference to Sophy's status as a famous Queen of the Circulating Libraries, she provided for her not a mouse-brown, but bright emerald green, which did nothing to flatter Sophy's looks at all. Nevertheless she gravely thanked her sister-in-law, catching Alexander's quizzical eye and daring him to comment.

Katharine glanced down ruefully at her cloth of gold farthingale dress, and white silk cloak with golden lining. It looked splendid, but superintending kitchen arrangements were not made the simpler by it and she was forced to leave Maggie and her assistants to their own devices. It was easier than she had feared at first. Her plan for an Elizabethan meal worked well, providing a talking point with which she could fend off any awkward questions about Luke.

'Not roasted swan, is it?' grunted Alfred, looking suspiciously at the spit.

'No. Fat capon,' she said laughing. 'And I've excused you the sucking pig, and porpoise in porridge.'

Alfred grunted.

As Maggie bore in the set piece, Katharine's work of which she was particularly proud, she glanced at Luke. It seemed to her he was deliberately avoiding her eye. So hope remained, albeit slender. 'It's

Plantagenet Pie,' she announced softly, 'in honour of –' his face turned swiftly to her '– the legend,' she concluded, and he visibly relaxed.

The crust of the huge raised pie was decorated on top with the Plantagenet badge and six heraldic pastry lions stood guard at intervals round the sides of the pie. As host, Luke cut into it and she held her breath. Inside set in aspic were crayfish from the Len, Kentish truffles and Whitstable oysters.

'It's based on the Gloucester Royal Pie,' she told her guests, as though this were any other dinner, not the one on which her whole future depended. 'It's still presented to the Monarch today by the City of London, as they have done every year since the reign of Richard III. That pie is a different recipe, of course.' She chattered on, aware that Luke grew silent.

'I'm so glad we've been able to use the old kitchens once before they go,' she said. Did the hasty importation of one kitchener into an empty room qualify as 'use', she wondered.

'Go?' asked Jeremiah, his mouth full of Elizabeth wine jelly. 'You mean you're starting to restore the West Wing?'

'No,' said Luke, not looking at Katharine. After all, he did *own* Bocton. 'We're going to expose the old roof in here first. Then finish the East Wing, leaving the West to last.'

'Not quite,' said Katharine with a smile. 'Those plans are changed now, Luke. I've not had a chance to tell you. Roderick and I have been talking to various builders and authorities, and our conclusion is that the West Wing is too far gone to save, so we are going to pull it down and rebuild it in modern style.'

'But –' Luke stared at her in complete amazement.

'And in here and the East Wing, rather than exposing all those beams which will make heating so difficult, we've decided to plaster over it again, perhaps make the rooms smaller, and more –'

'More what? Are you out of your mind, Katharine?'

She looked astounded. 'No, Luke,' she replied, puzzled.

'You can't do it.' He was on his feet, regardless of the interest of their guests.

'Please, Luke, let's discuss it later. This is a celebration for Bocton after all.'

'Now,' said Luke curtly. 'This is my house. *I'll* say what's to be done.'

'But I shall be living here, Luke, and I have to take expert opinion.'

'You'll follow my instructions.' His face was white with anger.

'Lovers' tiffs,' said Elizabeth brightly. 'Shall we leave the gentlemen to their port, darling? We remember these little quarrels, don't we, Alfred?'

'No,' he said shortly.

'Oh, Alfred, I am so pleased you remember our marriage as being one of unbroken happiness. So do I. And that will make it easier –'

'Make what easier?' he scowled.

'If I ever decide to return to you,' she said brightly.

339

'No,' howled her husband, but Elizabeth apparently did not hear for she had risen to follow Katharine. Transfixed, torn between amusement and concern, Sophy followed.

The gentlemen were some time at their port that evening, the glasses emptying rapidly as the candles flickered their shadows around them.

'Katharine is not serious, I trust, Alfred?' So abstracted that he was unconscious of rudeness, Luke broke abruptly into Alexander Bishop's account of the foibles of lady authors (excluding Sophy).

'Katharine usually is,' said her father. 'You should know by now,' he added in surprise.

Luke sank back, apologising belatedly to Bishop.

'It's an odd night, of course,' said Alfred, as if this excused Luke's eccentricities. 'This is the night that Nicholas Stowerton is supposed to walk – Midsummer's Eve. Goodness knows why since it must have been several days after Midsummer before Queen Bess got down here, but that's legend for you.'

'The ghost?' asked Jeremiah with interest. 'I wonder if he's with us now?' He glanced around uneasily in the eerie candlelight. 'Wouldn't catch me sleeping here,' he continued.

'Why not? When Katharine has finished her redecoration plans for the Queen's Chamber with floral wallpaper and whatnots and a modern brass bed, he won't recognise the place to haunt.'

'The Queen's Chamber?' said Luke blankly. '*The Queen's Chamber?*' He scraped back his chair.

'That's what she told me,' said Jeremiah without much interest. 'She's done it for you, and now you've seen it, that's enough. She wants a place she can live in comfortably, so she's going to divide it up, get rid of the old bed and get some good modern furniture in. Dark wallpaper to help her get to sleep, she says – where are you going, Luke?'

His son had by then flung open the study door, to stand trembling on the threshold. 'Katharine, what's this I hear about you redecorating the State Rooms?'

She rose and came to him with a worried look. 'Oh dear, I was going to explain it all to you later, but I'd better do it now.' She swished past him and up the stairs, passing interested eyes below. 'Your costume suits you,' she told him brightly, once inside the Chamber.

He blushed slightly.

'You've got the legs for it,' she added.

'Don't change the subject. What the hell are you up to? Bocton's mine,' he shouted.

'Mine,' she said calmly. 'I knew and loved it before you did.'

'No,' he reminded her, 'we grew up with it together. For my first seven years it was *mine.*'

'I've loved it and cared for it.'

'And I've paid for it. You won't alter a thing.'

'Then you'll have to stay here to stop me, Luke,' she said. 'For the moment you leave, I change it to what *I* want.'

He stared at her, calculating, trying to keep anger at a distance. She was bluffing, wasn't she? 'You won't,' he said at last. 'You wouldn't do it. You love it too much.'

'Not without you,' she said matter-of-factly.

'I still don't believe you.'

'Then I will start now,' she said, going up to the wall, taking the pictures of Nicholas Stowerton and Queen Elizabeth down and throwing them carelessly on the floor.

'Put them back,' he ordered.

'No.' She went to the bed, and wrenched vigorously at a curtain.

In a trice he was at her side, dragging her away.

'It's no use,' she said triumphantly, as he prevented her from making another attack. 'The moment you go I'll clear the walls and wallpaper the room, sell the bed –'

'No!'

'In fact, I could start tonight, after you've left.' She eyed the bed meditatively. Dear God, the strain was killing her. Surely he must see through her?

'You will not,' he said tersely.

'How will you stop me?' she asked, taunting him. *Please, oh please, believe me*.

He hesitated. Then: 'If you won't see reason, I'll put an injunction on you not to change anything in the house without my consent as legal owner. I'll see Pinpole tomorrow.'

'There's always tonight,' she said determinedly. 'I'll start tonight.'

'Then I'll sleep here, to make quite sure you don't wreak any havoc.'

She glared at him, thwarted.

'I'll start downstairs.'

'You will go home with Alfred,' he said quietly. 'No, better still, since you can twist him round your little finger, I shall get my father to escort you home, and make quite sure you are locked in.'

Luke saw with satisfaction that at last he'd got the better of her; her face was pale with shock and fear. Perhaps there would be no need for an injunction, perhaps now she would see sense.

They had all gone. He had watched Katharine leave, defeated and dejected. He was alone at last in Bocton. Luke Stowerton sank down, at first relieved, then a little disconcerted at the loneliness of this vast house. The candles in the Queen's Chamber seemed not so much comforting now as menacing. He heated up some water on the kitchener to wash. The embers had still been glowing on the hearth as he came upstairs, and outside it was a June night, Midsummer Eve, yet still he felt chilled. It was the night when girls saw their future husbands if they followed the rituals. All he was likely to see was the ghost of Nicholas Stowerton, he thought grimly.

If he had not been so angry, he might have laughed. Even now he could not quite believe he had known Katharine so little. Perhaps he had not reckoned on her determination to do something to annoy him.

Well, now he'd got the measure of her. He would thwart her in her plans for the Chamber, even if it had been all he could do not to seize her in that ridiculous cloth of gold farthingale, throw her on the bed and love away the quarrel between them; he would stop her mouth with kisses, taste on her lips the wine of happiness, kiss away the hurt of the previous years, till she laughed in pleasure and told him that she had meant nothing so ridiculous, so stupid.

But now he could not. She was gone.

He carried the water over to the old bowl on the stand, glad at least that the washstand had a urinal inside it so that he did not need to take the candle and walk the corridors to the bathroom. He thought of the old garderobe, and wondered how Her Majesty had fared for her sanitary arrangements, then shivered slightly as his candle flickered. The silence in the house was eerie after all the noise this evening. There was not even a clock. Nothing, but a moonlit night. Did ghosts like moonlight? he wondered, as he stripped off his costume, realising belatedly just how odd he would look, going home to the Dower House so dressed in the morning.

Ghosts, he thought again suddenly. Why think of them? He didn't believe in ghosts. Ghosts haunted your mind, nothing else. Ghosts of a love that once had been, of a dream that had never fully been realised; they were not creatures of the night, but of the day.

He opened the bed, the smell of lavender from the sheets greeting his nose as he slipped in. He was about to blow out the candle when the thought of darkness oppressed him. Quickly he ran to the window and pulled back the curtains. Moonlight flooded in. It would keep him from sleep awhile, but he was glad to feel that once the candle was out, there would be light of a sort.

He pulled up the sheets around his naked body, but sleep did not come. Sleeping in the Queen's Bed seemed, ridiculously, a treasonable act; perhaps her ghost would come along too, he thought wrily, aware of the tension in his body. When he had left Kent, there would be no more of these wakeful nights. He would sleep without longing to hold Katharine in his arms again. There would be other women, perhaps new loves. Or if not other loves, then relief . . . Somewhere he could hear a clock striking in the distance. Odd, for there was no clock at Bocton surely? Yet it was striking. Striking twelve. And on the last note he heard a sound. It was wood creaking. Wood did strange things at night. Yes, there was another creak.

Twelve o'clock, and Midsummer Day now. The night air smelled sweet through the window, the moon eerily distancing familiar trees. Suppose Nicholas Stowerton were indeed outside, waiting for entrance? Could ghosts enter through windows? he wondered. He shivered inexplicably. There *were* no ghosts, he told himself. All the same, he was glad, as if in propitiation to the ghost of Nicholas Stowerton, that he had put those portraits back on the wall.

Another creak. A mouse? A rat? No, merely the wood sighing in the night, as it did in all old houses. Or perhaps it was the ghost of Gabriel Arch. Directly up there he'd first fallen in love. And now that love itself was but a ghost of what had been.

But that noise was not up above, he realised with a lurch of the stomach. It was below in the study. Ghosts didn't make noise, he told himself. But how could it be human? Everyone had gone home, he'd seen them. *Everyone.* He was alone and the ghost was mounting the stairs to his Chamber. It was Nicholas Stowerton coming to present his rose. Luke tried to control such irrational fears, yet found himself sitting up, watching the panel, transfixed as the sounds grew nearer. He could do nothing, could not move.

Slowly, slowly the panel began to open and he almost screamed out, having convinced himself it was only imagination. A strangled yelp broke from him as it opened further. It *couldn't* be a ghost. They didn't exist.

It wasn't a ghost. It was Katharine. Katharine in her long, white-gold cloak with the crown of Anne Neville on her head. But this he hardly noticed, as she stepped into the room and cast off the mantle.

Between her white breasts hung the rubies of the Rose of Raby, in her chestnut hair blazed Burgundy's emeralds. In her navel another. Rings bejewelled her fingers, and diamonds her ears.

But where his eyes then rested the Pomfret diamond shone bright, flanked by two glowing rubies of Charolais amid the triangle of soft brown hair.

Luke caught his breath, as she came towards him, arms outstretched, and full of love. She halted uncertainly as he gazed transfixed at her naked body laden with Plantagenet jewels and stepped back, hiding herself in confusion. Then as she looked again at his eyes, what she saw there gave her courage, just as he threw himself out of the bed and came to her, gripping her so that she could not move.

'Why?' he asked, choking, seeing how much it had cost her.

'Because I love you, Luke. Because I've always loved you.'

'Always?'

'Always. Only like these jewels, it was hidden sometimes from both of us.'

He lifted up the rubies lying on her breast, letting them fall again gently against her creamy-white skin. He took the crown from off her head, touched the emeralds in her hair, kissed the jewels on her fingers and at last with a light touch on her lips plucked the glories of Pomfret and Charolais from their resting place, holding them aloft, then tossing them away, he knew and cared not where.

'Dangerous,' he murmured, laughing aloud in joy. He took her hand and, leading her to the bed, he sank down with her on the lavender-scented sheets, looking at her as if this might yet be the dream of a Midsummer Eve that might vanish with the dawn.

So she reached out to him, drawing him closer, crying out at the pleasure of his naked body next to hers once again. She trailed her finger down his chest while he caressed her breasts, the rubies' red glow cast over them. She kissed him on his lips, then on his chest, then further down till she felt the tremors running through his body, knew he wanted her but that he still held back. As her hands fluttered to caress, to kiss, to commit, he held them gently in his, taking them away from his body. Still that gulf. Still the fear. Even now?

'Why,' he whispered urgently, 'have you locked me out these past days?'

'Luke,' she cried softly, torn between tears and laughter. 'Ah, let me woo you now, as I choose. I never locked you from my heart. Have you not realised, do you not see, how I have led you to me?' Gently, tenderly, passionately, she pushed his hands away. 'For this, oh dearest Luke, has been but the wooing of Katie May.'